Fury

Rebel Wayfarers MC
Book #11

MariaLisa deMora

Edited by Hot Tree Editing

Cover image by Sara Eirew

Model: Gabe LaDuke

Cover design: Debera Kuntz

First Published 2017

ISBN 13: 978-1-946738-06-6

DEDICATION

Revenge is an act of passion, vengeance of justice. —
Samuel Johnson

For Kay, who reminds me in her unique and hilarious ways that sometimes long chapters are best filled with great stories.

Contents

ACKNOWLEDGMENTS

Ac-knowl-edg-ment
noun
plural noun: acknowledgements
1: acceptance of the truth or existence of something
"there was no acknowledgement of the family's trauma"
synonyms: acceptance, recognition, admission, concession, confession
2: the action of expressing gratitude or appreciation for something
"he received an award in acknowledgement of his work"
synonyms: thanks, gratitude, appreciation, recognition

There are some books that flow freely as they come to life. In those instances, I can sit in front of the computer with a broad grin, fingers flying across the keys as I try to keep up with the characters and their actions, dialogue, and plot twists. Those books are a joy to write, fulfilling in every way because when a story comes that easily there's a serene sense of assurance that it wants to be told.

This is not one of those books.

Fury's story came in fits and starts. I've never had as many separate files for a story before. My folder was filled with files! This chapter had a document, and that chapter had a document, and so on, but for the longest time I wasn't even certain in what order they should be placed. It started when I cut a whole section from the manuscript for *Duck*, back when Fury was talking loud and proud, and he shouldn't have been. I told him at the time, "Not your book, dude. Chill." So, he chilled.

He chilled to the point I wasn't certain he would even have a book. Frightening, but so what, I didn't have a cover yet, and while folks wanted to hear from him, I couldn't force him to talk, could I? Everything felt choppy, and forced, and I decided if I couldn't have the woo, I wouldn't do the story.

Meanwhile, I had things going on in my life, too. A surprise book or two, and baby those flowed. They had that effortless quality which always underscores my resolve to keep at this writer gig. In total, I wrote four stories while Fury chilled, quiet and silent as the grave.

Thankfully, it turned out he was just waiting his turn. Or should I say he was waiting on Bethany's turn. Up to that point she'd been quiet. Oh, I could pull sentences from her, but not a lot more than that. Once she caught her stride though? Look out. She was gone, man. Me and

Fury? We were playing catch-up for weeks. In the end, however, I think we have a balanced book where the main character, the hero if you will, is strong and firm in his beliefs, with a voice unlike any other Rebel. The main female lead is likewise strong, and has become one of my favorite chicks in the books. Growing up as she did, while carrying secrets as she does, and still she managed to seriously kick ass and take names. I like their story, and I hope you will, too.

So, the first thank yous go to Fury and Bethany, for not letting me give up on their story. They just needed time to find their stride and get in sync, and I needed to follow their lead.

Now on to the other acknowledgements, where I express gratitude and admit that while this writing is first conducted in solitude, it's not really a solo gig at all. Not by a long shot. I lean on a lot of folks for every story.

To my lovely editor, Becky Johnson, founder and CEO of Hot Tree Editing, and her team of professionals – thank you. You always make me appear so much more put together than I really am, and I truly enjoy how well we work together. (Should that be "how we work well together"? Grr. Now I needa ask Becky.)

Sara Eirew, photographer, and Gabe LaDuke, model – the image on the cover is phenomenal, and I'm proud to have your artistry adorn my story. Debera Kuntz, as ever, your interpretation of what I saw in my head is spot on. Thank you all.

For the gals who encourage me and listen to my whining when the words don't flow, who nip my woe-is-me in the bud and force me to look at the why so I can fix it – thank you. MirandaPanda, Jamey, Kay, Kori, and Megan – your voices echo in my head in a good way. My alpha team for this story was small, but fierce. Kori (yup, same one, I'm doubly blessed here) who read the story twice, Kelsi, and Megan – your feedback was valuable, and needed. Thank y'all smuchly!

To my cadre of folks in the life who gave insight on so many aspects of Fury and the various organizations he wandered through, thank you. It doesn't matter where I go, you know I take you with me. Even Tinker—much as it pains me to admit—I should confess I enjoy our interactions more now. Maybe you're mellowing as you age? Whatever it is, keep it up old man. Thanks for helping me see things through.

Woofully yours,

~ML

Simple things

Gabe

"In and out, shouldn't be a big deal. Just do your job." The big man lifted his beer and drained the bottle, staring at Gabe as he set it on top of the barrel. "You get my money, we'll be square."

We ain't ever gonna be square, Gabe thought. Dion Cooper wasn't the kind of man who would allow leverage to be lost. He'd been that way in the military, where Gabe had first met him, and had stayed the same after being discharged. Unlike most folks who'd served, Dion was proud of his bad conduct discharge, holding it up as if it granted him automatic badass status. BCD meant he'd spent time in military prison, and while Gabe knew that was true, he wasn't sure what the sentence had been for. *Coulda stolen toilet paper for all I know.*

Dion was a procurer. He found things you needed, or more usually, wanted. He'd gotten his hooks into Gabe while they were deployed in Africa, and the moment Gabe had gotten back stateside, the man had shown up, like a bad penny. *Shoulda never believed his shit*. But he had, buying a fortune of illegal drugs. He would have been fine, except the bag had gone missing out of his locker. That meant he was out both the money he'd borrowed to purchase the product, as well as the product.

"You hear me, Gabe?" Dion rapped the bottom of his bottle against the metal, switching it around in his hand. This being an unsubtle threat of potential violence.

"Yeah, I heard you. No big deal. I do this, and we're done." Gabe swallowed hard. *I cain't fuckin' wait.*

"No, not what I said. We ain't done." Dion tapped Gabe's shoulder with the bottle. "Said you get my money and we'll be square. Square ain't done."

"Same as." Gabe shrugged as he took a slow step back, moving out of easy reach.

"No, not same as. You get me my twenty-five K and we'll be square. Then we can see what's next in line." Gabe couldn't help his reaction, and his laughter was loud as it bounced back against the trees behind Dion's house. Scowl firmly in place, Dion clipped out, "The fuck do you think's so funny?"

"Twenty-five thousand? Are you jacked in the head? I owe you fifteen K. Fifteen thousand. Not twenty-five. Where in the hell did you come up with that number?" Gabe shook his head. This was why he couldn't ever get free from Dion. "You're insane, man."

"Want me to go through line-by-line? It was fifteen. Now, it's not. Inflation. Interest. What the fuck ever, dude. Now, it's twenty-five." Dion shoved the barrel out of the way, taking two steps towards Gabe. "Give it another week, and it'll be thirty."

I could take him. It would be so easy to just take care of this a different way. He shook his head, forcing those ideas away. They belonged to his father and the clan in the holler, not the man he'd been fighting to become his whole life.

"Where do you think...? There's no way this chick is gonna give me twenty-five thousand dollars. No fucking way." Gabe had thought it was a stretch at fifteen. "She's gonna know I am talking out my ass." Shaking his head, he tried to find an argument that Dion would listen to. "She's a businesswoman, in the music biz, and I'm a mountain boy. Fuck, Dion. Ain't no way."

"I got an angle." Dion always had an angle. Part of why Gabe had wound up so deep in his pockets. "She'll never see you coming. Pussy gonna be so quick to cash out for you, you won't know what happened. And then—" Dion leaned closer, poking Gabe's chest with a stiffened forefinger. "—we'll be square." Standing straight, the scowl wiped away, a smug smile in its place. "You ain't ever gonna be quit of me, though. I know where too many bodies are buried." Dion turned, walking towards the cooler on the ground near the backdoor, chin angled so he could see Gabe over his shoulder. He held up a hand and wagged it back and forth, fingers crossed. "You and me? Like this. We gonna stay tight, man."

***

Gabe stared up at the sign on the building: Iron Indian Records. It didn't mean anything to him, but he couldn't get the idea out of his head that it should. That the name was something he'd heard somewhere before. He rolled his neck, stretching and reached up to scratch his hipster scruff, running a finger around the inside of the shirt collar cinched tight as a noose around his neck. Sweat prickled his scalp; it was only nine o'clock in the morning, but Nashville was already stifling hot and humid.

Running the script through his head again, he tugged his shades free from the pocket of his shirt, flipping the arms out and shoving the sunglasses onto his face. Not a long con, this was planned as a short-term confidence shill. Six days preferred, but only two or three weeks, max. He just had to convince the business manager he could do what she needed, which was provide studio time. Recording opportunities at a studio he'd show her in a carefully choreographed dance during the absence of the real studio owner. For all she was young, this chick was smart and well thought of in the business industry, all of which meant she had integrity, which made her a good mark. Intelligent people who did the right thing always expected the best out of everyone.

Time to aim and let fly. "Showtime." Looking both directions, he crossed the street and confidently reached for the handle, pulling the door open. A welcome rush of cool air hit his face and he took a breath of relief as he stepped inside. That relief was short lived as he stopped abruptly, the door closing behind him and nudging him forwards as it tapped his ass, slipping into place. *Jesus, it can't be.*

Dion said her DJ gig used the handle of B.T. The paperwork for this place was all signed by a B. Taylor. Gabe knew sex, age, reputation, and work experience, but that was it. He hadn't asked for more, certainly hadn't asked for a picture. If he had, he would have vetoed this plan. Put the brakes on any proposal involving this woman. Someone he knew. Very fucking well.

Bethany Mason stood from the desk at which she'd been seated and came toward him, arm extended, broad smile on her face. Beautiful and poised, she was so different from the girl he'd last known, but the Mason genes bred true. Dark hair, gray eyes, square jaw—she looked like her mother, and more than a little like her brother. Gabe held his breath, waiting for her to out him. He was shocked when he heard, "Mr. Sorenson, it's good to finally meet you. You're punctual. That's always a good omen."

Fuck, she don't remember me. Derek Sorenson was his con name for this gig. Hearing it from her jolted him into action, and he wondered at the painful ache in his chest as he slipped his rough palm along her smooth one, clasping firmly but careful not to grip too tightly. *Can I pull this off? I put on weight and heft in the army. Fuck, some days I don't recognize myself in the mirror.* He pushed the curl of disappointment down, not letting it factor in the expression on his face. Bethy Mason had been the best friend of his little cousin, Tabby, and had been in and out of the Ledbetter household all her years growing up. But she'd known a much younger Gabe, one who wore a perpetual scowl. *I can do this.*

"Miss Taylor," he used the name she went by now, and he wondered for a bare moment if she was a shill, like him. Remaking herself once away from the hollers, taking on a false city persona that fit her better than the country girl she'd been. "I can assure you, the pleasure is all mine." He squeezed her hand again, then loosened his grip, trailing calloused fingertips across her palm as he released her. Seeing the flush climbing her neck to her cheeks, he threw away the idea that she was a con, too. "Nashville is a beautiful city, but I believe I'm looking at the prettiest thing in it right now." *Too thick?* The flush deepened. *Nope, not too thick. Just right.*

"Thank you, that's very sweet." *Oh, honey, I'm far from sweet.*

Instead of speaking his thoughts, he clamped his teeth closed, allowing the corners of his lips to curl up. "Are you ready for me?" So many meanings for that phrase, and as he hoped, she followed the words into the darker path. Dropping her chin, she looked to one side and pressed her lips together to hide a small smile. "For the meeting, I mean." *Damn, she's prettier than I'd have expected. Way prettier than I deserve.* That thought made him flinch.

"Yes, I am. I have everything set-up in the conference room. If you'll follow me?" *Through the gates of Hell, darlin'.*

Down boy, he told his twitching cock when her swaying ass preceded him up the narrow hallway. *Might be Heaven, not Hell.*

I'm done being stupid

Bethany

"It was never that, was it? Never real. Never going to be forever, was it?"

In her head, Bethany heard her trembling question on a repeated loop, remembered how it had echoed down the phone line connecting them through the glass. Saw again the expression Derek wore, cold eyes she didn't recognize staring at her over the mouth she knew so intimately. Dark stubble on his head, strange to see him look like this, his scalp had always been so smooth under her hands.

"Don't. Please. Don't lie to me. Give me that, at least."

Heard his response.

"No, honey. It couldn't be."

Twenty-year-old Bethany Taylor rested the heels of her hands against her forehead and pressed hard. Over the sounds of water splashing around her, she remembered the hollow clunk of the phone hitting the hook, the fluid movement of his muscles as he rose from the chair positioned across from her, and how he never broke stride as he walked away. Hollow inside, as she'd been since she left the prison after visiting the man she loved.

She'd left the prison and gone straight to the bank, shifting money and borrowing under her own name, not the business, funneling in every cent she'd lost. Only once that was done, did she pull in a breath that wasn't weighted with fear. All through the legal proceedings she'd expected her brother to show, expected him to swoop in like an avenging angel. Had woken with that fear choking her every day, slept but fitfully, plagued with the nightmare of having to explain to him how she'd messed up.

Now that everything was settled with the money back in the business accounts where it should have stayed all along, there'd be nothing to explain. *Better if Davy never knows.*

Tipping her head back, she used her palms to wipe the water from her face, turning to let the shower stream through her dark hair. If there was salt mixed in, no one would ever know. *Never again*, she vowed. *I'm done being stupid.*

So much to do

Bethany, six years later

"Ty," Bethy called, slapping a palm over her mouth and gagging as she stood in the doorway. She stared, looking around the apartment they'd shared for nearly ten years. "What in the hell is in those bags? A science experiment?" She waved a hand in front of her face, fanning to try and overcome the smell. "Jesus." Pushing the door closed with one foot, she walked into the room, dropping her purse on the couch. "Ty?"

"Yeah. Minute." This was called from the bathroom, and with confirmation that he was at least here, Bethy turned to what she thought might be the source of the stench—several black trash bags lined up along one wall. Using the toe of one foot, she pushed gently at the side of one bag, wrinkling her nose as it mushed in a couple of inches. The way it gave to the pressure felt wet and pliable, and wrong. She had just reached out to tug at the top, wanting to open it and see what was inside when Ty came out of the bathroom behind her. "You're home early."

"What is this? It stinks to high heaven, Ty." She tugged again, still unable to lift the bag, but each movement released a fresh wave of the overwhelming stench. "Jesus."

"Deerskins. Bought them from a rendering plant. Gonna take 'em to the cabin and stretch 'em out." Ty headed to the kitchen, and Bethy turned to follow him. "Make shit outta 'em. Sell it. Make some money."

"What kind of shit?" She hiked her bottom to one of the stools and stared at him. "They stink, Ty. You need help carrying them to the truck?"

"Tomorrow. I'll take 'em up tomorrow. Got a buddy coming over to help." Ty opened the refrigerator door and pulled out a beer. He turned to offer it to her, bringing out another one for himself. "It ain't that bad."

"Uh, yeah, it kinda is. I don't know if I can stand it all night, honey." She tipped the bottle, taking a long pull at the refreshing liquid. "Neighbors are going to complain again."

"Let 'em complain. I don't give a fuck." Ty matched her movements, but he drained his bottle, throat working hard to swallow the entire contents without stopping for breath.

Bethy sighed, knowing what this signaled. *Not the first time down this road*, she thought, and studied him.

"You go to group today?" Ty was a good friend and she loved him like a brother, hating when he struggled. He had served in the military with Michael Otey, the older brother of her best friend growing up. Most of the time Ty had his shit together. Most of the time he held down jobs and dealt with people. Most of the time. Sometimes, however, his PTSD would get the better of him, and he would begin floundering, caught up in the currents of his emotions in a way that could pull him far under. She ran their conversation back through her head, and now picked up on several red flags. *Screaming flags*, she thought, and prepared herself for a fight.

"Nope. New guy tweaks me." Ty opened the refrigerator again, bringing out a fresh bottle, seeming surprised when he looked at the one she held, seeing it only had about an inch gone from it. "He's an assclown. Can't stand assclowns. They get people killed."

"Ty, he can't get you killed. It's just therapy group." Picking at the label on her beer, she glanced up at him from underneath her brows. "You didn't quit your job, did you? Why do you need the deerskins to make money?"

"Assclowns there, too. I couldn't take it, Bethy." Drinking this beer at a slower pace, he didn't look up, didn't meet her eyes. There was a deep despair in his voice when he whispered, "I just can't."

"Ty, you know I love you." Bethy tipped her head to the side and waited for his nod. When it finally came, she pulled in a fortifying breath. "I'm going to call Sarge."

"No." Quiet and low, this was so much better than the shouting she'd expected. "I got this, doll baby. I know what's happening. That's why I want to head to the cabin. I gotta come to terms with my own demons."

"Not on your own, you don't." Sliding off the stool, she pulled her phone from her back pocket and dialed, saying only, "Need you, Sarge" when the call connected. She listened for a moment, caught the grunt of understanding, then disconnected and shoved the phone back into her pocket as she rounded the breakfast bar. Arms out, she waited until Ty matched her posture. Then she closed on him, circling him with her arms. "Not on your own. We beat it back together."

She didn't let him go, refused even when he tried to push her away as his shoulders jerked, chest heaving with each attempt to hold in his sobs. Still had him wrapped up when the door at her back opened, and she heard a deep voice call softly, "Ty, tell me what's going on." Slowly, she unclenched her fingers from where they'd been holding onto his shirt in a death grip, and shifting slightly, looked over her shoulder, knowing Ty's head hadn't risen from where he'd pressed it into the crook of her neck. Dwarfing the opening, an attractive man stood in the doorway, close-cropped hair accentuating the strong lines of his cheeks and jaw. She offered the tall man a trembling smile that faded when Ty's arms convulsed around her, holding tighter. The man she only knew as Sarge narrowed his brilliant blue eyes, letting his gaze roam over where Ty was wrapped around her. "Ty." He paused, then continued softer, "Brother." His brows drew together when Ty's arms convulsed again. "You gotta let Bethy go, man."

"Cain't." That single word was gritted from somewhere deep in Ty's chest, rumbling and raw when it hit the air. "Cain't."

"Yeah, you can." Sarge closed on them, and as he moved, Bethy saw two more men file into the apartment behind him. "We got ya, brother. Won't let you go. Bethy needs to step back so we can get you some help." He stood beside them, put a hand on Ty's bicep, and Bethy watched the fabric of Ty's shirt move, knowing that Sarge had squeezed him reassuringly. "Let her go, Ty." She echoed the movement with her arms, tightened and then slowly released. Ty clamped down for a moment, and her breath caught, then just as slowly, he let his arms fall away and lifted his head. She moved to the side and matched Sarge's position, her hand on Ty's other arm. Waiting until Ty nodded, indicating he was ready. She glanced at Sarge, then the other two men, offering them a small smile before she squeezed Ty's arm one last time and stepped away.

In less than five minutes, Sarge was the only person in the apartment with her. He stared at her and she waited, accustomed to his intensity. He ran a private charity that helped combat veterans dealing with PTSD, and seemed to take a personal interest in the men who had gone through their team-building weekend programs. Ty had been through the program three times in the ten years she'd known him, which meant she knew when she called Sarge, he wouldn't hesitate to jump in his truck and come over to help Ty. Now, she waited for him to follow the usual script. He'd ask, "Are you okay, Bethany?" Or his other go-to, which was, "Do you need anything, Bethany?" Never a "Do you want to fuck, Bethany?" Which was a question she would love to hear from him. *Hot and alpha just does it for me*, she thought. *Jesus, I'm as fucked up as Ty is.*

"Need help getting this shit out to his truck?" Sarge motioned to the bags and Bethy winced, having forgotten the odorous evidence of Ty's unraveling. "I don't have anywhere to take it, but I can at least get it out of the apartment for you."

"That'd be nice, thanks." She shuffled over and tugged at the top of the smallest bag, grunting as she lifted it. "Ty bought a bunch of deer hides, wanted to tan them up at the cabin." She hitched the bag up, trying to get a better grip, but the bag was difficult to hold, nearly slithering out of her grasp. "They're heavy." She gave a mental eye roll. *They're like a metaphor for so much in my life.*

Five more minutes, and she was thanking Sarge again, standing in the doorway and wedging one of Ty's shoes against the door to prop it open. "Gonna just let it air out a little. Thanks again." She took a breath. Then, because it felt like a betrayal, she stared at Sarge's boots when she said, "Pretty sure he quit his job." She swallowed. "Again."

"Pretty sure you're right, Bethany." She frowned, hating that the only time he called her Bethy was when talking to Ty. "I'll be in touch, let you know how Tyrell is doing." Nodding, she kept her chin dipped, remembering the way Ty had looked as he walked out of the apartment between the two men, glancing over his shoulder and telling her with his eyes how sorry he was that he'd fucked up again. He never believed when she told him it wasn't his fault. *It's not, though. Just because his PTSD isn't visible doesn't mean it's not real.* "You're plenty brave, you know that?"

She was so caught up in her thoughts, Sarge's words startled her, and she lifted her gaze to stare at him, unsure what he meant by that statement.

"Most women," he gestured towards her, "your size and age," his expression grew taut and intense, "would be afraid of a big man like Tyrell." He shook his head. "Not sure if you're that brave, or naïve. Whichever it is, I'm glad you called, Bethany. Never hesitate. You always make that call. Plenty brave."

"Of course, I make the call. He's my friend, and I want him to be okay." *I'm glad he never asked that other question now*, she thought, hating Sarge a little in that moment. *Asshole isn't an attractive look for him.* "I'm far from stupid, Sarge. Ty saw me through some of the worst days of my life. I owe him everything." He scoffed, immediately trying to cover it up with a cough, hand to his mouth. Now, she didn't just hate him, Bethany Mason-Taylor was pissed.

"You think you know me. You see me, what, a couple of times a year and you think you know me. Little woman, pitch a fit if she breaks a nail. No doubt you think me and Ty sleep together." He made a noise and she ignored it, forging on.

"Probably think I'm a stupid little girl who doesn't know what the big, bad, scary world can be like." She reached up, fingers tracing a scar on her breast through her shirt. "You don't know me." She pulled in a breath, then told him, "Ty's my friend. He gave me somewhere to stay when after two endless years I left the man I'd been forced to marry at fourteen." She didn't pause, didn't give him an opening to speak. "Ten years ago, I was sixteen and lost. He gave me somewhere to stay when I found out I was pregnant at sixteen. Gave me somewhere to stay while I carried that child, and he was in the room with me when that child was born. He helped me arrange an adoption that lets me see the boy, my son, but keeps that child safe from my own family. He pulled me back from the brink so many times. So very many times, Sarge. Ty deserves every ounce of my trust and love." She leaned forwards at the waist, needing him to understand.

"He's never, ever asked me for anything in return. Me loving him, being his friend, and helping him like this? It's the least, the absolute least I can do." Resolved, she tugged the collar of her shirt down, exposing the scar on the upper swell of her breast. Sarge's eyes fixed on the rough letters visible on her flesh. "This was put on me by my own father. Carved into me by a man I should have been able to trust, but who sold me into that marriage Ty helped me get out of. I was owned, Sarge. Bought and paid for." She released the fabric and stepped back. "I can't ever pay Ty back."

"Ty never said…" Sarge stopped to pull in a breath. Then eyes blazing, declared, "Hate that happened to you."

"Well, join the crowd, because I hate it, too." Suddenly nervous, self-conscious in a way she hadn't been in a while, Bethy avoided looking at him. "Don't worry about it. We'll pretend this conversation never happened." She swallowed. "Just don't let Ty know you thought I should be afraid of him. He doesn't need that to deal with, too. He's already conscious of how it looks, a white girl from the hollers living with a big, black man."

Turning, she kicked the shoe out of the door and put her hand on the edge. "I'm chilly now. I think the apartment's aired enough. Keep me updated if you have time." She swallowed again, her throat tight. "About Ty."

Sarge touched her, put his hand on her shoulder as he walked past her and out the opening. Bethy let the door swing closed behind him, ignoring how he'd paused and turned to look at her, not caring if he had another thing to say. Twisting to face the empty apartment, she loathed how her eyes burned, nose stinging from the tears she fought back, refusing them permission to fall. *Weak. Crying is weak.* Swallowing hard, she repeated on a whisper, "Join the crowd."

***

Forehead propped in one hand, Bethany stared down at the table in front of her. Silence surrounded her, then through the cans on her ears heard, "B.T., your intro. Pick it up."

Jerking her head up, she looked around the sound room, heard the soft background music that usually accompanied her gossip segment and realized she had ignored her cue. Glancing down at the notes in front of her, she said, "Speechless. That song by the Tufted Ottomans always leaves me just speechless." Scrunching up her nose, she rolled her eyes at the lame segue and looked up to see the laughing face of her tech through the window. "Gonna be a classic. One day. But now, for today, we've got a ton of stuff to talk about because there is a glorious rumor going around that the Wrapped Potatoes are in the studio and about ready to finalize their sessions. You know what that means, right? Means we're only weeks away from a new release and those guys are such good friends, they sent over a sneak listen of what will become the first single off that album." With that, she was solidly back on track, and the rest of her show went off without any more issues.

Hanging up her headphones, she waved to the guys in the other room, gathered her purse and quickly walked out, managing to avoid any conversation as she made her way down to street level. Stepping out from the studio into the warm darkness of a Nashville night, she paused a moment and tipped her head back, staring up at the black sky. It had been nearly a month since Sarge had picked up Ty, and all she'd gotten so far were terse updates that things were fine. This had been the fourth straight text that simply said, **He's good**. Eyes up, she glared at the first star she focused on. Less a wish than a demand, she muttered, "I don't want good. I want him well."

"You okay, miss?" An elderly man stood nearby, hand in hand with a woman of about the same age, and both were looking at her with some concern. Embarrassed, Bethy nodded, and he scrutinized her carefully, then nodded his own response. "Take care."

"You, too." Bethy watched them stroll up the sidewalk for a few seconds, then turned to her car. Off to her second job, soon to be her main one, if things kept working out the way they had been. Within a few minutes, she was pulling into the parking lot of a building. On the front, above the door, was the logo for Iron Indian Records, the recording studio and label she owned with her brother, Davis Mason.

As she climbed out of her secondhand car, two nearby vehicles disgorged their own occupants and she grinned at the men walking towards her. Aaron Rodneyns, Jed Neville, and Thom Dagwood were the voice, rhythm, and melody behind the rock group, Wrapped Potatoes. "Hey, guys," she called, wiggling the key into the deadbolt and twisting it, pulling on the door at the same time and holding it open with one hand. "Go on in, get set-up. I'll be right there."

"Hey, Bethy," Aaron called, leaning in to brush his lips across her cheek in a barely-there touch. "Heard the plug. You're amazing." She gave the air near his face a lip smack and then grinned at the other two men, angling out of the way of Jed's multitude of cases. She had a full kit set for him, but he always brought his own electronics, which was fine with her because those things were crazy expensive.

"Beautiful." Thom reached out, cupped a hand around the back of her neck and pulled her head forwards, dropping a soft kiss on her forehead. "How's it going?"

"It goes," she responded, shifting, getting ready to close the door when a feeling of being watched pulled every hair on her body upright. Scanning the lot, she didn't see any other cars. "This is everybody, right? You didn't bring any groupies tonight?" They laughed, and she grinned at them. But, the feeling didn't go away, and she scanned the lot again. The glint of a reflection in one dark corner slowly resolved into the shape of a motorcycle, and she shivered as she watched it pull onto the road and turn away, accelerating into the darkness. Brake lights flashed in the distance, and then the bike was gone. It looked like the same one she'd seen several times in the past couple of weeks. Never close enough to recognize the rider, but the bike itself looked the same. *Wonder who in the world that is*, she thought, knowing if it were her brother or any of his friends, they would have come in, or knocked on the door and greeted her at least.

Dismissing the bike, she turned and let the door swing shut. "I'll get some coffee going. You guys know where everything is." Frowning, she shook her finger at Jed who had pulled out a cigarette. "Nu huh. Not in here. You smoke outside, Jed. Don't make me hafta call your mama." Pushing past the men, she left them in the studio and went into the tiny kitchen, getting ready for what she was sure would turn into another all-nighter.

***

"Telling you, Davy, this is a great group. I hate to turn them away." As she walked through the apartment, Bethy balanced the phone on her shoulder, flipping through the pile of mail she'd just grabbed out of the box, most of it was for Ty, so she set those to the side to deal with separately. "I know we said we'd stick with just three bands until I had enough to hire someone, but I just know if I pass these guys up, they'll sign with someone else and then they're going to get jacked around."

"Bethy," Davy sighed. She heard noise on his end of the call, metallic sounds, and then a revving engine. "Honey, you're the hands-on person. If you think they're a fit, then you make 'em fit. But you know, if they don't fit, then it's on you to cut 'em loose. That's hard for you, honey." The noise suddenly muted and she knew he'd gone into the office of the garage he owned in Chicago. "We got plenty of bank for you to hire someone, so don't let that stop you. You just gotta find the right person. We need more bank, we'll make it happen. Whatever you need, Bethy."

She stood still for a moment and let the warm feeling in her belly sink in. This, the relationship she had with her brother, was something she had longed to have for such a long time. He'd left home when he was sixteen and she was twelve. Life had changed for her after he was gone. From the time she was little, she knew all she had to do was tell Davy and he'd make it all better. Make it right. Once he was gone, though, nothing was right after that. "I love you." He was silent, and she realized she'd blurted this statement, without anything to let him know what was going through her head. "Just that, Davy. I love you. I wanted you to know."

In a voice rough and gruff with emotion, he handed it back to her, proving that once again, he could make anything better. "I love you, too, honey."

She ended the call a few minutes later and stood, leaning against the countertop. Davy had always done what he could, done more than he should. Their father had his own path and used the whip of religion to drive his flock to what he wanted to accomplish. Even there, Davy had tried to save her.

An eleven-year-old Bethany lay on her stomach in bed, an unfamiliar ache low in her belly. She thought she knew what was happening. Aunt Barbra had warned her about what it meant to become a woman. Knowing that it was inevitable. They had talked about how to manage her body when she would become unclean. That was what Daddy always called it, and Bethy knew why the women sat to the side in church, and sometimes had to sit in the back, no matter who their husbands were. When women were bleeding, this condition their monthly reminder that they had much to repay for Eve's betrayal of God and her temptation of Adam, they couldn't be around the men. Unclean.

She rolled to her side and as she moved, felt something weird between her legs, a slippery warmth that was a lot like when the men anointed her. No one had visited her tonight, though so it couldn't be that. Bethy lifted the covers and looked down at her body in the shadows, seeing a dark stain on her nightgown. Touching herself there was forbidden, but she needed to know so ran her fingers along her hip, and dragged the blue cotton up so she could see her underwear. They were also stained. Between her legs was dark with what she knew would be blood.

A sound in the hallway, then the rattle of her doorknob had her rolling out of bed, standing straight. Her door opened. "Unclean," she whispered, looking up at the man.

"Fuck. Stay there, girl." Uncle Ezra closed the door.

A few minutes later, the door opened again. Bethy hadn't moved. She'd been told not to, after all. With a sobbing sigh, she threw her arms around her best friend. Tabby said, "Hang on, Bethy. Lemme get you to Aunt Barbra's. She'll see to you." In the hallway, Tabby pulled them both to a stop, and Bethy could feel her trembling, even though it wasn't cold.

At the end of the hallway stood two figures. Uncle Ezra, and Bethy's brother, Davy. In a voice filled with gravel that belied his fifteen years, Davy said, "Ezra, you do not want to let me catch you near her again." He moved a step closer to the older man, Davy's already broad shoulders nearly dwarfing him. "Not if you wanna stay breathin'."

"Your daddy runs this household, boy. Not you." That was Ezra's voice, filled with arrogance and disdain. The Ledbetters always wanted to remind folks that they had money, and influence. Aunt Barbra was blood, but the Ledbetters were congregation. Ezra wasn't really Bethy's uncle, but her daddy wanted her to call both Ezra and his wife, Loretta, aunt and uncle, to keep everyone happy. "He's the one who let me in tonight. You think you got more sway than your daddy?"

"I don't think Davy knows," Bethy whispered to Tabby, who nodded in response. "He can't know." Tabby shook her head, and the two girls turned around and headed the other direction. Davy would kill Daddy if he knew, she thought, remembering the men standing in a circle around her, touching her, touching themselves.

The girls eased out the front of the house, Bethy holding the screen door against the spring, letting it close quietly behind them. Tabby whispered, "If he knew, what would he do?"

Bethy looked over her shoulder, staring at the dark windows of the house. "He'd kill 'em all."

"They'd send him away like they did Mikey." Tabby reached out, gripping Bethy's hand. "You cain't let him know." The first time Tabby had

19

been anointed, one of the men had gone too far. Scared and hurt, Tabby had run away from the church camp, making her way through the woods, bleeding. Her big brother Mikey had found out what happened, found out who had hurt Tabby, and had almost killed the man. That was five years ago, and he had only been allowed home a few times since then. The girls loved when he did visit, because his uniform was a novelty. Each with a foot in his boots, arms around the other, the girls would clomp around the house Tabby lived in with Aunt Loretta and Uncle Ezra, laughing and giddy. "You cain't lose Davy."

"I won't tell. Not ever." Bethy's belly cramped, gripping her middle like a fist and bending her double for a moment. When she could straighten up, she looked into Tabby's moonlit face and swore, "Never."

Bethy shook herself, looking down at the phone in her hand, thumb already moving in a long-memorized pattern to dial a number from the past. When a woman answered the phone, Bethy didn't say anything. Didn't respond. Listened to the quavering voice call, "Hello? Is anyone there?" A pause, then, "Hello?" Bethy's eyes closed, and she stared into the darkness. "Hello?" A final greeting, then the sharp click of a disconnect.

Only then did Bethany allow herself to speak, voicing what she wished to God she could still say. "Hey Aunt Loretta, is Tabby there? I really need to talk to her." Fist pressed to her mouth, Bethy kept her eyes closed, tasting salt as the first tears slipped down her face. "Tabby girl, I miss you, baby. Miss you somethin' fierce. Wish you were here, honey. I left it too late. Too late and I'm so sorry." She swallowed convulsively, fighting against the sobs beating against her ribs, clawing at her throat. "I left it too late, too late. I miss—" Shoulders shaking, she bit her lips, unsuccessful in keeping the cries inside.

Movin' on

Gabe

"Good to see you, man."

That voice. That fucking, god*damned* voice he had hoped to never hear again.

Gabe sat still on his stool, elbows to the countertop in front of him, one forearm protectively framing the plate which held his meal. Keeping his chin down, he angled his eyes up, catching how the waitress was frowning at the man who had walked up behind him. Gabe hadn't seen Dion for years, not since Nashville went to shit, but still knew what the waitress would be looking at. Tall and broad, Dion had always held an edge of brutal in his face that foiled every effort to smooth it away. Skin puckered on one cheek from an encounter with a hot muffler, Dion wasn't handsome, not by any definition of the word. What he was, was memorable.

Shuffling the dish a little closer, Gabe leaned forwards, mechanically moving the fork from plate to mouth, and then back again, scarcely chewing in his haste. *He's not supposed to be here.*

Here was Raleigh. North Carolina being a place Dion had never talked about. So, when Gabe got released, he worked with his contacts to get himself to this town.

The cushion on a neighboring stool compressed, the sound of the air being pushed from the fabric and batting quiet, but telling. Dion wasn't leaving and probably wouldn't tolerate the silence for much longer. *Whatever, fucker.* Gabe stayed quiet, finishing his food, knowing now that there was no escaping this encounter. Fork clutched in one hand, he reached for the handle of his coffee mug, lifted it while tilting his head, and gulped at the hot liquid. It was robust, rich with flavor, something he had missed while inside. Like the food he'd ordered, eggs over medium, it was exactly how he liked it. Bacon crisp, cooked through. He'd even gotten wheat toast, not something he liked, but being able to order something because you wanted it was still a novelty.

"You been out what, a month? I'm hurt, Gabe." A cough, the air expelled was laced with the scents of cigarette smoke and decaying teeth. "You didn't even bother to look me up before you raced out of Tennessee."

"Don't give a fuck." Gabe let the words escape then clamped his mouth shut, being in the diner meant he was limited in his response, so much less than he wanted to give this asshole.

"Yeah, well, you should. You need to get square with me." Arrogance and confidence, two things he once admired about the man, were now traits that annoyed and angered.

Twisting his neck, shoving the empty plate towards the inside rail of the counter, Gabe glared at Dion, seeing his imagination had painted an inaccurate picture of the man. Lank, greasy hair pulled back in a loose ponytail, Dion's face looked sallow, cheeks sunken around missing teeth. *Life ain't treated him well. Good.* "We're square."

"Oh, fuck no, we're not." Dion's lips pulled apart, framing front teeth eaten nearly to the gums by meth. Somehow seeing that brought home to Gabe all the time he'd lost. Everything he'd lost.

He levered himself upright, muscles honed by hours of push-ups bunching in his arms as he shoved against the countertop. Looming over Dion, Gabe relished provoking an expression of fear that flashed across the man's features. "Yeah." Pulling his lips back in a snarl perfected over years in the open yard at Riverbend, Gabe leaned close, letting the weight of his rage free for just a moment. "We fucking are. Square—" He bent deeper, putting his face right into Dion's. "—and fucking done." Reaching for the wallet in the front pocket of his pants, Gabe laughed when Dion's eyes widened in terror. "Not going back inside. Not for something like you." Money tossed to the counter beside his plate, Gabe glanced at the waitress who had retreated towards the swinging door that lead into the kitchen. "Thank you." He held her gaze until she nodded. Leaning back towards Dion, he offered the only advice he would ever give the man. "Don't let me see you again."

***

Huddled under the thin blanket on his halfway house cot, Gabe let the movie spool out through his head. Like he had every night for six years.

"I think this is going to be a very advantageous arrangement." Bethany turned from the coffeemaker, carafe in hand. "I'm excited about bringing this to the table for my partner. He deserves for me to hit a home run." She smiled at him, leaning across the conference table and Gabe eyed the smooth globes of her breasts where they pushed against the soft fabric of her shirt. They'd been talking for hours, and she had taken off her suit jacket a while ago, draping it across the back of an empty chair.

Angled back in his chair, ankle across one knee, he lifted his gaze to her face to see she'd caught his open admiration. He'd done his job, keeping her off center all day, plying her with enough compliments that his attraction was clear, while piling on the details in a way that obscured the shallowness of his understanding of the music industry. He knew all the right words, had done his homework on that part, just the meaning behind most of them was gibberish. Today was laying the groundwork, and part of that was keeping her from talking to her partner.

Knowing what he did now, Gabe had no doubts that the partner was her older brother, Davis Mason. And Mason wasn't someone to toy with. He'd see through the ruse in a New York minute, which meant Gabe had to build up Bethy's self-assurance, make her believe that she was skilled enough to put together a deal like this. The damning thing was that she was smart. She was gifted and more than capable; she just lacked the confidence. So, in doing his job and building her up, Gabe knew he was ensuring that it would be a long time before she believed in herself again.

"Let's have dinner to celebrate." Gabe smiled up at her, reaching for the coffee mug she'd refilled. "I'd love to hit the town with a beautiful woman on my arm." If he kept her busy tonight, she wouldn't have a chance to call Mason. Tomorrow? If she went for dinner, that was already solved. He'd do a rinse and repeat, worming his way under her defenses a little more every day. "Leave your checkbook here, B.T." He couldn't bring himself to call her Bethany, afraid his accent or intonation would give him away, so he'd fallen back on what she called herself on the radio. "Tonight is on me."

She studied him for a moment, the confident exterior slipping slightly, and for the span of a breath, he saw the little girl he'd known. Tabby's best friend. Then she smiled, and he knew she was hooked. "Sounds really good, Mr. Sorenson."

"Derek," he scolded her, having already asked her to use his first name. "I'm ready when you are. Anything you need to do before we hit the town?"

She glanced at the phone, then turned back to him. "Nothing that can't wait."

Hitching the blanket higher on his shoulders, Gabe sighed, then rolled to his back, drafts of air stirred by the moving blanket softly caressing his heated skin. Just the thought of Bethy was enough to bring him fully erect in moments. Determined not to sully the memories, he had denied himself every time. *She's everywhere. Can't escape her when she's always in my head.*

The sound of her laugh swept through his thoughts, how she'd giggled at the shit he'd said. He smiled, remembering when she found out he was ticklish and spent an hour keeping him on edge, mouth around his cock, fingers tracing along his ribs and him never knowing when she'd dig them in.

Damn.

Throwing off the blanket, he shivered for a moment at the rush of being naked. Exposed. His body, anyway. With Bethy, his heart had been exposed. "Yeah, look how that worked out."

Swallowing hard, he clamped his mouth shut, not wanting to hear how desolate his own voice sounded in the tiny room. The air surrounding him was dead, no resonance, like he felt most of the time.

"I'll always say it like it is," Bethy promised him, chin propped on her arm folded across his chest. "And after four days, I can say I like you, Derek Sorenson." Gabe flinched and knew she assumed it was because of her statement. It was, sort of, because he found he wanted to hear his name on her lips, not the assumed persona he was using as a front. "Doesn't mean you have to return anything, Derek."

"Honey, you know I like you, too." Sighing, he let a tinge of melancholy slip into his tone. "I'll tell you that right out. But I'll also tell you that I'm not a settling man." He didn't want to leave her heartbroken at the end of the con. "I'm with you when I'm here, though." Gabe trailed his fingers up her spine, gripping the back of her neck in his hand. "And here is where

I want to be." Nothing in there was a lie, and he sold it as hard as he could. "Right here."

Toes digging into her mattress, she pushed up his torso until her lips covered his in a long, sweet kiss. "Good enough," she said when she pulled back, but he could see the pain in her eyes.

"Liar," he whispered, and she grimaced. "I like that you are willing to take what I can give, honey. I wish I could offer more."

"Damn." Cheek to his chest, she lay in his embrace. "I can't hide anything from you, Derek."

"I like that you're an open book, too." Pursing his lips, he kissed the tip of her nose. She moved to cover him like a blanket, and as they lay there, belly to belly, Bethany slipped her hand down between them. Angling his hard cock to her opening, she pushed and sat up, sliding him inside her.

Hand to his cock, Gabe groaned at the memory of how hot and tight she had been. How she moved over him, her hands on his chest, fingers digging into his muscles as she rode him. Her dark hair swinging over her shoulder when her head tipped back, a groan coming from between her parted lips. His fist moved fast on his cock, hips thrusting up into the tight grip that could never imitate how good she'd felt. That was why he never did this; he knew the illusion couldn't hold. *"Good enough,"* he heard her voice in his head, and he stroked faster, frantic now.

"Bethany," he groaned, feeling the spiral of heat in his spine. Ass cheeks clenching, his balls drew up to his body and a long jet of white striped his chest. Strangling his cock in a brutal grip, he didn't let up, embracing the pain and pumping hard as he milked his cock, imagining again that it was Bethy riding him. When he was done, he rolled his head to the side, teeth clenched, the heat of his ejaculate cooling on his belly.

Not good enough.

Iron Indian Records

Bethany

"Double latte, please. Skim milk." Bethy smiled at the woman in the food truck window. "That's all today."

"Child," Dorothea scolded, shaking her head. "You ain't gonna get no ass drinkin' no skim milk. And you got no ass, you ain't gonna get yourself a man. Lemme make you a real cup of coffee, with whipped cream on top." Even as her mouth moved, arguing, she was already assembling what Bethy had asked for. "And no muffin? Child, that's nearly criminal, with how good these banana nut muffins are today."

Rolling her eyes, Bethy laughed. "Dot, I'll give on the muffin, but you put whipped cream on my coffee, and I will not be coming back." She grabbed her purse, unslinging it from her shoulder. "And if you try to put butter on the muffin, we'll have words." Dorothea chuckled, and Bethy grinned at her, finding her wallet by feel.

"Put her stuff on my tab." Bethy didn't try to stifle her glad cry as she recognized the voice that came from behind her. Purse clutched in one hand, she whirled and threw herself at the man standing there.

"Davy." She felt his arms settle around her, holding her close. Then she laughed again when his voice rumbled in his chest underneath her cheek.

"But, Dot, if you put whipped cream in my coffee, we'll have more than words." He gave Bethy a squeeze. "How you doin', baby girl?"

"Better, now." The sadness from last night threatened to reappear, and she pressed closer when he would have released her. "I didn't know you were coming into town. When did you decide?"

"Coffee's ready, Miss Bethy," Dot called, and Bethany reluctantly pulled back from her brother.

"Thanks, Dot," she said, accepting the wax paper-wrapped muffin and paper cup of coffee. "You're my favorite."

"I'll remember that the next time you tell my son something I don't want him to hear." Dot laughed and shook her head. "My Ty thinks a lot of you, but you sic him on me again for my food choices and I doubt I'll still be your favorite."

Bethy felt her smile slip, and she waited for Mason to give his order for a breakfast sandwich before she asked, "Have you heard anything from Sarge?" It had been several days since the last update Bethy had gotten, but he usually kept in closer contact with Tyrell's mom. "Ty okay?"

"Yeah." Dot brushed at her forehead with the back of one wrist. "He said Tyrell is getting back on track. Every episode he has, my boy seems to come back from quicker, and that's good, Bethy." Dot reached out, sandwich in hand, waiting for Mason to take the food. "I'm glad he's got you to lean on. Matters a lot, more than you know."

"We always do better with good folks in our corner," Mason said. "How much do I owe you, Dot?"

"Not a thing, honey. Friends and family discount got you covered today." Bending over so she could see them through the low window in the side of her truck, Dot gifted them both with a broad smile. "Appreciate y'all."

"Back atcha," Bethy told her, then tried to hide a smile when Mason tucked a twenty-dollar bill into the tip jar on the counter. "See you tomorrow." Mason slung an arm around her neck as they turned to head up the block to the building that housed their business. "I didn't know you were coming in. Why didn't you tell me?" Careful of her full hands, she bumped him with her hip. "I like your visits, bro."

"I like visitin' ya, Bethy. I didn't know until late that I'd be headed down." She felt his lips brush the side of her head. "Thought I'd surprise ya." He huffed a laugh, then said, lips quirking into a smile, "Surprise."

"Good surprise." He released her as she juggled things, getting the key from her pocket and let them into the building, using her elbow to turn on lights as they moved through the receptionist area and into the office they shared. *Shared is a generous term*, she thought, looking around. Her desk was messy, clearly used and covered with folders filled with research on different artists and bands. Stuck in front of the phone were a dozen notes with names, numbers, and dates. The desk that faced hers, butted together as they were in the middle of the room, was a stark difference. Clear of everything except a notepad and pen, the telephone shoved to one side. She noted where the chaos of her area had bled across the line, edges of folders and papers extending into the pristine space.

"Tell me what that was about Ty." Mason shifted his chair and dropped into it, somehow managing to not fumble his sandwich or coffee this whole time. He set the coffee on the desk, laughing at her when she slid a coaster his direction. Ignoring that unsubtle hint, he unwrapped his sandwich and demanded again, "Tell me, baby girl," before taking a huge bite.

"I'd rather tell you about the group I want to try and sign." She settled into her own chair, pulling out the old-fashioned writing shelf to set her coffee down, knowing from experience that trying to make room on the desk proper was a doomed enterprise.

"I'm sure you would. But, you're gonna tell me what's goin' on with Ty first." He pried the lid off his coffee, and took a sip, grinning at her over the top of the cup.

"He's...away. Got a couple of things to take care of. I thought Dot might have heard from him." Bethy unwrapped her muffin, already knowing that Davy wouldn't accept that answer. She groaned when her fingers encountered the slippery coating on the baked goods. "She put butter on my muffin!"

"And cream, real cream in your latte. And she ain't wrong. You're too skinny, Bethy." He sipped his coffee again. Voice harder than it had been a moment ago, he observed, "You just lied to me."

Bethy's head jerked up and she stared at him, picking off a piece of the muffin and stuffing it into her mouth. He shook his head at her stall tactic and started talking. "Don't lie to me. About anything, ever. I know we weren't always close." She winced, because that was her fault. She'd blamed him when he'd left, only realizing years later that it was an act of pure self-preservation for a sixteen-year-old boy who, if he had stayed, would have wound up in a kill or be killed scenario sooner or later with their father. But him leaving when he did, and what happened afterwards? It had taken her a long time to sort that out in her head.

"Bethy, you know I only want the best for ya. You weren't asking Dot if she'd heard from Ty, you were asking about Sarge." He paused, staring at her, then shook his head. "Don't wrinkle your nose at me." Bethy rolled her lips between her teeth not even aware she was making a face until he said something. "I know about Ty's PTSD. Knew it the first time I came to visit y'all's apartment." That had been after Mikey's brother died, when Davy had come down for Darren's funeral.

It seemed so many of her interactions with Mikey had surrounded death and destruction. Like Tabby's death, the one that cost her so much, but gave her so much, too. Seeing Mikey's friend—the judge at the funeral—and having overheard her father and her husband talking that morning about their upcoming plans would have been enough to push anyone to desperate measures. Begging for help at the funeral of her best friend had been a mortifying tactic, but it probably saved her life. *Priorities. It got me off the mountain.*

She and Tabby had always promised each other they'd get out together. Out of the holler and away from the people who scattered careless pain like seed on a fertile field. Then Tabby died, and Mikey came home for the funeral, and she knew, somehow, that he'd catch her if she leaped. So, at the end of that long, long day, Bethy had been installed with Ty with Mikey's help. Out and safe for the first time in so long. Those first nights in Ty's apartment were scary, and the memories of him soothing her tears were reminders that she owed him so much. *Like I told Sarge, supporting him however I can is the least thing I can do.*

Then Darrie had died, the last of Mikey's family torn away from him. Loss after loss, all his life. Mikey had come home again, and as soon she'd gotten the call, she'd made her first return trip to the hollers. Panic twisted her belly the whole time she'd driven up that damned mountain. It hadn't mattered that Daddy was dead by that point, didn't matter that a vengeful Davy had worked to clear their home place from all the folks who had hung on every word that spewed from that man's mouth. Driving into the clearing had taken every ounce of courage she owned. And of course, that was the one time Davy had shown up, too.

Thank God. She smiled, remembering how angry she'd been to see him. In the end, the encounter had been the beginning of their renewed relationship. He'd met Ty the next day, staying in the apartment with several of his and Mikey's friends. The instant she'd gotten home, she'd pulled Ty aside and begged him to be quiet about what he knew, about what she'd had to do. She hated keeping secrets from Davy, but if he caught wind of what had happened to her…if he realized she had a child, he would lose his mind.

"He have a bad turn?" Davy's question startled her and she jumped, sloshing hot coffee over her hand.

"Shit." Grabbing for napkins, she dabbed at the darkening spots on her pants, then cleaned her hand. "Yeah, he had a turn. But he's better. Sarge is his guy when things go south, so I call him when Ty needs someone to talk to. He's got this place where he helps guys like Ty, vets who need somewhere they can just be, and not have to worry about civilians." She shrugged, feeling Davy's gaze like a weight on her shoulders. "He's been there for a few weeks. I'd just like to know for sure that he's okay."

Leaning back in his chair, Davy dug in his pocket, coming out with his phone. Laying it on the desk, he tapped at the screen for a moment; then she heard a ringing. "Who are you calling?" She took a sip and waited, rolling her eyes when he didn't answer, just grinned at her.

"Hello?" Bethy recognized the voice and shook her head at her brother, but she couldn't help returning his smile. "Mason, man, sup?"

"Watcher, how's it goin'? Got you on speaker, brother." When he answered, his voice had changed, even his posture shifting from Davy, her big brother, to Mason, the president of a motorcycle club based out of Chicago. "Bethy's here, man."

"Bethany." The pleasure was clear in Mikey's tone, and that made Bethy's throat tighten. The fact he could stay friends with her after how she'd failed Tabby, always amazed her. "How are you, honey?"

"I'm good, Mikey. You and Juanita coming back this way anytime soon?" His wife Juanita was a good friend of hers, and she talked to the woman as often as she could. "Family is always good to see."

"Probably not, honey. Bella's in school now, keeps Nita tied to the household more than before. Not that we're complaining." He was laughing at the last and Bethy heard Juanita's voice in the background, scolding him. "You could always come out here, see your goddaughter."

"Promise to do that soon. Give Nita my love." Bethy leaned back in her chair, blowing a kiss across the desks to thank Davy for letting her have those moments with her friend before he steered the conversation wherever he intended when he initiated the call.

"Hey, Watch." Davy jumped into the opening, as she'd expected. They made a good tag-team, which was why she always tried to have him in town for major negotiations. At least since that one fiasco. Not only was he intimidating as hell, even when he took off the leather vest and put on a suit, but he was smart as a whip, seeing past the words and fluff and into the meat of a problem. "You know a guy Ty's connected with called Sarge?"

"Yeah, Sarge is ex-military. He runs a halfway house for vets trying to put their lives back together. Sup?" Watcher's tone had gained intensity, and Bethy felt a niggling wiggle of fear. "Why you askin'?"

"Ty's had an episode." Davy left it at that, and Watcher filled in the blanks quickly.

"How long's he been gone? I got a couple of numbers I can call if he's dropped out entirely. See if we can find him." He'd made the wrong assumption, but it warmed Bethy's heart to know that Watcher would drop everything if their friend needed him.

"He's not gone like that. Sarge picked him up nearly a month ago, and I've gotten a couple of texts but…" She paused, trying to decide how much to share. "Sarge and I had words the night it happened, and he was different after. I just…Ty's never been gone this long and will usually keep in touch himself. He hasn't. It's been only Sarge texting me, and that's been just about once a week. I'm not really worried, but Davy got here just as I was asking Dot if she'd heard anything. You know Davy, he's all in to try and make every problem history." There, that had glossed over the near argument, and hopefully both men would focus on Ty instead.

"What'd you argue about?"

"Had words?"

Davy's question and Watcher's came at the same time, and Bethy shook her head, laughing. "I just want to know for sure that Ty's okay, guys. I'm allowed to have disagreements with people, you know. It's not a big deal."

"I know Sarge, and if he was pissed enough at you, he wouldn't hesitate to make it hard for you, Bethy. He's a good dude, but not a nice one." Watcher's words underlined what Bethy had been feeling, and she pulled in a breath, waiting. "I'll give him a ring-a-ling, see if I can't shake some intel from him on Ty. Would help if I knew what I needed to avoid talking about."

"He just...said something I took...look, it was a long day, followed by me getting home to be greeted with a half a dozen garbage bags full of rotting deerskins and Ty in the middle of a meltdown. Sarge just was a wrong place, wrong time thing. If you can find out about Ty, I'll pass it along to Dot, and we'll both owe you big." Bethy stared at her muffin, picking at the edges of the paper, studiously not looking at Davy. "Thanks, Mikey. Give both your pretty girls a hug from me, yeah?"

Silence from both men, and from the corner of her eye, she saw Davy nod. "Thanks, Watch. Talk soon."

"Will do. Let you know soon as I hear anything. Don't worry, Bethy." Watcher's voice softened. "Ty's good, or you'd have heard something for sure. Talk soon."

"Rotting deerskins?" Davy questioned after he disconnected the call.

Bethy tipped her head up and sighed. "Yeah, he had some idea about making things out of them and selling them. I don't know how much he spent on them, but I took the whole load to the cabin and dumped them into a ravine. They smelled so gross." Straightening her shoulders, she glared at him. "Now, if you're done ordering my life for me, can we talk about this group?"

Nodding, Davy told her, "Tell me."

***

"I like the sound," Davy said and held the door open for her to walk through. "You got a good ear. Brains of the operation, just like I always tell everybody."

Bethy shot him a grin over her shoulder, turning to use her key to lock the bolt. A sound on the lot across the street pulled her attention, and she twisted to see a bike slowly pulling out and into the street. A feeling of menace rolled over her skin, and she glanced at Davy to see him staring at the bike and its rider intently.

"You fuckin' know him?" Not a bit of softness in his voice, Davy barked the question at her, and she belatedly realized she probably should have mentioned the bike that had been following her around for the past couple of weeks.

"The bike? No." She shoved her keys into her purse, leaning over to link her arm through Davy's. "Want me to utilize my dubious cooking skills to feed you, or wanna get something edible from the diner?" Cuddling into his side for a minute, she stayed there until she felt his arm flex in hers, and knew he was past whatever anger he'd had. "I'm not saying I'm a bad cook, mind."

"You're also not sayin' you're a good one." He laughed and turned them so they were walking up the sidewalk.

"Mama always said it was wrong to lie." His arm tightened under her grip, and she immediately regretted the words. "Davy, I'm sorry." She scarcely remembered their mother, had only been four when she died of cat scratch fever. What she did remember was suffused through with a feeling of such safety, warmth, and love that it could bring her to tears. Things that had been missing throughout most of her childhood. "You ever think what life would have been like if she hadn't died?"

This time his feet stopped working, and he stood in the middle of the sidewalk, pulling her around so he could wrap his arms around her. Eyes squeezed tightly, he looked like he was in pain, and Bethy was suddenly afraid. "Davy, are you okay?"

"Yeah, baby girl. I'm good." He pulled in a breath and then softly brushed his lips against the side of her head. "I forget sometimes…" Davy's voice trailed off, and she leaned her cheek against his chest. "Let's go to your apartment. We can call for delivery or something. I got a…" He paused again to take in a deep breath and at his hesitation, she steeled herself for whatever was coming. "I got a story to tell you."

***

Feet to the balcony railing, Bethy lifted her clasped hands to her mouth, pressing shaking fingers against her trembling lips. She'd asked Davy for a few minutes of solitude, needing time to process the story he had spun for her tonight. Part of her didn't want to credit it as truth, but in a small sliver of her mind, she believed him outright. It backed up the remembered fear every time Daddy would march up to her standing at the mound of dirt, snatching at the scraggly wildflowers clutched in her dirty child's hand. He hadn't held any reverence for the gravesite. Other people had been laid to rest on the family's land, and he walked around those flattened patches, taking care with his feet and voice. When held up against those, something about her mother's grave never felt right. It had been off in a way she'd never been able to pinpoint.

I was twelve when she died, not four. Tears welled in her eyes again and she blinked furiously, trying to drive them back. *The year when things went bad.* That had been the year when old man Taylor had picked her out of the pack of girls to be his bride. *At least he waited two years to claim me.*

The door slid open behind her and Davy's hands landed on her shoulders, heavy and warm, holding her in place. "You doin' okay, honey?"

She nodded.

"Wanna talk yet?"

Shaking her head, she unclasped her fingers, reaching up with one hand to cover his, holding him in place, too.

"Okay if I sit out here with ya?"

She tipped her head sideways, nodding as she pressed her cheek to his other hand.

He released her to pull a chair over, and then turned hers, bringing her legs across his lap. He reached out, gripping one of her hands and resting their clasped hands on her thigh. Taking a deep breath, he said, "She loved you."

Swallowing hard, Bethy turned her face away, staring off into the darkness, watching the lights of the downtown buildings twinkle in the night.

"She did. You might not remember, but she loved you. Loved both of us." He moved, and she heard the scratchy noise of him rubbing his palm across his jaw. "Life in the holler is hard."

"I know it is. I was there, too, Davy." Blinking fast, she let the things she wanted to say go ahead and flow out, needing to know if she could. Needing to understand. "Do you know how she died?"

"No." The word came out on a hoarse croak, and she realized this was as hard on him as it was her, making him relive things he probably would prefer to stay buried. She gave his fingers a squeeze, smiling when he returned it. "Just know she's gone."

"And the man who took her, what was he to us?" The idea of her mother being taken wasn't as farfetched as he might believe it to be, and Bethy knew it from the inside out, being taken unwilling as she'd been.

"Nothing to us, Bethy. He's nothin' at all." Davy shifted in his seat, rocking her legs as he settled. "Justice Morgan is a powerful man, but he ain't nothing to us."

"You said she had another baby, a boy?" Bethany remembered the tingling feeling in her breasts as the milk intended for her child had let down, how it had made her cry to know she'd never hold him like that, never hold and nurse him. "I can't imagine how it was for her, being with us and missing him, or being with him and missing us. Pain no matter where she turned."

Ty scowled at Bethy from across the room, his brows bowing together. "You gotta tell him." He shook his head. "Watcher's gotta know."

She stood, trembling, arms crossed over her still-rolling stomach. That had been what betrayed her. Ty hadn't missed her nausea these past two weeks, and her claims of a bug only went so far. Bethy felt her lips quiver, tried to ignore how her chin bumped, but couldn't dam her tears. Hot and wet, they rolled down her face as she stared at him.

If Ty did this, told Mikey, then Mikey would be honor bound to tell her brother. She knew they were in touch. Mikey, now known as Watcher, had been clear on that when he set her up with Tyrell three weeks back.

"Please." That one word broke in three places, her voice betraying her. She sucked in a breath, then blew it out, trying to control both her belly and her tears. Accent thick, she pleaded with Ty. "You cain't. He cain't know. He knows, he'll tell my brother. Davy don't even know what Daddy

did. Don't know about what happened after he left. I've only talked to him a couple of times on the phone, haven't seen him for nearly four years. He don't know nothin' that happened. If he knew, he'd kill Daddy. An' Watcher'll hafta tell Davy." She willed him to believe her, to trust she knew the best path. Bending at the waist, she begged, "Don't. Please, God, don't. You know how this goes. I just gotta figure out what to do."

Ty's scowl deepened. Then he asked the right question. "You wanna raise this baby?" Sobs now shaking her frame, Bethy shook her head, having worked it out in her head that an on-her-own sixteen-year-old mother couldn't come close to giving this child what it deserved. "Want it to go to a good family?" Her head moved up and down so fast a wave of nausea crawled up her throat. That same wish had fled her lips nightly while she sat close to the open window, staring up at the cold stars overhead. "Then that's what we'll do, little girl." He took a step towards her and lifted his arms out to his sides. Disbelieving for a moment, she watched as the corners of his mouth curled up. "Come here, Bethy." She flew across the room to him, letting him wrap her up with his warmth and love. "Then that's what we'll do. But first, you're gonna tell me everything about this Taylor dude. Everything you can."

His voice had taken on an edge of rage when he finished with, "I'll take care of him, honey." He rocked them in place, soothing her with his words and body. "Then I'll take care of you. We'll do whatever you need, honey. I got you."

Davy moved again, pulling her thoughts from the past. She froze when he said, "That's a dark study, honey. Whatcha thinkin' about?"

Without lying, she answered, "Tyrell. He's been a really good friend, you know?"

"I know." Davy's other hand slowly stroked up and down her shin. His next words were careful. "Y'all are pretty tight."

Tipping her head, she looked at him and rolled her eyes. "He's my friend, Davy. That's all."

Not smiling, his eyes on her were serious when he said, "If it weren't...if y'all were more than friends, that'd be okay. I wish you weren't..." Davy sighed. "I wish things were different for you. I wish I could make things different."

Ty stood in the kitchen and stared at Bethy as she opened the thick envelope of papers from the Harrison County clerk's office. "That them?" She pulled out the sheaf of pages, scanned the top sheet and nodded.

"The annulment is official." Bethy shoved the certified forms back into the envelope, not wanting to look at them one moment longer than she had to. "It's all behind me." Lifting her head, she told him, "Weird that I get these the week after he died."

She'd heard from Aunt Barbra that Taylor had passed away. He'd been crushed when his tractor rolled over on top of him as he worked the side of a mountain. His body had laid out in the weather for days before anyone found him. With Bethy gone, there was no one else on his land. He'd died without an heir, which meant his land would go to the state and then up for auction. She'd had the option of stopping the annulment and being declared his widow, but she hadn't wanted the weight of that placed on her shoulders. Then everyone would have to know about the baby, which meant her father would know. Bethy rested her hand on her swollen belly. He'll never hurt you, little one, she told the child inside her.

Glancing up, she caught a look of rage and guilt on Ty's face that surprised her. She remembered his vow to take care of Taylor. "Ty, what did you do?"

"Only what needed doin', Bethy. Nothing for you to worry about." He grabbed her jacket and tossed it across the room to her, and picked up his sweatshirt, shrugging it on over his head. "Let's get to this class so they can teach you how to breathe right, yeah?"

Bethy only moved enough to pluck her jacket from the air, staring at Ty, fear crawling through her chest. "What did you do?" Her whisper was barely enough to stir the air, but he heard her.

"Man like that? What do you think I did? He had another girl all lined up, Bethy. I asked around, and he'd been hanging around at every one of the church camps. I know you know you told me what happened there. Know you haven't forgotten. He had another girl lined up." Ty lifted a hand and pointed to her belly. "That child's a girl, you gonna stand there and tell me you want her in the same world as Taylor? Breathin' that air?" Bethy shook her head. "That's right. And neither did I. So, I did something about it. Took care of it, like I told you I would." Breathing hard, as if he'd run a marathon, Ty stared at her. "Took care of it, Bethy. Takin' care of you. My little sister, I love ya, honey. Took care of it." One palm flattened on the table in front of him. His sober expression didn't change, having settled into rigid lines while he waited for her reaction. Held himself still, and the very air in the apartment was still, as if they were standing on a precipice. "Now, we going to Lamaze class, or not?"

For me. "We're going." She didn't move, holding her jacket as if it were foreign to her, an article of clothing she couldn't understand. Anything could tip things the wrong way, and she was suddenly terrified of things falling out badly. So she stood there, jacket in hand and let the magnitude of what Ty had done sink in. He did that for me.

"Then come on." Irritated and impatient, he slapped the table lightly, barely rattling the salt and pepper shakers. She didn't have any fear of him. He'd never hurt me. Gentle and kind, he'd never shown her anything other than the sweet giant he was inside. He did that for me. I can't ever repay him for knowing that shadow is gone.

"I love you, Tyrell." Bethy took a breath, feeling the baby move and roll around, shifting inside her. "You and Watcher, you've done so much for me, so much more than my family. And you...every time I turn around, *you're taking care of me. You're more my family than anyone else could ever be."*

"You afraid of me now?" He asked the question with a duck of his head like he expected the worst.

"No." Strong and firm, she laid it out for him. Never. "I am not afraid of you, Ty."

"Then what the fuck you doin' all the way over there?" He moved, coming closer, and took the jacket from her, shaking it out so she could slip her arms into it. "We got places to be."

"Tyrell has always been there. He's my friend." Bethy didn't miss how Davy flinched at the spaces between her words that shouted he hadn't been there for her. "I can't change what happened, Davy. We can't change the past. But you're here now." His hand squeezed her ankle. "And that counts for a lot, big brother." She paused, then carefully asked, "You think he knows about me?"

"He does. He knows he's got a sister. You want to meet John?" Davy had instinctively known who she was talking about and she smiled, shaking her head. "You change your mind, let me know, I'll set it up."

"Okay." A scene from last weekend flashed through her head, leaning against a tree and laughing, out of breath from chasing Michael through the park, his long legs easily outdistancing hers. *Do you want to know you have a nephew?* Bethany clamped her lips tightly. "Do you think Daddy knew?"

"Hard to think she'd keep it a secret from him. Probably why he was so damn mad at her all the time." Davy's voice had an edge of anger, his eyes focused on something in the past. "Not that the old man needed an excuse."

"I feel so sorry for her. She was in a hard place. With us, she missed him. With him, she missed us." His gaze snapped to her, and she stood firm. "I'll let you know about meeting him. It seems weird. I wouldn't know what to say."

Ty was in the room when she pushed her son into the world. His big hands were the ones that brushed back her hair, and he was the one who told her the baby was well and healthy. Ten fingers, ten toes, and gorgeous. He told her she'd done good. That she was brave.

She held his hand tightly, crushing his fingers as the pain hit when the adoptive parents held her baby. Not mine, *she tried to remind herself, feeling a welling ache in her chest. Then the woman turned and offered her a watery smile filled with such joy those words lost their sting.*

Angling the blue blanket so Bethy could see him, Martha Marshall said something so sweetly gracious Bethy loved her even more. This woman who had become like a mother figure to her, someone who so longed to be a mother, but nature had denied her the chance. Ty had found the Marshalls through mutual friends, and they agreed to an open arrangement. When Martha turned to show Bethy the baby, she said, "Look at our baby boy."

Michael Tyrell Marshall.

"Don't gotta decide today."

Early days

Gabe, four years later

"Fuck." The word gained extra syllables as he growled it into the darkness of the alley. He hadn't seen the blow that had finally taken him down. Gabe pushed against the ground, trying to get his feet underneath him. One arm buckled, sending him sprawling into the slimy grime along the edges of the cobblestone and he shouted with the pain, cheek pressed to the chill of the bricks underneath him.

"Stay down." Gabe froze at the command in that voice. The speaker had utmost certainty that he would be obeyed. He believed his words would be taken as gospel, and it sounded so much like Gabe's old man, he couldn't suppress a shudder that rolled through him.

Not my daddy. That was all the reminder he needed, and Gabe gathered himself for another attempt. "Fuck." He paused, got one knee on the ground and shoved again, staggering as he gained his feet. "You."

"Boy." Now the voice sounded faintly amused but pleased, like Gabe had done something unexpected and rare. "Takes some balls to climb your ass back up after the beatdown you just took. Should stop while you're ahead. Stay down. Just fuckin' quit."

Reaching back with one arm, Gabe tried to find the wall he knew had to be there, praying it wasn't far and that his legs would hold him up until he found the support. "I don't." He stumbled, and the movement woke a deeper pain. *Fuck.* "Quit."

"No shit, Sherlock." A different voice, this from beside him, and Gabe felt a shoulder shoved under his arm. "He's done, Shooter. Paid his dues."

Gabe's eyes had squeezed shut against the pain which seemed to be coming at him from all directions, swamping him like a metal johnboat in a sudden storm. Wave after wave, doing their damnedest to take him down. Flinging his head back, he forced his eyes open as he stiffened his legs, leaning on his unexpected supporter.

"Whatcha think, Gabe? Think you've paid your dues? Think you're ready to join the big boys?" *Shooter.* Now that Gabe had a name, he recognized the voice, one he'd spoken to over the phone several times in the past month. Gabe had been trying to extricate his group from the larger chapter in Louisville, and the man had repeatedly put him off, claiming multiple excuses that never seemed to hold water. Rumor had it he wasn't Diamante at all, but Outrider. Rumor was wrong.

Can't complain when you're the beggar, he thought. "Pretty clear—" He paused to breathe, wrapping an arm around his gut and grunting as the pain in his ribs hit him. "I'm sittin' out on the porch." Hissing in reaction to a movement from the man beside him, he grunted again. "For the duration."

"Tellin' you, he's done, Shooter. You leave him alive, we are assured of his loyalty." The voice had a faintly Mexican accent, a way of rolling the letters that sounded exotic.

"Fuck you, Chismoso. He ain't done until I say he's done."

Chismoso. Diamante from Juarez. If he were here, then crazy Lalo won't be far be—

Something hit Gabe's calf, sweeping his legs out from under him as his knees crumpled. He went down hard, unable to break his fall, arms instinctively going to protect his already damaged ribs. Another voice, this one gleeful as it shouted, "Again!"

Blow after blow stripped his senses, each sharp pain pushing him deeper under until there was just a noisy blackness all around.

"Tabby and Jonny, sittin' in a tree." The shouted rhyme came from a multitude of throats, the gaggle of boys on the schoolyard gravitating towards the ring of bodies already formed around a small girl huddled on the ground. Her too-big pants with ground-in stains from being pushed to the grass had pulled to gape at her waist, her shirt had rucked up and Gabe could see the livid bruise on her back. Goddamn Daddy to hell.

He pushed through the circle, shoving until he went to his knees beside her, reaching out and pulling her into his arms. Her tears wetting his chest, he glared up at the faces laughing down, their words and laughter trailing off as his anger made itself known. Silence descended, and the bell rang, the long rope pulled by the favored first grader calling everyone back to class.

She pushed against him, hands fluttering like butterflies as she tried to escape without touching his skin. A moment later he heard her utter a word and understood, hating that he did, hating even more that she did. "Unclean."

"Don't care about that, Tabbycat. I got you." He pushed to his feet, pulling her up alongside him and walked her to the side door of the schoolhouse. Calling the teacher over, Gabe explained, and they escaped together.

He got Tabby to talking, and she finally gave up the names of the boys who'd started hazing her. The next day was Saturday, and Gabe knew where the boys would be. He forced himself out of bed early to do chores so he could be at the fishing hole before they arrived.

At supper that night, he caught Tabby staring at his hands, knuckles scuffed and bruised from the lesson he'd delivered. When he finally got her to look at his face, he winked, and she ducked her head. But before she had, he'd seen the tiny smile. Work my fingers to the bone to see that.

After a time, even the noisy blackness receded.

***

"Fuck, boss. You took a beatin'."

Gabe shifted on his back, sliding to one side a few inches, twisting his neck so he could see the speaker. His side was one throbbing mass of pain so he rolled slightly, finding his flanks and low back were just as bad. *Gonna piss blood.*

"Jesus."

He tried forcing one eye open, making it into a bare squint. The blood, sweat, and fluids had dried and caked the upper and lower lashes together, so he could only open it a fraction of an inch. A round face hovered close, the man's features swimming in and out of focus while Gabe concentrated on maintaining that fraction of an inch long enough to see who it was. The voice was familiar, but nothing made sense right now.

Probably cuz my head hurts so fuckin' bad.

"Can you sit up?"

Ridiculous. He tried to snort a laugh, failing miserably when his ribs complained, his muscles seizing in a hard spasm. Frowning pulled every inch of his face painfully, so he let his features smooth out instead of scowling like he wanted. Blinking that one eye hard, he managed to gain another fraction of an inch open and the face above him resolved into someone he knew.

"Gator." His voice was weird. Soft and wispy instead of hard and angry, which was how he felt inside. "Get me up."

"Hang on, boss. Lemme make sure you aren't broke up." That preceded a painful process of touch and movement as his second's hands pressed and pulled, ensuring Gabe wouldn't permanently injure himself by moving.

"Get. Me. Up." No mistaking the impatience in his tone, and Gator responded like Gabe expected, an arm around his shoulders lifting and twisting, pulling him a few excruciating inches. Back against the wall, he leaned where Gator put him, not trying to move beyond getting his eyelids open. Best he could do was the one eye, but he managed to get that working, at least. "Head."

"Yeah, no doubt." Gator had read the message in the one word. "Side of your face is busted, bruised to shit and swollen enough I expect it hurts like a bitch. What…?" His voice trailed off as he glanced around the alley. "Chismoso called me, or I'd have never found you here, Gabe. What in the fuck did you do to piss everybody off like this? I thought we were in line to join 'em. This looks to be the opposite."

"Breathing." Clamping his teeth against a wave of nausea, Gabe said, "I'm talented like that."

"You mean you smartassed your way into a fucking beating?" Gator shook his head. "What are we going to do now?"

Gabe let his head lean back against the wall, resting his eye for a minute. "We go on. I got what we want. Nothing less."

"You mean you're willing to do this again? You are one crazy fucker." Gator crouched, one knee to the ground. "Stupid, too."

"No, man. I got what we want." He moved, bringing up one swollen hand to dig into the inside pocket of his vest. "Charter." He battled a cough, and won, knowing how badly that would hurt. "Lexington." Papers dangled from his fingers.

"Are you fucking kidding me?" Gator took the papers, unfolding them, looking at the handwritten message, blinking in surprise. "Fucking insane, man." Bringing the documents closer to his face, he asked, "Who the fuck's Fury?"

"Lookin' at him." Gabe lifted his swollen lip, stretching the throbbing flesh tight, grinning through the pain. "Got our own chapter."

***

Six months later

Fury blew out a frustrated breath at the idea of repeating himself yet again. *Why can't the man just listen?* "I told you. No, I'm not opening a second chapter in Fort Wayne. I just expanded the territory for Lexington. Bought a couple of businesses up there. Not lookin' to cause trouble for anyone, and Shooter gave a thumbs-up to everything. See, not out of line." The last sentence was hissed, and he knew the man on the other end of the phone had taken the warning as he intended.

"Didn't mean no disrespect, Fury." Painter, an officer in the Cynthania chapter of Outriders, backpedaled quickly. "Not intendin' no offense."

"Not sure what business it is of Outriders if I did decide to work up a charter. Not like y'all got shit all to do with anything in Fort Wayne." Fury bent double in his chair, leaning deep to pick up his coffee mug from the floor. Lifting it to his lips, he cautiously sipped at the hot liquid. "Not like y'all got shit all to say about Diamante, period."

"Not true, man. You know it. We got a princess in town still. We'll always keep tabs on Morgan's girl."

"She's shacked up with a Rebel. Y'all lookin' to poke that Bear? Everybody knows Mason's got a hella hard-on for Outriders. If y'all are keepin' track of what he now considers his, that won't go over well with him. You and I both know it." Fury shook his head and rolled his eyes, finding it hard to believe Morgan had gone that far.

"Still, she's ours." The words were said firmly, and Fury dropped his argument. *No skin off my nose.*

"Heard there's a professional guy in the area." Not a question, but he laid the statement out, knowing Painter wouldn't be able to ignore it if he knew anything.

"Yeah, bastard is something else." Painter laughed, the sound dark and fearful. "Woolfe is one scary motherfucker." Silence then Painter offered, "They pulled him in because there's something big going on up in Utah. Time and dime being spent up there like a bitch, and Shooter didn't have anyone to spare to deal with that shit in the Fort."

"What's going in Utah?" Eyes up, he stared at the ceiling, tracking a crack across the stained paint. "I could give a hot shit about Shooter, but Utah's interesting territory to be claiming."

"Got some plans for a compound or something. They needed a show of force. Heard your boy hit the area with a hard splash, had to be expelled." Painter chuckled, the sound grating on Fury's nerves. "Sent him out of there like a snot rocket."

"My boy?" With his ties to both clubs, Fury had no idea what Painter was talking about. Gator was the only one he really claimed as a friend and brother, and he was here in Fort Wayne. *At my side, like he should be.* "Whachu talkin' about?"

"Lalo."

Fury didn't try to stop the growl clawing up his throat, hearing the insane voice in a dark alley shouting, *"Again!"* like beating him was a thrill ride on a county fair midway.

"Yeah, figured you'd have that response. He's headed back Florida way, I understand." Silence for a moment, then Painter tried to get them back on track, obviously wanting the call to end. "Like I was sayin', Woolfe is one scary fucker."

Fury leaned back in his chair, taking another drink from his mug. "Any idea what he's doin' in the Fort?"

"Not a fuckin' clue. Man's a private contractor, so you know he's got a job or he wouldn't be in town. My advice? Keep your eyes open."

Draining the mug, Fury set it on the floor and stood, pushing the chair back and out of the way, giving himself a clear view of the man handcuffed to a set of rings in the wall. "No doubt. You hear anything else I need to know, shit like what's going down in Utah, bring it to me, yeah?" The call disconnected, and he tipped his head to the side, considering his captive. "You don't look so fuckin' scary to me."

Fury walked towards Woolfe and stopped out of reach. "You know how badly you've fucked up tonight? Just how fuckin' bad you screwed up?" He paused for a breath, then blew it out slowly. "You've screwed the pooch, man. There are a hundred men combing Fort Wayne looking for the man in the room up the hall. Lookin' for his woman, too. You don't know who you took, do you?" Using the toe of his boot, he prodded the sole of the man's foot. "Not a fuckin' clue."

"My boss is the same as your boss. We do what we're told." Woolfe shrugged as nonchalantly as he could be with both hands anchored over his head. "Pays the bills."

"Bought yourself a world of pain, man. That's Gunny. He's an insider. A confidant to the national president of the Rebel Wayfarers. You took him from his own home." Fury leaned down, letting his lips pull back in a feral snarl. "Brought him to my property. But that wasn't enough. Oh, no, not for you." He shook his head. "You had to bring his woman, too. And not only is she his woman, but she's also the sister of a friend of that same club. A friend who happens to be wooing the former president's old lady." Leaning in again, he clipped, "Fucked in the ass." Straightening, he stepped back. "You're right, though. Your boss is the national president of this club." Fury hooked a thumb at the back of his vest. "Means I needa do what I gotta do to haul your ass outta the fire before Shooter or Morgan get wind of just had badly you fucked up on my territory."

At the door Fury paused and turned back, staring into the Woolfe's eyes. "I guarantee you're a dead man. Gunny's insane enough to not let this go."

"Gunny and I go way back," Woolfe said cockily. "He ain't gonna do shit to me."

Pulling the door shut behind him, remembering the rage he'd seen in Gunny's face as he paced in the cell Woolfe had locked him in, Fury told the empty hallway the truth as he saw it. "You're wrong."

Taken

Bethany, six months later

Bethy yelled, lifting her voice so it echoed through the apartment as she reached down to pull her shoe on over her thick sock, "I gotta go to work. Heading to the studio, I'll be back later." Ty called something, the words lost in the closing of the door. Bethy was laughing as she walked out because, after almost sixteen years of living with him, she could safely assume it was a request for food. Pushing the button on her key fob, she climbed into her car and made her way through the streets of the neighborhood and out to the main road. Twenty minutes brought her to the darkened parking lot across the street from the studio.

She was already across the street and beside the door to the studio, reaching out to unlock it before she realized she hadn't heard the alarm on her car beep. Turning, she saw the driver door was open by a few inches, the dome light shining. "Dang it." Back at the car, she untwisted a kink in the seatbelt, letting it ratchet back into the frame of the car. Beeping her locks, she grinned and headed back into the building, locking the door behind her.

Cans on her ears, she was working at the mixing board when the lights went out. No flicker, no warning, just a hard cut of the electricity.

Groaning as she pulled the headset off, she laid it on the console, working by feel to find the door, knowing there would be emergency lighting in the hallway. "Jesus, that was a good track, too." She hadn't saved her work yet, which meant everything she'd laid down was lost. "Gonna have to invest in a backup system. I can't afford to lose work like this."

She didn't hear anything except the sound of her own voice. The building was eerily quiet without even the noise of the climate control system. No fans blowing, no equipment buzzing, just silent. Pair that with her being unable to see, and she felt strangely exposed, like someone was watching her. The hair on the back of her neck stood on end, and she swung around, turning in place, drawing in breath to scream when her hand hit something unexpected. Something big, and solid, and warm. The scream never left her lungs, silenced when darkness descended.

***

Terror had become a state of being. The only difference from day to day, or sometimes minute to minute, was the intensity of that emotion. She tried to keep it locked down, pushed far away. But sometimes it crept in on her.

Bethy sat on the floor opposite the locked door, eyes closed, belly quivering with dread. She'd found if she didn't look at him when he brought her food, she could hold onto her control a little. Even a little mattered, because he didn't like tears. Once she looked at him, as soon as she saw his eyes, the fear would wake, curling around her throat and chest. Bethy would start to hyperventilate and would feel her heart beat in her ears. His eyes, flat and grey, as lifeless as if he were a mannequin, but somehow familiar. Nothing else about him seemed to pick at her memories, nothing except his eyes.

Creepy Guy, she called him in her head, having learned the first day that it didn't pay to say anything aloud.

She knew she wasn't the only captive. He was holding another woman, brought in five days after he'd put Bethany into this narrow cell. The room was just wide enough for the cot and a bucket, the metal door had a window in it, meaning she could watch him through it if she wanted. Most days, she didn't want to. Seeing him meant trying to figure out why she was here, and that led her down dark paths. Paths filled with visions of her father, and Taylor. Of Uncle Ezra, and every terror-filled night of her childhood. Plus, if she could see him, the creepy guy, it meant he might see her. He left her alone most of the time, and as terrifying as the between times were, she was certain she didn't want him thinking about her too much.

Bethy had heard the other woman screaming at him more than once, yelling unintelligible words with an angry, strident voice, usually after he'd been gone for a couple of days in a row. There didn't seem to be any kind of schedule for his comings and goings. No rhyme or reason, each interval seemed erratic. He'd be here for two or three days in a row, then gone for two, then back here for a week solid.

The first time he brought in a grocery bag of food Bethany hadn't known to ask for water. Hadn't understood the why, because she didn't have enough data to know this action prefaced him leaving for an extended period. He hadn't put any water in the bag, so all she had was the one he'd given her for lunch that day. By the time he got back two days later, she was so thirsty and dehydrated she couldn't stand. He'd opened a bottle and poured it down her throat, uncaring when she'd choked on the unrelenting stream.

After that, when he brought in a bag, she would ask. Polite, eyes to the floor, feeling like the kid in an old English play, asking for more. Her only objective staying alive. She forced herself to picture Michael's face, imagine his voice telling her to stay strong, keeping him as her goal, a lodestone to lead her forwards. *When I get out of here, I'm going to tell him how much I love him.* Words she'd held back, never voicing them, because while he might suspect from her actions, she didn't want him to be conflicted in any way. *The Marshalls have given him a good home, and a good life. I'm so blessed they let me be part of it.*

When the man brought in a third woman, Bethy had scrambled to the window as soon as she heard the voices. Every time it happened, she was hopeful of rescue. And every time, she was also fearful he would bring his own brand of friends back with him.

He stood the woman in the middle of the room for a long time, not letting her move. Every time the woman would lift her bound hands to try and take the bag off her head, he screamed at her, hitting himself in the face. Shouting, he'd walked the perimeter of the large space, alternately talking to the woman and ranting at no one. Aggressively attacking things in the room like the desk, he'd overturned it with a crash, and then came rattling and hammering on Bethy's cell door while he screamed at her to get up and watch. Eventually, he seemed to exhaust the well of rage inside him and put the woman into the cell next to Bethy. The difference in sounds told her that the shouting woman was farther away, which meant he had at least three of these rooms.

When the lights went out, she crawled onto her cot and pulled the covers to her shoulders, curling into as small a ball as she could manage. So far, she couldn't see any way out, and without knowing why he had kidnapped her, she couldn't figure out if she had leverage at all. *Not enough data.* "Tomorrow." She whispered the single word, her voice rasping with disuse. *I love you, baby boy.* "Tomorrow."

***

The screaming woke her.

It had been seven days since the third woman was brought in, and the man had been uncharacteristically quiet most of that time. He would move a stool behind the desk and sit for hours, watching. Bethy had become adept at peering through a corner of her window with a single eye, keeping him in sight while feeling hidden. She knew it wasn't true, but as long as he didn't glance her way, she could pretend, at least.

Creepy Guy was the only person she'd seen in forever, and sometimes Bethy wondered if this was real. Hungry and thirsty, because he never left enough of anything for her, she felt faint a lot of the time. Maybe that's why it all seemed surreal. The whole thing. From being in her studio one minute, to shoved into a tiny cell the next. *Can this really be happening to me?* People didn't get kidnapped. That was a TV thing, done for drama, highlighted by eerie music. Here, other than the screaming woman, there were only limited noises and no music at all. Music, something she'd lived for since starting at the radio station the first day, was entirely absent. Now, yanked out of the lost space in her head, she lay on the thin mattress and listened, suddenly realizing all sound had stopped.

Bethy climbed out of bed, barely saving herself from falling headlong over the blanket in her rush to get to the window. Cheek pressed to the cold surface of the door, she strained to see something, anything. Moving in jerks and stumbles, the grey-eyed man came into view carrying something wrapped in rags, red liquid dripping in a stuttering stream to the floor. He was coming from the direction of the farthest room. The screaming woman's room. The screaming woman who was quiet now, silent as the...Bethy shook her head, not willing to finish the thought.

***

Hands over her ears, Bethy sat with her back against the door, trying to hide from the window as best she could. Not that she expected the grey-eyed man to come for her. Not after what she'd heard.

He'd done something unexpected today.

Bethy had been seated against the back wall when her doorknob rattled. Then she heard the latch make a clicking sound. That snick of metal sliding against metal terrifying because she never knew what it preceded. Would it be food and water? The hook on a stick to carry her waste bucket out? The dismembered hand she'd watched him toying with for most of a day? Death on two legs? Lowering her chin, she'd closed her eyes and waited for the sounds that normally accompanied him opening the door. Waiting. Maybe today would be when he came for her, like he had the screaming woman.

But, nothing happened. For minutes she'd sat there waiting, and nothing happened.

Eyes flicking open, her gaze had landed on the door that stood slightly ajar. Traced up and down the narrowest sliver of light that eased in around the edges. Waited for something to happen. *This isn't right*. Her door had always been locked from the outside. Always. Unless he was standing in the doorway with a bottle of water to throw at her, or shoving in a box of tasteless food. Always.

Noises had filtered in, tentative footsteps. No voices. The silence had been nearly suffocating.

When Bethy had stepped through the open door for the first time in nearly a month, she had seen two women. He'd come back a day ago with a fourth woman, locking her in the cell on the other side of Bethy's. And now, it had looked as if they were being released. That didn't make sense. Her mind had screamed at her, warning of a trick and she'd looked around, finally finding him perched on his stool in the shadows. Then the third woman had shocked her by knowing her name. "Bethy," she'd whispered, and Bethy had nearly given herself whiplash turning to stare at her. Then the woman told her an impossible truth, something the woman had clearly believed, and fit the few facts Bethy had put together, that this had to be tied to Davy somehow.

"I'm Willa, Mason's girlfriend. You're his sister, Bethany."

Jesus. Just remembering it gave her chills.

Things had happened fast, after that. He'd come close, talking to Willa like he knew her, and Bethy believed he did, because Willa had accused him of kidnapping her, comparing it to something in the past. She'd named the man, Luke Judge, and had put herself between where Bethy and the other woman stood and him as he approached. Protecting them. *Davy's girlfriend*.

Then Judge had gone crazy. *Crazier*, she thought, pressing her palms tighter to the sides of her head. He'd ordered her and the other woman back into their cells. For a moment, Bethy had thought about rushing him. Then he had his hand on Willa's throat, had lifted her to her toes, choking her. *He'd have killed her*. In the few seconds of indecision, Willa's struggling had already gotten weaker, her hands gripping his wrists instead of fighting him. So, Bethy had stared at the other woman. Then they had both backed through the open doors, pushing them closed.

But he didn't stop choking Willa, hadn't stopped. Bethy thought he was going to kill her, no matter they'd all complied with his demands. Yelling, screaming like she hadn't done since the first few days in her cell, Bethy had pounded on the glass. Little smears of blood attested to how hard she'd pounded, hoping to get his attention, hoping to make him stop. *I tried to save her, Davy*.

Then he took Willa into her cell, and it wasn't long before the other noises started. The ones that had driven Bethy to cover her ears. She'd been sitting like this for hours. A lifetime.

The sound of a gunshot ripped through the air and Bethy screamed, crossing her arms over her head. "Oh, my God. She's dead." Bethy didn't recognize her own voice. "She's dead." Holding her breath, she swallowed a scream, her head repeating the words she wouldn't allow from her mouth. *She's dead. She's dead. Davy's girlfriend. She's dead*.

Nothing happened for a long time, minutes ticking past while she waited for Judge to come for her. He had already killed the second woman, Bethy believed that because the woman had never been quiet, not for this long at least. *He's coming for me. She's dead, and he's coming for me.* She swallowed. *I love you, Davy. Love you, Ty.* She swallowed again, tears wet on her cheeks. *I love you, Michael. My son. Please know I love you.*

Shouting, yelling and screaming, her relief at recognizing Willa's voice countered by Judge's angry shouts which were so loud they sounded like he was right on top of her, and Bethy cowered on the floor. Then another gunshot. Hands pressed against her mouth, Bethy kept herself from screaming, repeating her litany of love. *Davy, Ty, Michael, I love you.* A noise, and for a moment she thought she'd blacked out. *Derek, I love you.* The door behind her pushed open, and she sprawled on her side, hands lifted to fend off the bullet she knew was coming.

Blinking, staring up, Bethy looked into the pale face of Willa standing over her, gun gripped loosely in one hand, a knife in the other.

***

"Hold up. Wait," Bethy whispered to Willa, slowing their run, trying to accommodate the slower pace of the third woman, who had introduced herself as Mica. "Wait for Mica."

"You know where we're going?" Willa's question was a whisper, too, and Bethy knew it was because her throat hurt. She was badly bruised; her neck bore dark circles where Judge had choked her. Shaking her head, Bethy didn't give another answer. There was no way she could know. It was slow going because Willa was injured, and Mica was dealing with the aftereffects from the drugs he'd used to incapacitate her while Bethy was weakened after her weeks in captivity. And, even after running and walking through the woods for hours, they hadn't come upon a road or even seen a building.

"Away. We're going away. I grew up in the woods, but these aren't Kentucky trees. I don't know where we are. So for right now, we're just going away." She leaned sideways, pressed a palm to the bark of a tree and looked over her shoulder back up the trail, thinking for a moment she'd seen something move in the distance. "I wish we'd brought the weapons." They hadn't, though. Willa had been adamant, and after what she imagined the woman had been through, Bethy hadn't pushed her. "Luke Judge was still locked up when we got out of there, but what if he gets out? We can't take the risk. We gotta get as far away as we can."

Willa looped her arm through Mica's, pulling the woman to her side. Whispering, she said, "Luke Morgan. That's his name, but people call him Judge."

Bethy stopped, staring at Willa, hearing Davy's voice as he told her, *"Justice Morgan is a powerful man, but he ain't nothing to us."* Slowly, she asked, "His last name's Morgan?" She pulled in a breath. "Do you know his daddy's name?"

Willa tipped her head to the side and chewed her lip. "John. John Morgan. People call him Shooter."

Bethy bent double, sucking in a hard breath. *My nephew was going to kill me.*

"Can we go?" That was Mica, and her shaky voice pushed Bethy to get herself back under control. "My husband and son are in Chicago. I need to...I want to go home."

"We will," Willa reassured, her voice raw and hoarse. She soothed Mica with the slow caress of her palm up and down her back. "We will, right, Bethy?"

Nodding, Bethy fought against tears. From the few things Willa had said, she knew Luke...Judge had raped her. Raped her, and still she had fought him. Fought him and gained control of the gun she'd used to shoot him. Forced him to release her. *She set us all free.* "We are all gonna go home," Bethy vowed. "Every one of us."

"Willa." A man's voice called from behind them, and all three women screamed, Bethy jumping to put herself in front of Willa and Mica. In her fear, it was Luke she saw coming at her, hands out. He was followed by another man, and she again cursed Willa for not letting her bring the gun. "Willa, it's Hoss, honey." Bethy blinked, the man's face gradually resolving into a stranger's, with warm brown eyes instead of the cold grey ones seen in her nightmares.

"Hoss," Willa cried, and then pushed past Bethy, running straight at the man. Bethy didn't know him, didn't know his face, but she knew he wasn't Luke. He planted both feet and wrapped his arms around Willa when she hit his chest. Crying, she was sobbing and hiccupping, asking for Davy. She went strangely still when he said Davy was waiting back at the compound.

Mica stood next to Bethy, arm around her waist as she said in a relieved voice, "We're safe, Bethy. Safe."

"Who...how do you know them?" Even before she finished asking the question she knew. Between Davy and Watcher, she'd been introduced to enough bikers they were friends with to recognize the type. Hoss and, she squinted, trying to read the name on the second man's vest, Gunny, had to be with Davy. A third man came into view, his red beard causing her breath to catch in her chest for a moment before realizing she didn't recognize him. Tater, his vest said. "Davy came for you, Willa. Like you said he would."

Hoss looked at her then, and said, "Bethany. We're here for all of you." He gestured behind her and Mica stepped forwards. "All of you. There's more back," he jerked a thumb over his shoulder, "there where y'all were. Watcher's there, so's Bones. You know them, right?"

Chin quivering, Bethy nodded, belief finally seeping into her belly. *Safe.*

On the plane headed back to Chicago and then Fort Wayne, Bethy sat beside Davy, recounting everything she could think of, wanting to purge it from her mind. As she narrated the past weeks, his tension was palpable, muscles all over his body tight. When she told him about Willa trying to protect them, and then in the end saving them all, his jaw moved as he ground his teeth, his jaw clenching repeatedly while he tried to hold onto his composure. Willa had retreated into herself after they got back to the compound. Bethy wondered if it was because Davy was there. Still, he made Willa feel safe enough that she could lean on him, quietly falling apart in his arms.

"She's pretty amazing, Davy." He nodded, eyes on a sleeping Willa, and in the intensity of his gaze Bethy saw how much he loved this woman. *So much more than just a girlfriend*, she thought, a little wistfully. *She's part of his family now. I love you, Michael.* "I want to go home, Davy. When can I go back?"

He leaned close and pressed his lips to the side of her head, answering absently, "Soon."

Still trying to make sense out of everything, Bethy mused, "What I don't get is why he brought Carrie and Mica. If he had known who I was, it would make more sense. I'd understand me and Willa, because, well"—she pointed at herself—"sister and"—she held her hand out towards Willa—"girlfriend. But why the other two?"

That was when Davy upended her world, showing her that he'd been keeping secrets as big as hers were. "Mica's been important to me for a long time. A long time. Since the day I met her." He paused a breath, then said, "Carrie was my boy's mother."

Davy has a son. Like her, but not, because from the way he spoke, she knew that his son was in his life. *Not like me.* "What? Your...boy? You have a boy? Davis Mason, you have a son? I have a nephew?" She knew her voice was loud and saw Willa stirring but couldn't stop, the pain in her chest fierce, consuming her.

"Well, yeah. I've been meaning to tell you—"

As if a child were disposable. A casual afterthought, when to Bethy it would have been a cherished being. "You've been...meaning to tell me? How long have you known about this boy?" The look on Davy's face was unreadable for a minute. Then pain flashed across his features and in that instant Bethy wanted to pull all her words back. He hadn't meant it that way, and the idea that she could believe he would had hurt him. Changing tactics, Bethy pulled on her DJ experience to drive the conversation in a different direction, picking humor as the only possible option. "Does the child have a name, or do you call him Boy? Like the cat you once named Kitty? Boy?"

Davy turned to Willa, murmuring to her, and Bethy saw this as a retreat she couldn't allow. She'd driven a wedge without realizing and needed to fix it. Jamming her elbow into his ribs, knowing she couldn't hurt him, she at least gained his attention.

"Well? Tell me now, it's as good a time as any. I'm a captive audience." Those were the wrong words to use, and she pulled in an involuntary breath that hitched, any words silenced in her throat. Davy seemed to realize what had happened, because he offered her the boy's name in return.

"Chase, his name is Chase. I haven't known about him that long. Carrie kept him a secret until Watcher found out about him and told me." *Watcher, who has a namesake and doesn't know it*, she thought, fighting tears again.

Forcing her lips into a smile, she murmured, "Chase Mason. How old is he?"

"He's sixteen now." That hit hard, because he and her Michael were nearly the same age. If she'd known about Chase, she could have spoiled and doted on him like she'd wanted to do Michael. *Damn.*

"Sixteen? I have a sixteen-year-old nephew? When did you find out?" Still trying to hide her emotions, she reached out and smacked Davy's shoulder.

Davy asked, "You wanna meet him?"

Time for humor again, B.T. Without hesitating she said, "Well, duh. Aunt Bethy, I kinda like it. What does he think about having an aunt?"

His words were quiet when he admitted, "He doesn't know about you. Things were fucked up with Sosa."

The screaming woman. Bethy had seen the bundle loaded into the belly of the plane and knew what it was. *Now I know why Luke...*her brain stuttered, and she lost the thread of her thought, caught up in what to call her dead nephew. *Luke. Morgan. Judge.* None of them seemed real. *Creepy Guy.* Chase's mom, killed by his cousin. *How sad.* "Poor guy, and now you'll have to tell him his mother is dead." She turned to look down the plane at Watcher, wishing she could tell him. *"Some secrets are harder to keep than others."* Ty had told her that, and she hadn't understood it at the time. *Boy, I do now.* "I always knew you were a keeper, Michael Otey. Glad you located him, and more than glad you got him to Davy. How long ago did you find him?"

Watcher grinned at her, and she recognized that look on his face. It was the one Tabby would have right before she would suggest something she knew would get both girls in trouble, but didn't dare do alone. *What in the world is he about to say?* "Oh, hard to remember. About four years ago? Does that sound right, Mason?"

"Are you kidding me? You—" She whipped her head to look at Davy and realized Willa was grinning at her, glad beyond words to see the expression on the woman's face. "—have known I had a nephew for four years? And you didn't think to mention it at any point?" *Hypocrite*, she thought, remembering the pictures from Michael's fifteenth birthday his adopted mother had e-mailed her two months before. *You're worse than a liar, Bethany.*

***

Fury

He stared at the blank wall. Blank, mirrored, or decorated with priceless art, it wouldn't have mattered, because Fury didn't see anything. His vision had gone red, and he was holding onto his control with the barest of grips.

Shooter's boy, Judge, had taken Bethany. Along with three other women, one name which made him flinch, because he'd known Carrie before she became a pawn in the Outriders' schemes, back when she was a fresh-faced girl working at her grandmother's produce stand along the highway. But the information that came closest to pitching him over the edge of his celebrated control was Bethany.

Put his hands on her. Memories of Bethy's smile as she lay propped on his chest mocked him. *"I like you."* His mind put his real name in her mouth instead of the fake one. *"I like you, Gabriel Ledbetter."* He knew he'd never hear her say those words.

"Brother, she's breathing. Mason's woman is hurtin', but she'll be okay. Mason's bringing his sister back here." Slowly he swiveled his neck, resting his gaze on Gator, who flinched at whatever he saw on Fury's face. "Jesus, brother. What the fuck is wrong? He'll get back, and we'll keep workin' our deal. No sweat."

"Bethy okay?" He wished he could haul those words back, but they were there lying on the air. Trying for damage control, he shifted the question to ask, "Are all the women save Sosa okay?"

"Yeah, they're okay. They're bringin' Sosa's corpse back." Gator shrugged. "Myron's figuring out what to do to deal with that pile of bullshit. They torched the compound, so there shouldn't be any blowback. But for Mason to give his kid closure, they need to figure out how to deal."

Fury reached into his pocket and pulled out his phone. He'd never stopped looking into Tabby's death, and over the years had found a surprising bit of information that might help them now. He dialed, then put in his security code and waited. A moment later Myron picked up, "Yeah?"

"Clean line?" Might as well ask, since he didn't understand the technology that'd been handed to him. A bridge between clubs, he knew this was supposed to be a secure way of communication, but using an app to call seemed risky.

"Yeah, talk to me." Full confidence in his tone, Myron sold his assurance.

"About Sosa. Your problem with what to do." Myron made a noise. "Got an idea for you to consider, that's all. There's a fuckton of wrecks in the mountains around Cynthiana where she lived. Get her in a car and sail it off a turn." Memories of Tabby's body edged into his mind, and he shoved them back. "She'll be so mangled by the time it stops pinwheeling through the trees, it won't even be questioned that she's mutilated."

"Copy that. Good idea." A hesitation, then came the words he wanted, "Thanks, much appreciated."

"No problem. You know when they'll be getting in? Me and Gator and some of the boys are gonna round up Chase, get him home from y'alls clubhouse, and then we'll lay in some supplies so Mason don't gotta leave." He stared at Gator who was looking puzzled. "Call it a goodwill offering. After an ordeal like this, he's gonna need some space, and I'll not be shoving my needs in his face. Having shit there will give him time to deal."

"Better than decent idea, Fury," the words came easier this time, and Fury smiled grimly. "I'll call once I know."

"Sounds good. Ride on, man," he responded, hearing Myron's return, "Shiny side," just before he disconnected the call.

"Gets us in deeper, every good deed." Since his men knew Fury was trying his damnedest to get them an entrance into the Rebel Wayfarers world, he knew that would be all the explanation Gator needed. He'd never know the satisfaction Fury would gain from selecting things certain to soothe Bethy. Favorite foods, the bath products he remembered her using. The idea of her wearing clothes he'd picked out sat easy in his belly. "Let's roll."

***

Bethany

Sitting on the edge of the bed, Bethany pulled on a shirt and then reached up to smooth her hair down, the scent of her shampoo a familiar comfort in this strange setting. "You might as well come on in," she called, having heard heavy footsteps pause outside her door. A moment later the knob turned and she had a shiver of fear. Then the door opened and Davy's face appeared. "Stop lurking."

He grinned at her testy order then came through the doorway, leaving it open behind him. The mattress lurched and shifted, and she rocked against him when he wrapped his arm around her shoulders. "You doin' okay, honey?"

"Did you call Ty?" Davy wouldn't talk to her about going home yet, and she understood his fears. Understood, and shared them, because right now she couldn't imagine being alone. "Just because I'm not fighting you on staying here a couple of days doesn't mean I won't be going home.

You know that, right?" *It won't always feel like this, so it's best to set the ground rules now.*

"I did, and he's ready to rip me a new asshole. Man's protective of you, girl."

She grinned. "He's a good friend." The smile tried to fade, and she kept it plastered on her face, holding it in place while gritting her teeth. "I bet he was worried."

"I fired your assistant." Davy's words shocked her and she twisted to stare up at him. "Asshole told everyone you were out scouting. Shit you do all the time. Ty never thought to check your room or we'd have known things weren't right." He paused, then swallowed hard. "You're gonna have to give me a few days. Me and Ty got some things in common. You being the main one, and guilt about this shit is another."

"Jesus, Davy. Do you know how long it took me to find that guy?" She leaned against his side, letting him take her weight, trusting him to hold on. "Thank you. He was kind of an asshole." Davy's frame shook, and she knew it was with suppressed laughter. "I like Chase." His arm tightened around her shoulders and she nodded. "Yeah. I'm gonna be the best aunt in the history of aunthood."

"A natural with him. I didn't know you were so good with kids." His words cut deeply, and she buried her face in his chest in an instinctive avoidance of the pain. "Honey, what'd I say?" *Can't pull anything past Davy.* "Honey?"

Now would be the perfect time to tell him about Michael. In this moment, with so much going on around them, he'd never blame her for keeping a fifteen-year secret. Bethy bit her lips, holding the words inside. *Michael's mine*, she thought, denying the words a voice. "Who bought me clothes? They're nice."

He had to know it was a diversionary tactic, but he gave it to her, chuckling as he responded, "Some of my friends volunteered. I can't imagine them trolling the bra and panty section at the mall, but they did it for me." He pressed a kiss to the top of her head. "For you."

"Well, whoever they are, tell them they have excellent taste in lingerie."

He laughed aloud at that, still laughing when he told her, "Yeah, not gonna be tellin' Fury that you like the panties he bought you."

Eyes dipping closed at the glad sound of his laughter—*maybe we'll come out the other end unbroken after all*—she smiled, slipping her arm around his waist and hugging him close. "Love you, Davy."

"Love you, too, doll. More than you know."

Protocol

Fury

Two months past the events in Utah, Fury sat quietly at the table in a Rebel-owned bar, trying hard to suck in air past the pain that closed his throat, watching as the RWMC member known as Hoss stalked away. The woman was already gone, fleeing out the door to the kitchen, but she wouldn't be returning. Nope, Hoss had sacked her where she stood. Because of Fury.

His path to this point had been long and bloody, dragging his feet through the corridors of three different clubs before finding one worth any risk, any cost. A club that was as loyal to its men as it expected the men to be to it. He had pursued that goal with every waking moment. Of course, the club he found had to be the Rebel Wayfarers, and as soon as he heard the first story of its bloody birth, he knew. Even if Bethy's brother, Mason, was at the helm, if the core of the club stayed as advertised, he knew he had found a home. Everything he had been looking for, tied up in the patch of a club so righteous that even their enemies spoke words of praise alongside cursing their name.

Tonight he'd nearly clambered to the wrong side of an exchange that could still hold the potential to fuck his plans in the ass. Hope was a waitress, and by chance, he and his men had sat in her section. Pure chance, nothing planned about the encounter. Fury had watched the beautiful blonde's tentative but graceful interactions with his rough men. Saw her gain confidence in herself over the hours, finally got to see her give back as good as she got from them. Saw her smile, watched her hips sway as she walked their orders to them, caught glimpses of the curves hidden by her apron when she leaned across the table to set a bottle in front of his brothers.

It wasn't that he'd wanted the woman so much as what she might represent. Enticing, but still a shadow when held up against his memories of Bethany.

Not that he'd been a saint since leaving Riverbend. He snorted at the idea. He liked pussy and hadn't missed many chances at finding a wet and willing hole in the dark. But he'd shied clear of anything that sniffed of a bitch that might have ideas above her station. According to him, that station was directly underneath him, and not a hint of anything else.

Hope, though. She'd been the light to Bethy's dark, still filled with a sweetness that called to him. She reminded him of something he had held in his hands long ago, a time when he was gifted with love paired with a naïve trust, and all of that wrapped up in a sweet and sassy package he could have spent his whole life worshiping. Back when he was just Gabe Ledbetter, con man.

I could still turn things around. Bethy can still be mine, he thought. Even as the idea passed through his head, he knew it wasn't even close to true. He could have a chance, but for his loyalty to his men and trying to find them a home that was worthy of their commitment and strength.

Not meant to be. Like every other good thing in my life, turned out wrong for me.

Hope's lilting laughter had echoed throughout the room. Charming, gentle, good. All the qualities he could wish for. Fury had watched, and ached, reminded of the woman he had loved, long ago. Still loved, holding his memories of her close. Those days before he'd betrayed her, and surely earned her hatred.

Mason had no idea who Fury was, or what had happened—what he'd done. No way, or Mason would have never let Fury get as close as he had already. He'd be taking advantage of Mason being on an extended ride with his woman, both of them healing from what had gone down in Utah. Any chance of recognition had to be avoided for the foreseeable future, giving him a chance to dig in deeper with the Rebel members.

Bethany had gone home to Nashville. Back out of reach, and his only glimpse of her, while she was in town, had been fleeting, a pale face rushed into Mason's house from the van that picked the party up at the airport. *So fuckin' far out of my reach.*

So, just for tonight, he'd watched.

Watched and wanted, and at the end of the night, finally decided he would try and take a little of that for himself. *I just wanted sweet. One more time in my life, I wanted a chance at sweet.* It didn't matter because the curtain closed on any options. *Denied again.*

For the span of a single minute, he'd held her brightness in his arms. The possibility of so much. Sweet and kind, beautiful. Cradled in his arms, him wrapped around her, memories burning through him. Wants and desires for more. Dreams he'd never expected to have again. Wounds reopened and bleeding, her bright hair shading to dark in his mind. *Bethany.*

Hoss had put an end to any thoughts by facing Fury down and declaring the woman off limits. When Fury looked at him—even without Hoss making his claim official—he could see the man had himself tied up in knots over the woman, and immediately Fury had backed off. If Fury angered Hoss, the man would take it to church. It'd be touch and go, but if Fury got a chance to speak, he could salvage things. If what he did pissed off Mason, he and his men would be up shit creek for certain.

So Fury ended it, setting Hope on her feet. But not before he had a taste of what she offered; saw clearly the beauty she held inside, the sweetness she could give. The bare taste he'd taken meant he *knew*. Knew in his soul. She'd set up a resonating echo inside him, pulling everything he'd wanted with Bethy back to the surface. Reminding him she'd been the woman meant to fill the hole inside him.

Nothing to do for it but stand back.

Wanting.

Watching.

Remembering.

Never real.

Sitting at a table in enemy territory, surrounded by people he trusted and those he might never trust, Fury remembered. He held onto the pain that came with those memories, drew it close, letting it simmer deep inside him. Then he blew out the breath he'd finally been able to pull in, throat raw with his shoved-down rage.

Bethany. After Riverbend, after dissuading Dion of any pursuit, he'd gone back to Nashville and kept tabs on her. Researched every fact and tiny bit of information he could scrape up. He found that she didn't date, didn't even socialize much. Couldn't find a boyfriend, not even a hookup. Her roommate—that man made him wonder, but he'd set that aside because in his selfish gut, he wanted her free. Wanted to believe he could swoop in and if she'd have him, he could have her.

He would park where he could see her, not too worried she'd recognize him if she caught a glimpse of him. Life had changed him from the Gabe she'd known as a kid, turning him first into the slick con guy who'd played her, and then finally into who he was now. *Fury*. Named for his ability to do what he'd just done, holding onto his anger in a way that made it a tool. A weapon. Not something that controlled him. Instead of going crazy when he got angry, now he went cold, his name an antonym.

Nashville had become a dream years ago. A lifetime. Memories of his dark-haired beauty. The one who slipped through his fingers. Her tortured darkness as deep as his had been, and he'd recognized that in her. Wanted to be the one who lifted it from her soul. Held to the course by threats and hatred. Lost her forever, because of who he was.

Betrayed.

Walking away from her had been the hardest thing he'd ever done. She'd sat there and stared at him, tears coursing down her face, her words empty of any emotion other than anguish. No more love, not for him. Not the man who had lied to her with every word, every breath. *Best thing I could do for her*, he'd told himself. It had taken him a long time to realize that moment defined him, because he had vowed never again. He'd kept his head down, done his time, and come out the other end a better man. One who knew what he wanted from life, who knew he'd held everything in the world in his arms at one time, and vowed to never settle for less than he'd had.

Eyes on the prize, he reminded himself, looking around the small table of suddenly-somber men. They were waiting to take their cue from him, but he'd been too lost in his own memories to notice. Deliberately softening his posture, he angled one elbow over the back of his chair and leaned to one side. Placing his mouth to Gator's ear, he pitched his voice so every man at the table could hear him. "Never seen a man so tied up in pussy. Glad I didn't fuck that up for him, yeah? She had a taste 'o' me, there'd be no going back." Nervous laughter circled around as he eased back upright. "Finish these, boys. We got a party to get to, yeah?"

Beer in hand, he used the bar's mirror to check the room. Hoss was nowhere in sight. Neither was Hope. *And in about thirty seconds, I'll be wind, too.*

***

Months later, a different patch finally in place on his back, Fury stood on a hill, staring down at the patterns created on the cold ground that stretched from fence-to-fence. Patterns of trust and uncertainty, drawn by lines of an alliance between clubs. Groups separated by just enough distance to ensure no conflicts would happen today.

He was glad they were being considerate. Putting aside grievances for grief.

Bingo had died, carried off this green earth by the cancer that had been eating at his insides for a while. He'd been a good man that Fury hadn't known long, but liked more than he'd expected. After only a few conversations, Fury had found he respected the man for his wisdom and experience, the miles the man had under his wheels, all the things he'd seen in his rearview. Old cuss of a member, a ground-pounder from decades ago, Bingo had been a past-president held in high regard by every man in the club, regardless of chapter. *Fuck, regardless of club,* he thought, looking down again at the dozen or more patches represented at the funeral.

Movement to one side drew his attention, and he turned to see Hoss standing there, staring down in much the same position in which Fury stood. He was surprised to see Hoss, and then twisted back to sweep the cluster of women close to the tent, seeing Hope there with her sister, Mercy.

Make nice with the man, he told himself with a grimace, walking over to stand next to Hoss. *It won't kill you to make nice with the officer who holds your future in his hands.* Even though Fury and his men hadn't been made to prospect like someone new to the life, as their sponsor, Hoss held responsibility for them and was in his rights to demand Fury acknowledge him. He wouldn't, but Fury felt it wiser to continue to offer it up unasked, letting the sincerity show. He was honestly pleased to wear the Rebel patch. Pleased, and proud.

Gaze cutting his way, then back to the men below, Hoss greeted him. "Fury. How's life treating you these days?"

Hoss' casual welcome shocked Fury, who knew the man had been through a world of shit recently. Hope's boy had been taken by her ex-asshole, and Hoss had to go all the way to Alabama to get the boy back, coming home only two nights ago. The kid had been found healthy and whole, thank God. *Man worked for and earned the woman, and gained a family*, Fury thought, hating the burn of jealousy that writhed through him.

Something must have shown on his face because Hoss' next words were a cautious question. "You got shit, man?"

Smoothing his features, Fury brushed it off with casual words, sorry he'd taken the time to walk over. *I'll just stand a minute, then head down to the boys*. His gaze swept the cemetery again, seeing his men standing in a clump to one side. Hoss was silent, staring down at Hope. *Enough of this shit*. Fury asked, "I'm gonna hit it. You want me to grab anything before I head back to the clubhouse?" Hoss didn't move, didn't change expression, and Fury wasn't sure the man had even heard him. With a grin, he repeated the question with the same result. Leaning closer, he asked a third time, laughing aloud when Hoss just continued to stare down the hill.

At his laugh, Hoss jerked and turned to look at him, asking grimly, "What?"

Fuck. Deep and dark with this man, too. "I've asked you three times if you guys needed anything picked up before my boys head back to the clubhouse, but you were staring off into space." Fury angled his eyes down, breaking their locked gazes. "Where were you, Hoss?"

Instead of answering him, Hoss said, "Our boys. Every member is ours, so you sayin' you got some special boys ain't gonna fly."

Fuck you. Clamping his lips tight so those words didn't escape, Fury kept his tone casual as he said, "Noted. You didn't answer my question."

Nothing could have prepared him for Hoss' answer. "Hope's pregnant."

With two words, Hoss ripped the ground out from under Fury's feet. Reminded again that for six short days he'd held in his hands what he wanted more than anything in the world. *Bethany.* A world away. Hooked her star to another man, any children she had wouldn't be Fury's. None of his jailhouse dreams of her would come true, all his imagining Bethy cradling a tiny baby, red hair contrasting with sweet grey eyes in vain. *Might as well wish on a fuckin' star.*

He stared down the hill at Hope, seeing happiness shining from her face. Hoss had never treated her badly. Never lied to her. Would never do to her what Fury had done to Bethy. *So fuckin' happy. Bethy deserved that.*

Hope's boy had run towards the tent by the graveside, coming back with one of Jase's kids in tow. The expression of love she wore when she looked down at her son was too much. Fury couldn't stand the thought of Hope's face appearing like Bethy's had, staring at him through the glass in the visitor's center, tears marking her shirt as they dripped off her jaw. Tiny rings of accusation, dark proof he broke everything he loved. *I caused that. That's mine.*

Stiffly, he moved, clenching his hands. Then he gave Hoss the advice he wished to God someone had given him. Wished he'd known the importance of holding on when he'd had the chance. Wanted to pass it along in a way that would resonate, so the man never lost sight of what he'd been blessed with. "Both hands. You find sweet and good like that, you hold onto it with both hands. Tight as you can. That is a fucking magnificent woman, and now she's carrying your babe. Both." He paused to take a breath, turning his head to stare at Hoss, willing him to understand the importance of the message. "Hands."

Without another word, he turned and walked away.

***

Marie's held the promise of oblivion. Delivered to his table by a curious Tequila, the requested full bottle of whiskey stood waiting.

Fury wanted it, hell, he needed it tonight.

Hope's pregnant.

Two words, and the resulting anger and grief of loss built a fucking home in his chest. *Something I'll never have.* He'd been swallowed whole by a wave of emotion so huge he had nearly missed Hoss' next words, that she was giving him a girl. Full family with a boy, a girl child, and a woman like that? *Fucking shit.* Hell, yeah, Hoss should be pleased and he'd sounded every ounce. In love, full to bursting with that pleased coming from so deep inside him, Fury could see how Hope had filled him right up, even if she didn't know. Hoss' whole world. Got her boy back, dealt with the dick that was her ex, locked her to him in a way that made the ties tighter than ever.

Fury harbored secret, dark dreams of having Bethany like that. Have her tied to him, any way he could. Now that he was patched into the Rebels, he had to keep his past closer to the chest than ever before, protecting what he could. At night, he would pull out the memory of holding her against him, feeling the way her soft curves fit into him. Only then could he remember how when he pressed his face into her neck and nuzzled into that soft hair, Bethany was all he could see. Buzzed as fuck, filling his lungs with the scent that was all truth, and nothing false.

Truth, not deceit. *Can't turn back the clock.* No matter how much he wanted. Her last words to him continued to flay him open. Two words he couldn't forget. *Never real.*

Yes, it was, he argued with himself, unsuccessfully trying to bury the memories of Bethany.

He'd breathed her in.

Drank her down.

Addicted in an instant.

Fuck.

Now, all that was behind him. Everything. All was solid and stable with the Rebels, life was good for his men. They got what they needed, what he wanted for them, every ounce of it. But... *Always a but*, he thought, forcing out a hard breath as he tried to push the memories aside. But, he would never have *that*. This day, standing on the hill at a good man's funeral, looking out at the respect and love paid that man, he'd felt hollow and empty instead of full. Hope was Hoss' whole world, and she handed that back to him. Full circle love. Like Bethany could have been.

Not mine.

His brain wouldn't rest, everything set to a simmer inside him. *I'll never have that kind of woman.* Not him. *Wasn't written in my fucking cards.* His one chance so far in the past, he was sure she wouldn't remember him if he were to walk in the room. Never again hear her voice cry out his name. *Fuck, never got to hear that anyway. She didn't know me.*

He grabbed the bottle from the table in front of him. Using the edge of one hand, he spun the lid off, letting it fall to the floor and lifted the bottle, drinking deep.

Anywhere but here

Fury had left town the day after the funeral. Rolling downstate, he'd been nursing a headache alongside a gutful of anger.

He'd headed to Kentucky to settle an old score. At some point that night, he'd decided it was past time to clear the debt with Dion. Wanted to give himself something tangible he could take hands to and deal with, rubbing out the problem. A problem that dragged its roots back through the years to where it sprouted from the first club takeover he had orchestrated.

Fury walked into the meet with a dozen of his most trusted brothers at his back, already knowing things were about to go bad for him despite Dion's promises. The North Carolina club he had been riding with didn't have the discipline to deal with threats like this one, and in the broad grins on the men facing them, he could see their expectations for the end results of the next hour. Dion wasn't here, oh hell no. Any chance of pain or consequences, and that man was ass in the wind. Didn't matter the cause. A straight-up fight like this promised to be, or doing a nickle in the pen because the money guy fucked up on the routing of a check. Dion would be vapor until things settled out.

Mentally evaluating the odds facing him, Fury rolled his shoulders, accepting that it appeared to be highly unlikely he would be walking out the door behind him at the end of this meet. Such an unlikely outcome, he decided to just go ahead and make the move they would all be making in about two minutes. As the canons of Sun Tzu taught, victorious warriors win first, and then go to war.

First, we cut off the head, he thought, lifting his arm with fist upraised, the signal bringing his group to a silent, shuffling halt. "Who speaks for Red Scorpions?" He asked the question casually, but the insult was out there because he implied it wasn't even worth his time to read patches, forcing the other club to identify their ranking officer in the room. Several men turned to look at a small man in the back of the group and Fury sighed, and then laughed aloud when a different man spoke.

"I do." The tone was arrogant, and he watched as the lips of several men twitched in response. This was a wanna-be officer, he decided, so he ignored him, turning instead to the first man who had looked around the room, the least member of the club he was about to go to war with. Fury aimed his words at that man, keeping his tone serious.

"You the president of the Reds?" Staring intently at the man, he still caught the movement of the small man out of the corner of his eye. Even as the low-ranking member shook his head, he heard the scuffing of boot soles moving his way. Allowing the man to get close enough without reacting was hard, but he schooled himself to stillness, pretending ignorance of the approach until the man was within reach.

In a single movement, he pulled his hunting knife from the sheath strapped to his leg, his thumb rolling the lock strap out of the way with a practiced twitch, bringing the blade out of the leather and into the air near his shoulder in a firm, underhand grip. Lashing out powerfully, with a short, sharp swing, he struck and then stepped to the side and out of the way as blood fountained from the man's neck. Reaching up with his other hand, he turned the man to face the Reds, coating them with their own president's blood. Within moments, the man had slumped to the floor, and Fury stood over the collapsed body, staring now at the only man *who had spoken. With a nod, he indicated the now-pale wannabe, "Guess you do after all, huh?"*

His words seemed to break the spell of shock, and both groups of men scrambled for weapons, surging forward to fill the gap that had previously separated them. Hearing the meaty thuds and pained grunts of hand-to-hand fighting, Fury allowed his men to flow around him, standing firm, watching as men slipped and cursed the blood that slickened the floor underneath their feet. When the first shot rang out, he nodded, reaching under his arm to tug his gun free of the holster holding it there. "Ain't no onesies, twosies here," he muttered, lining up a shot that took three members down.

At the end of the confrontation, there were four Reds standing and ten of his club. His gaze swept the group of men, those at his back and the few standing in front of him. "Whoever ain't with me, y'all want to walk away, drop your fucking centers right now." Calling for their patches would separate the real from lies fast, he knew and was ready when none of his men moved. Turning to the remaining Reds, he said, "If you ain't walking away, what the fuck you think you're going to do?"

"Join the Time of War," one of them said, naming Fury's current club. Fury watched as the man shrugged and shifted his feet to move away from the growing puddle of blood seeping across the floor.

"What the fuck for?" Fury asked, cocking his head to one side quizzically. "Dying club, why would you want to patch in here? And what makes you think I'd take a pussy who's so quick to drop his center?"

Looking confused, the man glanced side to side at the men to his left and right, then over Fury's shoulder to the men standing at his back. "If you didn't want us to patch in, why didn't you kill us?"

"Diamante," he said and heard the surprise of sucked air behind him. Not even his brothers knew what he had planned. Diamante was a growing club, spreading their influence across the central and southern

states. Strong enough to hold all claimed territory, they were serious one-percenters, breathing and dying by the bikers' creed to live free.

From that time to now, nearly a year after he folded in his Diamante chapter into the Fort Wayne chapter of the Rebels, he continued to evaluate every decision he made against that cost. No regrets for North Carolina, and absolutely no regrets for stripping the Diamante colors off his back. *Needful*, he thought, using one of Mason's favorite words.

Two of the men who had stuck with him were now planted, because they threatened his new family. Diamante members who didn't see the necessity of dropping their cuts, wanted to feed info back to the old club. An old club filled with old men who had betrayal down to a science. Vendettas against so many, they couldn't keep a fucking thing straight in their own heads. The past, for Fury. And those two members? In the past now, too. He'd dealt with their shit. Ancient roots brutally lopped off before they could grow and become a problem. Given a chance, he would do the same again. No remorse. No guilt. The only emotion was relief that he'd finally dealt with Dion.

"Told you we wouldn't ever be done." Dion leaned a skinny hip against the truck tailgate, staring out over the river. They'd met at the dam, in the parking lot near the spillway. A location Dion favored, because it meant he could give the necessary rundown for a con, send his minions off to do his bidding, and then get in some fishing. In the time Fury had known the man he had never, not once, done his own dirty work. No, what he did was find leverage with people he found valuable, and then worked them until they broke.

I'll try one last time, *Fury thought. He leaned against the fender of the truck, elbows propped on the top edge, steepled fingers in front of his pursed lips. Finally, all the words sorted in his head, he lobbed them at Dion, hoping to hit the mark with one of them at least. "I did time for you. Covered for you in a way that cost me a piece of my life." Dion shrugged, shifting to a more comfortable position, staring at Fury with an expression* of boredom. "I have run no fewer than ten successful cons for you. Made you more than a million dollars. For a while, I did everything you asked."

"And I know where every one of those bodies are buried." Dion paused and grinned, his remaining teeth yellow and uneven. "So to speak."

Undeterred, Fury continued. "You cost me the single most important relationship I'll ever have."

"Better off without the bitch. She'd've saddled you with that boy, otherwise."

Immediately alert, Fury barked the question, "What boy?"

Dion rolled his eyes. "Ain't your boychild. But if you'd hooked up with her, she'd have taken him back, that's for sure."

"She's got a son?" He'd seen no signs of a child in the days he'd known her, been in her life. None of his digging had surfaced any hint of a child. "Are you sure?"

"Yeah, I'm sure. Shit, you think I'm stupid and can't manage intel? Never did blame you for fucking the bitch. She was a hot piece. Maybe I should make a trip to Nashville myself, see if she's as good as your actions claimed. Mmhmm. Maybe I should." Not realizing he'd ensured his own death with those words, Dion turned to the truck bed and pulled his tackle box close. "Now, boy, if that's all you got to say, can we cut this short? I got your number. I'll be in touch when I need you next."

"There is no next time." He'd have to digest the info about Bethany later. Now it was time to deal with Dion, one final interaction. "We're done. I'm not your boy to come runnin' when you call."

Dion turned, pole in hand, playing the line out a few inches before reeling it back in. He took a step away from the truck and did a practice cast, backwards and forwards, flipping the weighted line in front of him. Reeling it all the way back onto the spinner, he shook his head. "Yeah you fuckin' will. That's the deal. I call—" He flipped the weighted line out *again, tugging when it became tangled in a set of bushes near the drop-off by the spillway. "Shit." He took another step, yanked the line without success as his feet moved again and Fury knew he'd never have as good a chance as this one.*

With a final glance around to ensure they were alone, Fury grabbed a ball peen hammer from the bed of the truck, gripped the handle with a sweaty palm as he rounded the tailgate, and took three steps towards Dion before bringing it down with force. The first blow took the man's knees out from under him, and Dion toppled forwards, hands up to break his fall, pole dropping to the ground. The second blow exposed bone-white skull, and he convulsed for a moment, legs quivering as his brain short-circuited. Not one to take chances, Fury lifted and let his arm fall again, then wiped the hammer on the man's shirt. "We are so done." Lying on the lip of the slope, one hard push with his foot and the body slid, then tumbled, free-falling the last thirty feet to the roiling water at the bottom of the spillway. Dion's foot had snagged on the fishing pole, dragging it along for the ride. "So done."

He hated having to be around Hoss. Hurt like fuck. Watching him with that perfect family he was making with his old lady, seeing him bonded firm and tight with her boy, that shit tore something loose inside Fury every time he witnessed it. And now, knowing Bethy had a child? It meant he mourned that loss of the possible even more than anything else. Loss of a dream.

That feeling in his gut meant that even though he had been absent for the better part of the past two months, he wasn't settled. As soon as Dion was in his rearview, Fury had headed to Chicago to ask Mason for a chance to move on in a permanent way. His intent had been to ask Mason to let him move away and settle in a different chapter, find some space to fucking breathe. Once he got there, he reconsidered, because begging a boon at this point would mean he'd owe a marker. *Something I surely do not want.*

This was where a Rebel named Duck was going to come in, because the club needed a security detail in the man's hometown and Fury wanted an invite. The possibility had brought him to here, putting himself in place to be called in for a meet in Jackson's, getting an eyeful of the family Mason had built for himself in the club in the process.

That was something else that was eating at Fury. Knowing how Mason had this for himself, and Bethy had been alone for a long time. Not now, because she had Ty for her family. But Mason had these riches at his fingertips, and Bethy looked like a beggar in comparison. Fury was pissed on her behalf, several times having to counsel himself against saying anything as the night went on.

Remember, it's just convenience on both sides of the equation. This assignment would keep him busy for at least a few weeks. After that, he and Mason could sort where to go from there. This would buy him some breathing space.

Duck had been hanging out in West Texas. Gossip said it was about his family business, not club. President of the Southern Soldiers, Fury's cousin Mike Otey had called and talked to Mason yesterday, going on about Duck having a woman in his hometown, sharing about his gut feel that Duck was hiding from them. Fury knew that because Mason had let him stay and listen in on the conversation with Watcher, exhibiting a level of trust that made Fury proud. Seemed there was lots to discuss, and Mason, thinking it was best done face-to-face, had set about recalling Duck to Chicago.

Tonight, sitting in a booth in Jackson's, seated beside the man who had hardly gotten his feet back on the ground after his plane trip, Fury wasn't willing to waste any time, ready to get this show on the road. Twisting his neck, Fury reached up a hand, fingers tangling in the long strands of his trademark red hair as he swept it back from his face. He glanced at Mason, then over at Duck and said, "Business here, or private room?"

***

Mason

Fury's agenda was different from his. The brother needed away from some kind of pain in his past, but couldn't look beyond the most recent hurt to see what was dragging at him so hard. He suspected the man resented what Hoss had found with pretty Hope, even if she wasn't a woman he ever had a chance with. Mason had heard the stories of their first meeting, heard from Hoss about that second time Fury had his hands on Hope.

Mason had been in the clubhouse over the holidays, seen for himself the love she held for the man. No question she'd bound her and her son's lives to in a way that shouted family to anyone who looked at them. He thought a lot of the woman. Loyal and hardworking, she had backbone that went on for days. If he had been picking a woman, she was just the one he would have selected for Hoss.

Fury, though? He was stumping Mason. The man might need a different kind of woman, maybe someone sassy, with a smart mouth to sort the man's shit. A woman who wouldn't be afraid of the club, or the life. Mason grimaced inwardly. *Now you matchmakin', old man? Leave that shit to Merry.*

***

Fury

Fuck. As he listened to Duck, Fury realized the objective of the trip changed. Duck had been forthcoming about his woman, and as he talked, Mason had visibly relaxed, lines of strain easing from his features. Then Mason had dropped a bombshell, having decided to allow the gathering of several citizens primary to the club and Mason in Lamesa. Chase, his son, would be playing a gig there with Slate's little brother's band. The lines crossed and blurred because Mica and Molly, two Rebel princesses who didn't deign to wear "Property of" patches would be there, too. Mason would be coming down at the last minute. All of this run by Duck's woman, which meant his Brenda would be included in those who might have a target on their backs.

Since joining the Rebels, Fury had wavered between disclosing his connections with the Masons or sitting on the information. At first, he'd been shocked that Mason didn't know, but then why would he? It wasn't like he'd been around much, leaving the holler at sixteen and scarcely looking back. Ledbetter was a common enough name. He'd been gone from Kentucky so long, that even if they did a quick check, they wouldn't find anything amiss. Just another ex-military guy. One of thousands who wanted the life of an outlaw, trying to better the circumstances in which he found himself.

So he hadn't talked about Kentucky. It would come out eventually, no doubt. Watcher's club in New Mexico was friendly with the Rebels, built on his strong friendship with Mason, that friendship stemming from their being raised side by side. Watcher had been Tabby's real brother, and the men had met often enough through the years that there'd be no hiding their relationship. *I wouldn't ask him to, either. Let it come*. It might even be a relief to have that secret out.

He'd have to come clean at some point about some things. *I can do that one and live*, he thought, lifting his beer and taking a sip. Reaching up to wipe the foam from his mustache, he ignored the pang that settled in his chest. Talking about what he'd done to Mason's little sister, however...?

It'd be a sure death sentence.

A breath later, without access to his thoughts, Mason let him know how long he had to live. "Hold onto your dicks, there's more, brothers. My Bethy will be there, too." Fury's breath froze in his lungs, solidifying in a way that wouldn't move, wouldn't flow, and wouldn't give him space to suck in air. *My Bethy will be there, too*.

"Jesus wept," Duck whispered under his breath. "All the Rebel royalty in one place. Our king, prince, princesses. Willa not going? Is the queen at least staying home, where she's protected?"

The front door of the bar opened, and Fury tore his gaze from Mason's grinning face, seeing half a dozen Rebel members he didn't know walking in. Keeping his gaze averted, he tried to beat Bethy's voice from his head. Tried, and failed. *Never real.*

It was fucking real. More real than anything else in his life had been. For nearly a week, they had been real.

Gabe sat across from her at the small table, one he had specified when he called for the reservation. That had been when this was a calculated play, the intimate setting designed to keep her focus on him. He was glad of his forethought, but not for the normal reasons, because halfway through the conversation at the studio this had stopped being a con. Her obvious intelligence and quick wit made him laugh. Really laugh in a way he hadn't for a long fucking time. And pretty? He let his eyes drift over her features, watching as her expression changed throughout the story she was telling, going serious and soft by turns, her grey eyes dancing when she laughed.

By the end of the night, when he returned to the parking lot across from the studio so she could retrieve her car, he was sunk. The only way he'd been able to stay in his rental and watch her drive away was because he knew they'd be having breakfast together.

Their third dinner started differently. He asked to follow her to the apartment she shared with a roommate so he could pick her up. "I wanna make it a real date, B.T." Eyes wide, she'd stared at him for a minute that stretched to two, and then slowly pulled in a deep breath.

"A date?" The questioning lift at the end of her words told him so much. She wanted this but hadn't expected to get what she wanted. She'd been disappointed in the past, but he shoved aside the thought of his

Bethy with someone who didn't take a care for her feelings. He reminded himself, She wanted this. Wants me.

"Yes, ma'am. A date." Leaning forwards, he settled his hand over hers, gaze to that joining, feeling her clench as he threaded his fingers between hers. "I'm asking you out on a date. If you're interested." His answer was another involuntary clench of her fingers. "Please be interested."

"A date." Repeated, but now this was a statement. Her trying on the words to see how they fit, and he lifted his gaze to her face, seeing a rising flush in her cheeks. Staring intently at her, he felt a smile curl the corners of his mouth. "Okay."

"Good." No room for a repeat of her question, he wanted it clear that he hadn't been willing to accept any other answer. "Now, let's get out of here." With his free hand, he gestured at the sound room of the recording facility they were touring. "And we'll begin."

"Begin?" Breathy and soft, this question revealed a brutal insecurity that lived just below her skin. Right there, waiting to pounce. He knew how that felt, hated she had that inside her. The weight of knowing you weren't enough.

"The date." Shaking his head, he dropped his gaze to their hands, watching and feeling his thumb sweep across the satin bumps of her knuckles. "With me."

"With you." Another statement, and he didn't lift his head, looking at her from under his brows. She made an amused sound, and repeated, more firmly. "With you."

Mason's voice broke in on his memories, and Fury looked up when he said, "So yeah, need y'all rolling down. Watcher's going to have a scoot for me to straddle while I'm in town, but I'll want you there day after tomorrow. Twelve hundred miles, means you gotta drop at least four today yet to make it there."

No chance of getting out of this now. "Fuck. When we leaving?"

"Right the fuck now."

Occupy Yourself

Bethany, Lamesa, Texas

Standing on the elevated porch outside what had temporarily become the media room of the rodeo grounds office, Bethany shook her head. She was in Lamesa to help her most recently signed band work promo stuff with the radio stations before the opening of the rodeo. Taking an early plane into Midland, she'd driven over and was about to walk in on the group. Bethany Mason-Taylor, manager and promoter for Occupy Yourself. *I still feel kinda like a fraud*, she thought, then plastered on a grin and pulled the door open.

Chase was sprawled on the only armchair in true teenaged-boy fashion, legs over one arm, head tipped far back on the other, tossing corn chips in the air and catching them with his mouth. He paused, and slowly rolled his head to look at the door and then bolted to his feet, "Aunt Bethy!" It only took him two steps to get close enough to wrap his arms around her, picking her up and whirling them both around. Bethy was laughing hard by the time he stopped and put her feet back on the floor. Weaving for a moment, she grabbed the front of his tee for support.

"You swarmed me," she accused and looked up into a carbon copy of Davy's face grinning down at her. *I'll never get used to this*. Chase had the

Mason trademark dark hair and grey eyes, and over the past months, she'd seen a maturing in his face. A defining of his already square jaw, giving him just rugged enough features to ensure he was called handsome and not pretty. He looked a lot like her son, the cousin he'd never get to meet.

My nephew, she marveled. As she had every time she'd seen him. The day they met, he'd been slightly more reserved than today, but only until she had put him at ease by picking on Davy. She hadn't been aware of the boy's full story then, and when she'd learned that was his first real introduction to how a family could tease and play, it broke her heart all over again. *That's why I gave Michael up, so he'd have a normal life.*

Those had been hard days. Not her darkest time, but close.

And here I am, nine months later, virtually okay. That was her sales pitch to herself, anyway. Her dreams put the lie to that every night, but no one would ever know. *Except for Ty, and that doesn't count. He's still got his own demons.*

"Okay," she said, slapping her palms together. "Tell me what you've done, and we'll sort out what's left for me. Get everything lined up." Swinging the laptop bag off her shoulder, she looked around for an outlet, finding one beside a small table. "Hook me up, boys." Her energy set the tone for the next several hours, as she took calls and worked bookings around the other things already scheduled. One after the other, calls, e-mails, interviews—the never-ending cycle of promotion for a band relaunching their brand.

Resting her butt on the arm of the couch, she looked around at the group, grinning at the self-imposed labor divisions she saw. Benny Jones, the lead singer, was going over a printed spreadsheet, marking things in pink or yellow. That would be the swag delivered here yesterday. Armbands, beanies, buttons, drumsticks, and a few T-shirts would be handed out to VIP guests, or sold at a merchandise table. They'd been assigned a spot near the concession stand for the table, and that would be Bethy's focus tomorrow.

"I know there are a few more things I should deal with today, but I'm beat, guys and gals." Six faces turned and looked at her. "Two more interviews and I'm calling it, going to head to the hotel. This trip piled on top of a few busy days back in Nashville means my bed is calling."

"You must have been up before daybreak to get to the airport," Chase said, reaching over and grabbing a handful of chips. "No wonder you're beyond tired."

Looking around the room, she noted the band members had all stopped their activities. Apparently, her announcement provided the permission they needed to switch back to lounging around, bottles of water and soft drinks in hand. *At least their nerves were eased by today's early interviews.* Benny was an old hand at this, but the rest of the group were less polished. Bethy glanced over at her nephew with a grin, thinking it was a good thing Mason hadn't told Chase about the gig ahead of time. As it was, the young man looked wrung out. She knew if he'd had even a couple of extra days to worry and fuss, he would be a whole other level of exhausted. She was about to offer to take him to the hotel too when the door abruptly opened.

Bethy's breath caught in her chest as she watched a striking redhead walk in, complete with a full, thick beard and an attitude of owning all the space around him. *It's just not fair*, she thought, assuming he was one of the radio promoters. *Why are the good-looking ones always in out of the way places like Lamesa?*

Benny stood, hand out, evidently thinking the same thing about the guy, but before she could move forward, Chase was hooting with laughter, yelling, "Fury, *dude*. Totally didn't expect to see you here!" He turned to her, a delighted grin in place on his face as he introduced them, "Aunt Bethy, this is Fury. He's one of Dad's trusted few in Fort Wayne." Twisting, he held out a hand to point at her, speaking to Fury, "This is my best Aunt Bethy. She's the coolest. She runs the record label for Dad, and signed Benny's band."

Standing slowly, she took the look Fury was giving her, half-appraising and half-aggravated. She held out her hand to shake, and when he wrapped his fingers around hers, she felt a zinging awareness of him zip through her and watched his eyes widen and then develop a laser intensity as he studied her. Shoulders rising and falling as he pulled in a deep breath, he reintroduced himself, "Fury. Otherwise known as your escort while in town."

With a nod, she responded, "Bethany Mason-Taylor, otherwise known as the awesome Aunt Bethy."

He smiled at her, white teeth flashing in the midst of that dark red beard and she found herself smiling back at him. *Damn*.

***

Fury

Damn, she's still so fuckin' pretty, was the thought that trailed through Fury's head when she introduced herself after the fiasco of Chase's mouth running ragged. *Always so fuckin' pretty*.

It had been the moment of truth, a scene he'd been dreading since rolling out of Chicago, and the weak fizzle of nonrecognition burned. *Nothing at all like I thought it might go*. It killed him that he so clearly remembered her, had held on to every moment he had with her, and she didn't recognize him. Not a bit. *Again*. Her eyes were clear and without guile, and without a single ounce of acknowledgment. A decade and a half was a long time, and he'd changed, sure. Remade the businessman she'd known for that week in Nashville into the outlaw standing before her. Still...*shit*.

He wasn't sure what he'd expected and knew even less what he'd hoped for, but it sure wasn't being forgotten—cleared from her life so completely that she didn't know him from a fence post.

Pretty, and hella smart, but he already knew that. She'd been running one of Mason's businesses for nearly half her life. Lifting his chin, listening to Chase being a chatterbox, he tried to convince himself he could pull this off. *I'm still a con man, right?*

Fury stood at the back of the room for the next half an hour, keeping all occupants within view as Bethy finished the final interviews scheduled for today. He had been pissed when he came through the door, ready to tear someone a new asshole. Chase had flown in early but didn't wait at the airport for his ride; the resourceful little bastard had grabbed a cab, leaving Fury searching the not-large, not-small airport fruitlessly because his charge had fled the scene. So, he hadn't been in the best of moods when he walked in.

At least until he had seen Bethany. Seen and watched her, liking everything she showed him. Loving everything he saw. The years had changed her, but in only good ways.

All the hard in Mason had found a soft counterpart in this woman. Lips, cheeks, jaw...the only piece of her that matched her brother were her eyes. As with Mason, when she looked at you, it was with certainty that you would be doing whatever she desired. Those eyes saw way too much; they looked deep inside where you would prefer the shadows remain, but she picked her way around those feelings, giving you an assurance that all would be well.

Chase adored her, that was clear, no matter that they hadn't been acquainted very long. He'd only known her since Utah, a marker in time that every Rebel club member knew well. Shooter was doing time in Cali right now for kidnapping and damaging his own daughter, while Judge, the nephew, had been put to ground.

"Can I have everyone's attention for a moment?" Fury swept the group with his gaze, marking each member of the group from the information Myron had fed him. So many more ties to the club than most folks would see at a glance.

Occupy Yourself was an up-and-coming restart band, having done well on the charts and the tour circuit for several years, before imploding because of the addictions of their lead singer. Ben Jones, baby brother to Slate, Fort Wayne's chapter president, had rolled into town and promptly drank himself into rehab, leaving his brother to clean up his mess. Something Slate seemed good at doing, as if he had a lot of practice somewhere in his past.

Not just fucking up his band, Ben had managed to piss off some important people when he'd borrowed a fuckton of money, bought some heroin, and then skipped town out of Denver before repaying that money. The way the stories ran, there'd been Mexican mob and Chicago mob involved, as well as a big-ass Mexican MC, but somehow Slate had cleared all that shit up so his brother was still suckin' air, and not doing it through a tube.

This show in Lamesa was to be the kickoff of their relaunch tour, with mostly new members, and entirely new music. Bethany must be good at her job because these days, you couldn't listen to a rock station on the radio for ten minutes without hearing one of Occupy Yourself's songs.

So there was Ben Jones, lead singer, not quite two years sober. Sitting on the couch next to him was Lucia Foscan, daughter of a past Rebel member. A jacked-up betrayin' club member, who also happened to be very dead. That had opened the door for her and her three brothers to be adopted by another Rebel member, Bear. A man whose old lady was Mason's goddamned fucking niece, the same one whose father saw her as a pawn to his ambitions. The tight pull of family in each of those ties.

The band's drummer was a good old boy, southern born and bred, Victor Montrose. No one's high school prom king, all through school Vic worked every spare moment to make enough money to support his crappy garage band. He'd skipped college, gone straight to Nashville and picked up studio gigs where he killed it, his genius finally recognized. Good kid, real straight shooter. He didn't put up with any of Benny's shit and would probably be the reason when Slate finally let Ben's sober companion resign. Until then, they had Mercedes Gruffudd along for the ride, too. She was sprawled on the floor near the wall, legs angled straight up against the surface, ankles crossed primly.

Bonnie Dupont played bass for the band, and she was as nasty as Vic was sweet. Tatted up one side and down the other, her rebellion against everything played out over her skin, and she had a fucking attitude to match. Talented, sure, but from Fury's perspective, no pussy was worth all the drama she brought to the band.

Dmitri Glass was the only original band member to hang with Benny through everything. He and Vic had kept the gear out of hock while Ben was in rehab. Big, muscled, and tattooed, all that topped with matted and felted dreads, he looked like a fucking badass, but Fury had watched with disbelief as Glass teared up during ballads at one of the band's gigs in Marie's in Fort Wayne.

Then there was Bethany, Mason's baby sister. When Fury had worked her in Nashville, she'd been going by just Taylor, but he'd noted she hyphenated it now, introducing herself as Mason-Taylor. He suspected no one had the full story behind her marriage, but he'd been there at Tabby's graveside when she exposed enough of what went on in the Mason religious compound for a judge to take action on her behalf. Sixteen at the time, already two years into a forced union.

Jesus, why any man would let that walk away was hard to fathom. As soon as the thought rippled through his mind, Fury tried to clamp it down. Tried and failed. *I was that stupid. I had her in my bed, and I fucked up. Had her so close I knew every breath she took. If I hadn't fucked up, I could have fulfilled every wish, not even making her say them aloud.*

"My role here is to make certain you are all safe." The faces turned his direction were transparent, every emotion and thought showing plainly. Interest, caution, dismissal, and from two, fear. Bethy didn't surprise him, but Benny's expression was just short of terror for a moment. Interesting. "I will have another dozen men later tonight, and we'll be camping out in your space for the duration. You done fucked up and pissed me off this morning,"—he pointed a curled finger at Chase, shaking it for emphasis—"ditching me at the airport. Don't do that shit again. If you want to know the threat, tell me, and I'll share with you what I can." Scanning the group, he noted a puzzled look on Bethy's face and saw she was intently focused on him. Not what he was saying, but on him. Huh.

The message had to be delivered, so he forged on. "We've got two nights until the show, and then you're all in town for a bit following. We've got a couple more folks coming in tomorrow, or the day of the show, and I'll be adding to the detail at that time." He reached into his pocket, pulling out the cards Myron had made. "This is my cell number. I expect you to text me in the next five minutes with your name. I can access your info in other ways, but it's easier like this. Make sure you get me in your contacts, so you know it's a safe call to answer if I need to get ahold of you." He twisted his neck, scanning the group again. "From here forwards, at a minimum, you buddy up. Do not go off on your own. My plan is for you to stay at the hotel, and not on the bus. Do not answer your suite door at the hotel without confirmation you know exactly who is on the other side. Do not answer calls from people you don't know."

Bethy rolled her eyes, and he scowled at her. "Serious as fuck, Bethany. I get that this is your business, but my business is keeping you safe." When he said her name, she'd frozen, going stiff as a post, slowly relaxing as he kept talking. "Help me do my job."

"My brother's a pain in my ass." She shook her head. "But we'll do what you need. I won't try and make things harder than they have to be, because God knows this gig is going to be hell enough. The heat alone…" She trailed off, fanning her face with one hand, and smiled at him.

Fury didn't know how he kept it together, how he managed to nod at her, but he did. *Beautiful, smart as fuck, sweet...*his thoughts stuttered to a stop as he watched her reach over and slide her fingers through Chase's hair. She pushed it back off his face, leaning in to press her lips to his forehead, eyes closing with what seemed to be sadness.

After dealing with Dion, Fury had made it his business to dig up every detail about that little revelation, finding out all about her son in Nashville. He'd even seen pictures of her with the family the boy lived with. Boy was a Mason through and through, which meant it wasn't her roommate's kid. He knew name, birthdate, and how often Bethy saw the kid, which was often. More than you'd expect an adoptive family to put up with, but the Marshalls seemed to welcome every visit with open arms. He'd heard a lot from sources in Nashville. What he hadn't heard was boo about that boy from Mason. He hadn't pegged the absence as odd until just this instant, but he realized he also hadn't heard boo from Chase. Chase, who couldn't put a filter on his mouth for anything, would have surely said something by now.

The look on her face right now gave so much away, the expression of love and longing exposing her pain. Her features said she was pleased for her brother, happy he had this, a son he doted on, but there was something else there. She wanted this for herself. Eyes on her face, Fury thought to himself, *Want that for you, gal.* At the idea of her with a child, his cock woke up, fattening in his jeans.

Uneasy, he rolled his shoulders, the familiar creak of the leather vest reminding him of his words to Hoss. *Both hands*, he thought. *Already fucked that up, so many years ago. Ain't got no chance of recovery at this point.*

When the music of her laughter filled the room, rolling across his skin with a stroke he could feel, he took a quick half step towards her. Greedily drinking in the way her head tilted when she laughed again at something

Chase said, the column of her throat working with that sound, hair falling down her back. Open and relaxed, easy joy on her face. *Fuck, yeah.*

So beautiful, and he remembered everything about her. Every sound she made when he slid inside her, the way she'd cried out the time he took her in the shower. How she'd snuggled into him after fucking, drawing circles on his chest while they both tried to control their breathing. *Beauty in my hands.*

Mason-Taylor.

His next footfall didn't happen, and he shuffled his boots on the floor, edging back to the wall, leaning into it.

Mason.

Off limits. Not in so many words, but he knew how Mason felt about his baby sister, had heard the man talk about the weight of guilt he carried from pulling her into his world even a little. No way in hell was the man ever going to stand down from protecting her. And if Fury started anything with Bethy, he knew the past wouldn't stay secret. Everything would come out in the open. Would have to. All the things he wanted to forget. That meant it was not smart to even contemplate what it could be, to think about how it would feel to have a different look directed at him, one that could make him feel as if he held the world. *Had that*, he thought. *I had that and threw it away.*

Want that for me, he thought, lifting his gaze from her face with an effort, scanning the room.

Forbidden.

***

On his bike and rolling through town, Fury headed towards the bar he'd been told Watcher owned for the Southern Soldiers. After deploying three Soldiers members both inside and outside the rodeo grounds media room, he'd left them with orders to split the civilians into three groups for transport back to the hotel. While Lamesa might be Duck's hometown, Watcher owned it in every other way; his club had the region sewn up nice and tight.

His movements on autopilot, Fury's mind wandered to Mason. From the first stories he'd heard told across tables and bars, he'd been impressed by the man. For years he'd studied Mason, working to build an image slowly pieced together fact-by-fact. Discarding the obvious lies, Fury had dug into each elaborate legend of the man until he found the meat underneath, the real story. Dug until he believed he knew Davis Mason inside and out, understood him better than anyone else did, except maybe the man's cousin DeeDee, or Tugboat.

Intel on Mason had been the framework half of Fury's strategic movements, something he had built around for the past five years. Getting a Diamante charter, then moving that charter closer to the Rebel territory. All of that happening at a time when the Rebels were spreading their sphere of influence both east and west of Chicago. *Timing is everything*, he thought, flipping on his blinker and turning at the next light.

Then Utah happened. Fury had been circling things in Fort Wayne with the Rebels, trying hard to earn his place in a new club. Earn a place for his men, too, those who had followed him for years. Utah, an event entirely orchestrated by one of the men Fury hated with everything inside him. Deacon.

From what he knew, Deacon and Dion had become friends sometime during the period Fury'd been in Riverbend. Cut from the same cloth, they'd latched onto the evil in the other in ways that tore through the North Carolina town Fury had been living in. This was in the days when he was still toying with the idea of the biker life, riding with men who claimed outlaw status, without actually earning it. Deacon horned in and took over the group and Fury watched how he did things first with disbelief and then anger. He'd ripped in two what Fury had tried to build.

Citing police harassment, Deacon picked up stakes and moved the club entire. But taking their show on the road to Florida hadn't changed anything except the scenery, and it hadn't been long before the police had been sniffing after them there, too. Sex slaves and labs were how Dion made his money, and Deacon offered not only the facilities to do whatever was needed, but he also organized much of the activity, too.

Deacon had been friends and enemies with Morgan, an old guy from California who had his own fingers in so much it wasn't funny. Morgan's son was crazy, Fury knew that for a fact, but had been surprised to find Shooter had a hard-on for Mason that wouldn't quit. That shit had bled down to his son, Judge.

He'd known something was up in Utah, but not the what. No details. Didn't keep him from kicking his own ass over how things had shaken out. Thank God Utah had been a cluster from the beginning, and it was definitely one Fury had been glad to see fail. Still, once Bethy had gotten caught up in it, it didn't matter that she'd escaped relatively unscathed.

Throughout all the rumors flying through the MC community, Fury had found out most people didn't know Mason had a sister, not until Utah happened. He'd kept his mouth shut because if he'd appeared to know of her, to fuckin' *know her*, there might be questions about the how of that. Questions he couldn't afford at the time. So Bethy became a detail in Mason's past that Fury simply filed away. He figured he'd sit on it until he had time to consider the ramifications of a hidden relationship, but that time never came, when things just went from bad to worse in the Diamante club. Everything fucked sideways by Shooter and Judge.

Noting the addresses on the street signs, he slowed and moved to the outside lane, seeing his target building coming up on his right.

Fucked sideways hadn't taken long. Within five months, his chapter was no more, folded seamlessly into the Rebel chapter in Fort Wayne. That was the best move he'd ever made. So much better than their lives before, and he had no complaints about how Mason and the Rebels had dealt with them.

Still, it meant his men were his to command no more, but equal brothers to every patched Rebel. That was how he'd wanted it, but Fury had nearly chewed his tongue in half the first two weeks, biting back orders and arguments, reminding himself he was no longer the man in charge. No longer an officer, no longer someone with leverage. *Member.* He had stepped backwards into a role that never sat well with him. Just a member, one of the foot soldiers, expected to do as you're told without argument, without thought, with only a willing acceptance that you don't know everything, so whoever is giving the orders must have the right of it.

Slowly, gradually, without even meaning to, he had earned his way into meetings. The important ones, where long-term strategic talk happened behind closed doors. Once he was in and tasted the rich wealth of intelligence and planning the Rebels boasted, that's when he actively set his mind to earning a higher place, determined to regain a position of prominence because that simply was who he was. It had taken months, but he did it. Mostly by demonstrating his dedication repeatedly, and earning respect all through the ranks with his unwavering loyalty to the Rebels. *All in.* He snorted. *Had to be, no goin' back.*

Gunny and Hoss had proven great allies, and with everyone knowing the real story behind how Gunny wound up in his compound—*not yours any longer*, he thought, surprised the thought still burned, *lease canceled, all the shit moved to the Rebel clubhouse*—the fact the man was easy with him went a long way to reassuring everyone about everything else. Hoss, too, was an officer in Fort Wayne and was such a respected member in that town, hell in any Rebel chapter, that for Fury to claim his friendship was a big deal. *Worked at that shit, too.*

He punched the gear lever with his toe, downshifting as he rolled to a stop, hands working the clutch and brake. Chin to his shoulder, he watched behind him as he shoved the bike backwards, walking it to park pipes to the building. Still on mental autopilot, he killed the engine with a flip of his thumb, heeling the kickstand down so he could lean the bike over and stand up. Stepping through the front door of the bar, he scanned the area, nodding at a couple of men who were clearly in the life. Fury couldn't see their patches, but given where he was, it was probably safe to say they were Soldiers. Then he saw Duck's dark hair, saw the top rocker of the Rebel patches over the back of the chair he was seated in. Positioned with his back to the room, it spoke to the level of comfort he had with the man seated across from him.

Fury didn't hesitate, with long strides he moved towards Watcher, his cousin from the mountains of Kentucky. It felt almost like going back in time, the weight of decades lifting, and he felt light, off-balance. Watcher stood, followed by Duck, and both men stared at him. Well, Duck's was more of a glare than a stare. *About to blow your mind, man. Show you something about me even Mason don't know*, he thought, then he'd reached Watcher who held out a hand for a warrior's grip. *So much people don't know about me.*

Watcher's laughing question clearly shocked Duck, "You're Fury? Fuckin' kidding me?" Standing a foot away from the only family he claimed, Fury looked into Watcher's face, seeing age and a somber heaviness he hadn't expected. Mike Otey carried profound responsibility, and it was written into every scar and line on his features. *Jesus*. Shaking his head, he ignored the outreached hand and wrapped Watcher into an embrace, holding tight, feeling gratified as the man's arms closed around him. *Family*. Pulling away first, Fury left one arm wrapped around the man's shoulders, then dragged him into a headlock, knuckles rubbing in what he knew was a painless noogie. Mike struggled, still laughing as he demanded, "Goddammit, Gabe, let me the fuck go."

And there's the first break in the dam. Fury watched as wordless questions flowed across Duck's face. *Deflect? I need to delay, at the least.* Or, he could put Watcher on the spot, revealing their relationship and see what the reaction was from everybody in the bar. Loudly, as if Watcher weren't right beside him, he called, "Cuz. Nice place." Grinning at Duck, he said, "Brother, good fucking mattress, man. I slept like a baby." With carefully calculated movements, he stepped between the two men, facing Duck as he reached out a hand. They'd gotten into Lamesa last night, and Duck had been up the stairs and into his woman's bed like a man on a mission. Fury hadn't even seen him this morning, getting himself out the door early to meet Chase's plane.

Duck snatched his hand out of the air, grinding down painfully on his knuckles as he pulled him close. Lips to his ear, Duck muttered, "This would appear the exact opposite to fostering good relations, *brother*. Wanna explain what the *fuck* you think you're doing?"

He really didn't know, Fury thought, laughing as he pushed back to glare at Watcher. Hands to the side, Fury postured and pushed the fake outrage hard, wanting this to be a story told for a long time.

"Watch—" A calculated pause, then he continued with, "—Michael," Fury called, "you keepin' secrets, cuz?"

Another few moments of standing and chatting, then Fury wanted to get the meeting back on track. So, beer in hand, he settled into a seat next to Watcher, and traded pieces of stories with Duck. The Rebels had a lot of things going down, and Mason had been clear that nothing was to be held back when it came to Watcher. So much unreserved trust between the two presidents, and even at the member level between the two clubs. With that in mind, Fury asked about something he'd only heard about in passing a couple of weeks ago. Video footage of Watcher's compound had been found, and technological wizard that he was, Myron still hadn't been successful in tracking down who was responsible.

Watcher shook his head, lips pressed together in frustration for a moment. Fury noted how the muscles of his arms had tensed. This was not going to be a good story. Watcher said, "Had someone put up cameras at my place." He continued, telling them about tracking the signal to a truck, equipment in the bed. They'd staked it out for two weeks, waiting on whoever had strung up the equipment to come back and retrieve their investment.

"About two weeks into our stakeout, it took a burst of power from something. Zapped the entire rig. Fried everything." Fury watched intently, seeing the strain on Watcher's face as he drank deeply from his beer. "When we realized it was useless, we went to move it. Fuckin' IED under the wheel. Blew a crater and sprayed my guys with shrapnel."

Fury opened his mouth, but had no words. He'd been overseas, knew what an IED was from up-close. Couldn't imagine having that happen on US soil.

Shaking his head, Watcher continued, "Afterwards, we found a battery under there with a sensor. That's what had fried the rig. It was hooked to the frame. Whoever did it was able to kill the system remotely by opening a connection. Set a trap." He paused for another drink of beer, draining the bottle, stress twisting his expression into hatred. "Found a room...a cell buried under the truck. Two women. Devil," he named one of his officers, "figured they'd been dead about four days." Rage building in his voice, Watcher continued, "We sat on our asses for two weeks while they starved to death. Sat there eating chips and drinking beer, watching a fucking truck in the middle of the desert while two women starved to death in a metal fucking box under the truck. A truck filled with videos of my house, and my wife and daughters."

Voice harsh with anger, Watcher stood, pushing his chair back, "So no, I don't consider that shaking out okay." Fury didn't speak, and neither did Duck. They just stared at Watcher. After a moment, he said, "Back in a minute, just need...some air."

Fury waited for him to hit the door before he asked Duck, "You know any of that shit?" Duck's head shake was slow, angry. "Fuck. He had guys get hurt, but those women. Gonna fuck with him for a while. And vid in his house? His daughters on that vid? Bastards are lucky they didn't show at the truck. He would've killed them."

"Yeah, and so would you or I. That's fucked up." Duck leaned forwards, elbows to the table, eyes intent on Fury. *Here it comes.* "You wanna explain to me exactly who you are, *Gabe*?" The emphasis on his government name was telling, and Fury winced.

"Mike's my cousin. He went one direction, I went the other. Nothing to tell, brother." Fury shrugged, keeping his gaze level, not looking away. "We weren't close. He's older. But we're blood."

"Mason know?"

Fury pressed his lips together and shook his head side to side.

Duck ran a hand through his hair. "Fuck, Fury, you know I gotta say something to him before Watcher calls, right?"

"Oh, yeah, I know you do. Ain't a big deal." Still holding his gaze, Fury handed him the next piece. "Mason knows my name. Gabe Ledbetter. He just didn't put it together. Watch's mom and my mom were sisters, so it's close. But Watcher's sister lived with us when he went into the military, so that's a little closer."

"Tabitha?"

The sound of her name spoken aloud caused Fury's head to jerk back. He corrected Duck, knowing she'd always preferred her nickname. "Tabby. Yeah."

Changing direction, Duck asked, "You get everything squared away with Chase and the band today?"

Fury nodded, picking up his beer again. "Yeah, they're all tucked in by now, I hope."

Then Duck made the one connection Fury had hoped to avoid. "Bethy know you?"

"She didn't recognize me, no."

"No, I mean did she know you back in Kentucky?" Duck's question wasn't hard to answer, because she had. He nodded. "But she didn't recognize you?"

"Nope. I'd like to keep it that way. I'm Fury. That's the long and the short of it." Carefully setting his empty bottle back on the table, he stood and said, "I'm gonna go see if he's ready to come back inside."

**

Sitting and drinking a beer after supper, Fury was surprised at how much Duck's house reminded him of home. The desert had its own set of sounds, but being surrounded by acres and acres of empty space let a silence settle in, just like the mountains of Kentucky. Noises of animals settling down echoed, strengthening the illusion. *I could get used to something like this again*, he thought, tipping his head against the back of the chair, comfortable in a way he couldn't fake. Eyes closed, he yawned and relaxed, knowing the home of a brother would be safe.

Brenda, Duck's old lady, was full of surprises. Things even Duck didn't know, it seemed. She'd spoken of her early childhood being in Kentucky, not New Mexico, and something she said snagged Fury's attention. From Cynthania, so close to his hometown, and she'd lost her parents in a car accident. That wasn't shocking, wrecks happened all the time, especially in the mountains where a moment's inattention could result in a fall of hundreds of feet. But she survived because a Good Samaritan had pulled her from the wreckage. Not just pulled a little girl out of a smoldering pile of scrap metal, but carried her to the local hospital. Then left her there, making an anonymous deposit onto a gurney in the ER. *Fuck.*

He'd heard that story before.

Watcher's sister had taken a dive off a high curve and died. Little Tabby, raised as his baby sister for years. *Fuck.*

Everyone thought she'd killed herself. Thought she'd had enough of living with the knowledge that her body had been defiled in a way that should never happen to a woman, never happen to a girl—and never, ever happen to a child. Thought she'd sailed her truck off a mountainside to end the pain inside her mind.

Not my Tabby. That had been the refrain he couldn't shake. *Not my Tabby.* She wouldn't have done that to him. Wouldn't have done that to her best friend, Bethany. Wouldn't have done that to her brother, Mike. The day before her funeral, Fury had been in the right place at the wrong time, and overheard an enlightening conversation between his daddy and Preacher Mason. That had been the catalyst to getting himself unassed and out of the holler.

Daddy's voice was solemn and quiet, but Gabe could clearly hear every word said between the two men. He'd seen old man Mason and Daddy walk to the barn, seen the shady looks Daddy had cast around the clearing before he closed the big door. Whatever this was, the men didn't want to be seen doing it. Tabby's death was eating at Gabe, and he'd heard Momma on the phone this morning saying the coroner had finally released her body. Funeral was tomorrow, and Gabe didn't know how he would be able to stand going. Seeing the box that held her body, knowing the light that always shone from Tabby was snuffed out.

Everyone on the mountain knew what she'd suffered. Parents dead, and her mother's death an unsolved mystery. One the TV shows liked to talk about, reporters and cameras arriving in town every few years to capture new footage of the storefronts and any local resident who'd talk to them. Their somber questions echoing through the streets, "And no one knows who killed Mrs. Otey?" As if the person responsible would be jumping up and down in the background, waving their hand and shouting, "Me, I did it. It was me!"

With everything going on, when he'd seen the men's secretive movements, Gabe followed. He slipped through the narrow door at the back of the building, walking silently on the loose ground, tracking their voices through the darkness with ease. He'd been hunting and trapping the mountains since he was eight years old. Stalking two old men through a barn wasn't difficult enough to tax him. Close, so close he could have reached out and grabbed old man Mason's coattails, Gabe crouched and listened.

"Ezra," Mason said, his voice a growling slash through the dark, "you better take care of that kid." He puffed a breath, taxed by his emotions. "We don't need no repeat of before."

Gabe tipped his head, wondering what the man was talking about. He didn't have to wonder long.

Daddy spoke into the silence, his manner obsequious, greasy sounding, like someone with something to hide. "You know that was a fluke, Irving. We've got the suppliers under control this time. The boy won't surface. I fixed it good last time, and you know I'm right."

Gabe barely had time to wonder, Suppliers? Then his father was speaking again, the words stripping the air from Gabe's lungs. "Tabby never knew what hit her, right? You did it quick?"

Old man Mason's tone was dismissive, angry at being questioned. "I told you she wouldn't suffer. I'm not an animal, Ezra. My man dealt with her with compassion, like I promised. He got the kid out, too, just like before. Innocents shouldn't suffer for their family's mistakes. You know I did my part, and now it's all on you. You park that kid, and you park him deep if you want him to keep breathing." Mason moved, and Gabe stared through the crack in the wooden wall to see the man's hands were clenching and unclenching, seemingly frustrated at his inability to do something. "I do what's needful. Morgan's grandbaby lived, that's all he needs to know. You park him deep, and I'll leave that boy alone. You don't, and there's gonna be hellfire to pay. I'll tear your family to the ground, Ezra. You'll lose more than you ever thought possible."

Daddy shuffled closer to the preacher, craning his neck to look up at the big man. His words were half plea, half ultimatum, but full of fear. "And my family, with this, Irving, we're out of it. I'm telling you we are out."

Mason's laughter was dark and filled with humor. "You ain't never gonna be out, Ledbetter. Dug in deep, you're stuck with me. We're in the pits chipping away at the walls around us. You know that, better than most. I'm leaving. You're just wasting my time with all this bullshit, and I don't take kindly to people wasting my time."

Gabe's father stood silent for a moment, and it was his turn to impotently clench his fists. When he finally spoke, his words were quiet but vibrating with anger. "You done took from me, Mason. You know that. Took from me and mine. I had one slip, one. And you hold that over my head like I was your lackey, setting off to do whatever the king bids. I won't lose more. Not this time. I'm warning you—"

He didn't get anything else out. Mason moved so fast Gabe scarcely tracked him, and had his hand around Ezra's throat in a heartbeat, had him lifted and pushed against the wall. Leaning close, choking him with his strength and weight, old man Mason rumbled the words, "You do not know what's been taken from me. My wife. My children. That man took them, and took them, and took them. He's taken the last thing he'll ever have. His man is bedding my daughter." Mason's voice broke, and Gabe's fists tightened. Bethany, he was talking about Bethy. *"Do not speak to me about how much has been lost. That man ain't going to see the light of day once I get done with him. I'll bury him a mile deep. And I'll plant you there beside him, if you buck me on this. Ledbetter, you do what's needful. You park his grandson where he can't get at him. You do it in a way that he gets the message. And when I get my wife back, I'll think about letting you out. Not until then. Not a bit of it."*

Fury pushed to his feet, suddenly unable to stay inside another moment. He muttered something, it didn't matter what, as long as it got him out and into the nighttime air. He pulled in a deep breath, shocked for a moment at the absence of rich earth and deep woods on the air. Tabby hadn't killed herself. That was knowledge he'd lived with for a long time. He'd had to see how it ate at Bethy, how it ate at his ma. Tabby hadn't killed herself, hadn't taken herself away from them. The knowledge had run him from the mountain and to the military, where he'd found a costly mix of friends, leading him in the end to Dion.

It had run Bethy from the mountain, too, and Fury had been there that day, his mouth closed tight because of fear. The last time he'd allowed himself to be ruled by that weakness. Bethy had faced off against her father, told him she was done, and then she left the graveside of her best friend in tears, Mike Otey's arm wrapped around her shoulder.

At home that night, Gabe had heard his mother's cries, heard the smacking of the strap and knew his daddy would be coming his way next. If the man didn't get what he wanted one way, he'd get it another. He always had. That was when Gabe had packed, taking his knife to the pillow and dumping the feathers on the bed before shoving his sets of smalls and pants into the empty case.

At the last minute, he'd heard his father's footsteps coming up the hallway, a staggering gait which sent the man running into the walls, bouncing back and forth between them in a telling way. Easing over the windowsill on his belly, Gabe had stared at the turning doorknob as he reached up to silently close the window. Feet firmly on the ground, he'd cast around for a few seconds to find the bag, heart in his throat. Then he'd been running. Barefooted and free, tearing through the woods, crashing down the mountainside and to the road where he'd ridden his thumb to Lexington. Showing up at the recruiting office like he had, the only reason the men didn't call the police on sight was because he'd thought to grab his papers. With his birth certificate in hand, they couldn't turn him away. Right hand raised, he'd stared into the eyes of the man in front of him, repeating the words that would take him away from there.

Tabby didn't kill herself. His daddy knew who had. Even if old man Mason was dead and gone, nothing but ash and dust in the ground, Ezra Ledbetter knew who had killed her, and he was still suckin' air. Fury turned to look at the house behind him, seeing the shadows of Duck and Brenda come together behind the blinds, then move as a unit deeper into the house. Lights came on in a room on the second floor, and he stared as they came together again before darkness descended on the night. *Duck's a good man. His woman didn't deserve to lose her folks.*

"Park that boy deep." He remembered old man Mason's words.

Facing outward again, Fury leaned over and toed a rock out of the dirt, scuffing it back and forth with his boot. *Things can be dug up.*

The pain on Watcher's face as he recounted the story about his family today haunted Fury. That was a man who deserved better, too. He needed to know Tabby hadn't killed herself.

Just gotta dig shit up.

Brenda's parents hadn't died in a random crash. She deserved closure.

Fury let his mind go back to today, standing in a room with Bethany Mason, forget her married name because that hadn't been a real marriage. That had been her daddy selling her for silence. She was Bethy, the first girl he'd ever loved. Bethy.

Tabby's best friend. The look on Bethy's face at the funeral had never left him. One of those scars he could pull up at will, ripping off any healing scabs, keeping it fresh because you knew, with one look at her, Bethy wouldn't be moving past the moment. Not ever. And from talking to her in Nashville, she hadn't then. After watching her today, it was clear she still bore the pain. She deserved closure, too.

Fury pulled out his phone and thumbed the screen. A moment later the call connected and he waited through the usual pleasantries, then said, "Gunny, got something in Lexington we need to look at."

Saving Bella

Fury

Fury stood in the bar, watching as men rapidly cleared out, the slick leather of their soles skidding on the floor as they ran to the door. He heard motorcycle engines roaring in the parking lot as the first to respond chased the stripes down the highway. Swallowing hard, he stared down at his phone. His alert had been different from the Soldiers' brief, preceding theirs by only moments. He hoped like fuck they had more information than Myron did, because a text that said, **Soldiers princess lost**, wasn't nearly enough to roll on.

Once silence settled back into the room, he dialed Myron, only to get voice mail. That action earned him another text, an instruction: **Call Duck**. Within seconds, the call connected and Fury heard the sound of the wind—ever present in this part of the country—then the noise quietened at the slam of a vehicle door as Duck said, "I'm headed to Las Cruces. You're here in Lamesa. Thinking this is a dividing tactic, pulling all the Soldiers from here like this."

Fury grunted and responded, "And I'm thinking you're probably right. Seeing as they were all we have in the form of backups and those backups just rolled west. That leaves just you and me. So, being as you're the only other soul in that equation, what in the hell are you doing going to Las Cruces, same place those men are headed?" He shook his head, walking to and through the door, squinting at the bright sunlight. "We got Rebel royalty already here." He slung a leg over his bike, shoving the key into the ignition. "And even more coming in. Brother, you stay with me."

An engine roared where Duck was, and Fury knew he was in a truck and heading out, no matter the outcome of this conversation. *Fuck.*

The quality of the call changed, and Duck's voice sounded like he was in a tunnel when he said, "Mason ain't comin' down. Willa's in labor. Means you got Chase and Bethy to worry about. That's it."

"Fuck, that timing's a bitch." Fury leaned over, staring down at his tank, thinking fast. If Mason was tied up in Fort Wayne, he wouldn't be directing assets down this way. He'd be keeping everything close, in case there was a threat to club or family there. "What about Mica and Molly, because we got the cousin. They still coming?"

"Shit, yeah. Essa's here. I wasn't thinking. Shit." Duck was quiet for a minute, and Fury racked his brains like he knew Duck had to be. "You'll have to improvise."

"Improvise, hell. Not like I'm handing the prince a pistol and setting him to guard himself." Fury considered the other band members. "Benny, maybe. Wouldn't want him at my back, though. No offense to Slate."

"He'd be the last one to take offense, brother." Duck's voice was tight, concerned. "Bethy's roommate." Startled, Fury sat straight, wondering why Duck would be referencing Bethy's man. "He's ex-military. He'd be on a plane in a New York minute, you call him. Get Ty on the horn, talk to him. If you can't raise him, get creative."

Fury barked a laugh, the lack of humor matched in the one he heard from Duck. "Creative. I'm good at that. Travel safely, brother. You need me, you reach out. This puts you on the road alone, Duck. I'm liking that just as little as the shit you're leaving behind here."

"Back atcha, brother. Catch you on the flip." A pause, then Duck asked quietly, "Check on my family when you have a minute?"

The call disconnected without giving him a chance to respond, and Fury bent to his phone, tapping out a message to Duck that simply said, *You got it*. Then one to Myron. He hit Send just before he started his bike and rode towards the rodeo grounds. Time to pay the piper when it came to Bethany.

Quacks in the wind. Royalty on a short leash. Updates go both ways.

Thirty minutes later he heeled down the kickstand as he checked his phone and saw a brief affirmative response. He climbed off his bike, standing in the parking lot at the rodeo grounds office. Looking around, he saw a bus parked near the outside fence and recognized it as the one for the band. Through the tinted glass of the windshield several figures were visible, but he couldn't tell who they were. Twisting to face the other direction, he took in the large, clear windows that circled half of the upstairs office. It had an outside staircase, an interior chute for winching things up or down, and it seemed as if the building was structurally sound, but would be an absolute nightmare for security. He spun again, looking at the bus with new interest. It would make them mobile, but vulnerable to fire and explosives. Not more so than a building, though. Self-contained, it even had a gas generator for when the motor was off. The bus was fitted out with a decent-sized kitchenette and bathroom, even had bunks.

Shit.

That motherfucker looked big, but was small inside. He counted bodies in his head, coming up with way too many to be comfortable.

Fuck.

Fury put his hands in the front pockets of his jeans, shoving them down an inch while he thought. He came to a decision and shaking his head, yanked his phone out and composed a message to Myron. He hit the Send button. Then he walked up the stairs to the rodeo office, ready for whatever fight he would have on his hands. Just before he jerked the door open, his phone buzzed and he pulled it out to see a response. **Consider all reasonable precautions approved.**

Fury pulled his lips back from his teeth, glancing over at the practice rounds going on in the arena. "Yee haw."

***

Bethany

"Are you crazy? I can't do my job from anywhere except here." She stared up at the man, thinking to herself again that he looked oddly familiar, then shook off that feeling and focused back on his insane directive. "I'm not moving my entire operations to the bus. That's for the band. They live and sleep there. It's their space and I respect that."

"Step outside for a minute, please." Bethy saw the muscles in his jaw flex and knew he had gritted his teeth in an attempt to keep a civil tone. *You failed, buddy.*

"I have too much to do." She stood and walked to the wall, squatting down to match box numbers to the spreadsheet she had in her hands. Glancing at the dumbwaiter set-up, she was mentally calculating how many trips it would take to get everything downstairs so she could get the merch table set-up, when a band of iron circled her arm, lifting her. Instinctively, Bethy tried to get her feet under her. "What?" That was all she got out before Fury hauled her towards the door, heels of her sandals dragging on the hard floor. "Stop it." He ignored her and Bethy twisted frantically, prying at his hand with her fingers. "Let me go." Chase turned and watched their path, not trying to hide the grin on his face. "Stop it!" she shouted, louder this time, while she tried to get her feet under her enough to brace herself to stop. "*Jesus.*" They were outside now, on the porch, and she looked back through the windows to see five very curious sets of eyes on her. "Asshole."

"Yeah, been called that one." The mutter was the first thing he'd said since he grabbed her, and she hoped it meant he was less focused, finding she was wrong when she tried to pull away. He shook her almost absently, marching quickly towards the broad staircase. "Need to talk to you. Now you've made this a thing, we need to get some privacy." Halfway down the stairs, she stumbled, and he caught her effortlessly, holding her front tight to his side as he cleared the last few stairs. He looked around and saw her rental car, immediately aiming them to the vehicle. "Good" was his only word when the door opened under his hand. She felt a palm on top of her head and he angled her body into the backseat. "Stay." He fiddled with something for a moment then the door slammed. She yanked on the handle, but the door didn't open.

A moment later the driver door opened and slammed as he folded into the front seat. She was headed towards the other door when he turned sideways, and looked at her. "We got a situation." Those quietly spoken words captured her attention. *How could they not, after what had happened only a few months ago?* She nodded slowly. "All our security's been pulled. I'm all you've got. I know you're smart, so it's not going to take you long to realize the reason they've been pulled is because shit's going down somewhere else. You with me so far?" She nodded.

He pointed to the office, and she looked up to see five heads silhouetted against the lights inside. "The band depends on you. They take their cues from you. You give me shit, they'll shovel it ten times worse. You didn't earn it, but you've experienced being in the middle of club shit going wrong." She swallowed hard, and knew he'd seen something because the expression on his face softened slightly, and she had another sudden moment of almost recognition. Then it was past because he was talking again. "Benny has been in the middle of club shit. Chase has seen the results of it, even without knowing that was what he was looking at. The other two are babes in the woods when it comes to real shit. And Bethy, this is *real* shit. This is war."

He paused, and she took the chance to ask, "Is my band in danger? My nephew?"

"I hope not," he answered with honesty, which wasn't quite what she wanted to hear, but she liked he wasn't pulling punches with her. "I can't say for certain. This other club, they're going after family. Watcher's daughter is missing, and the consensus is that they've taken her."

Bethy's heart jolted and she shook her head. "Bella? Oh my God, where's Mikey?" *Little Bella, I changed her diapers. Tiny Bella, the child who climbed me like a monkey, wanting a hug from her Aunt Bethy. Bella kidnapped. Kept in a tiny room, held behind a metal door for days.* She clawed at the door handle again, yelling in frustration when it wouldn't work. "Juanita, I need to get to Juanita."

"No, Bethy. You need to stay here." She stopped yanking on the handle at his firm words, staring at him. "They've pulled every resource possible to find her. Maybe it'll just be a college kid being adventurous." She shook her head, knowing Bella would never do that to her papa. Fury frowned, then continued, "But this club we're set against, they've been known to do family." He paused again, his gaze traveling over her face, making a study of looking at her and Bethy realized why he looked so different. *I can see his eyes.*

No sunglasses. Every time she'd seen him over the past two days, he'd been wearing sunglasses, even inside. Without them, he looked even more familiar. Shaking off the feeling took more effort this time, but she ignored her gut, which was sending off huge warning flares, and instead focused on the immediate issue. "Why can't I go to Juanita? She has to be devastated."

"Because I'm one guy. Chicago boys are busy, and so are the Fort Wayne members. Willa's in labor…" She sucked in a breath, and he at least had the good grace to wince when the news came out so baldly, holding up one hand. "I don't know more than that. But as you can see, we've got a few angles working right now. So if you don't want to be locked in a hotel suite, then we need to move everything to the bus. I'm just one guy," he repeated with another shake of his head. "And your brother is counting on me. I call you guys the Rebel royalty, because it's true. So right now I've got three princesses and one prince in town, and I can't do more than what I'm doing. Mica and Molly are being directed to find me. I need somewhere to put them."

Bethy nodded, hating that he was right. "This all makes sense, in a nonsensical way." Brimming with anger, she needed to turn that emotion to the ones who deserved it, knowing she sounded crazy and not caring. "What kind of people do this? Put innocent children at risk?" She shifted, looking out the car windows towards the arena. "I'm sorry." She stumbled, his name sounding foreign in her mouth, but she forced it out, "Fury. I know you're being considerate. Um, do you think the hotel might be easier to handle? Are you sure you want us on the bus?"

"You can't do your job at all from the hotel, can you?" The concern in his tone surprised her and she looked at him, shaking her head. "Right now, the show is still on for tomorrow. I don't want to jack this shit up for Chase or Benny," his voice lowered an octave, the sound of it scratching along that what-the-hell line in her head, "or you, Bethy. I think the bus will be fine, and it keeps you here where you need to be. As soon as I know anything, or if anything breaks loose, we'll be back on track."

"Mica's in town?" She hated how tentative her voice sounded, hated the queasy roll of her stomach at the knowledge. "Here?"

"Yeah, her cousin's competing tomorrow. Mica and her sister, Molly, are here. I met them along with Essa twenty minutes ago over at Duck's place. I don't think Essa expected them to show, but she was excited to see them."

Bethy's hands shook. She noted the marked tremble when she laid her palms on her legs. Mica had been in Utah. After that thought breached her defenses, it only took moments for the memories to sweep over her, rolling her under the tide of a desperate fear she'd lived inside for weeks.

I'm alive, she told herself. The chill of the cement floor bit into her skin as she sat and stared at the tall, thick, and dreaded door, waiting for the man to come back and kill her. That was what he would do, she knew it. Her death his eventual goal, so every breath she took was another moment deferred. Each day he didn't kill her seemed an eternity. Another set of hours spent in the hell of not knowing. Not knowing why, or who, or if she could do anything to stop it.

She curled up, pressing her head against her knees, blocking out the sight of that window set in the door. The damned, damned door. That was where she'd see him, see him coming for her. The door. That would be the last thing she got to see before she died.

The floor moved, and Bethy was flung against something hard and warm. She pushed, trying to get away. Clawing and shoving, because the door was there. The door would open and he would kill her.

***

Fury

He wrapped his arms around Bethy from his position sprawled halfway in the backseat. They'd been talking about the security situation, and it seemed like he'd gotten through to her. Then she'd gone quiet, chin dropping to her neck. He'd spoken to her several times before she started rocking and trembling. Still unsure, he'd spent another few moments trying to figure out what was going on. It was her whispers that had pulled him from his position behind the wheel, faint and trembling on the air. He'd had to stretch out to reach her because the moment he'd opened the door, she'd scooted as far away from him as she could get. Ass to the floor, back to the opposite side of the car, she'd used her feet and nails on him, trying to keep him away.

"Kill me," she whispered, and he sucked in a breath, shocked. Her teeth chattered, clicking together violently as shivers racked her body. "No. Please, no. I'm alive."

Fury tightened his arms around her again, yanking to tear her hands free from the door. He somehow got her into his lap so he could wrap her up, hold her close. As hot as it was outside—and in the car it was worse, an oven that had him soaked with sweat—but her skin was chilled and she shook as if she were freezing. "Kill me. He's gonna kill me."

Fuck.

PTSD. He'd said something about Mica, and she'd latched onto that, somehow vaulting into her head so she thought she was back in Utah.

At least she wasn't fighting him anymore, but her sagging submission was almost worse. "Bethany," he called, putting his mouth near her ear. She didn't move. Didn't acknowledge him. "Bethany, you're safe." He tightened his arms around her. "Safe, honey." Nothing. Shit.

"Bethany Mason, you're safe." She shivered, and he thought he could hear her muscles creak with the movement.

"Kill me. He'll kill me. Gonna kill me."

"No, honey. You're safe." He would repeat it as long as she needed him to. "You're safe."

Adjusting his grip, he eased her up his legs so he could pull her tighter against his torso. "You're safe." She shook, her hair flying all around her head. "Safe as toads. You're safe, Bethy."

A shadow at the door startled him, and he looked up to see Chase in the process of crouching down. "Give her to me," the boy said, his voice firm. He put actions to words, not giving Fury time to argue before he had pried her away, lifting her to his chest. "I got you," the boy muttered, and turned, stalking towards the bus, covering ground with long strides. Fury realized the rest of the band was standing in front of the car, staring at him. Scowling at him. The look on Benny's face was livid, an angry tension evident in every line of his body.

Fury climbed out of the car, slammed the door, and turned to watch Chase as he disappeared into the bus, Bethany in his arms. The accordion doors closed and without turning, Fury demanded, "Someone want to clue me in on what's going on there?"

Bonnie Dupont was the first to speak, her voice low and furious. "She has flashbacks."

He swung around to stare at her. "No shit, Sherlock. How long has this gone on?" If Mason knew, there was no way he'd have her out here on her own.

Benny turned on his heel without speaking, heading back towards the office.

Dupont said, "Since I've known her. She'll be okay. Chase is good with her."

He looked back at the bus, the large vehicle seeming to crouch at the edge of the lot, waiting. The way Bethy had quivered in his arms had sunk into his head, into his body, setting up a sympathetic vibration all through his frame. Every atom strained towards the bus, and knowing she was hurting pulled at him. "She said anything to you about what happened?"

Vic and Dimitri walked away, also towards the office.

"Bad mojo." Dupont stepped around the car and into his line of sight. "Give him a few minutes with her. She'll be okay." She took a step, then a running skip, then pelted towards the office, catching up with Vic at the bottom of the stairs, swinging on his arm a moment before he turned with her to walk into the shadows of the arena.

I've officially lost control of the situation.

Her voice had been broken when she spoke, despair coating every word. The time in Utah had been harder than anyone knew. A true Mason, she'd been adept at hiding how deeply it had impacted her.

She will not be okay, he thought. *There's nothing okay about what I just saw. I was about half pissed she didn't remember me, but now seeing this, I'm glad she doesn't.* He didn't want to be another thing that caused her to break like that.

***

Bethany

She sat on the bench that ran across the back of the bus, in the salon space behind the bunks. Curled into a ball, Bethy rested her cheek on her knees, looking out the smoky back window with her legs pulled tightly to her chest. On the ledge near her head was a bottle of water and a pile of sour jelly beans. She was always exhausted when she came back to herself, as well as sick to her stomach, and Chase knew it. He'd set things up for her without even asking this time.

This time. That thought made her stomach roll, because she didn't want there to have been a *this time*, because that implied there'd be a *that time*, and then a *the other time*. She just wanted to be done with all of it. "Beat it back," she whispered, feeling her hair sweep across her arm as she adjusted her grip on her legs. *Only so much a body can beat back.*

Now that she was past it, she could look at the things she thought she'd seen when she blacked out, and pick out the imagery that didn't belong. The cement floor and window in the door, those were real. Had been real. Had been her world for three weeks while she waited every day to die. The eyes that watched her every move, those were not real. Neither was the feeling of safety, like she'd found her own personal angel. Not real. The imagined Kentucky woods, strong hands reaching to turn over a fallen log, and a long, pointing finger showing her the toad crouched there. *Not real.*

"Safe as toads." That had been something her aunt had said, using the phrase to calm a frightened girl in the middle of a violent spring thunderstorm.

In the distance, she saw Fury walking up the staircase, moving slowly, as if the heat lay heavy on his shoulders. Fury reached the door at the top of the stairs and paused, running his hand over his head in a gesture that felt so strikingly familiar, but she couldn't put her finger on it. It looked like he was surprised to find a full head of hair. Like he would be more accustomed to bare skin.

In her head, she heard his voice, almost as clearly as if he'd been seated next to her, "Safe, honey."

Right after that, she heard the voice from her older nightmares, Derek's voice. "No, honey. It couldn't be." *I'm going crazy.*

"Chaser." She tried to shake off the unease plaguing her and called out as the bus swayed in a way that told her Chase was walking down the long hallway towards where she sat. She had to focus on what was important. *Watcher and Juanita. Bella.* The words Fury had said started flashing through her head. Davy and Willa. *I have to tell him.* "Come here."

"'Sup, Aunt Bethy?" He pushed through the folding door and fell to a slouch on the couch beside her. "You put back together?"

He'd been the one to find her after her first episode at the house in Fort Wayne, when she'd been cowering in a closet, waiting for the man to come and kill her. At first—and this told her how hard his life had been—he'd assumed she had taken drugs, his disappointment rough as sandpaper while he talked her through it. Afterwards, he'd seemed relieved when she explained it had just been her head trapping her in memories. The spells didn't come as often now, nor did they last as long. She well remembered how Ty had struggled with his bad turns, and eventually had drawn comparisons between Ty's behaviors and her own.

Chase had become her rock, and she felt guilty for leaning on the young man, but telling Davy wasn't an option. He needed to see her as strong and able, or he'd pull the business and put someone, anyone else in charge.

"Willa's gone into labor." That was the most important information, because if he wanted to go back and be there, they'd need to get a flight lined up for him quickly. "Do you want to go home?"

He stared at her, then one corner of his mouth pulled down as he made a face. "I should want to, right?"

"You don't have to." Reaching out, she stroked the back of his hand as she shook her head. "What's right for me is different from what's right for you. I want to, but I'm here for the show. It's bigger than me."

"I don't want to. He'll have enough to worry about without me being there." She narrowed her eyes, focusing on his face. *Not quite as inscrutable as Davy.*

"Liar." He winced and she knew she'd gotten it right. "You want to go, but you're being smart and adult about it, even if that sucks. Because you know you're not a problem, and you wouldn't be in the way. You're right, though. If you're there, he'll worry about you, too. This way—" She paused and shook her head. "This way he can focus on Willa and the baby, and being a brand-new dad. Something he didn't get to experience with you." Bottom lip pushed up into a bow, Chase nodded. "Okay, I can see that. Love this selfless side of you. So much. But, if you decide to go, if you change your mind, that's an easy adjustment, okay?" He nodded again. *God, he's a good kid. He'd love Michael.*

"Now, let's get everyone on the bus so he-man will be happy. He's got some other news he'll share once we're all on here." Chase lifted his chin, staring at her with Davy's eyes, the familiar intelligence shining through was uncanny. "And then, once the show's over, you can tell me what you know about Fury."

Don't laugh at me

Fury

Leaning his hips against a rest area picnic table, Fury waited on Bella to come out from the bathroom. Glancing at his phone, he realized she had been gone nearly fifteen minutes. With a sigh, he straightened and turned, about to head inside and check on her when she appeared in the doorway. Face angled down, the edge of one hand shaded her eyes against the glare of the sun, boot-clad feet moving slowly as she paced along the walkway towards him.

They would be stopping for the night soon, but he wanted to get another hundred miles down the road before that happened. To urge her onward, he swung his leg over the seat of the bike, making it obvious he was waiting. He felt compassion for her ordeal, knew what she went through would have to fuck with anyone's head, much less a just-into-her-teens kid, but he needed to get her to Chicago where the full weight of the Rebel ranks could take on the responsibility of keeping her safe.

It might make him paranoid as fuck, but the skin on the back of his neck had been creeping since they left Lamesa. Even before then, he had the tech guy for the Soldiers sweep his fucking bike before they headed out. He had also switched phones, churning and burning the technology, carefully texting the new number to only three people: Mason, Watcher, and Bethany.

Ready for it, he didn't move when Bella's glove-covered hand settled lightly on his shoulder. The bike shifted underneath him as she placed her foot on the peg, swinging over and seating herself behind him. Two days into the trip, this was their routine, nothing needed explaining or discussing. She had grown up around a club, so she knew he was simply doing as he was told. Just like her. "Get on this man's bike and ride with him until he hands you off to someone else I trust." Those were the basic instructions her father had given her, and Fury could see what it cost the man to send her away after he had barely gotten her back. Saw the price in his clenched jaw and narrowed eyes, taking in Fury at a glance and nodding. Family cared for family, and blood mixed with club loyalties meant an unbreakable tie between him and his cousin.

Getting her out of the firing line seemed the smartest thing to do, especially since the particular brand of crazy they were dealing with didn't seem to hold anything back. Where many clubs, hell, most clubs would never consider targeting families, Deacon and his minions like Shooter, Judge, and Lalo, all seemed hell-bent on causing the greatest amount of damage possible, regardless of the innocents caught in the crossfire.

Back on the highway, he felt her curl in behind him, her body slumping against his. Fury braced as he took her weight. *Two hours*, he thought, seeing a mile marker sign fly past. Two hours and they would rent a double in a cheap motel, cash only. No phones, no pool, no problem— they wouldn't be there long enough to use them anyway. Just long enough for them both to catch a few hours shuteye, then they would be back in the wind.

Fury knew when he got to Chicago, he had another two days of riding before he would be back at his assigned post. *Turn and burn*. But, by then, the concert would be over, the rodeo would be over, and fuck...for all he knew, Chase and Bethany would be gone from Lamesa.

Bethany, he thought, feeling his lips curl up in a smile. The prettiest woman he had ever been around, hands down. She had accompanied the group to dinner the last night he had been there. He and she had wound up seated side by side, and conversation between them had been relaxed and comfortable. Almost like she was trying to catch up with an old friend. The idea sent a shiver up his spine, because Fury knew if she had realized who he was, she would have found a stake to tie him to and burn him.

Instead, it hadn't been strange, hadn't been weird. She'd pulled Chase into the conversation often, letting him bear the weight of talking when Fury felt himself getting too close to critical secrets. She had a million questions about his life, but was just as happy to talk about herself and her career. It had been fun to watch, how she had worked at giving him glimpses into her world in a way that she thought kept some mystery, her clear goal to ensure his interest remained piqued.

Even more than before, Bethy knew the music industry inside and out, and it was clear she wasn't afraid to bust balls when needed. She'd laughed it off, saying it was a hard lesson learned, but her bands benefited from her education. That had stung, because he knew she was talking about him, and the days they'd spent together.

He found she had a soft side and got to witness it over and again as she loved on Chase. A woman he had always been able to see himself with, and one who seemed as cautiously into him as he could be her. *If her brother wasn't my fucking president*, he thought as the smile faded into a scowl. *If I hadn't already fucked her over.*

He considered all the details he knew about Mason. The biker, the businessman, the city councilman, the father, the brother. Would there be any possibility he could consider someone in the life for his baby sister, or would that be a no-go? All Fury knew was that since seeing Bethy again, all thoughts of any other woman had fled his mind. He didn't consider himself a fickle person, his plans usually were laid months in advance and he lived by his lists. But now, Bethy consumed him, his dreams filled with her grey-eyed gaze, that zing of electricity from their first touch still seeming to ricochet around in his body every time she was near.

Seeing an approaching off-ramp with a motel nearby that would fit their needs, he slowed and prepared to exit the highway. *What would work best with Mason*, he wondered. *Frontal attack, approaching him with the ask? Or a sidelong campaign, sneaking in the side door belonging to his sleekly attractive sister?*

Pulling up in front of the doors of the motel, he waited for Bella to dismount, and then with a glance, cautioned her to stay by the bike as he went inside. *Bethy's too smart and sassy.* She'd never submit to Mason if he went against her. Fury dragged his wallet out and tossed bills onto the counter, fingers slipping across to snag the old-fashioned key on a plastic fob. Finger to his brow, he saluted the man behind the desk, turning to see Bella obediently waiting, chin tucked tight to her chest, eyes focused on the ground at her feet.

Poor darlin'. He eyed the healing scabs on her face and forearms where she bore the wounds of her captivity. "Here's the key," he said, offering it to her. "Go on in and get cleaned up. I'll knock when I'm back with food." Her gaze flicked up, locking on him and he saw her warm brown eyes fill with tears. *Oh, honey.* "Swear. You're okay, Bella. I won't be gone five minutes. This place is safe." Her fingers were shaking as she reached out for the key, obvious reluctance in her stance. He remembered she'd thought her apartment was safe, too. She'd do it, what he was asking, but she would be in fear the entire time.

"Okay, sweetie. No worries, yeah? Together," he said softly, pulling the key back and shoving it into his pocket. "Ride with me for food, we'll be back in a minute and you can rest."

Now her gaze filled with gratitude, and he heard her voice for the first time, liquid tones sweet in the air. "Thank you."

***

Three days later, Fury stood in a hotel doorway back in Lamesa, dusty boot toes just over the threshold, fingers clenched onto the wood at the sides. He watched as Bethany stalked across the suite towards him, grey eyes flashing with anger. He had never seen a more beautiful woman than she was right now, pissed as hell at him.

"What are you doing? I don't need security, Fury. I don't care what my brother thinks." She stopped about five feet away and cocked out one hip, resting her hand on her waist. "You're here and then gone, but it doesn't matter. I've been taking care of myself for a long time now. Not sure what changed that he forgot all that."

"After everything we got going on, he's just worried about you, that's all." He took a single step inside, reaching for the door handle as he moved to one side, pulling it closed behind him. "Chase and everyone else has their own detail. It just worked out that I'm yours."

"You came in." She stated the obvious with disbelief in her voice.

"I did," he responded, struggling to keep his eyes on hers and off her tempting curves. *Damn, this woman is the whole package.* Sassy and sweet, beautiful and rounded in all the right places. *Perfect.*

Grey eyes blazing, she reminded him, "But, I just told you I didn't need security." When her head tipped to one side, he couldn't help himself, feeling the corners of his mouth curling up. "Do *not* do that," she ordered, her head snapping back upright.

"Do what?" He fought against the smile, knowing he was losing ground with every second that passed. *She's just so fucking cute.*

"Laugh at me." He watched a shadow of some dark emotion chase across her features as she said this, then saw the anger settle back into place, now recognizing it as a defensive maneuver on her part. "Don't laugh at me."

Her words had stripped the humor from him, making it easy to answer. "Not laughing at you. I just like what I see, makes me happy." He shrugged, looking away from her and around the suite. "Pleases me." Her belongings were strewn across the sitting area and he found himself again struggling against a smile when he saw no fewer than six bras, all different colors—some of which looked familiar—draped across the backs of chairs and the couch. "Oh, yeah, I like what I see," he muttered, stepping around her and farther into the room. *God, this is such a bad idea*.

"Fury," she called. "Did you not hear me tell you that I don't need you? That I don't need someone like you?" He rocked to a stop and turned to face her at her words. *Someone like me*. Thank God, she didn't know who he really was, or her cuts would be ten times deeper. "I didn't mean…" She turned her head to look at her purse when her phone went off, then looked at him, because his had started ringing the same moment.

"Yeah," he answered without looking at the display. Didn't matter, only club had this number. And Bethy, but that was beside the point since she was standing five feet from him and didn't have her phone in hand.

"Get on Bethany right now." Slate spoke the words in a tone that brooked no argument, and it wouldn't get one from him. He might have been lying five minutes ago when he told her that her brother wanted her covered, and while this gave him a legit excuse to spend time in her space, he was honest enough with himself to know he would have been doing that anyway. Just on the high he got from being in the room with her. In her space was exactly where he wanted to be, and Slate had now granted him permission.

"On it," he responded, disconnecting the call, carefully watching Bethy as she spoke into her phone. Chin down, she wasn't paying attention to him, and he took full advantage of the chance this gave him to look his fill. So beautiful and put together. Even surrounded by the chaos of life lived out of suitcases, she was perfect.

"Yeah, I'm safe, Mason," she reassured her brother. "I promise, honey." She listened, and then her gaze cut up, locking with Fury's as she nodded. "Yeah, Fury's right here."

Sorry for your loss

Fury

Their back and forth argument hadn't stopped after the calls, but instead had slowly slipped sideways back into the sweet comfort they'd started building before he'd been sent to Chicago with Bella. Bethy exposing a bit more of herself with each exchange, and Fury found every glimpse into her private life enticing. He also found out fast that he'd been wrong about her relationship with Tyrell, the roommate.

For Fury, the specter of her flashback in the car haunted his thoughts, and he was on edge, watching for symptoms that all of this had continued to fuck with her head. He'd tried to find an in but never seemed to hit the right words to make her understand. Not wanting to make her self-conscious, he'd spoken of his time in the military and how it still impacted him at times. He might not have diagnosed PTSD, but like with so many military who'd served in front of, or behind the wire, that hyperalert edge was always within reach, curling closer depending on the setting.

That had been the thing that opened the dam. Ty had a dose of it, a big dose, if what Bethy conveyed was right. Story after story about the man and how he'd learned to deal with the monsters haunting his mind had segued naturally into Fury gently urging Bethy to talk about her own. He sat and listened, but more than that he'd watched her.

When she'd nearly curled into a ball, still talking about Ty while making herself as small as possible in the chair, he'd had all he could stand. His abrupt ejection from the couch startled her, and he watched her eyes get wide when he stalked closer. Pushing his arms underneath her, he'd only begun relaxing when her hands wrapped around his neck, instinctively holding on as he lifted and twisted. Ass in the chair, he'd cradled her in his lap, cupping the back of her head to hold her in place.

He'd waited, expecting an explosion about being manhandled, figuring she'd need to rant at him about how she didn't want to be touched. He'd waited and then was glad he'd braved her wrath because she jerked in his arms. Not attempting to get away, just trying to swallow the torrent of sobs struggling to force their way up her throat. "Shhhhh." Speaking softly, lips to the curve of her ear, he soothed her, "I got you, honey. Shhhhh."

"You saw me." Not a question, and he didn't treat it as one, just left it there between them, hoping she'd keep talking. "The day Bella was...kidnapped." Uttering the word caused a rolling, full-body flinch in her, muscles moving involuntarily to a threat that existed only in her head. Whispering, she said, "You saw me lose it."

"I saw a strong woman pushed too far." Tucking her face under his jaw, she shook her head. He knew he had to make her hear him, or she'd never stop pushing him away. "Yeah, Beth, that's all I saw. A strong woman who'd endured a nightmare. The kind of nightmare that doesn't end when a sun is rising, doesn't let you wake safe in your own bed because it was a dream. The kind of nightmare that sticks around, waiting for you to drop your guard so it can sweep the legs out from under you." Her body hitched and he ran his hands over every inch he could reach, soothing her muscles, feeling them twist and jerk under his fingers. "I saw a strong woman who needed a moment to remember her nightmare was over, and once she did, she climbed back up on her own two feet. You helped get everyone moving, got everyone on the bus without me having to be a shitheel about it." He stroked her back, liking how she arched into him. "Made it so I could do my job and keep everyone safe, made it so I could concentrate on that important work without having to fight. You did that." He paused, but she didn't fill the silence. "You did that, Beth, and that proves just how strong you are."

Her question, when it came, made every muscle in his body lock up. "Who were you, Fury? Before you met my brother, I mean. Who were you?"

"What do you mean?" Shuffling to cover his lapse, he pushed a brusque tone into his voice. "I'm just a biker. Nothing else."

"Nothing to see here, kiddies, move along," she sang the words like a midway barker and he laughed, the sound harsh and hard. "I call bullshit. But fine, keep that secret." His belly sank, thinking she might have already guessed. "You're too nice to be just a biker. And it's weird, how you can be whatever is needed in the moment. Biker one minute, security guy the next, comforting friend when demanded." She wasn't far off the mark and he schooled himself against flinching. "So if you won't tell me who, tell me what? What were you before you met Davy."

"You already know. I was in the military. Quit school and joined up soon as I turned legal." *Fuck.* He hadn't meant to give her anything, and yet there it was, his mouth moving without regard to keeping the secrets she'd accused him of.

"Do you know Mikey? Um, Watcher?" Her head lifted from his chest and she angled to look up at him, intelligent and somber grey eyes peering at him from under a dark wing of hair. *Fuck.*

"Not from the military, no." He didn't lie. "I've met him, yes." Still not a lie. She seemed satisfied by his answer and rested her cheek on him, cuddling close with a sigh. They stayed in that position for a time, such a long season of quiet that his mind began to wander, going over all the irons in the fire the Rebels had, and where those lined up with the Soldiers. He was on item four on his mental list, talking to Watcher about Spider because the man didn't ring true for Fury, when Bethy stirred.

"What time is it?" Her voice was quiet, thick in a way that let him know she'd been dozing. Fury liked knowing she felt secure enough to fall asleep in his arms.

He glanced at her phone on the arm of the chair. "Nearly ten." That surprised him, because no way did it seem as if he'd been here for more than five hours. *She's gotta be hungry.* He realized he didn't know her itinerary post-concert. "When do you fly out?"

"Wow." She stretched and yawned, then folded herself back against him, clearly unwilling to give up her spot in his lap. At the movement and friction, knowing it was a soft, round, female ass resting on his crotch, his dick started to harden. "That late already? Um, two more days? I had to change my flight out of Midland with everything that's happened. The band's already on the road, well you know that, don't you?" She shifted and it felt deliberate when she put a welcome pressure on his cock. Yawning again, she kept talking. "I'll follow Chase to Fort Wayne, get to meet my new nephew."

He expected the reminder of who she was to Mason to be an ice bath on his libido, but no such luck. Her yawning and stretching had her twisting and moving under his hands in all the right ways, and one palm wound up on her ribs so the pads of his fingers cupped the lower curve of a breast. *Fuck me.*

"You hungry?" If one of them had to get up to call room service, that would be a natural interruption to where he saw this going otherwise. If she didn't get still or get out of his lap, he'd be hard pressed to hide his arousal for much longer.

She moved, sliding her ass across his thigh so she could lean back and look up at his face. Lips slightly parted, her eyes had gone a dark grey he recognized, and she blinked at him. The tip of her tongue swept her lower lip, leaving a glistening trail behind. *Jesus, she's turned on.* "Baby," the endearment slipped out and he felt her shiver. "You want this?" Blood engorged, his cock was painfully hard, wedged between them, stuck behind a fold of his jeans, and when she nodded, it still gave an eager jerk. "Be sure, Bethany."

"I'm sure," she whispered.

"Be real sure, baby," he whispered back.

She blinked again and hesitated, and for a moment he thought she would throw the brakes on. Then, she turned the tables on him in a way he didn't expect. "I don't usually do casual sex. But I've wanted you since the moment you walked into the office." He pulled in a breath, slipping his hand up her side, holding her waist tight. "You walked in and my first thought was 'why are all the handsome ones in out of the way places' because I thought you were a promoter from the area. Then you smiled, and I contemplated what it would take to move to Lamesa." Staring into her eyes, he saw them get bright, crinkling at the corners with a suppressed smile. "Then I found out you were with my brother, and I took a mental marker to your name, crossing you off any potential partner list." He tipped his head to the side, and she did smile at that, the edges of her mouth curving upwards. "What I'm saying, in my blunt and sidelong way, is I've given this significant consideration, Fury. So yeah, I'm sure."

And there it was, the Bethany he remembered. Laying it out there in real talk, making certain he couldn't mistake her interest. "You might be the bravest woman I've ever known." She was laughing softly as she shook her head. "Yeah, baby. Putting it out there like that, ready to take a hit if I shut you down? Brave as fuck."

"How about you? Are you sure?" Not quite a dare, still the edge of a challenge was in her voice, goading him to say what she wanted to hear.

Guided by his thousands of dreams, assisted by the times he'd run the movies of their lovemaking through his head, he lifted a hand to her face, tracing across her lips with his fingertips. He glided them up and across the bridge of her nose, between her eyes to bury his hand in her hair, stroking out and down, slowly. Arranging locks of her hair on her shoulder, he flattened his palm on her chest, tracking a line down her sternum until he could cup her breast in his palm. Lifting and squeezing with his fingers, he grazed the pad of his thumb across her nipple, feeling it harden through her clothing as she gasped.

Gaze back to her face, he took in her features. Sharp desire burned in her eyes. The expression on her face was pure, exposed need. "Yeah, baby." Bending close, he brushed his lips across her mouth and along the edge of her jaw, pausing when he neared her ear. "I'm sure. I wanna fuck you. Have since I walked in that room and saw your face turned my way. Unexpected beauty. Then I got to watch you over the past few days, here and there, always takin' care of others. That's an unforeseen boon, baby. I wanna see how you take care of me, but more—" He paused, sucking her earlobe into his mouth and toying with it for a moment, then pressed his mouth to her throat. "I wanna take care of you." He kissed her throat again. "You gonna let me do that?"

"Yes." Her response was breathy and immediate. She'd gone rigid in his lap, holding herself still as he spoke. "I want that."

He shifted and found her mouth with his, not having to fight for entry because she opened for him right away, as eager for it as he was. Tongue sweeping against hers, the slick glide a promise of what was to come, he took his time, exploring and reacquainting himself with her secrets. Head angled, she gave back as good as she got and in moments, the kiss was blazing through him. He stood with her in his arms, never breaking that connection, her hands on either side of his face, her hold fierce. Down the short hall and through the door to the bedroom of the suite, he saw the covers were smooth and flat, unmarred. Wedging her against him, he reached with one hand and flipped them back, exposing the sheets.

Laying her across the mattress, he followed her down, chasing that mouth, needing more of her taste, of the feel of her under his lips. He trailed a palm up the inside of her thigh, pushing to spread her before wedging a leg between hers, his hand continuing up her belly to her breast. Frustrated by the clothing between them, he flicked the buttons open on her shirt, fingertips tracing the swell of flesh along the lacy edge of her bra. She moaned into his mouth and arched up when he shoved his hand into her bra, lifting her breast over the edge. He framed it with the fabric and moved fast, bending deep and latching on. Her fingers landed in his hair when he sucked hard, fingertips and thumb gripping and lifting, his movement unceasing as he fed her into his mouth. Her breathy mutter barely stirred the air, "Jesus, Fury." She clenched and his scalp stung as he shifted so he could angle his eyes up, looking at her. Open mouthed, she stared at him as he worked her over, breathing hard and moaning again when he bit down lightly. Every reaction was honest, an echo of their lovemaking from twelve years ago. Releasing her slowly, he bathed every inch with his tongue, lapping and nipping at her flesh, pulling her nipple between his lips and bearing down until she moaned again.

Lifting up on his arms, he stared down at her flushed face. "Goddamned beautiful, baby." Pushing away from her, he unfastened her pants, tugging them down her legs, taking her panties with them. She was already working on her shirt and bra, so he took the opportunity to remove his vest, folding and placing it on the dresser before stripping bare. Laying one wrapper on the bed at her hip, he tossed a spare condom to the nightstand, watching how her eyes tracked it before returning to him, a smile on her face.

Covering her, he kissed her hard, biting at her lips in a way he knew would leave them puffy and red, then made his way down her body.

Pushing underneath her legs with his shoulders, he positioned her like he wanted and buried his face in the joint where her leg met her body, breathing deep and finding everything he wanted. Sweet scent, soft flesh, and willing woman.

Starting there, he licked his way across to the other side, flicking and dipping into her opening, finding her wet and ready. She didn't need him to prime her. *Coulda just fucked her*, he thought with a grin. *She's hot for it*. Flattening his tongue, he licked up her center, pressing hard on her clit. *Still, wouldn't give up a chance to have my favorite meal.* He teased her, flicking and circling the nub of responsive flesh with the tip of his tongue until she cried out, shoulders rising from the mattress as she clutched the back of his head, holding him to her.

Tearing free from her grip, he lunged up her body and kissed her deep, tongues dueling as she eagerly took what he gave. Tiny whimpers fell from her lips when his hand found her center, spreading her before spearing her with his middle finger. Pumping deep, curling and coaxing her with each stroke, he shoved his other hand underneath her shoulders and up, threading his fingers into her hair and gripping hard, holding her in place while he kissed her.

He jerked reflexively when her fingers curved around his upper thigh, trailing across to his cock, slipping in the fluid leaking out of the tip. She slicked up her hand and stroked him, then explored down, cupping and tugging his sac, pulling a shout out of him when she broke the kiss, pushing up to put her mouth on his shoulder and bit down.

"Move your hand, baby," he warned her as he opened and rolled the condom on, moving sideways between her legs, loving how they fell apart, letting him slot into place. Cradled with her limbs, he pushed against her, feeling her outer lips part for him, gliding up along his cock, wetting him. She'd moved her hand to his hip and now pulled, tugging in a clear demand.

Mouth to her neck, he set his teeth in the muscle there and bit, sucking hard as he lined up and pushed. She arched up and made a sound that made him slow, pausing to work his cock in and out those first couple of inches, letting her get used to him. Stretching around him, so fucking tight he groaned, mouthing her neck. "You good, baby?" He got a muffled response and lifted so he could see her face, shoving his forearms into the mattress on either side of her head. "You good, baby?" he asked again, keeping the same rhythm of shallow thrusts.

"You're big." She breathed the words and wiggled her ass, pumping up against him, forcing another inch inside.

"You're tight," he responded and she grinned. "Not complainin', baby. Feels fuckin' great."

"Backatcha," she whispered and wiggled again. "I'm good."

He worked his way inside her slowly, advancing in small increments, having to pause the action for a moment here or there in order to hold his control. Staying in that position, he examined her face as she took him, seeing the tiny frowns when the stretch would burn, watching as they smoothed out and she'd nod, indicating she was ready for more.

Gave this up, he thought when he was seated fully inside her. *Gave it up once*. He moved, and she shifted with him, their rhythms naturally in sync. *Can't give it up again*. Arching up against him, she dragged her full breasts across his chest. Teasing and nipping, she ran a hand up his neck to grip his hair, pulling his mouth down to meet hers. *Won't give her up*.

Sweaty and slippery, he moved over her and in her, bringing her along with him as he followed the thread of true desire he'd only found in her bed. Over the past decade, every time he'd lain with a woman, the only way he could get off with any satisfaction had been to think about Bethy. Now that she was the woman under him, he found his dreams had fallen far short of reality. She was so much more, so good, so sleek, so wet and tight, vocal in a way he liked, her whimpers and moans floating on the air around them, feeding into this goddamned feeling of making his woman feel good with his hands, his mouth, and his cock.

When she broke, he raised his head, gaze fixed on her expressive face, and she didn't try to hide from him. Mouth open, calling out, she didn't hide anything, gave him everything, let him know how what he gave her was good, let him have the knowledge of how she liked it. He shifted gears then, driving in harder, knowing she would take it for him, take him however he gave it to her.

Hands under her ass, he lifted to his knees, bringing her up to meet his thrusts, fingers tight around her hips as he pulled her onto him. Her breasts shifted on her chest and she didn't try to control anything, she lifted her arms over her head, palms flattened against the headboard as she pushed back, taking him deeper, exposing everything to him and it was that trust that finally took him over the edge. Knowing she'd given him that, was giving him that, took him there. Collapsing on top of her, he shoved a hand under her back, curving around to put a hand at her hip, holding her in place as he clutched the pillow with his other hand, burying his face in her neck and shoulder, grunting through his release.

***

Fury looked at his phone in disbelief. Not even twelve hours ago, he had received a group text with a picture attached that made him smile, even as his throat tightened with an ache. *Our brother's bundle ... Faith Inez.* That brief message of joy, with an image of radiant mother and infant daughter, framed in the smiling father's arms. Now a new message to the same broad group, but with an entirely different tone. Similar to a dispatch received only four months ago, it consisted of few words, crafted to convey the loss. *Hoss' old lady passed.*

Beautiful Hope.

Golden hair, a laugh that could light up the room, filled with stubborn and love in equal measures. He had seen devotion on her face towards her old man and her kid, a singular focus that only made her more beautiful.

Gone.

Fuck.

Chest tight, he thought about the times he had seen her over the past year and a half, from the first vision of her beauty and poise in Marie's, to the last time, watching her walk from Hoss' arms towards her car in the clubhouse lot. She had turned to wave at her man, fingers pressed against her full lips to toss him a playful kiss, belly rounded with a child who would now be motherless.

He jerked, so lost in his thoughts he startled when a hand settled on his shoulder. He tossed the phone to the floor beside his jeans, and lying back in bed, twisted to look in her face, seeing the question there. "Death in the family," he offered quietly, not wanting to explain more. She took what he gave, nestling her face into his neck, fingers playing idly with his beard as Bethy whispered, "I'm so sorry for your loss."

He reached down, lifting her chin to see her face. *Has she guessed yet? Got it all figured out?* It would almost be worth telling her, just to end the uncertainty. Dipping to press his lips to hers, he told himself he'd tell her tomorrow. Lay it all out there, let her know the truth about the three men she knew, and how they were all him.

Her hand slipped down, flat along his belly, fingers playing with the hair along his midline until his belly was jerking underneath her touch and he felt her lips curving as she smiled against his mouth. Then her hand was on him, fingers folded around his cock, thumb slicking through the fluid eagerly dripping from the slit. He kissed her hard, cupping the back of her skull to hold her in place, tongue thrusting deep in her mouth while she jacked him steadily.

"Jesus, baby," he muttered when she ripped her mouth away for a breath, hand moving faster on him now. "You wanna ride me?" Her face lifted to his again and he saw her eyes go wide, pupils dilating. He flung off the sheet, urging her to straddle him, hands on her hips lifting her into place. "Fuck me, honey."

He liked that he could see her face as she slid him into her this time. Liked seeing the tiny indents her teeth made in her bottom lip, watched with reverent attention as her lids slipped to half-mast, from the edges of his vision caught the way her belly sucked concave when she ground deep, bottoming him out inside her. She paused there, sleek heat all around him clenching and pulsing. Then after blowing out a slow breath, she placed her palms flat on his chest and lifted, careful not to lose the knob of his dick as she rose over him. The flare of her eyes warned him, and he was ready when she dropped on him, slapping her ass against his thighs in a rush to bury him inside her again. The concussion of the hit throbbed deep inside him, and he tightened his muscles, jerking his cock against the inner walls of her pussy.

"Mmhm. Yeah, fuck me. Just like that."

She shivered at his words, a movement he saw and then felt as she quivered and tightened around him. Then she lifted slowly before dropping again. Another pumping hit followed by a grind that pulled his cock in all the right ways, dragging it down and up again. Hot, slick fluids made by both of them gave the motion a slippery sound, and he listened as the wet slapping echoed in the room. "Fuck me, baby."

He let her ride him at her pace, getting off on her gasping moans every time she took his cock deep. Her fingers curled, nails scoring bright stripes on his chest and still she lifted and fell, rocking in a steady rhythm that made his ass clench with the need to drive up into her.

"Baby," she whispered, and he felt it, saw her nipples tighten and peak on her breasts as they swayed with her movements. Lunging up, he captured one in his mouth, his hand pressing between her shoulders, arching her back. Pulling deep, he tongued the hard nipple fast, lashing it as he bit down gently but firmly. His other hand slipped between them, finding and pinching her clit, rubbing tight circles.

"Fury," she called, and that word nearly stopped the show because that wasn't what he wanted to hear. Then she was coming and all words were lost, only primal, babbling sounds that flowed from her mouth as he whipped her to her back and drove deep. She was coming down, movements less urgent underneath him as he felt the first curling threads of his own climax. She wrapped one leg around his hip, and he reached down, wedging his arm behind her knee, holding her leg up and out, keeping her open for him. Deep and fast, he pumped, thrusting faster, her hands slipping up his back to curve around his shoulders. "Baby," she called, and he felt her pussy quiver.

"Fuck, yeah," he grunted, then ordered, "gimme your mouth." She twisted, and he kissed her hard, panting breaths mingling in their open mouths while she orgasmed again. He plunged deep, holding there, feeling heat pooling around the head of his dick inside her. Lifting up, he locked his elbows, staring down at her before dropping his head to place a kiss at the base of her throat, licking the salt from his lips as he rose up again.

"You wanna shower?" There were few things he'd like to do more than lay beside her in bed, something he'd done several times as Derek. They'd talked, and she would cuddle close, the sweat on their bodies drying against the sheets. Fury hated he felt this need to make things different now, because if she hadn't figured it out and didn't know who he really was, he wanted to draw different figures in her head. Build good associations with him here, now. He moved, pulling out and rolling towards the edge of the bed, ignoring the grumbling noises she made at the motion. "I'll shower first, then."

He brought out a washcloth, wet with warm water from his heating shower, washing first her face, and then her breasts before cleaning between her legs. By the time he got back from his shower she was fast asleep, dark hair tamed into a twist under her neck. Climbing carefully into bed behind her, he wrapped his arm around her waist and pulled her tight against him, smiling at her groaning sigh until it ended on a name that froze him in place. "Derek."

***

Bethany

Bethy sat on the edge of the unmade bed, covers still rumpled from the activities of the night before. Phone in hand, she was locked in place, staring at the messages glaring up at her from the screen. Several were from her brother, and several, including the one that held her attention in a brutal way, were from Fury.

"How could I be so stupid," she muttered, one hand raking through her hair, pulling hard against the snarls her fingers found there, wincing at the pain as her scalp was tugged. "Naïve isn't pretty at my age. Stupid me. Stupidly thinking stupid things I had no business thinking."

Mason's communications were, as ever, terse and concise.

Nashville.

That would be his command for her to head home.

Promo OY tour.

She had already intended to continue to promote Occupy Yourself's tour, using the media attention from the rodeo performance as a springboard, but evidently, Mason didn't think she was moving fast enough.

He ain't no good for you.

With Mason as a brother, and now having an idea of the pull and power he had, it shouldn't have been a surprise that he would be capable of finding out she had spent the night with one of his men. It shouldn't have been, but it was, and her cheeks flamed at the thought of her brother knowing what they had done...what she had done in bed with Fury.

Love you, Bethy.

Regardless of anything happening around them, Mason always— *always*—ended every communication, written or spoken, with those words. He had told her once that life was too short to make people wonder if they mattered, and he always made certain she knew just how much. This, all of this, made her both irritated as hell at Mason and filled her with gladness he was her brother.

Brother. *Blood of my blood*. Something that meant more than outsiders knew, back in the holler.

Protector. *Each time I've reached out in need, he's been there*. He'd bent luck more times than she could remember, making certain she had what would make life better. *If he knew about Michael...* She thrust that thought away.

Friend. She smiled. Over the years they'd moved from being strictly siblings who worked around birth order to a solid relationship, one that she cherished.

Family. *Back to blood*, she thought. More though, because he was family she claimed. Unlike some of them.

Mason was all of that and more. Raised the way they were in eastern Kentucky, bonding together was the only way to survive. With only four years between them, they had been each other's sounding board for plans and dreams, so she knew what Mason wanted to build, the family he had begun gathering almost as soon as he left the legacy of mountain and holler. He loved her, she knew it, and he made sure she knew it. He also tried to keep her safe and made sure she knew that, too.

Fury's messages were no less short, just as concise, but they left a chill in her chest that didn't feel as if it would ever work its way out.

Was fun.

Yes, what they had done could undoubtedly be called fun, even the bits where they were arguing. Total fun.

Recalled to Chicago.

She suspected this meant he was no longer in town, which surprised her because they had made plans for tonight. And tomorrow morning. And tomorrow night. Plans that she had been looking forward to in a big way.

Then came the final message, three words to underline the good time part of their contact.

See you around.

Time to start digging
Bethany

She'd been seated at the table in the window of the coffee shop for an hour, waiting. When she reached out to pick up the oversized mug, Bethy studied her fingers impassively, watching the tremble caused by too much caffeine. *If she's not coming, she would have texted*. To prove to herself that the girls' lunch they'd planned was still on, she picked up her phone and unlocked it, going to the last message from Dot. Nope, still just the **See you there** that was a definite meeting notice.

Tipping the cup, Bethy lifted it to her mouth, draining the contents. The next time the waitress came by she shook her head, declining a refill for the moment. *Come on, Dot*.

The door opened and she looked up, smiling when she recognized Ty's mother. Rising to her feet, she opened her arms for a hug, sighing with relief when a moment later she was wrapped in warmth and the soft scent of Dot's favorite perfume. "How you doin', Miss Bethy?" The whisper in her ear was light, airy, and Bethy returned the soft greeting.

"I'm well, Dot. How are you doing?"

While she'd been in west Texas, Ty had another turn. Without her there to look out for him, it had gotten bad before help was called. Dot had walked in on her son casually playing a version of Russian Roulette, and the bullet hole Bethy had patched in the apartment wall testified to how close things had been.

"Oh, you know me. I'm fine, honey. Just fine."

Bethy narrowed her eyes, assessing, and then called Dot on her lie. "No, you aren't. Have you heard from Sarge?" They pulled apart, and Bethy flicked a finger at the girl behind the counter, getting a nod in response. Dot was looking down, avoiding Bethy's eyes as they seated themselves. "Dot, have you gotten an update from Sarge?"

"Tyrell is doin' fine." Dot was still looking anywhere but at Bethy. She murmured her thanks when the girl placed a cup of coffee in front of her, studiously adding three packets of sugar to the drink. "He was hurtin', no denyin' that. But he's going to be fine." Dot's eyes darted up, then down. "What did Sarge tell you?"

"Just that Ty was back in treatment at his place, and I had a mess to clean up when I got home." She had, too, Sarge hadn't lied about that. There had been at least two weeks' worth of takeout trash and spoiled food to dispose of, followed by a couple of hours of dishwashing and tidying. "He's always terse with me, so I hoped you had a better update."

"Tyrell was bad, Bethany." Dot's gaze lifted, focusing in on Bethy's face. "Real bad, honey." Tipping her head to one side, Dot asked, "Anything you want to tell me?" On guard now, Bethy shook her head. "You sure, honey? What happened in Lamesa?"

"What do you mean?" She shrugged. "We had a concert. Then I stayed over a few days to sort out details."

"Ty said he got a call from a man asking him to come out and help guard you." Bethy froze. "When he asked the guy what was going on, the man told him that you were in danger. Put my Tyrell into a tailspin, knowing his best friend was in a situation like that and hundreds of miles away."

"Oh, no." Bethy blinked fast, clearing the stinging wetness from her eyes. "No."

"Yes, Bethany." Seeming to change directions in the conversation, Dot waited until Bethy had herself under control to ask her next question. "Who is Michael?"

The bottom of Bethy's coffee mug clattered against the tabletop as she tried to set it down without spilling. Dot's warm hand settled over hers, fingers curling tightly, holding on as Bethy folded in half, bending far over her knees and breathing deeply. "Honey." Dot's soothing voice settled on her like a blanket. "Baby girl, what's happening? What happened in Texas? Who is Michael?"

With holes punched through her words by sobs, Bethy told her. Ty was the only one who'd known, the only one she'd ever spoken to about Michael. There were the Marshalls of course, but they weren't her family. Ty and his mother were closer to her than anyone other than Mason, and Bethy would never be able to tell *him* about Michael. So she told Dot the story, how she'd been pregnant when dropped on Ty's doorstep, how he'd helped her every step of the way, been there for her and for Michael.

And Dot returned the favor, telling her how Ty had sobbed, explaining to his mother that it was only Bethy and Michael who had kept him from taking that final step. Dot reached into her large handbag, pulling out the album Bethy and Ty maintained, something she hadn't even missed when cleaning the apartment. He'd been holding it in his lap the night Dot found him, cradling it to his chest like a child.

"So you already knew who Michael was?" Bethy tried to keep her chin from quivering, feeling somewhat betrayed.

"Yeah, honey. I knew. But he's yours, and you deserved to be the one to tell me." Dot shook her head, a small, sad smile ghosting on and off her lips. "And I deserved to hear it from you."

Shame and pain swept over Bethy, and she twisted her neck, trying to bury her head against her shoulder to hide her tears. A moment later and strong arms circled around her, pulling her close to Dot's chest. "Hush, now, honey. No more secrets between friends. Life's better when lived in the light."

"Oh, Dot," Bethy cried, turning to return the hug, resting her wet cheek in the curve of Dot's shoulder. "This is how I've lived my whole life, hiding my secrets in the dark. I don't know how to be in the light anymore."

"Sure you do, Bethany. You are the light, most days. Just gotta pull the curtain back a little bit, show it to the world." Dot paused and her arms tightened. "I'm surprised as anything, Mason and Mikey letting you give that little fella up."

"Not so little anymore. Michael's sixteen. He gets his driver's license in another week." Bethy licked her lips, trying to take in a breath that didn't hitch or break, and failing. "He's sixteen, Dot."

"Just a baby, still." Dot's words were firm. "Still, doesn't answer my other question about your brother. He's got a boy the same age, right? What does Michael think about his cousin?"

Shoulders shaking, Bethany admitted, "Mason never...he doesn't know. Neither does Mikey. I had asked so much from both of them, I couldn't...Ty's...he's the only one who knows. Michael...his adoptive family is so good to him, I never wanted him to know where I came from. He doesn't know I have a brother, much less a cousin."

"Oh, Bethany." Dot's voice was soft with sympathy. "Just a babe yourself, taking so much on your shoulders. My Tyrell loves you like the little sister I never gave him. That boy'd do anything for you. Even keep a secret like this." Her arms squeezed and Bethy's convulsed in response. "So, tell me what your next steps are?"

Bethy pulled in a shuddering breath, glad her tears had stayed relatively silent instead of the braying cried that had tried to escape. "Call Sarge, see if I can go see Ty. I need to see for myself that he's okay. Then," she leaned back slightly, looking up at Dot through her clumped lashes, "I'll have a chat with Michael."

"And then you talk to Mason, and Mikey." Dot shook her head. "Juanita's going to be fit to be tied, you keeping her from being able to shower your child with presents."

Bethy smiled, lips still trembling. "Then Mason and the rest."

***

Bethy waited, ringing phone held to her ear, eyes closed against the afternoon sunshine. Still slightly swollen from her afternoon crying jag, they burned every time she opened them. A final ring and then voice mail picked up, Sarge's voice brusque and gruff as it demanded, "Leave a message."

"Sarge, it's Bethany." She'd stick with the name he most often called her, hoping he would pair her voice and name, and come up with the right person. "I'm coming up to see Ty. I'll be there this evening. Call me and let me know if there's a time that's best. Otherwise, I'll aim at around seven." She disconnected abruptly, without a farewell. By not asking permission, she'd hopefully taken away Sarge's ability to deny her access to Ty. It wasn't something she'd ever demanded before, but she knew where the facility was, having picked Ty up more than once.

As she'd predicted, right at seven she wheeled her car up the long, sweeping drive that wound between trees. She parked next to a muddy SUV with a comical spare wheel cover that read, "If you can read this, call help" in upside-down lettering.

As she was unfolding from the car, stretching after the two-hour drive, the front door of the cabin opened and Sarge walked out to stand at the top of the steps, staring down at her. "Hi." She waved, slamming the door and stepping to the side. "I'm here to see Ty."

"So I gathered." He didn't move, and where he stood with arms folded across his chest, she would have to push past him to gain access to the porch, much less the building. "He's not in a good place, Bethany."

"I know." She decided to offer him a little more information, hoping he would understand it didn't matter what condition Ty was in mentally, she would always be his friend. "I spent some time with Dot, so I know how things were when you came and got him. I wasn't there." She swallowed, trying to shove down the guilt that followed that statement. "I've always been there, and I wasn't. Please." She swallowed again, holding her eyes unblinking, trying to force away the sudden tears by willpower alone. "I need to see Ty."

"He ever talk about being here?" Now she blinked, because that wasn't what she expected him to ask. She shook her head, and then nodded, because Ty had, once.

"Only one time. He said your methods of helping your men"—they were all Sarge's men, whether they'd served together or not, once he took them in they became his—"were unorthodox, but he also said it helped him and some others so much more than they'd ever gotten from the government. I don't care what's going on, what you've got cooked up in there, as long as it keeps making Ty better."

Sarge's eyes had narrowed as she spoke, his lips flattening in reaction, but she didn't know him well enough to read that expression. It could be anger at Ty for talking at all, or satisfaction that she was placing her trust in him.

They continued to stand like that, in opposition both figuratively and literally. Bethy refused to allow her gaze to drop, so she stared at Sarge and she waited. His lips flattened even more and he sighed. "Okay." She smiled and reached for the handrail, putting her foot on the first step. "Wait." She froze, because when Sarge said anything in that tone, it paid to listen. "I have more men here than just Tyrell. I won't compromise the privacy of my other men by allowing you inside." Tipping her head towards one shoulder, Bethy waited in silence as he sighed again. "I'll talk to him and bring him outside." He took a step back and pointed towards a sagging upholstered armchair wedged into the corner. "Wait here." She nodded and sat. Pulling out her phone, she brought up a word guess game she'd been trying to beat. Wordlessly he stalked past her and inside.

Her phone's battery was at 50 percent when the door opened again and a sleepy-looking Ty stumbled out, Sarge's hand clamped on his bicep. She jumped to her feet, then felt the smile on her face crack, sliding away as she looked at Ty. His lids were drooping over badly bloodshot eyes, and that paired with his faltering gait told her he'd been smoking a great deal of pot. The grin he gave her was pure Ty though, and his arms opened in an invitation she would never ignore. Even as he folded her against him, arms curling tight around her, Sarge was maneuvering him to sit in the chair she'd abandoned. Ty pulled her down with him and she didn't argue, just crawled up into his lap and rested against his broad chest.

He held her for a moment and then let out a sigh that seemed to begin at his toes and work its way up his body, muscles relaxing in a wave. "You always feel like home, Bethy." She smiled, her face hidden in his shirt. The interlude lasted a few seconds more then he tensed and she knew what would be coming next.

Shaking her head, she leaned back and squinted at him. "Don't." The sober expression on his face didn't change. "Just don't, Ty. None of this is your fault."

"I shoulda called Sarge earlier." Bethy felt her brows draw down into a scowl, but he just looked at her. "I shoulda. I knew it, and thought to myself, 'Oh, hell. I can do this.' But I was wrong, Bethy. I'm always going to need someone to help me see when things start to fall back on themselves."

"And I'll be there." Ty shook his head as he tightened his arms, one big hand traveling up to cradle her head, pulling her against his chest. She didn't fight him, letting him hold her as he needed even as she argued her point. "Every time it's a little better." He didn't say anything, just shifted so he was more comfortable and stayed seated, her in his lap. "I'll be there, Ty."

The shadows of the trees around the cabin had lengthened, working their way up the outer walls and shrouding much of the clearing in dim twilight when Sarge spoke. Ty had gone to sleep long ago, his arms still wrapped around her even as he slumbered. "He'll do better in one of my homes." Bethy tilted her head, cutting her eyes so she could see his shape as he leaned against the post. "I have staff there all the time, and he'll be around the other guys he knows. Being on his own is something he'll have to work back up to, Bethany."

She knew it was best. It was something Sarge had talked to Ty about in the past, and Ty had always turned down the offer and come home, telling her he didn't want to move. Maybe staying in that apartment was holding him back. She could keep the place, she made plenty of money with the studio, so that wasn't a consideration. *I've never had to be alone.* Other than the scant times Ty had spent up here at the cabin, she'd never lived alone. She'd gone from her father's house to her husband's at fourteen, then to Ty's at sixteen, and lived there since. The prospect was terrifying, but for Ty...*I'll do anything.*

"It's not your fault, Bethany, any more than it's his." With one sentence, Sarge had hit on the emotion that kept swirling around her. She'd spent nearly the entire drive up here muttering various renditions of, "If I'd only been there." Logically, Bethy knew she couldn't take the blame, because her extended stay in Lamesa hadn't been in her plans. *Still.* "He's managing better than before. Take strength from that."

The soft tone in his voice hit her like a stick crashing down on the overstretched head of a drum, breaking and shredding the faltering control she had. Bethy didn't lift a hand to wipe the tears, trying to keep them silent as things from the past week battered at her. Threats, actual threats against her family, real enough to warrant frighteningly tight security; Fury, there and gone again, leaving her with a series of texts that stripped their encounter of anything important; Mason, always the puppeteer, pulling her strings yet again; Ty, needing her and not finding her, so far gone in his head that his mother's voice trembled when she spoke of how she'd found him. *Too much.* Her shoulders shook and she heard a choked noise, realizing it came from her throat. *It's just all too much.*

"Hey, Bethany, he'll be better." *I won't be.* Strong arms shoved underneath her, peeling her away from Ty's chest and Sarge backed up against the wall, sliding down to sit on the porch, her in his lap. "Don't cry." She tried, clamping her lips to keep the cries inside, holding herself stiff and trying to touch him as little as possible. "Hey, don't cry."

Rough fingers touched her chin, hooking under the edge of her jaw and lifting. Before she could take a breath, his mouth was covering hers, the brush of lips light and gentle, delicately working across to the corner of her mouth. "Hey." Sarge pulled back and she opened her eyes, staring at him. He looked confused, as bewildered by his behavior as she was. "I'm sor—I didn't mean to intrude, Bethany. I just." The pad of his thumb glided in front of her ear, and down the side of her throat. "I don't like it when women cry."

She snorted a laugh at the idea and then reached up to wipe her tears finally, chasing the feeling of tightness across her cheeks. "So, you kiss them?"

A haze of red began to creep up the curve of his ears, matching color blooming on his cheeks and neck. "Not generally, no."

"I'm the lucky winner of the lottery, then?" She shifted and froze, her ass cheeks sliding across his very evident erection. "I just...had a shit week, Sarge. No application of kisses necessary. That's part of the problem, anyway." She decided to ignore his physical reaction and pushed on his chest, intending to move to sit beside him, but his arm tightened around her waist, holding her in place. Ty let out a groan, and she glanced over at him, catching sight of his face, slack-jawed and about to...a loud snore broke the quiet and she laughed quietly.

"What happened in Texas?" Sarge pulled her attention back to him, and she studied his face for a moment before deciding to continue the path of truth she'd begun with him so many months ago.

"My brother's in a MC. You know what that is?" He nodded. "Well, he had one of his men acting as my 'security' while I was in Lamesa." Bethy rolled her eyes as she gave the word the air quotes it deserved. "I fucked up and slept with him."

"Bad deal, mixing business and pleasure like that."

"No, shit. I knew better, but there was just...Fury, that's the guy's name, he seemed familiar somehow. Safe. And I thought it was..." She sighed. "More. But it wasn't."

"Fury? He military? Ex-mil?"

She angled her head to better see his face. Sarge had something more than polite curiosity on his features, but she couldn't tell what it was. She nodded. "He said army."

"Huh." After a nearly silent grunt, Sarge tipped his head to look at Ty, then back to Bethy. "Ty know this guy?"

She shrugged. "I didn't ask."

"Redheaded dude?" Bethy stared at him a moment before nodding. "Talk like Watcher does? Backhills country?" She shook her head. "No surprise, Ledbetter always a good conman. Could bend himself into anyone, putting on a mask for whatever was needed. I knew him, and knew of him. He ran with some shady folks overseas, heard he carried it back home with him. Spent a nickle in Riverbend. Figured he'd clean up after that."

The world swam, loud buzzing in her ears finally resolving to Sarge's voice asking, "Bethany, you okay?"

Hesitantly, she opened her mouth, afraid for a moment that the things she'd put together in her head would fall apart once spoken aloud. "Gabe Ledbetter?" Derek's face flashed in front of her eyes, not the slick-talking man who'd shared her bed, playing her body exactly as well as Fury had, but the last time she'd seen him, through the glass in prison at Riverbend, dark red halo around his head where his hair was growing to cover his skull. Barely older than she was at the time, the Gabe who left the mountain to make his way in the world been a half-grown gangly kid. Clean-shaven, but his hair had been a deep russet, like the heavy cones that fell from the pine trees. Fury's hair was lighter, brighter, and his beard so much fuller and longer than Derek's scruff. *How could I have missed it?* "Gabriel Ledbetter is Fury?" she asked for clarification because Sarge was staring at her. Tabby's brother, for all intents and purposes. Watcher's cousin.

She watched as Sarge's chin dipped and lifted, the single motion of his head setting her anger in motion.

Rumors and secrets

Bethany

Sitting in her favorite chair in the apartment, Bethy tilted her head up, looking out the window at the breeze-stirred leaves of the oak trees along the greenway. A few minutes later, silence in the room brought her back to herself, and she turned back to the laptop propped on her knees. The demo track had finished playing, and she not only didn't know when, but she also didn't remember anything about the music she was supposed to be evaluating. "Shit."

Restarting the track was a moment's effort, and one click of the cursor had the opening swell of music filling the room. Closing her eyes, she tried to dig into the sound, separating the different artists' efforts to see what would make it memorable, saleable. Something people would call or text radio stations to hear.

It wasn't long before she found herself staring out the window again and set the computer aside with an irritated huff. Lifting her hands, she roughly scratched across her scalp, fingers tangling in her long hair as she gathered it on top of her head. After they'd gotten Ty inside, Sarge had insisted she stay the night, bedding her down in a small room in the cabin. She hadn't rested well, strange sounds kept her awake until late, and it had been a relief when Ty had come in early the next morning to talk. More coherent than he'd been the night before, they'd had a pleasant breakfast shared with three other men staying there. Sarge had been conspicuously absent, and with the other men joining them, she couldn't really ask Ty anything about Gabe.

Bethy released her hair, letting it fall around her face. "Derek." The name spoken aloud startled her, and she snapped her mouth closed. *Or Fury, whatever.*

Her phone rang and she picked it up, a curl of fear crawling up her spine at seeing Martha Marshall's name on the screen. "Martha? Is everything okay?" Michael's adoptive parents didn't call her. Martha texted when there was news to share, often sending pictures along with a recounting of the various successes Michael had seen over the years.

"Well, yes, and kinda no, Bethany." Martha's no-nonsense attitude was one of the things Bethy liked best about her. That, and the fact she loved Michael as if she'd carried and birthed him. "Can you come over? Maybe tonight?"

Bethy glanced at the clock and frowned. Late afternoon was an unusual time of day to receive an invitation for the same day, but Martha was acting odd enough to warrant accepting no matter what she had to reschedule. "Absolutely. What time do you want me there?" She had two station interviews set for six o'clock, but they were taping to play later in the week, so she could arrange to do them later.

"As soon as you can manage it." Martha's breath in was audible, and she blew it out in a shaky stream. "Michael isn't ill, so you don't have to worry about that. But we need to talk. There's a...situation, and I want you to help us sort out what comes next."

"Is everything okay?" Bethy repeated her question, then followed with, "I can leave in ten minutes. I'll be there soon, just tell me if he's okay."

"He's fine. My boy is fine." Bethy's head snapped back, and she froze in the act of rising from the chair. Martha had always, always called Michael theirs. From the first moments of his life, she had promised to share him as best they could. This was the first time Martha had laid sole claim on Michael. Then she kick-started Bethy's heart into beating again by saying quickly, "Our boy. Our boy is fine."

"Be there in a few minutes."

True to her word, Bethany pulled up to the Marshalls' home and was out of her car within the time she'd offered. Martha met her at the door and pulled her into a quick hug, then backed away, hands still clasping Bethy's. "He's upstairs. I want to talk to you before he comes down. He's—" She interrupted herself and then followed up with a simple, "Come sit."

Seated on the couch beside Martha, Bethy glanced at the ceiling when she heard a thumping crash followed by the unmistakable driving beat of a rock song. "Lord. He's been at it all day," Martha muttered, then pulled in a breath, turning to stare at Bethy. "You're his birth mother." Bethy nodded. "He knows that. We've made no bones about it. You've had a…" Martha trailed off, searching for a word and finally landing on something acceptable, "challenging year."

She hadn't told anyone about being kidnapped. Couldn't, as Davy had explained it because there'd been no reports to the cops, no official version of events, and so many things that couldn't be explained. Not legally. Work and friends, everyone got the same story of a sudden illness on tour, weeks of recovery in place. She'd been so skinny and pale when she got home, it was an easy sell. Everyone except Ty. Bethy nodded.

"Tyrell called Michael." Bethy froze in place, and Martha arched an eyebrow. "Oh, yeah. Tyrell wasn't having a good day." They knew about Ty's PTSD, he had been a fixture in much of Bethy's life, and by extension Michael's, too much for her to hide something that could disrupt his life for weeks on end. "He talked to Michael about a lot of things. Michael said he was rambling, mostly. But he told him something about you. Something I think you've tried to keep a secret, not wanting to upset anyone."

"What? What did Ty say?" Bethy's palms were sweating, chilled and damp when she clasped them between her knees, trying to hide the shaking that had set up in her fingers. "What did he tell Michael?"

"You have a brother?" Martha's soft words weren't a statement, she was giving Bethy an out if she wanted to say there'd been a mistake, that Ty had misspoken. Bethy couldn't do that. She remembered Mason's face as it had looked on the plane as they traveled home from Utah, talking about his boy Chase. Chase, who she'd seen take to a stage last weekend as if he'd been born to it. Chase, who loved his Aunt Bethy so much, it shone from his face. Mason hadn't gotten the chance to be an uncle to Michael, but he probably would love it as much as she loved being Chase's aunt.

Bethy nodded and Martha pulled in a lungful of air. "I see." Another loud thud from overhead, then the screeching sound of something heavy being dragged. "Michael is unhappy he didn't know."

"I'm gathering that. Martha..." Here Bethy had to be careful, because she had worked hard to stay in Michael's life, worked hard to cultivate a sustainable relationship with his adopted family. She had never regretted her decision, but every day she'd longed to have been given the chance to make a different one. Martha and her husband had provided the best of both worlds, loving and raising Michael as their own child, while acknowledging that Bethy had a claim, too. "Does he want to talk to me about it?"

"Yes." Martha breathed the word out in clear relief. "He very much does."

"Should I go up, then?" Martha shook her head, and Bethy offered a different solution. "Want me to go back to my car and call him? I can tell him I'm outside?" Martha nodded. "Okay. I'll make it right."

Martha smiled and leaned forwards, lifting her palm to cover Bethy's cheek. "Honey, you've always had his best interests at heart. He'll see this as more of the same." A loud thud rattled the pictures on the walls, and the music got louder, booming down the stairs. "Sooner or later."

The young man who climbed into the passenger seat of her car fifteen minutes later didn't resemble Michael as she'd last seen him. Dark hair longer than he'd ever worn it, he slumped into the seat with a teen's boneless ease, grey eyes cutting her direction as he rolled his head to the side. She sat a moment and waited until he finally deigned to buckle, her persistence provoking a sarcastic sigh.

She pulled out and turned at the first opportunity, deciding to cruise aimlessly for a bit. It was a tactic she'd used on recalcitrant band members before, and she knew it would eventually work. *He'll be easier to manage if he's a captive audience.* "So, you're pissed at me."

She got a grunt, followed by a "whatever" shoulder shrug.

"If you want to know the story, I'm happy to tell it. But you need to let me know what you want."

"You've got a brother."

"Two. One of which I've never met." Before the words escaped her mouth, she hadn't planned what to say, but clearly her subconscious wanted to go with truth.

"Why haven't you met him?" Michael shifted in his seat so he could watch her. "Any sisters I should know about?"

"I haven't met him because my family is complicated. John is my half-brother and was raised in California." She sighed as she stared out the windshield. "No sisters that I know of. I always wanted one, but no luck."

"Your dad left and went to California?" He sounded shocked, but she was about to rock his world a little.

"No, Mom left us. I was just little. She went to California and had another family." For a moment, echoes of Mason's voice sounded in her head, retelling the story of their mother's death. She pushed that aside for now. "Daddy raised me and my brother."

"You've never talked about having family, Bethany." As it always did, her name sounded funny coming from Michael. In her dreams, he called her mom. "Why's that? I've never met anyone from your past."

"You say past like I've lived some sordid life or something. I don't keep in touch with anyone except my big brother." After Tabby died, after Bethy had left the mountain and hollers, she hadn't answered a single call or returned even a Christmas card. "You've met Ty."

"Ty's from here, not somewhere in Kentucky."

"Right." She turned onto a larger street, then took the next road to the right, knowing it was a winding thing, edging along old homes and buildings.

"I'm named after him, right?" Bethy glanced at him, seeing Michael's focus was on his fingers, gripping and twisting together in his lap. "How'd you meet Ty?"

"If I'm going to tell that story, then I'm going to have to start at the beginning." He didn't say anything, so Bethy plunged in. "My daddy wasn't a good man." Might as well turn out all the pockets on that suit; she'd never get a chance to dig out the dirt any other way. "He made me marry a friend of his when I was fourteen." A shocked inhale told her he was listening. "My brother had left the family farm several years before, so he never knew."

Michael got out a stuttered, "What?" but she talked over him, needing to get it all out at once. Questions could come later.

"Things were bad up there back then. So much worse than anyone knew. When I was sixteen, my best friend committed suicide. I knew if I didn't make a change, I'd risk following her footsteps. So I got some help from an old family friend. Her brother, actually. His name is Michael."

"Like me?"

She nodded. "Mikey was like a brother to me. He got me out of that situation and brought me here. Ty knew them because he'd served with Mikey in the military. All I cared about was it was safe, and not where I grew up. I don't know why me and Ty hit it off, but we did, and I moved into his apartment." She took a breath. "Three weeks later I knew I was pregnant."

"Wow."

"Yeah, kind of a mix of the worst and best kinds of wow. Did you know Ty was in the delivery room? He's known you all your life."

"So I'm named after Mikey and Ty?"

Bethy nodded, steering the car around another curve. "The two men who saved my life. Seemed fitting, and your mom and dad were willing."

"Martha and Rodney." He didn't say anything else, and she wasn't sure how to take that statement, so she left it alone for now.

"My brother had left home already and had all kinds of his own problems to tend to. He hadn't known about what daddy did, and he didn't know when Mikey rescued me." She slowed the car, waiting for a cat to complete a deliberate promenade across the street. "He didn't know about the pregnancy, either."

"You mean me, he doesn't know about me." She shook her head. "Is it because of who my fa—the man was who got you pregnant?"

"No. He doesn't bear the burden of why I've never told him. That's all on me. Michael, I was sixteen and grieving for my best friend, torn willingly away from everything I'd ever known. But some of the lessons we learn when we're young never go away. Like picking up your socks." Something she'd heard Martha tell him countless times, and it earned a humorous snort. "I was told to suck it up, dust myself off, and figure things out." She shrugged. "So I did. I'm really good at that. I knew if I told him while I was pregnant with you that he'd do his level best to help me do what he thought I wanted...I was so young, but I knew you deserved all the best things. Afterwards, if Martha and Rodney decided to close the door between us..." She shook her head. "But they didn't. Then, like with all deceptions, the longer it drags on, the harder it is to change the outcome."

"You were sixteen?" The heaviness in the air had been gone a while, his questions and her honest answers clearing things to a point she felt lighter than she'd been in years. Pulling the car into the parking lot of the nearest diner, she nodded. "That's...young."

"It is." She gathered up her purse and turned to face him, bracing herself for the look of disgust she expected. Instead, she just saw Michael, intelligent grey eyes studying her from under the fall of dark hair. She smiled, and his lips twitched, sliding sideways in an attempt to remain stoic. "Let's go inside and eat."

"One more question first?" He waited and she nodded. His mouth opened and closed. Then he narrowed his eyes and opened it to speak. "If he knew, would he want to meet me?"

Bethy couldn't help herself, laughter ringing in the enclosed space as she reached out, grabbing one of Michael's tightly clenched fists. She squeezed and he turned his hand, wrapping his fingers around hers. "Oh, yeah. He's going to want to meet you. He's also going to rip me a new one when I tell him."

"You'll do that for me?"

Suddenly sober, she blinked fresh tears from her eyes. "Baby, I'd do anything for you."

I am what they made me

Bethany

The weight of his silence battered at the room. In her mind's eye, she imagined the paint peeling, ceiling sagging in response to the oppressive atmosphere. Raw and agonized emotion bared on his features brought her to tears, and she lifted a hand, palm up, as if that could stop the waves of disappointment. She knew how he felt, and knowing gutted her. "I am what they made me." His words tore through her and wrenched her to her knees. "I cannot be anything else." Head bowed, she slowly crept towards him until she felt the heat from his body radiating out. Fingers working at the fastenings of his jeans, eyes to his face, she released him and waited. It felt like the touch of an angel, the grace of pardon when he cupped the back of her head, guiding her mouth to his cock.

Bethy's eyes opened and she stared up at the dark ceiling, fighting for breath, every nerve in her body firing. The sensation so similar to the moment Judge had tasered her, Bethy found her muscles locked tight, and for an instant, she was too terrified to move. Just in case.

The dream had taken her by surprise. Right after coming back, she'd dreamt of Gabe often. Her brain refused to call him by his club name, and most of her memories of Derek had been buried for years, so Gabe was how she thought of him. *Back to our roots.*

Pulling up an image of him in her head, she compared the Gabe of now to the boy she'd known, still shocked she hadn't made the connection. Might never have made it without Sarge's voice in the dark, drawing lines between past and present in an undeniable way.

Derek. A thing the prosecutor had said about how the lies of Kentucky had invaded the courtroom made sense now. At the time, she'd held onto hope it meant Derek wasn't guilty, but now, she wondered if it was because he knew who she was at the time, even trying to hide behind her married name.

God. So many layers. Anger at Davy for not being there when she needed him had pushed her to reject the name they shared, and it was only after their nephew kidnapped her that she took ownership back, introducing herself to Benny Jones with a hyphenated name.

Maybe it's time to ditch the Taylor part. She pulled in a startled breath when her door creaked, swinging slightly as the air conditioning kicked on, dark shadows leeching into her room from the hallway. "You agree with me, right?" Her question asked the air, because she'd been alone in the apartment since coming back from Texas. Ty had left Sarge's cabin and gone to communal housing where he had access to other veterans and more intensive therapy than she'd ever been able to make him accept.

Turning to her side, she ignored the aching throb between her legs, a reminder of her dream. Gabe had been in the military too. Maybe he brought back more than she knew about. Dot's pictures of Ty before enlisting were more a match for the Gabe she remembered. Tall and lean, where now he was muscled and bulky. He'd often called it his armor for what might come after him.

Maybe Gabe's behaviors are his armor? He'd confessed, preventing a drawn-out trial, keeping her out of the papers, because she would have had to testify. It helped her keep things from Davy, too. Still, there were his words at the prison. Maybe that was more deflection, not wanting her to come and see him, not wanting her to wait. *Or maybe he faked that, too.*

Bethy flopped to her back, shoving the sheet and blankets to the foot of the bed, impatient with the confinement. In Texas, Gabe had his own set of defenses. He'd hidden behind protocol of the club and the demands of her brother.

Except in bed. As both Derek and Fury, Gabe had shown a tenderness and care that she didn't think could be false. *He likes me.* His text messages were a smokescreen, like his words to her through the jailhouse phone so many years ago. She reached up and twitched the curtains to one side, staring up at the winking stars. *Please let me be right.* With a sigh, she closed her eyes, letting her hand fall back to the bed beside her. In Texas, everything he'd done had been with her well-being in mind. Before they slept together, before he'd taken a rescued Bella to Chicago...she could look back and see where she'd come first. *I think he likes me.*

She smiled, skin heated from the vision of him moving over the top of her, hands cradling her face while he stared into her eyes as if he needed to memorize something important. *Maybe more.*

Hours passed as she lay there, running every conversation she could remember through her head. Gabe, Derek, Fury—she passed each word through the sieve of what she knew now. As Gabe, he'd been the near-brother to her best friend, an ever-present protector she and Tabby both depended on after Mason left the holler. But her memories of him then were tied up in the doings of things. A grin flashed alongside a creek as they collected crawdads, the weight of his arm across her shoulders when she found out Davy had left.

When he was Derek, the memories were more complex. Remembered tension between them had been colored by the outcome for so long, it was hard to pick the threads of that lens away, leaving her the moments that lay between. His startled laughter when she gave an unexpected answer during their first dinner together, hand darting out to cover hers then yanked back as if her touch was acid. That avoidance giving way over the course of the evening to an incredible connection she'd embraced, and he had clearly fought. Fought and lost. *He didn't come to me with the intent of seduction.* After examining their moments together, that much was clear. There'd been a plan of wooing, but he had not intended for them to wind up in bed together.

The same in Lamesa when he came to her as Fury. He had kept his distance for days, treating her like an unwelcome chore assigned by a project manager. In many ways, she guessed that much was truth, because Davy had set him on her. *Davy can't know who he is*, she thought, and that awareness gave her a moment of toe-curling terror. Because if Davy didn't know and eventually realized, then found out what had happened in Nashville, he would be…furious was probably too small a word. *He'll kill him.*

Even after coming back from his trip with Bella, Gabe hadn't intended for them to sleep together. *That was all me.* He'd held her as she came apart, lost in the nightmare of her memories, willing to stay with her through the worst of it. If there'd been any seduction in that hotel room, it had come from her side of things. He'd even asked her more than once if she'd been certain it was what she wanted. Once they were in bed, and even before—after she'd been able to clearly articulate her definite interest—he had been all-in, fully present in the moment. *Exactly like he'd been with me before.* Tenderness covered his fierce hunger like a thin veneer of civilized, but she had no doubts sleeping with her had been on his mind. He'd admitted as much. *He just wasn't going to act on it.* Either time.

Outside influences. The idea trailed through her head, and she turned to her side, tucking her hands under the pillow. In Nashville, he had conned her out of money, pretending to be something he wasn't. But in bed, he'd shown her exactly who he was. It had been a lot of money she couldn't easily afford to lose like that, but she'd made it through okay. No lasting damage. He'd gone to jail, paid for it with five years of his life. A bad exchange on his end, no doubt. When he'd gotten out, he hadn't come to her. Hadn't found her and explained or apologized, but—Bethy snorted, *I would've shot him on sight back then*—it was probably a good thing.

The lessons had been hard but served her to this day when she approached negotiations. *Not that I'm excusing his behavior*. But without that experience to guide her, there were a dozen more situations that would have been even more costly, both emotionally and monetarily. *Never again* had become an instinctive mantra, repeated until it was an embedded part of her psyche.

In Texas, he had again clearly set out to deceive her about his identity. *Who wouldn't?* He had no idea how she'd dealt with things, and she knew from talking to Chase that the man Fury had worked his ass off to get into her brother's club. If she'd recognized him, it would have screwed everything up for him. Self-preservation because of outside influences. *Am I justifying what he did because I want more?* She didn't think so. There was only one way to find out. *Road trip*.

"I need to talk to Davy anyway, telling him about Michael needs to be a face-to-face conversation." She rolled to her back, eyes adjusting to the faint light easing into the room around the curtains. Reaching up she twitched them aside again, the breaking dawn not quite erasing the brightest stars in the sky. *Please make Davy not kill him*.

First one then the other

Mason

"I want you to bring her the fuck to me," Mason roared into the phone, hand tightening down on the device as he swung to glare at the men in the room, all now frozen in fear of whatever he had heard over the phone that could bring him to this level of rage. "You bring her right the fuck to me."

Disconnecting the call, he twisted and scanned until he saw the faces he wanted. "Slate, Deke, to me," he clipped, stalking towards the secure room in this Ohio clubhouse where they conducted business and church. A thought hit him, and he paused, then pulled his phone out of his pocket where he had thrust it and dialed. They needed to make sure there weren't any bugs in this clubhouse since it wasn't one that he used frequently. "Myron, Ohio sweep. Who?"

There was a pause as his tech and money wizard caught up with his shorthand speech and then he heard, "Gunny."

Disconnecting, he dialed another number, barking his question as soon as the call connected, "Where are you?"

Not cautious, because he never held back with Mason, not anymore, Gunny said, "Fucking my woman. My own bed." He sucked in air audibly, then clipped, "Where you need me?"

Tipping his head to look at the floor, his tone more moderated this time, Mason said, "Sorry, brother. Need you in Ohio yesterday. Need you to bring cleaning supplies when you come."

There was noise in the background, a soft feminine moan that made Mason wince, then a loud, fast, slapping sound of flesh against flesh. "Goddammit, Prez." The moan came again, and Gunny hissed. "Fucking hell, babe, you comin' again? My fucking pussy. Hell." His breathing sounded hard and fast in Mason's ear. "Fifteen minutes, in the wind," Gunny grunted, and the call disconnected.

Mason reached out, deliberately locking and placing the phone face down on the table near him, seeing Deke do the same.

Altering his direction, he strode to the door, stiff-arming it open as he walked into and through the yard surrounding the farmhouse that was now a biker clubhouse. Surrounded by cornfields, the house looked like any other all along the blacktop country road, except for the chosen mode of transport for the occupants. For five minutes he walked out into the field, hearing the footfalls of his brothers behind him, listening to the sibilant sound of the corn shocks sliding across their leathers, slipping past the denim of their jeans. He came to an opening in the field and stood beside the wellhead sprouting from the ground like a mutant crop, and cocked one hip out, propping a foot on the metal pipe.

Looking at his two men, he knew they understood things had gone to shit, and saw their bone-deep belief that he would, that he *could* fix it. His mind whirled, stuck in what he had heard on the phone call earlier.

"Feds in our phones," he said, and they nodded. Expected, when you were involved in a one-percent club, when you were national, when you were leadership. "Feds in our houses." Picking up bugs when you did sweeps meant you were on someone's radar, something he didn't like but knew it also was expected. That invasion of their world, where they lived, existing alongside the citizen lives, but taking up a whole different kind of atmosphere, was anticipated.

"Feds in our ranks." He said these words quietly and saw the shock on their faces. *Fucking Bethany*, he thought, *only Bethy could fuck a Fed's informant and not know it*. In his head, he imagined he heard Bingo, not cutting him any slack, saying, *Only an arrogant boy would patch a fed's informant and not know it*.

Deke's voice was low, riding dangerously close to the edge of control when he asked, "Who?"

"Fury," he said, his voice just as measured for the moment, but that control was slipping further out of reach with every breath. "Pike heard something, followed up on it, found a lead."

"No fucking way." Slate spoke immediately, shaking his head, rejecting the idea. "No fucking way, Prez. Pike's always seeing conspiracies in his mind. You know that."

"I do know that, but this has legs," he gritted out. "You think I'd have this chat without at least following up on this shit?" Pike was the president of the St. Louis chapter, his hold on that charter tenuous at best, having been brought to the floor only two weeks ago. Recalled to Chicago, he hadn't come willingly, and once there hadn't played the conciliator; instead, he'd barked laughter and threats. Mason had already regretted giving the man the president nameplate, and now deeply regretted letting him roll off the parking lot that night still breathing.

Still, when he'd called claiming info, Mason had picked up the phone.

"No fucking way," Slate repeated himself firmly, and Mason had a moment of uncertainty. Then Deke spoke, and that uncertainty fled like clouds before a storm.

"I can see it," Deke said. "I don't like it, but I can see it. Him coming up the way he did. How all-in he was with folding his boys into Rebels, more than pulling his weight on shit jobs for months and gaining trust, easing into the leadership on a fast track." Deke took a breath, then cut his gaze to Mason and ventured, "Fuckin' the national president's sister."

"She showed in the Fort. Tequila's bringing her here." Mason swung his gaze, looking at the corn moving and swaying in the breeze. Life all around them; dust in his heart. He had seen pictures of how she was with Fury, seen how the man was with her. Looked at her like she held his heart. Fury looked at Mason's sister the way Mason knew he looked at Willa and that sucked. It sucked hard, mostly for his Bethy, because now he knew it didn't mean anything. "Feds all up in our shit. Our boys'll be bringing her in hot. Then she and I will have a fucking chat. Gunny's comin' to sweep the clubhouse, need that done before I talk to my sister about the fucking CI she was with."

Slate shook his head again, still resistant to the idea of Fury being on the wrong side of the blue line. "Walk me through what Pike has, boss."

"Pike has Memphis. We knew shit was bad there, knew it when we sent Hoss in. Knew it when he settled things out as best they could be, but we kept Memphis." Memphis had been a mistake to charter from the get-go, that town drowning in corruption from so many directions there wasn't enough territory to support shit. All of which meant any space they carved out, everyone else in town wanted.

The shit there had finally been cleared by Hoss, who went down for a day and stayed three weeks, leaving twenty-two bodies in his wake, spilling blood that ran deep. "Ling had papers on him." Ling was a longtime dealer in that town, had fucked more people over than they had the population for, but he kept on. Until he wasn't able to anymore, seeing as how he had a hole in his head that couldn't be plugged. "Had papers on Fury from Lalo."

"You see those papers, boss?" Slate asked the question casually, but they all knew it was important. Mason shook his head, waiting. "No papers, just Pike's word? Really, Mason?"

"Could do without the shit from you today, Slate," he gritted his teeth as he spoke, frowning when he saw Slate again shaking his head.

"Pike's a fucking liar. We've caught him more than once. Shoulda cut him back when we found his charter fucking the laws, boss. You've seen him fuck brothers' women, laughing as he handed them back, feeling he was above it all." Slate leaned in, his face tightening as his voice came out tense and harsh. "Did you make a call based on Pike's intel alone?"

"*Fuck.*" Mason's hand reached for his phone and only then remembering he had left it inside, fearful of the ears he knew might be listening. Slate grinned and reached into both front pockets, pulling a phone from one and battery from the other. Grabbing them, Mason quickly assembled the phone, tapping in a memorized number. "Stand down," he said into the phone, waiting for the shouted instructions on the other end to be passed along, glad the meaty smacks of fists against flesh stopped immediately. "Bring him to me."

Mason looked down, then back up at his brothers. "He's fucking my sister. I fucking hate his ass."

Slate grinned, then tossed another rock onto Mason's grave as he said, "Wait until Willa gives you a baby girl, see how you feel about someone fucking your baby."

***

Bethany

Bethany was nervously checking her mirrors yet again because there were three bikes trailing her car. They had been behind her for fifteen minutes as she navigated her way through Fort Wayne, headed from her hotel to the clubhouse where she would be finally able to see Fury and decide if this was more than a one-night stand. *Hopefully*.

She glanced into her mirror again, same three bikes still reflected there. She recognized one of the riders, the other two she didn't. At the next light, the one she knew roared around her and swooped back in front of her car, then slowed down, the rider making insistent motions towards a store coming up on the right. She followed his bike in, keeping her eyes on him as he pulled to a halt in an empty section of the parking lot. She had barely gotten the car in Park when her door flew open; Bethy shrieked and lurched away, her seatbelt preventing any real retreat.

"Phone, keys, wallet." The mass of black leather standing in her door said the three words as if they made sense, and she tilted her head, looking up at him. He scowled, the tattoo on the side of his neck jumping with his visibly racing pulse. Growling now, he snapped, "Don't like repeating myself, girl."

"What?" She was confused because he hadn't really said anything, then things became clear when he leaned into the car, snagging the keys from the ignition. His head moved, scanning the inside of the vehicle and he reached out, pulling the cord from her phone and dropping it to the floor of the car before putting the phone along with her keys in his pocket.

"Wallet." Down to a single word, she realized what he must want and quickly grabbed her purse, handing him the whole thing, shoving it into his hands. "Good enough," he said and took a step back.

Hoss moved forward into the opening, holding out a leather jacket. "It's chilly today. Put this on, Bethy," he said, and she took the garment from his hands.

Holding it protectively in front of her, she asked, "Where's Mason?" This wasn't an ambush in a dark hallway, but even standing in the open in a parking lot she felt the terror trying to claw its way up her throat.

"Takin' you to him, sweetheart," Hoss said gently. "He called this in, wants you where he is as fast as we can get you there." *What if Mason's hurt?* They'd tell her if he was hurt, she felt certain of that. If he was okay, that meant it must be someone or something else.

"Where's Fury?" That question caused him pain, and he had to look away before he answered.

"Not with Mason. I'm not sure beyond that. Put on the jacket, Bethy." She did, and with a hand on her back, he pushed her steadily away from the car. She looked back as the door closed and saw the lights blink once, heard the beep as the locks engaged. Glancing over, she saw the man with her keys stuffing them and her phone into her purse, watching bemused as he shoved that into one of the saddlebags on his bike.

"Climb on behind me," Hoss said, and she saw more pain move through his face, remembering it was only two months since his wife had passed. That passing sudden and brutal. If Hope were still here, she would have been riding behind him. Bethy knew that, and couldn't wrap her head around the fact that today, he wanted her there.

"You're taking me to Mason?" She wanted to hear him say it plainly. Flat-out, she wanted, no *needed*, that certainty. Holding to her control with a brittle grip, close to losing the battle with her fears, she waited.

Straddling his bike, Hoss held out a hand as he nodded. "Yeah, takin' you to him."

Wordlessly, she swung onto the seat behind him, reaching up and gripping the sides of his waist.

Within minutes she felt frozen, her fingers so cold she didn't know how much longer she could hold on. Glancing forward over Hoss' shoulder, through wind-whipped tears she saw the speedometer hovering around one hundred, and decided she didn't want to know if they went faster. Hunkering down behind him, she tried to protect herself from the wind as best she could. An hour later they slowed, their procession of one entering a small city, riding sedately to a small house on a small street, unremarkable in any way.

Standing up off the bike, Hoss offered her his hand, supporting her when her legs would have given way. Arm around her waist he walked her up the cement path, onto the porch, and into the house without even a knock. She saw a startled woman's face appear and then disappear in a doorway, Hoss walking them straight through the house and out the back door. Stepping off the small back porch, he strode directly to an older model truck sitting in the driveway. He reached out a hand to open the passenger door and gently, wordlessly, urged her to get in.

Once convinced she was settled, he slammed the door shut, walking around and climbing into the driver seat. Fingers to the visor overhead, he pulled out a set of keys and shoved them into the ignition. Twisting them, starting the truck, he never even looked back at the house as they drove away, but Bethy did. She saw the same woman's face in the window, fear stark on her features.

Twenty minutes later, they were on a remote back road, tall fields of corn surrounding them on either side. As he slowed and turned into a driveway, she stared at the house they were approaching. Well kept, its yard yellowing from the late season. Still she noticed two things that struck a chord of disquiet in her chest.

It looked like a family house, but there were no kids' toys in the yard. No tire swing from the oak tree in the side yard, no swing set, no bikes. No family lived here; this was a different kind of place. And regardless of them being so undeniably in the middle of a corn field, there were no outbuildings to speak of. No big barn, multi-level and built up, set-up for animals on the earth-sheltered ground floor, farm implements situated on the main floor, driven up the ramp and inside to keep them out of the unpredictable Ohio weather. No barn, no silo, no garage next to the house, just a small storage building at least a hundred feet from the back door of the house.

Her eyes focused back on the house as the truck rolled to a stop. *Mason.* Her brother stood on the porch, his presence giving truth to Hoss' words. *Healthy and whole.* She didn't recognize the feeling clenching her chest as fear until it was gone. Fear that she was being taken to his deathbed, the feeling remaining coiled in her throat until it was no longer a possibility.

Tears streaming down her face, she shoved and pushed at the lever holding the door closed, finally working the mechanism and rolling out of the truck at a run. Mason met her at the bottom of the steps and wrapped his arms around her, holding her tightly against him, soothing her with soft words. Each moment that passed put more distance between her and a panic attack, and Bethy felt herself beginning to tremble in a delayed reaction.

After a time, when she felt she could speak without tears, she lifted her head from where it was buried in his chest and looked over his shoulder. What she saw caused all the air to leave her body in a big whoosh. Fury stood nearby, hands on his hips, watching her and her brother. There were vivid bruises on his face and an expression of pain on his features as he silently stared at them.

That pain receded when he caught her eyes, and then he held out his hands, opened his arms and she couldn't extricate herself from Mason's grip fast enough. Four running steps later, she was up the stairs and in his arms, hearing his pained grunt as he took her weight, but all that mattered was this. The connection they had, the care in his touch, and she knew her feelings were there for everyone to see when she lifted her face to him, when he took her mouth, kissing her hard and long. *Love.*

***

Mason

"Serious as a heart attack, Bethy. You hit me one more time and I'll give you something to regret," Mason growled, scowling down at his little sister.

"You basically had me kidnapped." She yelled, not quite a shriek, but then again they had heard those already. "Kidnapped. Most people don't get kidnapped once in their lives." She leaned into him, face twisting with anger. "Much less twice. And, both times by blood."

He jerked, the pain of that ripping through him, but before he could respond to that blow, he heard Fury reprimand her, words slightly slurred from the swelling. "Baby, no. Bring it down a notch. It wasn't even close to the same. Not even close. You need to shut it."

"Kidnapped." Now they were firmly back into shriek territory, and Mason saw Fury wince. "And, he had you beaten up." She leaned into Fury this time, giving him her pain when she hissed, "Beaten all to hell and back, baby. On some stupid man's say-so. My man, beaten all to hell."

Fury's voice was dangerously quiet, rumbling around the room when he asked, "Your man?"

"Yes, *my man*." She was exasperated and didn't hesitate to show it, giving him the point of her jaw as she lifted it. "He didn't even give you a chance to defend yourself. Just picked you up and worked you over. Then he had me picked up, dragged more than a hundred miles on the back of a bike into the wilderness of bee-eff-eh Ohio. By *Hoss*. And Hoss is scary. He's scary standing still, but let me tell you, he's even scarier at a hundred miles an hour. A hundred. Miles. An hour. A hundred miles an hour on the back of a bike is scary. Scared the juice out of me. I wasn't sure what—"

Still quiet, it sounded like he was testing the words when he interrupted her, repeating as a statement this time, "Your man."

"Yes, my man. Keep up, Gabe." Her hands hit the air even with her shoulders, then fell back to her sides in exasperation. Now Fury was getting the edge of a little of her angry vibes and tone, and from his face, he didn't mind a bit, lips curled up at the corners, white teeth flashing in his red beard.

"Get the fuck over here, woman," Fury growled, and Mason grinned as Bethy's mouth fell open, for once no noise coming out. "Come kiss your man again, baby."

Love and then loss

Fury

A week later and it still felt surreal.

A week out from the day he had barely walked into the Fort Wayne clubhouse and heard his name called from the office area. Four men had waited for him there, faces he knew, men he trusted.

Fury stood and stared, the atmosphere in the room heavy with anger. He moved towards the couch along one wall and Bear broke the silence, "Don't get comfortable." The door hadn't shut behind him, and Fury turned to see a scowling Rebel member standing there, arms crossed, taking up the opening with his bulk.

Fury nodded. "Brute." He looked back to Bear, giving him a chin lift and stilling when he received nothing in return. "PBJ, Pinto." None of them said anything, no one spoke, and the hair on the back of Fury's neck stood on end. "Wanna give me a fuckin' clue as to what's going on here?"

"We"—Bear indicated the men in the room with the stir of one finger— "are going to escort you downstairs." Downstairs meant the basement, where the wet rooms were. Standard issue blood drains in the floor, caged

lights on the walls, no outside doors or windows. "Then we"—Bear stirred his finger again—"are going to have a talk."

"Talk about what?" Fury took a step back and to the side, clearing the arm of the couch and putting his back to the wall. "What exactly do we have to discuss that requires the use of a room in the basement?"

Pinto shook his head. "Don't make this harder, Fury."

"Harder than what, Pinto?" He glared at the man. "Harder than what, exactly? From where I stand, you all got me backed right into a fuckin' corner. But—" He dropped one shoulder, angling his body slightly, telegraphing to anyone looking that he was prepared for a fight. "—do not expect me to go easy."

Brute started his direction with the intent to pin him away from the door and Fury grabbed the top of the couch, turning it over on the man's legs. He jumped over the side and ran across the upholstered back, balancing himself with one hand on the wall. Shouts and curses rang out, the noise bouncing off the walls of the small room. Two strides from the door he saw a shadow approaching him from behind, and he put on a burst of speed. Then his boot went through the fabric, tangling with the springs and wooden frame for a moment. Not long, but enough for Bear to grip the back of his vest.

Fury ducked and twisted, putting his head and shoulders underneath Bear's arm. He stood and twisted again, completing his turn and yanking his cut out of the man's hand. It would have been easier to skin out and leave the man to deal with a handful of empty leather, but Fury'd worked hard to earn the right to wear this patch and he'd be damned if he'd give it up without a fight. Through the door and to the left, he ran, furiously trying to recall the details of the clubhouse's layout. Another left turn put him in the kitchen and he ran into someone's back, bouncing sideways, trying to regain the lost momentum. Hurley turned, eyes wide, holding his hands out to try and keep Fury from falling.

Then a hand clamped on his arm, another on the back of his neck, a third man swept his feet and Fury went down with a shout of anger. So fucking close. *Pinto groaned when Fury's elbow found his ribs, then the man landed a crippling blow across Fury's kidneys as he gritted out, "For the record? This is you making it harder."*

They'd taken him to the basement and started with questions first. *Well,* he shook his head, *they started with tying my ass up, and the questions came second.*

Nothing had made sense. Memphis wasn't on his radar, ever. He'd been fresh from Lexington, tucking his men into their new places up in Fort Wayne when that went down, trying to manage Shooter's varying moods and instructions. He'd heard about it, yeah. Wasn't a man in the life who didn't hear about the Rebel Wayfarers sweeping in and cleaning house, then staying to have meetings with a dozen clubs who wanted reassurance that the activity wouldn't be bringing federal attention their way. Most of his notice about the whole thing went to Hoss being out of town and out of contact, because it was a critical delay in the negotiations getting them to where they were today.

Bear and PBJ had led the questioning, Brute and Pinto providing the muscle needed to keep Fury in one place. Fury hadn't worried about what the outcome would be, not really, because he knew he didn't have any connection to whatever they were looking for. Not in Memphis. Not ever. Nashville, yeah. Lexington and Louisville, hell yeah. Little Rock, yeah. Raleigh and Charlotte? Yes, and yes. He'd run cons or clubs in all those towns. Not Memphis. So he hadn't worried. They hadn't used more force than necessary to get him downstairs, hadn't retaliated for his struggling, probably because they all knew they'd be the same. Then Captain came downstairs.

Every man in the club had heard the story of how Captain had dealt with trouble sent the Rebels way from out west. A cancer set free from Shooter, a member named Birdy had pulled some bullshit, beating up a stripper. Bad, but not a death knell. No, that had been rung by repeated threats against Captain's old lady, and family. A bruiser on the ice in his previous life, Captain had systematically taken the man apart, leaving him to drown in his own blood on the floor of the same room Fury had been sitting in. So when Captain came in, things got serious.

They stayed serious for about three hours. Fury hadn't blacked out, and while there was no real damage, that didn't mean they hadn't hurt him. He'd known from experience it would take a while to heal, and had slept for most of this week. Which was good because every time he pissed and Bethy saw the blood, she got angry all over again.

Bethy stirred beside him, scooting backwards in her sleep until her ass pressed against his hip. He smiled and reached across, sweeping a strand of hair out of her face, tucking it behind her ear. He'd heard her story several times. Grinning, he tweaked the tip of her nose, smirking as she jerked away to press her face into the pillow. *Several, several times.* She'd recounted it often, each rendition providing a new reason to rage. She might never forgive Mason at this rate.

For his part, Fury didn't hold any grudges. He'd bought the five officers and members a beer the next time he'd seen them in Marie's, letting them know he understood. As president, if he'd been handed the same intel from a chapter president, he would have acted quickly to investigate, too. Rank and file were just doing their jobs, and that's what the club needed them to do. Not question, just accept and move forwards. Mason had been harder to convince, but the man had been dealing mostly with Bethy, and she was still angry.

He dragged the pad of his thumb across her temple, continuing down to her cheekbone, caressing her softly. She'd been on her way to him. Through some miracle, she'd pieced things together, and instead of picking up the phone and calling for his head, something her brother would have been all too happy to hand over, she wanted to talk to him. She'd said she needed to see his face. For his part, he was stunned.

Thank God for Mason.

Mason had learned of their involvement in Lamesa and hadn't been pleased with the knowledge that a member had fucked his sister. Add to that the lies spewed by whoever—Mason remained tightlipped on the who, just voiced a loud what, and since everything went down, that whoever had backpedaled like a motherfucker, claiming all innocence— and it's a wonder Fury lived to walk out of that basement. By the time she'd driven to Fort Wayne and broadcast she was looking for him, Mason already had him locked down.

The look on her face when he stepped to where she could see him had made his knees weak. In an instant, he'd flashed back to Nashville, all the years in between swept away like cobwebs by a freshening breeze, her face shining, smiling down at him as she laid it out, "I like you."

He'd fucked her over in Nashville, then ditched her attempt to reach out with a cut that went deep. He'd seen how deep he'd hurt her in the seconds before he'd turned and walked away. They hadn't spoken since west Texas. He'd sent her a shitty text and hadn't called. Had known she wasn't for him. And she'd persisted, coming to him. *She was coming to me.*

She'd spent two weeks putting the puzzle together and talking to people who knew him along the way. Tyrell's advocate had served with Dion and knew Fury by extension. Told her he knew Fury was in over his head but wasn't in a place to step in and help. She found and spoken to Gator, who hadn't known to keep his mouth shut. After all, she was the big boss' sister, and apparently in the know. According to Bethy, Gator had painted a prettier picture than she'd expected but hadn't glossed over the fact that Fury might have fucked up, but he was a man who wasn't afraid to take responsibility for his actions. She'd apparently dug up a dozen people who sang the same song, and that, along with her gut feeling about them, decided her, putting her in a car alone driving from Nashville to Fort Wayne, and determined to find him. By the time she'd made it to Indiana, her mind was made up, and she was already on the path of forgiveness.

That didn't mean they hadn't worked their way through a ton of shit. For days now, every time he opened his mouth he had waited for her to say, "Know what? Enough. I didn't sign up for this." But she didn't. She'd held his hand as he talked through his journey, and he'd held her while she cried because of the days and months they'd lost. Between Nashville and Lamesa, he hadn't been the only one in her bed, but nothing had gelled—*thank fuck*—and she'd always walked away, looking for what they'd had together.

Jesus. Everything he'd ever dreamed of, right here lying next to him. *If I'm asleep, I'll gladly stay here 'til I fuckin' die.*

His fingers played with a curl of her dark hair, smoothing it across the bare skin of her shoulder, teasing the tiny strap out of the way. The baby doll nightie she wore was sexy as fuck, and she knew it, giving him a smirking half smile as she sauntered to bed last night. They'd had a failed attempt to fuck on day three, her riding him, but even the slight sway of the mattress had started his injuries singing, and once she saw the pain in his face, she'd climbed off and refused to let him even get close to getting her off.

Today would be a very different story. He'd woken feeling considerably better, and strung out with his need for her. *Lemme drink at your fountain, baby.*

"Beth," he murmured, lips following the trail of his fingers on her skin, deliberately dragging his beard across. Soft curves pressed against him, he wanted to devour her. "Wakie, wakie." He slipped his hand under the covers, finding the hem of her nightgown with his fingertips, trailing along the heat of her thigh. Mouth to her neck, he pressed kiss after kiss to every inch of flesh he could reach. Sketching slow circles on her shoulder with the tip of his nose, he dipped his fingers under the satin fabric, dragging it up the few inches until he could cup her mound with his palm.

Hot, so heated when he gently wedged his hand between her legs, he sucked in a breath of anticipation.

Bethy mumbled something and moved in the bed, arching back and lifting her leg slightly. He shifted his hand slowly back and forth, then changed position to find the top edge of her panties, slipping underneath to trace the lips of her sex with his fingers. "Fucking wet, baby. You dreaming of me?"

"Always, Gabe." Her voice was whisper-soft, a barely there exhalation of sound that reverberated inside him. He'd wanted to hear his name from her lips for so long, wanted and imagined how it would feel. *So much better than anything I could have dreamed.*

He moved, stripping her panties down her legs, gripping her thigh in one hand and lifting it so her calf draped over his hip. He might not be able to fuck her properly yet, but he'd be damned if he waited another instant to be inside her. It was the work of moments to position himself at her entrance. "Bethany?" She responded with a slow pump of her hips, still half asleep but aroused by his play. "Baby, you with me?" A soft hum was his answer. "Beth," he dragged the head of his cock through the wetness she'd given him, "are you with me?"

"Yes, Gabe. I'm right here." Now she sounded peeved, and he grinned at that because a peeved Bethany was an awake one.

"Bethany?" She turned her head finally, a tiny frown drawing her brows together as she glared at him. When he didn't say anything else and didn't move, she shifted slightly, angling the top of her body away so she could see him better. Her brows lifted, arching up towards her hairline and he grinned at her. He moved then, thrusting into her, feeling her pussy part and give way, accepting his invasion of her body. Her lids drooped, those gorgeous eyes heated and her lips parted as she pulled in a breath. Midstroke, he gave her everything. "I love you." Her eyes focused on his face. "I've loved you for so long, baby." He saw wet gathering in her eyes. "I'm never giving you up. You're—" Bottoming out inside her, he ground deeper, finding comfort in every inch of skin that touched along their bodies. He pushed her nightgown up, palm sliding over her breast, fingers wrapping around to caress and plump as he pumped into her again. "Mine, forever. You get that, right?"

"I know, honey." She lifted a palm to his face, thumb sliding along his bottom lip, fingers threading through his beard. "Forever." Catching her lip between her teeth, she hissed as he thrust hard, pussy pulsing around him. "Gabe."

He rolled her nipple between finger and thumb, tugging and playing just how she liked it best. He remembered every moment spent in her bed and used those memories now. Shoving his other arm under her, he wrapped his hand around her hip, stroking down until his fingertips were pressing on her clit. Timing his thrusts, he alternated between tweaking her nipple and flicking her clit, watching as her eyes closed, then opened, finding his. "Bethany, you know I love you?"

"Uh, huh." She nodded, hair wisping across his face as she moved, hips pumping back against him. "Love you, too, honey."

"My name," he growled, bending his neck to graze the side of her throat with his teeth. "Say my fucking name."

"*Gabe*." Whispers filled with urgency, she called, "Gabe, honey."

Sweat slicked her skin, and he stopped torturing her nipple, wrapping his arm around her waist to drive her down onto his cock. Her pussy pulsed and rippled, every change in tension and pressure pulling him closer to the edge. He worked her clit, first slow, then fast until she gasped for air, mouth opening as she threw her head back, turning to bury her face against his neck. On a rising wail, she cried out and her body tensed in his arms, her hands gripping his wrist, holding his hand still as he pressed hard, hips moving fast. Driving deep, he clamped his teeth into the muscles of her shoulder, brutal in his chase towards climax. She cried out again, and he heard what he'd been waiting for. "*Gabriel*."

Deep inside her he held still, balls tight to his body as his orgasm poured from him, the heat around the head of his cock intensifying until he had to move again. Another thrust, then another, slower, feeling her relax into him, turning into an exhausted ragdoll in his arms. Still he glided in and out, slowly, filled with the indescribably beautiful sensation of being inside the woman he loved more than life.

"Baby?" He kissed the indents left from his teeth, wincing to see how deep they ran, knowing she'd bear bruises tomorrow. "You okay?"

"If by okay, you mean bonelessly satisfied and exhausted? Then, yes. I'm that." She sighed and then froze. "Gabe, your spooge is leaking out of me."

He grinned, pressing his forehead tight to her back, hoping he was out of elbow range. "Yup."

"You spooged in me?" He tried to bury his laughter, unsuccessfully, and when he chuckled, she twisted in his arms, turning to see his face. "You spooged in me?"

"Yup."

She reached up and touched one corner of his mouth. "Stop smiling." He shook his head. "I'm serious, Gabe. Stop smiling." She lifted both hands and tugged on the corners of his mustache, trying to pull his lips into a somber line. "Stop smiling. I can't be mad at you if you're smiling like that."

"Like what?" He leaned in and brushed his lips across hers, watching her nose crinkle as his softening cock slipped out of her. "What am I smiling like?"

"Like you're six years old and someone told you that Santa and the Easter Bunny were real things."

He kissed her again, trailing his lips up her jaw to press a final caress in front of her ear. Whispering, he told her, "Better. I got told that you're mine, forever. I'm just working to seal the deal."

She pulled back, studying his face, her expression one he hadn't seen before, equal parts terror and hope. "I'm not on birth control."

When her fingers touched the corner of his mouth again, he knew he was smiling. "I know."

***

He stared at Mason, not certain he'd heard correctly. "Come again?"

Grinning, Mason lifted his beer and tilted his chair back in the same movement, leaning backwards on two legs. "Fort Wayne." Slate snorted a laugh and matched Mason's posture, his balance wavering for a moment. Then he collected himself and took a long pull from the bottle in his hands.

Fury looked around the room, narrowing his eyes as he realized the men had been handpicked to be there. In addition to Mason and Slate, there were national and chapter officers, a couple of members, and one prospect, Hurley. He ran through the names again, and any humor or goodwill fled when he realized every man who had witnessed Mason's distrust of him was here, Bear, Brute, PBJ, and Pinto. Turning back to Mason, he stared at the man for a moment, then asked, "Why are you fucking with me?"

Mouth flattening, Mason shook his head. "Not fucking with you. And, gotta say," he let the legs of the chair thump to the floor, "most men got told they were having a promotion like this, they don't much argue."

"Most men aren't me." Fury was intensely aware that he'd deposited his phone and weapons into the lock box before coming into this room, the lightness of his vest pockets making him uneasy and that uneasiness pissed him off. *I shouldn't be like this here. These are my brothers.*

"Wanna start from the top, and maybe begin with why this isn't going to be a voted change?"

Mason shrugged. "Hand-picked successor." He pointed a thick finger at Slate who grinned around the mouth of his bottle. "Slate suggested, and I agreed."

"Why are you suddenly willing to step down?" This was directed at Slate, and he saw true amusement in the man's eyes as he thudded the legs of his chair down in turn.

"Nope. Not sudden. I took over from Bingo, you know that. He and Mason lassoed me into it, kinda like he and I are doing to you right now. Bingo had too much going on, kids and everything, he couldn't spend the time to deal with all the bullshit that comes to the president's plate." Slate twisted his head side to side, looking at each man in turn. "Not that I wouldn't trust any of y'all, but Fury's got a vested interest now." He turned his crooked grin to Fury. "Bangin' the boss' little sister and all." Mason's face hardened, and Fury glared at Slate, who broke out in laughter. "Seriously, Fury. It's not sudden. I've been talking about it for a while, and with Ruby blessing me with another pair of twins, I cannot be both the man she needs, and the president the club demands. Not now, and not for a while. Turns out being a parent isn't a transient event." He shrugged. "Who knew?"

"Me?" Fury locked eyes with Mason, holding their gazes until Mason nodded slowly. "I accept, of course, with the understanding that the office is not dependent on anything outside of the club."

"More in spite of, than because of," Mason assured him. "Lotta men gonna be hatin' on you for this."

Fury let the idea settle in his mind. President of the Fort Wayne chapter was a large step up from a no-voice member just over a year ago. Mason was right, of course, there would be dissent. *I'd worry more if there wasn't.* He glanced around the room, letting his gaze rest on each man, much as Slate had done moments ago. Support and excitement on every face except one, and Hurley looked more confused than anything. *Probably about why he got invited to this little powwow.* Fury shook his head. "Thing about haters? They're a lot like noisy bugs. Chirp, flap, and crap all fuckin' day but when you walk past 'em, they shut the fuck up." He shook his head. "Tell me what I need to know."

They spent the next twelve hours going over many plans and projects already underway, and Mason unveiled a few that he'd been holding close to the vest. Timing was a bitch on this change, because of how many irons were already in the fire.

Fury yawned, and Mason laughed, leaning back in his chair, stretching his arms overhead. "My fuckin' brain is mush." Mason leaned back and hammered on the door, telling the prospect who opened it to bring in the lockbox. Phones and weapons were passed out and Fury checked his phone, groaning to see five missed calls from Bethy. "Can we pick back up tomorrow, brother?" He waggled his phone. "Got some explaining to do to the old lady."

Mason stared at him for a minute, face expressionless. Slowly he shook his head, reaching up to pinch the bridge of his nose. "Never for a minute thought I'd hear that applied to my sister." Without looking up, he said, "She's about used up her vacation. What are y'all going to do when she goes back to Nashville?"

Fury knew better than to let his amusement show, so he kept it clamped down as he said, "Business is between her and her partner. I'm no part of that." Mason grunted and flattened his palms on the table, pushing to his feet. "As her old man, though, I'm strongly recommending she have a conversation about hiring a local manager for the Nashville part, and sticking to what she does so well, the tour management."

Nodding, Mason looked thoughtful for a moment, then said, "She'll still spend a lot of time away. She gonna be okay with that?"

"I doubt it, which is why the second argument I have is for her to stay home and be barefoot and pregnant with my babies." Mason's chin lifted, and he stared at Fury. "She won't go for that either. Seriously, she's got to sort it out. I can listen and tell her what I think, but it's on her in the end."

"Real mature attitude." The words should have been a compliment, but they came out sounding like an insult instead. Fury knew where Mason was coming from though and didn't take offense.

"I'm just"—he thumbed over his shoulder—"gonna go give my old lady a call."

"You do that. I'll do the same. We'll circle back around tomorrow, brother. Set some timelines on things here in the Fort."

Fury nodded, his attention already on the phone in his hand. Two rings and Bethany answered, voice breathless. "Hey, honey."

"Baby."

"I'm going to make myself some dinner. If you can let me know when you'll be home"—he caught his breath, liking how the word sounded in her mouth—"I can have a plate ready for you."

"Baby, did I tell you yet today?"

When she answered him, her voice had softened, growing warm in a way that made him smile. "Yeah, but I'd love to hear it again."

"I love you, baby." He heard her sigh through the phone's speaker, knowing she liked hearing the words. "I'll be home in twenty, so wait for me and we can eat together. Whatcha makin'?"

"Just some fried squash and skirt steak. Nothing fancy."

"Sounds good, I'll be there soon."

"Can't wait."

It's a little strange, he thought as he straddled his bike, waiting a moment after starting it to allow the engine to warm up, *how quickly we've settled into this*. As he pulled out of the lot, lifting a hand to the prospect who was manning the gate, he tried to shake off the feeling that it had been too easy in the end.

***

"Brother? What's happened?" Fury wordlessly waved Pinto away, needing a minute to try and make sense of the info he'd been force fed. Mason's voice echoed in his head, the words chasing each other around and around.

"Watcher wrecked out, brother. He's gone."

Followed by a guilt-ridden explanation of the scene that lay before Mason, those words, choked to life in a tear-thick voice, wouldn't lay down and be still. They kept clawing at his chest, working their way underneath his skin until he twitched in place. *He's gone*. It didn't seem real, and he could only hope this was a nightmare, a restless night followed by a startled waking filled with relief.

"Brother? Fury?"

Squeezing his eyes closed, he ground out the order, "Call the officers in." Mason had asked for face-to-face and phone calls, such a loss was not something to be disseminated in a text message, or, God forbid, first seen on social media. Pinto's presence receded, and Fury knew he was going to do as asked. With the sirens in the background, it was unlikely Mason had finished calling chapter presidents before he would have to conduct a different kind of interview, so once he'd told the officers here in the Fort the few, sparse details he had, he would call Myron, then Bones.

Shuffling footsteps behind him, then a heavy hand on his shoulder. He turned to see Gunny standing there. "I just got off the phone with Road Runner. We got news, brother." Fury gestured towards the seat across from him. "I found records," Gunny started, pulling the chair out and turning it around, seating himself on it backwards, arms crossed on the wooden back of the chair. "Records going back a few decades, about wrecks in those mountains. You told me to dig deep. Well, brother, I dug fuckin' deep. You remember how you said Duck's Brenda was left in a hospital with a note pinned to her coat, transported up a ravine from a burning car and across two county lines to land in that ER?" Fury nodded, finally realizing what Gunny was going on about. He'd asked the man to look into the wreck that killed Brenda's parents, and to look at what Fury had put together about Tabby's wreck, trying to find a connection. It seemed he had. "I found another one just like it. This one was Watcher's little sister, Tabitha."

"Tabby," Fury interrupted. Her name was a punch to the stomach, the memories of her loss piling in on top of what Mason had told him. "Call her Tabby."

"Tabby," Gunny acknowledged, eyeing Fury curiously. "Her wreck wasn't no accident. You're right about that. She was dead before her truck went off the road. What you didn't find was the boy."

"What boy?" Fury's memory of the conversation between old man Mason and his father swam up to taunt him. "Which boy are you talking about?"

"Night of her wreck, two counties away a little boy was laid on a gurney in an ER hallway, note pinned to his coat. Said his parents were dead, family that had been raising him were overwhelmed, couldn't do it anymore. Got made a ward of the state." Gunny stared at him intently. "Handwriting on the notes is identical. Same person wrote both, years apart."

Fury waited a beat for him to continue, and when he didn't, made an irritated gesture. "Get on with it." So much to do, and this was likely the least important part of anything.

"Five-year-old kid, not hurt but drugged unconscious. His name is Christopher Camp." Gunny paused again and when Fury just stared at him, shook his head. "Camp. Deacon's name is Camp, Ryan Camp."

"You sayin' Tabby had Deacon's son with her that night?" The words didn't make any sense even as he spoke them. "That doesn't compute, brother. I don't understand it, but need to tell you now, we gotta put this aside. We're about to go to the back room and I got news to lay on you."

"Age ain't right for a son. Not unless he was masterful at hiding things. Best I can tell, he had just one boy, James. Lived in California with his mother." Gunny shook his head, pushing up from the chair as the room began filling with men walking towards the meeting room behind the bar. "I think it's his grandson. That fits what you heard, right?"

Struggling to keep his composure, Fury nodded. It didn't quite fit, because all this time he'd been assuming old man Mason and his father had been talking about Morgan. Then he put that information aside and turned to see every face pointed his direction. There were a dozen members in the room, too, and suddenly he couldn't stomach the idea of telling the story twice. "Let's do this out here, brothers. I'll just—" He walked towards the bar and pushed as he jumped, twisting to sit his ass on the bar, putting him head and shoulders over nearly all the men. "I got news, and it ain't good. Y'all know about the run to New Mexico, right?" Nods around the room, features sharpening as men went on alert, knowing that whatever was coming, it warranted attention. "About eight hours out from Las Cruces, they encountered a group of Diamante." Involuntary movements placed hands near weapons, just the mention of their enemies' name enough to bring the level of tension in the room up about a dozen notches "There was a wreck. Watcher went down." Chins lifted and shoulders squared, bearing the weight of the knowledge he was laying on them. "Mason said he's the only one on our side lost."

"Watcher's dead?" The question echoed from a half a dozen throats, in varying degrees of disbelief. Fury nodded and waited.

Slate's voice asked, "You're sure?" Fury couldn't see them, not a single face, not now, because the staggering pain in Slate's words plunged a knife into the wall of his grief. *Mikey's gone. How can that be true?* He nodded.

"I don't know much more than that, but Mason asked we do a call and tell, no texting. Watcher was important enough to a lot of us." His throat tightened, and he felt a hand settle in the middle of his back, fingers pushing deep to help hold him together. "All respect, yeah?"

Gunny was behind him, his growling question asking what a number of men were probably wondering. "He wrecked out, wasn't taken out by Diamante?"

Fury lowered his head, feeling hot tears tracking next to his nose. He shook his head. "Wrecked out. Mason said he got his target, took out Lalo. Went down in the process." Murmurs now, and those fingers on his back flexed. "Gonna miss that motherfucker." Dragging in a deep breath, he steadied himself and blew it out slowly. "Cops were showing while we talked. Mason was sticking tight. Said he'd see Watcher into the bus, then he'll head on to the compound in Las Cruces. Juanita"—*Jesus, Bethy has to know this. She's going to want to go to Juanita*—"deserves to hear it from him."

Bear asked something Fury hadn't even considered. "Merger still going to happen? We still gonna fold the Soldiers in as a westerly chapter?"

"Far as I know. I'd be surprised if they didn't, because, with Watch gone, Soldiers will need help to stay together. So—" He lifted his head, taking a moment to blink until his vision cleared, looking out at the ring of men who appeared as devastated as he felt. "—make your calls. Slate and I will touch base with the chapter presidents, in case Mason didn't get a chance to call 'em all. But you can call who you need. Respect, because he'd been a friend of the club for years, and in all but one detail was already a Rebel." He took another breath, then began the phrase, knowing the men wouldn't leave him hanging, "Rebels forever—" Every man's mouth opened, and the words rang out loud, filling the room, "—forever Rebels."

***

"Baby," he crooned, cradling the back of Bethy's head, his other arm curved tightly around her waist, holding her in his lap. When he'd walked into the house, she'd taken one look at him and come straight over, wrapping herself around him.

When he'd pulled her close, she'd demanded, "Tell me," sounding so much like her brother it was almost funny. He'd told her, starting with what he knew, and then answering her broken questions as best he could. The tears had flowed in earnest, and she'd held on like her life depended on it, Fury welcoming the tight grip she'd maintained.

"Baby, you gotta get a hold of it." She hiccupped and then sobbed, shoulders jerking with the force of the emotion driving her. "Oh, baby."

"All gone, every one of them. They're all gone." Twisting, she buried her face against his throat, and he felt the wet heat of her tears on his skin. "All of them."

"Baby, you aren't making any sense. Who's gone?"

"First my Tabby. Little Tabby who would have never hurt a fly. Gone before she even lived." She shifted, cupping the back of his neck with her palm. "Then Darrie, and that was so sad. He never got his feet back underneath him after he came home." She sobbed again, and he tightened his arms. "And now Mikey. Oh, Gabe. Why? What could have...I'm so pissed at him. Why?"

"Why won't ever be answered, baby." He shifted, scooping an arm underneath her legs. "We should go to bed. Tomorrow's going to be a long day." Standing, he lifted her with him, keeping his grip tight.

"Juanita. God, I can't imagine." She shook her head, arms twined around his neck. "He was her whole world, has been since he found her. What will she do?"

"She's got two girls to look after. That'll keep her somewhat occupied." He angled them through the doorway and stepped into the bedroom, placing Bethy on the mattress. "We'll sort it all out, tomorrow." He slipped off her shoes, then unfastened all the buttons on her jeans. She lifted and wiggled as he pulled them down her legs. "Tonight, we're going to sleep." He wadded the jeans up and tossed them to the side, near the wall.

"Bella, does she know?" He nodded, leaning in to brush a strand of hair back from her face. She looked as exhausted as he felt, and all he wanted to do right now was get her to rest for a few hours.

"Tater, the brother she's hooked up with, he got a call so he could break it to her gentle like." Pressing his lips to hers, he pulled back. "Diamond is with Mela. He got a call too. They should be at the compound by now."

She sat up, nearly bumping his nose with her head. "Ty! Oh my God, *Ty*. He and Mikey were tight. I need to call him."

"Tomorrow," he soothed, taking advantage of her position to grip the hem of her shirt and lift, forcing her to raise her arms. "We'll call him tomorrow." He glanced at the clock. "It's going on midnight, baby. Let him have his rest. Tomorrow is soon enough."

"Will you go to Kentucky with me?" She looked up at him as he crumpled the blouse, tossing it on top of the jeans. "His family plot is there, so that's what he'd want."

"I'll go anywhere with you, baby." She smiled, the expression so sad and wan it made his chest clench. "Climb under the covers. Let's go to bed." Staring down at her, he was struck again by how lucky he was. *Never would have called this one, not in a million years*. The idea that she could be here, with him, in his bed? Impossible. That she could have forgiven him so easily, put aside the lies and betrayal, because she loved him? Even more impossible.

In his bed, dressed in the sexiest set of lingerie he'd ever seen, the woman of his dreams. *Pinch me*. She moved, pushing up near the pillows to shove the blanket and sheet down, slipping underneath. "I'm gonna go lock up. Be right back."

She smiled and smoothed the pillow next to her head in clear invitation, then gave him a gift he never would get accustomed to receiving. "Love you, Gabe."

"Love you, too, Bethany." He bent, pressing his mouth to hers then stood. "I'll be right back."

***

Bethany

She was still, curled small as she could manage while Gabe lay wrapped around her. He'd come back to bed as promised, then succeeded in distracting her wonderfully for a length of time. Sweaty and out of breath, he'd gathered her close to his side, caressing her with fingertips and lips until slumber claimed him. With heavy limbs, he'd turned in his sleep, his movement forcing hers. Then he crowded close like he did every night since she'd come to find him. Even in sleep he kept her close.

The third day in Fort Wayne, the first she'd surfaced from being with Gabe, Willa had sought her out. Mason's wife had become a friend and confidant, reaching out often just to keep in touch, doing a much better job than Mason or Bethy had ever done, lending them both her innate resilience and strength in different ways. Willa's son, Garrett, was the spitting image of Mason, something Bethy had been very glad to see given the timing of the pregnancy. She'd never asked and Willa hadn't offered, but the relief had been clear on her face when Bethy had come to visit and could answer that yes, Garrett looked a lot like Mason's baby pictures as she remembered them. Willa doted on the boy, taking him everywhere with her, even to work once she started back.

So when Willa showed up at Fury's without Garrett, Bethy knew it was an orchestrated visit. She smiled at the memory of how Willa paled when asked her reason for visiting. One thing about Willa was you knew exactly where you stood with her, and Bethy knew Willa liked her, but at that moment, she hadn't liked Fury at all.

"Why don't you come with me? We can go get some coffee or something." Willa leaned her shoulders against the door, seemingly unwilling to move away from the opening. *"I brought the car and everything."*

Bethy eyed her sister-in-law for a moment, taking in the level of discomfort showing on her features and then slowly nodded. "Let me just change clothes and tell Gabe where I'm going." Willa's face scrunched up, a movement Bethy would bet money the woman didn't know she was doing, but it coincided with Gabe's name, and surely telegraphed her feelings louder than a shout. This was an intervention.

Not that she hadn't expected one. To the outsider, this would seem intensely fast, because most people only knew about Lamesa. To the uninformed observer, her tracking him to Indiana then Ohio and facing down her brother, and then turning around and calling Gabe "her man" would seem the highest of folly. Those people, Willa and Mason included, had no clue about what had happened sixteen years ago. They didn't know she and Gabe had a history, good and bad, and to Bethy, the good outweighed the bad by a large measure.

So, sitting in a café across from the woman her brother loved more than breath, his words, she laid it out for Willa. Not all the bad, there was no reason for anyone to know that part. It would forever be between her and Gabe. But talking about the holler and how he'd been the sweet boy who was her best friend's sorta brother figure, and then how he'd happened on her in Nashville so many years ago. How they'd fallen into a sexual relationship that was just getting deeper when business tore them apart. She spoke about how she'd dated since, finding herself measuring every man against Gabe. Him always coming out ahead, even though he wasn't there.

Willa had nodded at that and smiled, shyly sharing her first encounter with Mason and how, even if she'd put herself out there to give him her number, that hadn't gone anywhere for months. How, when they started seeing each other, there was always something getting in the way, something pulling them apart. Bethy knew in that moment that Willa got it, she understood, and she'd do her best to make Mason understand, too.

So with that handled, they spent the next hour talking about Willa's pregnancy, how that was advancing. Willa was excited about the chance to build their family, but her stories about Mason's nervous concerns were hilarious. Bethy grinned, knowing she'd be leaving this little sit-down with a dozen new jabs in her arsenal.

"Do you have siblings?" Bethy watched as Willa's eyes warmed, her face softening as she shook her head.

"Always wanted a brother or a sister." She twisted the handle on the mug holding her decaf. "Gar has Chase, of course, and I couldn't ask our sons to be better brothers." Bethy smiled to hear her say it like that, liking how Willa took ownership of Chase. "But there's a huge age gap."

"Mason and I have eight years between us, and we seem to get along."

"Chase and Gar have twice that. Once this little one comes along, I'll have to figure out how to keep Chase from feeling like he's part of a different family." Willa frowned, then set her shoulders back, lifting her chin. "I'll do it, though. He's too good a boy to need to wonder where he fits into the whole family."

"If…" Bethy paused and took a breath. "If I tell you a secret, can you keep it from Mason, just for a little while? I want to tell him myself." Willa frowned again, this time more exaggerated, not hiding how that request made her feel. "Just for a couple of days until I can figure out how to tell him."

"Are you pregnant? Because that would be kind of a miracle if you already knew, unless it's from Texas?"

Bethy laughed, shaking her head. "No, I'm not pregnant. Can you keep my secret, Willa?"

"Just for a couple of days?" Bethy nodded. "Promise?" She nodded again. "Okay." Willa held up her hand, palm first. "Unless it means you're putting yourself in danger. I can't stand thinking of something happening to you." She reached across and cupped Bethy's hand, wrapping her fingers around and holding on tightly. "We've been through too much together. I can't stand it, Bethy."

"Promise you it's nothing bad. It's something from years ago, but I need to sort things first, then tell Mason."

"Okay," Still holding Bethy's hand, Willa lifted her other one and sketched an X across her chest. "Cross my heart." She wrinkled her nose. "I don't say the rest. I'm way over any kind of wanting to die."

"Agreed." Bethy took in a deep breath. "I have a son."

Head tipping to the side, Willa repeated her words. "You have a son?" Bethy nodded. "A son." She nodded again. "As in a flesh-and-blood boy, not a wooden Pinocchio thingie?" With a laugh, she nodded a final time. "Jesus. How old is he? What's his name?"

"Michael, his name is Michael. He's sixteen this year. His birthday was just a few weeks ago." Willa squeezed her fingers. "Michael Tyrell Marshall."

Willa's head tipped the other direction. "Marshall? Not Mason?" Frowning, she shook her head. "Wasn't your husband's name Taylor?"

Bethy dropped her eyes to the tabletop, not wanting to see Willa's face. "Yes. But that marriage was annulled, and a farce. You don't know how bad it was, Wills. Michael...I was sixteen. Same age he is now. I didn't know much, coming from the holler like I did." She darted a glance up, then back down. "I never even graduated high school. I was in a town I didn't know, living with a man I didn't know, and about the only thing I did know was I was in no way equipped to raise a child. So, I found a couple who wanted a baby and were willing to do an open adoption. That way I could stay in his life, even a little bit." She swallowed hard, then rushed to defend the Marshalls. "They've been great, better than I could have ever expected or asked. They invite me to everything, and I've seen how much Martha and Rodney love him. But he found out about Mason a couple of weeks ago, and now Michael wants to meet my family. He'd been thinking I was alone, and now that he knows differently, he wants to meet everyone."

She'd finally run out of steam and words, and the silence collected between them, the gap bridged only by Willa's unwavering clasp on Bethy's hand.

"You and your brother are so much alike. More than you'll probably ever know." Bethy looked up, seeing tears on Willa's face and realizing her cheeks were wet, too. "Holding your secrets close to the vest, not wanting to give anyone any ammunition to hurt you. I hate how you were raised." Willa's voice quivered with anger, red rising to flush her cheeks. "I hate your daddy. I'm glad he's dead. Never thought I'd say that about anyone, except...you know." She drew in a noisy breath through her nose. "I hate him. He hurt the two of you so much, and in ways that still seep poison. Wounds running deep and keeping you from helping each other heal, because what if that pain is contagious. God."

"We just do what's needful," Bethy told her, surprised when Willa flinched.

"I hate that word, too. It's a cover for things that hurt, for pain." Willa shook her hand, thumping Bethy's knuckles on the tabletop. "He loved Mica, you know that? Mason. He loved her but wouldn't let himself go there, and I'm thankful every day, even as I know he loves me more. I know he loves me more, because though he loved her, he never told her about you. He didn't tell her about Chase, either. He held close the people he loved the most, not letting even Mica have an ounce of knowledge about you two. But—" She leaned forwards, shaking their hands again. "—he told me. You're right. You have to be the one to tell him. If I said anything, it would be a breach between you that would take years to heal. I love you both too much to see that happen. But you have to tell him."

"I will." Willa narrowed her eyes, wrinkling up her nose in exaggerated disbelief. Bethy smiled, feeling it waver for a moment before settling into place. She told Willa, "I promise."

She hadn't though. One thing led to another and then he was caught up in business that didn't have a place for her. Tears clogged her throat and she forced down a sob, holding herself to a rigid silence as she wept. *Mikey never knew.* Never knew she'd loved him so much she'd given his name to her child.

Tomorrow, she would force herself on Mason, even if it was a phone call, and tell him. *Things that matter shouldn't wait.* Then once she told Mason, she'd find a way to tell Gabe.

Meeting Michael

Bethany

Bethy lifted the laundry basket to her hip, navigating the door into Gabe's home. "Hey," she called, hearing a muffled response from deeper in the house. She stopped in the bedroom doorway, not sure what she was seeing. Gabe stood at the foot of the bed, rolling a pair of jeans before he stuffed them into the open bag in front of him. "Whatcha doin'?"

She crossed the space to the bed, setting the basket on the mattress. Her suitcase lay next to his, clothes already packed except for the couple of shirts she had just pulled out of the dryer. Gabe flicked a look up at her, gaze steady behind the fall of hair across his forehead. "Packin'."

"For what? Where do you have to go?" Tucking the last articles of clothing into her suitcase, she lifted the other clothes from the basket, carrying them to his dresser. In the weeks she'd been here, she'd shifted his things around to create space for hers, and he hadn't said a word. She smiled as she pulled what she now thought of as "her drawers" open and put away things.

"Nashville." Turning, she looked at him, taking in the serious expression on his face.

It was a week after Mikey's funeral, and true to her vow, she hadn't wasted any time talking to Mason. Catching him between other business calls while he was still in New Mexico, she'd petitioned for ten minutes of his time, scheduling through the guy who seemed to run most of her brother's life, Myron. That ten-minute conversation turned into more than sixty because Mason had a wealth of questions, once he got past the initial confusion and anger about how she could have been strapped with what he saw as such a burden for so long. With everything else going on, he'd given her his time generously, listening as she cried with the guilt of never telling one of the men who had mattered so much to her. Mason waited until she'd cried herself dry, then reassured her they'd be revisiting this topic, and ordered her to bring Michael to the funeral in Cynthiana.

She'd demurred, arguing that throwing a sixteen-year-old boy into that kind of intense emotional situation wasn't the best idea, and to her surprise, Mason had backed down. Before the call had ended, he'd garnered her promise to bring Michael to Fort Wayne the following week. Mason would be going to Chicago after the funeral, but he would be back with Willa within a couple of days.

Then Bethy had made an error in judgment. She later blamed it on the extreme situation, but still could have kicked herself. She'd sought out Gabe without thinking, crawling into his lap and only then calling the Marshalls, talking first to Martha to secure permission, and waiting impatiently while Michael came to the phone. Telling Michael she'd talked to his Uncle Mason had caused Gabe to go still underneath her, his arm around her waist turning into an inescapable band. Turning away from him, she'd continued the conversation, discussing the timing of his visit to Fort Wayne.

That phone call had been uncomfortable, but what came next surprised her.

"Already knew you had a boy, Bethy." Plucking the phone from her hand, Gabe didn't release her but didn't try to make her face him, either. He told her in his own way that she had the right to hold Michael close. "Wish I'd known you then like I do now. Things would be different, baby. Can't change the past. Can't, so it's not worth arguing or worrying about, yeah? Looking to the future, if we can swing it, he'll be in our lives however makes you happiest. Whatever that looks like, I'll make it happen. You know all my secrets, every dark corner I could dig out I've shown you. You know, more than anyone else, what it's taken from me to be where we sit today." He paused, and she twisted, leaning in to rest her forehead against his, the heat from his breaths ghosting across her skin. "Know where all my skeletons are buried. I've known about Michael for a while, and any decisions you had to make to get him where he is, and get you to the woman in my arms, you have my full backing. All confidence in you, baby. No matter the road, you'll do what's needful."

She knew then why Willa hated that word. It was used in so many ways by the people she'd grown up alongside, covering all manner of things people raised differently would be shocked or terrified of. In Gabe's mouth, it meant he knew she'd work her fingers to the bone to take care of those she loved. "I love you," she said, then shook her head. "I don't want you to ever think that's not something I think about before I say it. It's not something to fill a silence, Gabe. It's me—when I say it, that's me giving you me."

"I know, baby. Take you as you can give yourself. And part of that was you needing time to tell me about Michael. I want to meet him, too. You know that, right?" She nodded. "Now, we need to sort out getting ourselves to Cynthiana. I don't want to ride down. We're gonna take your car. Wanna be with you and have you where I can keep my eyes on you. We leave tomorrow night, we'll get there about the same time as Mason and the men riding in from Las Cruces." He gave her a squeeze. "You need to make another call, baby. Call Juanita. She needs to hear from her girl, and you need to talk to her." Pulling her close, he handed her the phone back. *"Stay right where you are, let me take as much of this from you as you can give. Hadn't reconnected with him long ago, but I'm gonna miss him. Let me grieve with you, pull it from both of us, yeah?"*

Seeing Juanita the night before the funeral had them both weeping, Bella crowding close, arms around both women. Fury, Bones, and Tater had stayed nearby, waiting to be needed. It had been cathartic for all of them in a way, but when Bethy asked about Mela, fear rose in Juanita's face like a wave battering the shore. Carmela had been with a group of bikers headed from Indiana back to New Mexico, and none of them had made it. No sign of them anywhere, and Mason had everyone looking.

Then it had been over, and like Tabby's funeral, the whole thing seemed both rushed and drawn out, leaving her exhausted and sleeping in the car all the way back to Fort Wayne. Gabe had surprised her by giving her space to sleep and then cry, only touching her when she'd reach out—he seemed to understand that after the services, after seeing the hole in the ground, casket suspended over it by the fragile bands holding it aloft, after standing close and throwing her clod of dirt into the grave—she needed time to sort out all the hidden terrors and pain dragged to the surface.

That was five days ago, and today she was driving to Nashville to pick Michael up. She intended to swing by to see the studio first, pick up any messages or mail that hadn't yet been forwarded, and then spend the night in her apartment. The plan was to get Michael early tomorrow, making the return six-hour trip to get back in time for dinner at Mason's. She wasn't looking forward to the night alone. It would be the first in weeks, and she hadn't been very comfortable in the apartment after Ty had moved to the group home. She was expecting a sleepless night and had already cataloged a dozen ways she could keep busy.

"Why are you going to Nashville? I'm assuming you mean with me, but why?" Zipping the suitcase closed, she found her hands brushed aside as Gabe lifted it, setting the wheels on the floor.

"Because I want to?" He grinned, and the sight of his smile breaking through that damned, beautiful red beard made her smile in response. "Come on, Bethy. I don't want to sleep alone. I'm betting you're the same way. I'll come with, we can do dinner out, both get a good night's sleep, and then I can meet Michael."

Staring at him, she saw nothing but earnest desire in his eyes. Nodding, she offered, "I bet if I call ahead, he could do dinner with us." Gabe's expression brightened and his smile grew broader. "You really want that?"

"Fuck, yeah, I want that. He's your kid, baby. Nearly a man grown, and I want to get to know him." He leaned in, kissing her softly. "See what he thinks about being a big brother at some point." His palm settled on her belly and she grinned, feeling his lips move and knew he was smiling too. "Even if it takes us a while, we'll get there. I want to know he's cool with it."

"Pinch me." He laughed at her request, giving the skin along her hip the tiniest tweak. "Swear to God, Gabe. I can't believe we're here."

"Believe it, baby. Told you, mine forever. That means you come with a boy half-grown? Cool. Means we have a half a dozen rugrats? Also cool." She rolled her eyes, and he laughed, head back, mouth open, sounds of his humor pouring from him to fill the room. He sobered, staring into her eyes, earnest love on his face. "Means we never get the chance to parent together, except what we can do with Michael? Much as it would kill, that's cool, too, because I'd be here with you."

***

Fury

Bethy was wringing her hands in her lap, the movement unconscious but consistent. Nervous as she was it would be a wonder if she could eat anything, and a second wonder if what she ate would stay down.

"Relax, baby. I already know I'm gonna love him." Her face lifted to his and he saw tears trembling on her bottom lashes. That looked like a lot more than nervousness. "What, Beth? What's wrong?"

"I just really, really wish Mikey had gotten to meet him."

He steered the car into the parking lot of a shopping center they were passing and parked. Unbuckling, he reached over and popped the button on her belt. Lifting and pulling, he brought her into his lap, shifting his seat backwards as he held her close. They sat like that for minutes as she cried into his shoulder, the fabric of his shirt dampening, getting wet, holding the weight of her tears. Silent through it all, she gave a tiny hiccup that he knew signaled her crying jag was on the downward side.

This was something he hated. Not her crying. Well, yeah, he hated that, because so far it had been him doing stupid shit that had caused it, or it was like this, and something he couldn't fix. Couldn't get his hands on to make better. No, what he hated was the long-lived evidence of how their life back in Kentucky had scarred her. Crying silently so she wouldn't be heard, no matter what was done to her.

Voice trembling, she broke the silence. "I'm sorry."

"For what, lover?" He gave her a squeeze.

She snorted a watery laugh. "For being such a girly girl."

He squeezed again, slipping one hand down to her thigh to stroke up and down. "I like you being a girly girl."

"I'm not usually, so don't get used to it." That had a little bit of her sass back, and he smiled against her hair to hear it. "We should go."

"We should," he agreed, not moving. That earned him another snort, this one less tear-filled. "We will. Just let me have another minute of you, yeah?"

"You only want a minute?"

Eyes closed, he held her, feeling the way her breath still hitched occasionally, and liked how her weight in his lap felt perfect, as if he could sit here for days and not get tired of holding her. "I'll take a lifetime, one minute at a time."

Michael was waiting on the porch of the large house as Fury pulled the car to a stop. Tall and angular, he seemed to be all elbows and knees, big mitts of his hands dangling at his sides. Dark hair curled at the back of his neck, hanging down into his face to partially hide intelligent grey eyes. He looked exactly like Mason had at that age. Even before Bethy could unbuckle, Michael had her door open and had crouched down, looking into her face with an intensity Fury could feel from across the car. The boy didn't say anything for a moment, just stared at her. Then when he did, it wasn't anything Fury would have expected.

"You've been crying." Michael moved, angling so he could glare at Fury. "Did he make you cry?"

Whoa. Bethy had told her son she was bringing a friend, and when questioned by Michael had given him the information that Gabe, as she called him, was more than a friend. She hadn't mentioned him being upset by the news, but clearly this was a wrinkle the kid wasn't excited about.

Before Fury could respond, Bethy got there. "No, honey. Gabe didn't make me sad. I just had a good friend die. I told you that. I had a moment on the way over, that's why we're late. Gabe had to stop the car and take care of me." She lifted a hand to curl her fingers around the corner of Michael's jaw, angling his head so he had to look at her. Pointedly she said, "Hello, Michael. I've missed you."

Lurching forwards, Michael wrapped his arms around her with a sigh. "I missed you, too. I was afraid I'd made you mad with all my questions. With my wanting...I just missed you."

Fury gave them a minute, looking around at the neighborhood. It was nice, filled with well-kept homes, clearly a bedroom community of families by the piles of bikes next to some of the garages. Movement caught his attention, and he saw an older woman come out of the house they were parked in front of, the door opening behind her as a man joined her on the porch. "Beth, looks like Michael's parents want to say hello, too."

Michael pulled back, looking around Bethy again, this time with an embarrassed expression on his face. "Hi, I'm Michael."

Bethy filled in, "And he's sorry about what he said before."

Fury scoffed. "No, he's not, baby. He was makin' sure someone he cares about was okay. Can't hold that against him." He stuck out a hand and Michael gripped and held, solemnly pumping up and down. "Hey, there. I'm Gabe." For the second time in a few minutes, he unbuckled Bethy, this time pushing her ass to slide her towards the door. "Out, babe. Let's meet 'n greet, and then get some food. I'm starving."

She rolled her eyes as Michael laughed and stood, holding his hand out to help her up. Gabe liked seeing that, how the boy held her in high regard, ready to do battle if someone hurt her, and making even a casual gesture caring. He joined them at the porch, following Bethy up the sidewalk, winning the battle to keep his eyes off her ass. *Probably wouldn't go over well with Michael's adoptive parents if I strolled up lookin' like a lech.*

Five minutes later they were back in the vehicle, Michael in the backseat. He was so tall he could lean up between the seats, and did, hand to the radio in a way that spoke volumes to how comfortable he was in Bethy's car. That started a good-natured argument about what radio station they'd listen to, Michael coming out on the controlling side of the buttons well before they pulled into the restaurant Bethy had selected for their meal.

At the table Michael was well mannered, courteous, and curious, something he didn't bother trying to hide. She'd been gone a long time, and he had questions about that, about how she was handling what had evidently been a difficult conversation with Michael before she left, and who Fury was to her. All his questions made Bethy anxious, and she kept tripping over herself to give him the answers he seemed to need. He wasn't rude, not a bit of it, just persistent in a way that made Fury smile. His questions continued through the meal, circling back to Bethy's family again and again, and Fury finally understood the kid was not just inquisitive but was nervous at the idea of meeting people who meant something to this woman he clearly loved.

Leaning forward, Fury tapped his water glass with the handle of his fork, pulling their attention to him easier than if he'd tried to interrupt the intense conversation. Leveling the fork at Michael, Fury told him, "Get this, yeah? Bethy's family is good, decent people. I've known her brother all my life, known Bethy the same. They're the kind of folks where, once you're in, you're in. No worries about them changing their minds. Mason's already decided you're in, or he wouldn't have pushed her to bring you up. He would have come down and done an on-site assessment, so to speak, figuring out if you're worth the time and effort." Bethy's head jerked back, and her eyes went wide as Michael's expression mirrored hers. Fury grinned. "Him tellin' her to bring you up, letting you close to his wIfe and kids? No doubt about it. You are in, boy. Family. Cousin Chase will be happy to have someone around his age to talk to. And, I bet you won't always get along, but that's okay, because family doesn't set you aside just because you argue." He shook his head, stabbing a piece of meat with his fork and lifting it to his mouth. "I won't set you aside just because you like country music, either. Just sayin'." He shoved the bite into his mouth and chewed, watching wave after wave of emotion cross the boy's face. Relief and fear, followed by a longing so intense he wondered if Bethy saw it, too. A moment later she leaned towards Michael and spoke softly, confirming his suspicions.

"Gabe's right, you know. I don't tell him that often, on account of it goes to his head, but he's right about this." Michael turned to face her. "I've fought to stay part of your life through the years, because I wanted you to know me. Now, I want you to know my family. All the people who are as important to me as you are. They're going to love you, Michael."

"I'm a little nervous," Michael admitted and she nodded.

"I know. So are they, honestly."

"Nervous? Why?" The kid looked confused.

"Because they're going to be meeting someone who is very important to me and they care." Michael offered her a one-sided grin and she returned it, reaching out to ruffle and then smooth his hair. "You can't blow my cover, though." Michael cocked his head to one side and she laughed. "Chase thinks I'm cool. I wanna keep my cool aunt status for a little longer."

"You are cool." Michael was quick to defend her, and that made Fury grin. "She is!"

"Okay then, I'm cool. You're cool." She looked at Fury. "Are you cool, honey?"

Stabbing a piece of meat off her plate, he grinned at her immediate scowl and then laughed aloud as Michael eased his plate away, moving it closer to his side of the table. "Oh, yeah, baby. I'm cool."

Right don't mean easy

Mason

He stood in the open garage door and watched as the car swung into his driveway. Squinting through the glare of sunshine, he made out the form of his sister in the front passenger seat, Fury driving, his red beard the most visible thing inside the car. The door leading into the house opened behind him, and he glanced over his shoulder to see Chase walking towards him. For a moment Mason was struck by how mature his boy looked these days, not the first time he'd had that thought. Not quite as tall as his daddy, still Chase had the thick, dark hair from the Mason side of his family, and a build that showed he spent time working out.

Good lookin' kid, he thought, shaking his head. Late teens were a hard age, but Chase had pulled himself together over the past year and a half. Mason had talked about it with Jase, because the man seemed to have a sixth-sense when it came to kids. They'd decided it boiled down to Sosa being killed. Taking her out of the equation allowed Chase to explore being happy with Mason and Willa, without feeling guilty about that happiness.

The multiple slamming of car doors announced their visitors were on the move and he shifted to look outside again. Bethy walked his way, arm around a boy who towered over her by several inches, putting him nearly eye-to-eye with Mason. Fury had her hand in his, walking slightly to the side, but keeping that connection.

Nearly fucked up with that one. Mason had never been one to hold others accountable for his mistakes, and this was no different. Pike had been full of bullshit, and if Mason hadn't been so thrown by the idea of little Bethy being with one of his members, he would have seen it. All the time he'd spent grooming Fury to take over from him, nearly thrown away in the space of a few hours.

Bethy laughed, neck twisting so she could look up at Fury who tipped his head to steal a kiss as they walked the last few feet to where Mason stood. *She loves him.* Mason knew what love looked like. He was blessed to see it in the face of his wife every day. He knew there was something else in their past, but if Bethy had buried it, as far as Mason was concerned, it could stay buried. *Good enough.*

Chase stopped next to him as Mason stuck out his hand towards the boy who had to be Michael, and wasn't that a kick in the teeth. Bethy still felt guilty about never telling him or Watcher about the boy she'd birthed, even if her reasons were sound in her mind. Watcher would have been thrilled at his namesake, would have bent the world into a pretzel to get Bethy whatever she needed.

Michael gripped his hand, and Mason clamped down, jerking the boy towards him, Bethy making a tiny surprised sound as her arm slipped away. Then Mason had Michael in his arms, holding him close, talking fast into the boy's ear, wanting to make an impression before he lost the upper hand. "Know you're nervous, boy. Don't be. We're family here, every one of us, and we'll bleed ourselves dry to get you whatever you need." Mason gave a squeeze, and Michael made a sound that echoed

Bethy, making Mason grin. "Proud as fuck to meet you, Mikey, I'm already thinkin' you're a little bit of all right."

A wheeze, then near his ear, he heard Bethy's son whisper, "You're my Uncle Mason, right? Pleased to meet you, sir."

He laughed, the loud sound echoing off the inside of the garage as he stepped back. "Pleased as fuck to meet you, Mikey." Looping an arm around Chase's shoulders, he pulled him forwards. "This is my boy, Chase. One of my boys. The other one ain't much of a conversationalist yet, but Chase'll talk your ear off." Chase reached out and Michael shook his hand. "Bethy, come here, baby doll. Need a hug from you, too." He released Chase and brought Bethy close, kissing the side of her head. "Fury." He nodded at the man who had stayed back a few steps. "Good trip?"

"Good as it can be in a cage." Fury grinned and Mason returned the expression. "You got beer?"

"Yeah, let's move this inside." He dipped his knees and before Bethy could react, had her up and over his shoulder, arm wrapped around her thighs to hold her in place. "Brother, wanna bring the boys in with ya?"

"Will do." Fury laughed, the sound barely audible over Bethy's howls of anger, partly fake, mostly real.

"Mom?" Michael called and Bethy went rigid, still and quiet. "Can I go with Chase? He's going to run to the store quick for Aunt Willa."

They were inside the house before Bethy answered, her voice breathy and quiet. "Sure, honey." The door closed behind them and Mason heard the roar of Chase's truck exhaust as the engine started.

Mason set her back on her feet, looking down into her face, seeing tears welling in her eyes. "What's wrong, Bethy? Did I hurt you?" She shook her head. "Then what's wrong?"

"He called her mom." Fury's words broke the stillness that had been holding Bethy in place and she turned, launching herself at Mason, wrapping her arms around his neck. "I'm betting it's the first time."

Mason closed his eyes, holding Bethy close, feeling her body shake. "I can't imagine how you're dealing with all this, Bethy. I lost twelve years of Chase's life, but once I was in it there was no questioning what my role was. You've had him all this time, but still not. So fuckin' strong, baby sister. Love you."

"It was the right thing to do," she reminded him, telling him the same thing she'd explained when she called to confess. "I know it was."

"Right don't mean it was easy." He gave her a squeeze, then cocked his head. The sounds coming from the baby monitor told him Gar was awake, which meant Willa would be, too. She'd been struggling with the pregnancy, and he'd been encouraging her to sleep more. Mostly by exhausting her a different way. *Doctor's orders*. He smirked. "Serious as fuck, Bethy. You doin' what you had to like that. I fuckin' hate I wasn't there." He sighed and stroked the back of her head, smoothing down the sweep of her hair. "You done bawlin'? I still gotta get your old man a beer."

"Got it." The sound of the refrigerator door opening and closing mocked him and Mason shook his head.

"I love you, baby sister."

She tensed, arms going tight around his neck and then she told him, "Love you, too."

Common ground

Fury

"No fuckin' tellin'. But we're gonna do it." Mason slammed a coffee mug onto the countertop as he growled out the words in response to a question from Bear.

It had been a month since Fury and Bethy had brought Michael up to visit. That weekend trip had been followed by Bethy taking him home and then staying in Nashville to work on projects that required her presence there. After a week, she'd been talking about setting up a studio in Fort Wayne, after two she had actively called real estate agents, that lasting until Chase introduced her to Benny's brother, Slate, and she'd been shown the studio he'd built, converting his garage over so his brother would have a place to play and record. After three weeks, she had hired an up-and-coming producer to begin taking over for her in Nashville while they worked to expand the business. She would be here in three more days, and every time he talked to her, he liked how she said the word home when talking about his place here in the Fort.

Those weren't the only events for the month. Not by a long shot.

It had taken three long weeks after Watcher's death, but Carmela had finally been located. Her kidnapping had been treachery from within.

Diamond, a long-time member of the Southern Soldiers had taken her, working hand-in-hand with the old Rebel enemy, Deacon. A founder of the Rebel Fiends, he'd been ousted by Mason decades ago, still holding a grudge more than a mile wide. It wasn't widely known in the Rebels that Diamond was actually Deacon's son, but that was the truth. *Weird world*, Fury thought, holding out his own coffee mug for a refill.

So the month had seen Carmela rescued, Juanita reunited with her girls, Bella deciding to stay in Chicago with Tater, Hurley moving to Las Cruces, and that was just the events surrounding Watcher's family. Within the Rebels, they'd uncovered some oddities with a Las Cruces member. Spider, a long-time Soldiers' member, and one who had opposed the joining of the two clubs. Opie, so recently forced into the top role in that chapter, was investigating that side of things for the club. And Mason had discovered what looked like a blood sister down in Florida, following clues laid by Morgan.

Maybe the most shocking piece for Fury was the defection from the Diamante of a large group of men well known to him. One of them, the biggest piece in the puzzle, had saved his ass in an alley long ago. That was what they'd been discussing for the past hour, why Chismoso, who was dead Lalo's cousin, would drop his full set of patches and roll away from a club he'd been in for years. In leaving, he'd taken fully two dozen men with him, and they'd ridden straight to Chicago, working a meet with Bones to see if they'd be welcomed. *Not fuckin' likely*, Fury had thought at the time, but now it was looking like the tides had turned in Chismoso's favor.

"Then why would we want to patch them? If we can't hold guarantees of their sincerity, how do we trust them?" Bear pushed Mason, asking his original question again, clearly hoping for a different answer. "Where do we see this going in a month, or two? What's the benefit for Rebels?"

Mason cut his gaze towards Fury, who realized this was his cue to show how he was on the same page with Mason, and could see beyond the immediate to the future.

"In a month, we'll have a good idea if they'll stick. In two, we'll have broken their clique into smaller and smaller groups, scattering them to the winds, because if their loyalty lies with the club, it won't matter to them where they are posted. If it's to the group, then we'll play a different tune on their ribs." He took a breath, looking around the room. "Benefit is the addition of more than two dozen men who aren't prospects, not in the normal sense of the word. They don't have to try the life on for size to see how it fits, they already know how well that motherfucker rests on their skin. We let them earn trust, giving them chances to fuck up, because you can't make a splash and gain approval without having a chance to really fuck shit up. In the end, if Chismoso is playing us false and he's a plant, we'll eliminate him from the equation and see if we can salvage the other two dozen."

"Gonna be a fuckton of work, brother." Bear had turned to glare at him, and Fury saw the flash of Mason's smile behind the man. "You sure you wanna back this play, Prez?"

Fury nodded, and Bear's scowl broke apart, a smile filtering up like a slowly brightening spotlight. "Okay."

"Okay?" Fury glanced around the room, seeing nods all around. "All righty, then. Someone get Bones on the horn. We got shit to talk about."

After the conference call, something Fury still had problems getting used to, seeing the crisp images of the men on the screen via video, he dug two beers out of the cooler and went in search of Mason. He found him in a quiet corner of the clubhouse, phone to his ear, clearly on a call with his old lady. "We got a few more weeks, baby. I know you're tired of it, but you can't quit on me now. I'll be home in a couple hours. We'll watch that fuckin' TV show you're always on about." He paused, and Fury watched as his face transformed, softening in a way that was hard to describe but allowed the love he had for his woman to show to anyone who cared enough to look. His voice was rough when he spoke again, broken by emotion. "Most beautiful woman I've ever seen, my Willa is. Precious and loved. Never. Don't ever forget that." Another pause, and one corner of his mouth crooked up. "Oh, yeah. Still wanna fuck you. I got my ways to get around that belly, woman. Now stop talkin' dirty to me. I got work to finish before I can come take care of your horny ass." Fury chuckled, and Mason looked at him. "And I got company now, so unless you want me talkin' about your pretty pussy where my brothers can hear, we need to end this now." He laughed. "Love you, too, babe." Fury took advantage of Mason ending his conversation, hooking one of the chairs out from under the table and seating himself without waiting on an invitation.

"You need something, motherfucker?" Mason clipped as he shoved his phone into his pocket, reaching for one of the beers Fury held.

"I think I need to hit up Little Rock again soon." He'd been down last week, collaborating with the local president, Stan, on an upcoming national event they were planning to host at the Arkansas chapter's house. "Make sure we're good. I know I can call the man anytime, but there's something to be said for some face time of the real-world sort."

"Work it around anything you got going here, and roll. I ain't gonna question you on shit like that." Mason tipped his beer up, taking a long pull at the bottle. "Good job earlier. You hit the nail on the head with how you handled Bear. He's in your pocket now, because he believes in your vision."

Fury felt his head jerk back. "In my pocket?" That was usually a good thing, because it meant a member or officer would back any play without any kind of politicking. "You sure about that?"

"Fuck, yeah. You got a pocketful of posies here, man. I count three officers who act like they've already made the leap. Makes me feel good, knowing I picked well."

"So you say." Fury sighed, not quite sure what he wanted to express.

He was saved from having to decide by Gunny. "Boss?" Fury and Mason turned, both responding with, "Yeah?" Gunny laughed, pointing to Fury. "That boss."

"See? See what I mean? I'll just sit here and pretend to be important." Mason was grinning as he lifted his beer.

"What's up, Gunny?" Fury reached out and tapped Mason's shoulder with his fist. "Whatcha got for us?"

"Nothing good, man. This is Kentucky." The feeling in the room changed, and Fury knew he wasn't the only one who felt it because Gunny stood straighter, and even across the room Bear and Slate lifted their heads, turning to face the small group of men. Tension rolled off Mason, and every man in the room tuned into it. "You had me looking, I've kept looking. I don't stop looking until I've found everything there is to find." He made a face. "I think I found it." He flicked his eyes to Mason. "You ain't gonna like this. It ties to LaPorte."

Justine LaPorte was a Fed in Florida who had twice arrested Lalo and cut him loose. Chismoso had shed some light on the encounters, but she'd been a black hole for a time. Not anymore, a picture of her had turned on the spotlights, because she and Mason were dead ringers for the other, given the differences forced on the Mason mold by gender. Or, Morgan mold, as things were looking. Fury knew it was something Mason was struggling with, the idea that Justice Morgan was his father, making him a full brother to Shooter. So Gunny saying Kentucky was tied to LaPorte was surprising, and yet not, all in the same breath.

"Spill." Fury didn't look away, kept his eyes on Gunny, waiting.

"Told you what I found with Tabby's wreck." Fury nodded. "You remember what I found with Deacon's blood, left in a hospital same night. Note just like Duck's Brenda?" Fury waited. "Ryan Camp was Deacon." Bones had killed Deacon in California, ridden him to the ground and beaten his head to a broken, bloody pulp. Backed into a corner, Deacon had killed his own kid during the last few hours before the Rebels found Carmela. From everything Fury heard, the scene had been entirely fucked up, Bones and Opie helping make sense of a senseless mess. "His kid, James Camp. Jimmy." Gunny angled his chin towards Mason. "You remember the kid from Chicago, right?"

"Barely. Wasn't until I pulled out a picture Bones wanted that I even thought of Deacon's kid. Nearly took us too long to put it all together." Mason drained his beer, yelling across the room, "Bring me one, prospect." There were three prospects behind the bar, all three jumped, and Fury was briefly amused as they appeared to tussle over who'd get to take the beer to Mason.

"Deacon's old lady got pissed off about the French chicks." Mason nodded at Gunny's words, but Fury was confused.

"French chicks?"

"Canadian whores, Fiends bought and paid for flesh. That was the last straw for me, started me on the path we're still on." Mason shook his head, reaching for the beer the prospect held out.

Fury watched as the kid—they all looked like kids these days—retreated to the bar, one of the only safe places in the room for someone of his level when there were so many heavy hitters in the room.

"She got pissed and went west, wound up in California. She...liked her some biker, man. Hooked up with Outriders out there. Not Morgan," Gunny added the last part quickly, in response to some subtle shift on Mason's part. "But she was around, a lot. Meant Jimmy was around a lot, too. Friends with Shooter. Friends with a lot of the Outriders, which was his intro into the life. It was about that time when Morgan moved one of his many women into residence at the clubhouse." He gestured at Mason. "Your Justine's mother, looks like. And Justine came with. That's about the time Shooter's old lady took a runner, hiding her and Eddie for a time.

Everything's a muddle in some places, but in others, Mason, I got a clear thread to follow."

Mason's eyes closed slowly and he stood for a minute. Eyes still closed, he said, "Justine LaPorte was living in the Outrider clubhouse?"

"Yeah."

"What else?" Mason's eyes opened, then narrowed on Gunny. "She and Diamond, Jimmy...they were about the same age, right?" Gunny nodded. "And you found a boy in Kentucky who was abandoned about the same time Tabby died?" Gunny nodded again. "That boy Tabby's kid?"

"Nope." Gunny shook his head, hands on his hips. "I think it was Justine and Jimmy's kid. Morgan and Deacon's grandson."

"Jesus *fuck*." Taking a deep breath, Fury leaned sideways, putting one shoulder against a column. "Is there anywhere those men don't have their fingers dug deep?"

"Seems like it, I know. Still, this Christopher Ryan is the right age, has the right name, and, Mason—" Gunny turned slightly. "—pictures of him as a teen? He could be Chase's big brother, man."

"For years, I thought Bethy was the only family I had." Mason's voice was deceptively mild, calm, but Fury could see how his clenched fists trembled. "Now, I got blood coming out of the woodwork." He pulled in a breath, lifting his chin. "Got anything else for us? This Chris is what...thirty now?"

"Twenty-seven, married, with two kids, and he's an accountant in Louisville." Gunny shrugged. "He's about as vanilla as a citizen can be, brother. I think he got stuck somewhere and then left there, and he's totally ignorant of his heritage."

"So you think he's gonna be a product of nurture? Leaving nature out of it?" Mason laughed, the sound hard and brittle, breaking against the walls around them. "Fucking shit, brother. I vote we leave him the fuck alone. Leave him to his life."

"Seconded." Fury lifted his beer, making a face when the warm liquid hit his tongue. He swallowed it down, forcing the bitter along with everything else.

Florida fiasco

"Jesus fucking Christ." Fury stared at the screen, watching the video Myron had queued up. They'd allowed only officers in the room, and other than Myron, it was the first time any of them were seeing what had gone down in Florida three days ago. Fury jolted as he watched Bones fall, neck twisting involuntarily to flinch away from what he was seeing. Even knowing Bones was okay, pissed as fuck but recovering temporarily at the clubhouse in Little Rock, this was hard to watch.

Fury flexed his fists, every bone, knuckle, and muscle in his hands and arms complaining. Things had moved at warp speed over the past few days, and he was still coming to terms with everything.

He'd spent nearly a week in California, trying and failing to get in to see Shooter. The intent had been for him to deliver a message in the clearest possible fashion, while assuring the club that one of their greatest enemies was still securely behind bars. That visit to a prison wasn't anything he'd wish on anyone, and just making the walk up to the visitor intake building had nearly sucked his courage dry. Then, when things went sideways, and he'd been detained for three full days, Fury had nearly lost his mind. Not in a cell, things never went quite that far, but just knowing he wasn't free to leave had played havoc on him. He'd been allowed no calls, so he didn't know if anyone even knew what was going on. In the end it was for nothing, because not only didn't he get to see Shooter, the man hadn't even been in Cali, as evidenced by subsequent events.

On the screen, the pixels that represented Mason stood over Morgan for a moment. Words were spoken, the sounds indistinct, speakers in the coffee shop blown out by the concussions of the earlier shots. Morgan made a motion towards where Shooter lay on his back, head tilted at an unnatural angle, eyes already turning cloudy. Bones lifted his gun at the same time Mason did, both men reacting to whatever it was Morgan had said, and the speakers clearly picked up the sounds of four shots. Morgan's body jerked and he fell backwards off his chair, elbow catching and turning over the table where he'd been sitting. Stillness on the screen for a moment, then the speakers picked up the shrill screams of a girl. Fury knew that was the barista, barricaded in the bathroom, at that point already on the phone with the police.

"Jesus fucking Christ," he repeated, shaking his head. "We know what was said?"

Myron nodded. "Mason wants to wait to brief everyone on that when he and Bones are back in Chicago. We'll be calling a national meet for officers, and he'll go over everything there." He stopped fiddling with the laptop in front of him. "I've got to get back to Chicago tonight. Ester is with Road Runner, but I promised her I'd be back in a few hours." Ester was Bones' old lady, a quirky, flighty woman that Fury found himself liking for the man. Bones' stick-up-his-ass attitude melted clean away when Ester was in the room, and seeing him like that humanized the myth somewhat. *Who knew I'd wind up liking the asshole?* Myron got his attention again when he said, "Now we need to hear about St. Louis."

Fury clenched his fists again, the ache returning and blooming into a more acute pain.

"St. Louis," he repeated Myron's words with a sigh. "Fuckin' nuts, man. I was leaving Taft, fuckin' finally, after they'd jacked with me for too long, and you—" He angled his head, nodding at Myron. "—had me head there instead of back to Mother." Pain shot through his hands, and he realized he'd been clenching his fists again. "I found a situation I still don't rightly understand. Pike—" He glanced around the room to see recognition on every face, so they at least knew who he was talking about. "—had crossed over to the deep end of crazy, and made threats to national officers and the club. I investigated,"—he'd searched rooms and pockets, talked to a dozen men, consulted with key Rebel players— "and found the local officers' concerns were warranted. They'd secured him." Pike had been held in the basement, in a small room, dark and smelling of old piss and bleach, lights buzzing from behind their cages. "Pike had already removed his patches, tossed them on the floor, and demanded a beatout." Fury shrugged. "I'd already talked to officers who had indicated that might be expected. So I delivered. Dyno moved from SAA to President, and they're filling the hole with another local member Mason sanctioned. That's"—he shook his hands out, tucking one thumb into a back pocket to try and stop himself from the compulsive movement—"what went down in St. Louis."

"Did you know about Pike before you went there? What he'd done?" Bear's distinctive New Jersey accent didn't show its face often, but it was there now, signifying the tension surrounding this question.

"What he'd done to his sister's husband? I think everyone knows about Harddrive, brother." Fury shook his head. "That's family, not club. Did not factor."

"What he fuckin' did to you, man. Did you fuckin' know?" Slate was behind Fury, and he twisted in place, turning to face the man, shaking his head.

"Pike never did anything to me. I didn't like him, but that was more his attitude than anything."

"Entitled asshole, through and through." Gunny threw his opinion in the ring and Fury nodded. "We've all seen how he'd wander in, lording himself over the members and prospects, trying to wow the women. He's a fucktard, no doubt, but the question on the floor"—with that, Fury realized this had turned from a witness conversation about what had happened on the screen to their national president, and into something else, a niggling trickle of fear curling around his balls, drawing them up tight to his body as he remembered the beating he'd taken in the basement of this building. *Will I never move past that?* Gunny continued—"is did you know what Pike did to you?" Fury shook his head. "Nothing? Not a clue?"

"Asked and answered, brother." Fury squared his shoulders, turning to face the big man. "Spit out what you got to say. You're wasting my fucking time."

"He don't know." Slate leaned back in his chair. "Fuck me runnin', he really don't know."

"Already said that, more than once. You a fan of makin' me repeat myself?" Now Fury was pissed, crossing over the line from annoyed to angry. "Not sure what you're talking about, and I do not appreciate the way you're trying to put me off balance. Spit—" He leaned forwards at the waist. "—it out."

"Pike is the one who called Mason. Told him you were a Fed plant. Told him he had papers from Ling in Memphis that named you. Pike twisted shit and twisted shit, and played it out until Mason didn't have any choice but to call you in." Myron closed the laptop with a snap, turning it upside down and removing the battery before putting it in a messenger bag. "Pike coulda gotten you killed with what he played. They...we were wondering if you'd put that together before you hit St. Louis." Myron looked around the room, fingers working to fasten the buckles on the bag. "Pretty clear to me that wasn't the case. Which I already told all of you. Only six of us knew who had made that call. Damn sure I didn't talk about it after Mason gagged us. Pretty sure you were the same." He turned back to Fury. "With it not proving true, it wouldn't do for there to be division in the club." He shrugged. "You get it, and Mason knew you would if it ever came out."

"Oh, I get it," Fury gritted out between clenched teeth. "Don't mean I like it." He swung his gaze around the room, pausing on each man, forcing them to meet his eyes. "This has me thinking Mason was wrong. Slate was wrong. And me? I for sure was fucking wrong." He shook his head. "This isn't the first time you've called me to the floor." Slate sat up, twisting to face him, mouth open to argue but Fury cut him off. "Don't mince words, man." He deliberately withheld the word he would normally use, considering this was beyond the pale and he was infuriated. "What you orchestrated just now? Same as, don't deny it. You don't trust me, because I came in from Diamante and you're warring with them. You don't trust me, because I got tangled up with what went down with Gunny. And now, you don't trust me because some of you beat the fuck out of me on the say-so of a man who's turned into a goddamned cut." Angry, he was so angry he could feel the blood pounding in his temples, hear every beat in his ears. "So you've called me out, questioned me in ways you would never have dared do with Slate, Bones, Tater, *fuck*— anyone. You want me out, you'll have to take my patch, but it won't kill me to explain to Mason why I'm handing back the office plate. Fuck you." He pounded his chest with a closed fist, knowing his anger was misplaced, but not willing to put a halt to his words. "I know the kind of brother I am. You don't, then that's your goddamned, *fucking* loss." He turned to walk out only to pull up short, Myron standing in his way. "Move, man."

"Nope. You're stuck here. I know you. You won't turn your back on the club, this chapter, or a single brother in this room." Shaking his head, Myron lifted his arms to the side, palms forward. "They went about it wrong, but they meant well."

"I don't like it."

"You don't have to." Myron shrugged. "What you said means there's a void in St. Louis, and we have a mouth on the loose that we might not want to leave that way. I say we set a hunter on Pike, bring him back into the fold." He glanced at Fury. "I can't make that call, though."

Pike. Fucking Pike. He hadn't recognized the man until St. Louis, but he'd been one of Dion's cronies. That meant he might know what Fury's gig had been back before the MC life. If he knew and flapped his lips, it could bring everything down. *A life built on lies. Fuck.* "I don't think there's a man in here wants me to make *that* fucking call."

"You're wrong." That was Gunny, and what must be his footsteps sounded until he stood behind Fury.

"I agree." Bear's twang had subsided, but his voice was still distinctive. "Your call, boss."

Myron held his gaze unflinching, waiting.

Fury sighed. "He's been playing alongside the boys who don't hesitate to pull in family." Fury was thinking aloud at this point, wanting every man to follow his reasoning so there wouldn't be any questions. If they were determined to make him do this in spite of a demonstrated lack of confidence, he'd give them the demanded show. "We know how Diamante and the Outrider holdouts are." When Shooter went to prison, some of the Outrider chapter folded, some of them shifted away from the things he'd driven them towards, but a few chapters had held the line, maintaining they were the loyal ones who would be rewarded when Shooter got out. *Ain't no rewards comin' their way now.*

"They'll bring blood right back to a man's doorstep, putting it in the way of everything we have. If he winds up in the wrong place, wrong time, he knows a fuck of a lot of info about all of us." Pike had been a Rebel for years, made regular visits to some of the clubhouses. That meant he had friends or at least acquaintances he might reach out to. "With everything that's happened, we didn't do a general notification about him being out bad. I think we need to do that now, see what it stirs up." *Beth's forgiven me, even if I can't forgive myself. If it comes out, it comes out. I won't kill a man to save my ass like this.* "He betrays us in word or deed, if we heard even a breath of him talking out of turn, we hunt him down. Until then…" He looked at the faces of the men, seeing agreement written there. "…we let him dig his own holes."

* * *

"But I dun wanna." The slurred words caught his attention and Fury glanced to his right where Bethy leaned against his shoulder. Eyes closed, her lips were pursed in irritation. Mikey was sprawled in the backseat, head against one door, feet stretched out towards the other side, earbuds in place a silent protest to Fury's commandeering of the radio. Windows down, they were on their way from Nashville to Adken, Florida, where Mason would meet them and facilitate the introduction of the two sisters. With the windows down, the moving air had teased strands of Bethy's hair free from her attempts to tame it. Fury smiled as it moved across his skin, as if even in her sleep Bethy was caressing him. She shifted, and he glanced at her again, seeing her nose wrinkle and her lips pull to the side. Whatever she was dreaming, it wasn't making her the happiest camper on the block.

There had been a lot happening, and not all of it good. In fact, this trip might be the best thing in a couple of months, since Mason and Bones came home from this town that Fury was willingly driving towards now.

Myron had worked his magic on the video the Feds had of the coffeehouse, inside and out, and in the end, the only thing that said there'd been more than Morgan and Shooter on the premises was the eye-witness account from the terrified teenaged employee. *Well, and Bones' blood.* He smirked.

The man was pissed he had a hole put in him, and in his unique way of communicating had said as much. "When four men of varying skill are battling as we were in a closed environment, it is no wonder when three of the four have the bad luck to step in front of a bullet. What I do not appreciate is that it was Shooter, already dead on his feet, who had the audacity to be aiming at me at the moment his hand clutched the gun like a lover's breast. The only thing worse would be to have been injured by a ricochet from Mason's weapon."

Engaged as he'd been with things within the club, and then with the burgeoning relationship with Bethy, Fury had somehow missed the memo about what Mason had found in Florida. Not just a sister, which was trippy enough when you thought about it, but his and Bethy's mother. The story as Mason told it was convoluted. Shooter had always been unstable, his moods written off as edginess in a world where men made up their own rules. Morgan had recognized it for what it was, and when Shooter made threats against his own mother, Crystal, Morgan had taken steps to make her safe. He'd faked her death, displaying a mutilated body that somewhat resembled her in order to convince Shooter. It worked, and he'd moved both Crystal and Justine's mother, Lori, to Florida.

According to Justine, something had happened about ten years ago to break both Lori and Crystal's hold on reality. She had suspected Morgan because he visited the women regularly. Mason didn't disagree with her. That lined up with the troubles Morgan's original club was having with the cops, and both women would have had a wealth of knowledge about a variety of his crimes. Myron was researching what compounds would have been available, pairing the information with knowledge about the other things that Morgan might have had going at the same time. Mason had said he wasn't holding out much hope, but it was easy to see he had some.

Mason and Willa had brought their three kids down a couple of weeks ago to meet Crystal, and it had gone well. So well he'd agreed it was time for Bethy to make a visit. Bethy had immediately petitioned to bring Mikey, and that brought Fury back full circle to the car full of sleeping people. He smiled, reaching out a hand and placing his palm on Bethy's thigh. Just the feel of her leg under his hand was enough to have his cock fattening, and he shifted in the seat, fingers tightening. *Jesus.*

He'd stopped at a rest area, rolling up the windows and locking the doors, leaving his sleeping charges in the vehicle. It was winter, but the chill wouldn't creep in too quickly, not with the sun out like it was. Flipping his shades back into place, he started down the walk to the car, seeing Bethy standing beside it, arms over her head as she stretched. She saw him and waved with one hand, looking adorably ridiculous, and he swept her into his arms, holding tightly as he pressed his mouth to hers. Pulling back, he watched as she blinked up at him, the movement slow and sleepy. "Hey, baby. You need to pee?"

She nodded and covered her mouth with one hand, yawning wide. "Yeah. Should we wake up Michael?" He didn't release his hold, just reached out with one hand and rapped on the window next to Mikey's head, grinning as the boy sat bolt upright, looking confused. A moment later he was on the receiving end of a Mason specialty, this being one of the darkest scowls he'd seen in a while. "Guessing that's a yes," Bethy said with a giggle.

"Yeah, baby. Go, take care of business, let's get back on the road." He kissed her nose.

"Where are we?" Mikey shoved his phone in Bethy's face and her eyes crossed, then focused as she tried to look at what he was showing her. "Map shows us in a swamp."

Fury reached out and gripped Mikey's shoulder, shaking him back and forth. "Swamps are good for a lotta things." Bethy moved to Fury's side, wrapping one arm around his waist. "Like hiding a teenaged boy's body if he doesn't get a move on and go pee."

Mikey rolled his eyes and grabbed Bethy's hand. "Come on, Mom. Before he leaves us behind."

This had been happening more often than not, but every time Mikey called her that seemed to hit Bethy hard. This was no exception and her eyes closed for a moment, a soft smile on her face. "Okay, okay. I'm right behind you." Tipping her chin up she stared at Fury. "Back in a minute."

"I'll be here."

The rest of the drive was unremarkable, except for Mikey's choice in music. Even Chase's influence hadn't shifted the boy from his love of all things country music. If it wasn't boot stompin' with a twang, he had no interest. Fury found himself hiding a smile from Bethy as she lectured the boy in a way that sounded practiced, and he was certain he was listening to a conversation they'd had many times before. *This*, he thought, *this is what it means to be with someone.* Not the hot-as-hell fucking they did every night, although that was part of it. Lives together were built on this warm sense of comfort felt when someone you loved wanted to share themselves with you.

Fury changed lanes, seeing the hotel sign ahead and both Bethy and Mikey clammed up, their nervousness coming to the fore again. Fury rested his hand on Bethy's knee, squeezed once to get her attention and told her, "She's excited to meet you."

Grinning at him, eyes bright, she whispered, "I have a sister."

"That—" He turned into the parking lot. "—you do." Myron had made the arrangements, booking the hotel and reserving a private dining room for the meeting. The plan was for Fury to check them in while Bethy and Michael went to meet Mason and Justine. He'd give them a few minutes of privacy, then join them, thinking it would be easier on Justine that way. "I'll get the bags, y'all go on inside." He thumbed the button to open the trunk and leaned close, cupping his hand around the back of her neck. Pulling her in for a kiss, he told her, "You're going to do great. You have a sister."

She smiled and repeated his words back to him. "That I do."

Several hours later they'd moved their party poolside. The adults watched Michael as he did his suave best to impress a couple of girls about his age, swimming side to side across the pool underwater, and treading water beside the girls, his mouth never ceasing its movement.

"Did you know where they were keeping him?"

The sound of the kids playing mixed with the manmade waterfall at one end of the pool, working to obscure their words from casual eavesdroppers. Fury had used Myron's tool to sweep the area before they all sat down, ensuring there were no electronic devices in play, just in case.

Even with the noise and assurances of privacy, Justine still looked over her shoulder before answering Mason's question, the long-time habit kicking in. Him, in this case at least, meant Christopher Camp. The heartbreaking story she'd told over dinner had curdled Fury's stomach, and the look Mason and Bethy shared told the tale. They were both pleased for once that Morgan's paternity claim meant they weren't any kin to old man Mason.

"Irving told Daddy"—Mason grimaced, making it clear hearing about the two men who had ruled his life for so long wasn't his favorite thing. Justine continued—"that as long as Daddy left you two alone, my son would be unharmed. He gave Daddy back Luke, my nephew, and then said it would be the last thing Daddy would ever get from him." She shook her head.

"I didn't know where he was, and Daddy exhausted all his contacts unsuccessfully. Chris was just...gone." Her neck twisted and she glanced at the pool, eyes on Mikey. "After I joined the DEA, I kept quietly searching. I never found anything. As far as anyone knew, he had disappeared off the face of the earth, gone."

"How'd they get their hands on him?" Mason's question was quiet, respectful, but filled with a hard edge of anger. Fury eyed him, gauging his reaction. He suspected if old man Mason wasn't already dead, his breaths would be numbered on the smaller side of the ledger.

Justine sniffed, wiping at her nose with the back of her hand. "I was stupid. So stupid." She shook her head. "Jimmy wasn't the sticking around kind of guy. I should have known, but when we started things we were both so young. Young, stupid kids. Things got bad in California. John's wife left him. She took their daughter."

Mason supplied the name with a nod. "Eddie. Moved her girl away from the club, trying to give her a normal life."

"Yeah. Made things difficult for me and Mom, because John was always a little crazy, but after that happened, he really fell off the edge of the earth." Mason nodded again, and Fury remembered some of the stories he'd heard about those times. Death and destruction following John around, him earning his club name of Shooter by killing a friend of Mason's. Blood and pain were the watchwords for those days. "Mom knew Crystal, liked her." Justine shrugged. "The club was a different kind of life. I didn't realize how different until after I got to college and found out that not everyone had a second mother figure, both sharing a bed with your father." From the corner of his eye, he saw Bethy flinch and put that reaction aside, deciding to follow up on it later.

"Crystal had talked about Kentucky, talked about the two of you. When Jimmy and I decided to leave with Chris, we didn't have anywhere else to go. I didn't expect to find trouble waiting." Justine shivered, picking up her cardboard container of coffee and cupping her hands around it. "Crystal had been gone for a couple of years, and Mom was...she saw where things were going. Every night, it was the same thing. I'd sit nursing Chris, and she'd come in and talk, telling me I needed to go before Daddy had a need for me. Everyone is always just a tool for him, he's—" She interrupted herself and looked at Mason, bleakness bleeding from her eyes. "He's dead, right? Really, really dead?"

As an active federal agent, she hadn't claimed a relationship with Morgan, and he wasn't listed anywhere in her personnel file. Since the shooting was still at the local level, it hadn't hit her radar for a couple of days other than a ten-second blurb on the news. That meant with a little influence from a few Benjamins, Morgan's autopsy had been completed and his body released to family before she knew about his death. Mason had arranged for a quick cremation of Shooter's body, and with Myron's assistance, Morgan's as well. Justine hadn't seen the body. After watching over her shoulder for decades, it was natural for her to not trust the news.

"Yeah, honey, he is." Mason laid a hand on her shoulder, thumb and fingers digging in, holding on. "Very much dead." Fury didn't know what kind of details Justine had been given, but he doubted very much that she'd ever know Mason's had been the finger on the trigger.

"It's just hard to wrap my head around." She sounded apologetic, and Mason shook his head.

"Nothing to worry about. If you want the ashes, I'm happy to hand the urn over, honey." His gaze landed on Fury as he said, "I got no love for the man. Got no need to have anything around to remind me of him." He looked at Bethy, then at Mikey, and finally at Justine. "I got only to look at the two of you, and my boy or yours"—he nodded at Bethy—"to see the mark he left on us. None of us are hard on the eyes, 'cept me." Everyone laughed. "Let that be his only legacy." Fury saw the fabric of her shirt move and knew Mason had squeezed her shoulder again. "How'd they get Chris?"

Her chin dropped. "Jimmy missed...pretty much everything to do with the club. He fell into a group of friends in Lexington who wanted to start one. He reached out to Daddy, who granted whatever approvals were needed. It wasn't long before Ezra—" She stopped talking and stared at Fury when he reacted to his father's name. "You know him?"

He nodded, glancing at Mason and Bethy. "We all do." He hoped they wouldn't make him claim the man, not until she got everything out without filtering anything.

She stared at him for a moment longer, then picked up her story. "Ezra and Irving came to the house. I didn't have anything to do with the club. Had no desire after what I'd seen in California. I'd just passed my GED and was starting to work on college applications. Chris was in his high chair in the kitchen and I went to answer the door. They stood on the stoop and wanted to talk religion. I didn't know who they were, didn't know that was the man Daddy would rage about for days on end. Had no idea. There was a noise, so small I nearly missed it, but I turned to look in time to see the back of a man walking out my kitchen door. I had the high chair where I could see it from where I stood." The coffee in her hands trembled, threatening to splash out, and Fury plucked it from her grip with one hand, the other closing around her frozen fingers. She didn't seem to notice, continuing with her story.

"The high chair was empty. I screamed and started running, but they grabbed me. Irving put his hand over my mouth and told me if I knew what was good for me, I'd shut up and listen." She paused, breaths coming fast, mouth open as she panted through the pain of the memory. "'You want your boy to live, you say nothing.' His mouth was by my ear, on it. His breath smelled like a septic tank. I smell that in my dreams, sometimes. Foul and dank. Like death. I always thought Irving smelled like death. I didn't know who he was then. Not then. But I learned, oh yeah, I learned. 'You want your boy to live? You're a good momma? Tell Justice this evens the scales. You go to the cops, your boy dies. You do what I tell you to do, and you'll do it without him in your arms, but knowing he's warm and breathing somewhere. Tell Justice this evens the scales.' I didn't know what that meant. Didn't know why he'd want me to give Daddy a message. Why he'd even know Daddy." Her posture had changed as she'd spoken, back rounding so she was hunched over in the chair, protecting herself from a danger decades in the past.

"I knew, though. Knew better than to call the cops. He didn't even have to tell me, I just knew. I called Daddy and told him. Told him everything. Told him how my baby boy was crying as they took him away.

Crying out for me, wanting his mother. All my daddy told me was to stick tight, stay close to the phone, and not tell anyone anything. I did that. Not sleeping, not eating, even when Jimmy tried to force me, I stayed with my hand on the phone, waiting for his call. Five days later he called. Five days." She looked up into Mason's eyes. "Do you know what it's like to lose part of your soul for five days? For twenty-five years? He called, and all my daddy had for me was sorry." Her voice changed, pitching lower in register. "He said, 'I'm sorry, sweetheart. He's alive, that's all I can tell you.' I asked him, what can I do? How do I get my boy back, my son? He didn't have any answers for me. I did everything I could think of, short of going to the cops. Jimmy left. He told me I was obsessed and he needed a wife, not a scarecrow mourning something that never should have been born. He said that to me. Chris is our son. How could a father say that to the mother of his child?" She took a deep breath, mouth covered by one shaking hand.

"I didn't find him. You know that much. Never found him. After a while I told myself he was dead. That was better than wondering what was happening to him. I'd looked for a long time, asked all kinds of questions. So I knew, better than most, what kind of outfit Irving had on his mountain. His kingdom, where he thought he could do anything he wanted and no one could touch him. Better dead than there, that's what I told myself." She leaned away from the table, taking long moments straightening her body out, shoving her shoulders against the seatback.

"In college I focused on criminal justice. Everyone always laughed, Justine studying justice. I wanted to make a difference, to help some young mother who had her child stolen, help a child find their way home. Those were the worst dreams, you know? When I'd dream of a five-year-old or ten-year-old Chris crying, screaming out for me, looking for me as desperately as I was trying to find him. I got assigned to the Florida office after I graduated Quantico. About three years later was the first time Daddy showed up. I thought I was clear of him. I thought we were clear. The next time he came, Jimmy's dad was with him. I learned Jimmy had a wife and three kids. He'd moved on from his failure with me. Mr. Camp's words meant to hurt, and they did. That's the last time I saw Daddy."

"Why did you let Suches go?" Fury asked his question slowly, taking time to formulate the right words to hit the tone he wanted. "We've heard from his associates that you had him on house arrest at one point, and then arrested him again, several weeks later. Both times he was released, and when I look for the papers on the actions, I not only can't find a warrant, but I can't find any kind of record of his arrests."

Justine's gaze landed on him, heavy with anger. Not at him, but at something in the past. *Suches? Morgan?* Fury waited.

"I have a good team." Her mouth drew sideways, the smile as familiar as anything because it was one he'd seen on Bethy's face more than once. Wry and crooked, with Bethy it meant she was being self-deprecating. "My team had word that Suches was teamed up with another man, Gordon Tucker—" Once again she interrupted herself to stare at Fury, his reaction unmistakable. He carefully unclenched his fist from around the crumpled cup, shaking drops of liquid from his fingers. "You know him, too, don't you?" He nodded.

"We'll talk about that later." With that promise, she continued, "So Suches and Tucker were teamed up and seemed to be set to stir trouble all across the south. Suches connections in Mexico were tightly associated with one of the Mexican drug cartels, and he was bringing in all kinds of drug components that were then processed into one of a dozen designer drugs. They'd sell to US dealers, who would in turn sell to the local addicts. Tucker had different connections. He was in tight with Camp and his ilk, including my father. The two men together were building a business that threatened the stability of communities all across Florida's panhandle."

She made a noise, and he caught the tail end of an eye roll. "We federal types know we can't kill the drug trade. So we try to unofficially regulate it in lots of ways. Tucker was disrupting everything we'd worked out with the locals about safety and quantities. I wanted to see if there were vulnerabilities I hadn't considered, but I knew pulling Tucker in would get people involved I didn't want to see. Namely Daddy and Camp. So, I picked Suches to discuss things with. It was a waste. He didn't know anything of note. Tucker, however, had all the connections we needed to break. I never did get my hands on him. Last I heard he'd retreated to Mexico, but relations between the countries has deteriorated to the point I can't even pick up the phone and call folks I used to work with weekly."

"You think Tucker's in Mexico?" Mason's question sounded offhand, but Fury was looking at him and could see the tension in his face.

"I know he is. Border agents on this side of the line are all primed to tell me when he moves back across to US soil. I've not heard anything." She shrugged. "So, he's still in Mexico."

***

"It's just so weird."

Fury was toweling off after a shower when Bethy's comment came from the master bedroom of the suite they'd booked at a local hotel. Michael was in the adjoining bedroom, talking on his phone and doing whatever it was teenaged kids did these days. *These days*. He snorted. *I sound like an old man*. Staring into the mirror over the sink he focused on his face in a way he normally didn't take time to do. Tanned and weathered skin; wrinkles at the corners of his eyes because he didn't like sunglasses, preferring to squint into the sun instead. Reaching up, he ran his fingers through his hair. *No gray*. He snorted. *Not yet*. Smoothing his beard down, he examined it and found only the same deep red color he'd borne all his life.

"I look at Justine—and man, that name's a mouthful, don't you think—and she looks just like Davy. Different mothers, but you'd never know it. I always wanted a sister, and now I have one full grown. So weird."

"Mmhmm." He picked up the shaving cream and stared at his face again. *What'll she think when I'm old and gray?* There were only four years between them, which amounted to a drop in the bucket. Tipping his chin up, he squirted lather in his hand, then smoothed it on his neck. He was just starting to work it into the skin when his hand was slapped away. Backing up quickly, he turned to face Bethy and saw she was scowling at him, razor in hand.

"You," she leaned closer as she shoved the razor behind her back, "are not shaving—" With every word her voice increased in volume until by the end she was shouting. "Your beard!"

"Baby, no." He shook his head, laughing. "I'm just cleanin' up my neck. I'm not shaving."

"You're not?" She looked abashed, then pushed, "Promise?"

"Promise." He reached around her and plucked the razor from her fingers. "I like it too much. It makes me look…like me."

It was there and gone before he could isolate the expression, but he saw it. A fleeting change in her face that told of pain and anger, betrayal and hopelessness. *I put that there.* In that moment, he knew she was remembering him as Derek, scruffy and bald, and playing her in a way that had left a deep and lasting scar. Written in that short-lived expression was the story he most feared for their future and he knew. Down to his bones, he knew. She wasn't over it, hadn't forgiven him. No redemption.

I can work for it, he promised himself. *I will* work for it. He was willing to do whatever it took to earn her trust.

She was worth it.

***

Bethany

Absently threading fingers through her hair, Bethy encountered a snag and flinched, uttering a soft, "Ow."

"What's wrong, baby?" Gabe's question coincided with a flexing squeeze of her knee, covered for the last hundred miles by his large hand.

Once they'd gotten together, there were two things she'd realized about Gabe. More than two, she mused, working the knot free as she smiled at him, saying, "Hit a tangle." His return smile was so tender if she'd been standing, it would have weakened her knees. One of the soul-deep truths she'd come to believe was that he loved her. Devotion was present in his every action, each gesture or word reinforced her decision to take a chance on them. His love was both emotional and tactile in equal measures. If she were near, she would find him touching her, holding her hand or stroking her skin with his fingertips. She wondered at times if it were as much to assure himself they were real, as if he still couldn't believe his luck.

The other thing that stood out was how he watched her every move. More than a focus on her comfort, the level of attention could be intimidating. *Like today*, she thought. She knew he saw everything, even reactions she'd rather hide. *Same as Davy*. She turned to the window. It wasn't constant, wasn't even every day, but things still tripped her up. Between life in the holler and what had happened in Utah, she had her share of demons. *Between Gabe and Davy, I'll be confronting them until every fear is slain*. She had been at breakfast this morning when Davy cornered her with questions.

"Hey, sis." Bethy looked up, fork finishing its path to her mouth as Davy's hand landed on her shoulder. "Sleep okay?"

"Mmhmm." She smiled at him as he angled himself into a chair at her table. "You?"

"Yeah, decent. Your boys bein' lag-a-beds this morning?" She smiled at this statement, more evidence that the changes in her life were the new normal. My boys. He turned a coffee cup over, setting it upright as the waitress showed up with a half-full carafe. "Just the coffee, honey, thanks." He waited until she'd moved away. "What was your deal yesterday? You had a turn when Jussy was talking about livin' in the MC clubhouse out west."

"Jussy?" Bethy grinned. "I like it. She know you renamed her?"

"She ain't complained." He sipped his coffee with a slight smile.

"Fits better than Justine." Bethy wielded her knife and fork, cutting the waffle on her plate into bite-size pieces.

"Yeah, that's a mouthful."

"That's what I told Gabe." She ate in silence for a moment. "It's good she's so cool with everything." He made a soft sound of agreement. "Can I ask you something?"

"Sure, honey. Anything."

"Did you know John well?" She'd never gotten to meet him, something she'd realized yesterday as Jussy—Bethy gave an internal snort at her easy adoption of that name—talked to Davy about their father. Never met either man. But I was entirely too acquainted with Judge. If those men had been the same, maybe her lack of knowledge was a blessing. "Yesterday, it sounded like you were friends once."

"Not really, not ever." He set his cup down.

"Do you think Mom was happier out there? If Justice was our father, why would she leave us with...in Kentucky?" Bethy's emotions were tangled when she thought about the things revealed over the past few weeks. Jussy was her sister because they shared a father, but John was her full brother. Like Davy.

"What'd you ask her, Mason? Baby, what was that thought?"

Bethy looked up, startled by the questions. Gabe stood beside her chair, glowering down at Davy. She'd left him dozing in bed a half an hour ago, expecting to take him a cup of coffee back to the room. "Morning."

He cupped the back of her head, running his fingers through her hair. She tipped her lips up and he bent to brush a kiss, pressing his mouth to hers. "Morning, Beth." He kissed her again. "Now, what was that thought?"

"We were talking about Jussy and John." Gabe nodded as he settled into the chair next to Bethy. Davy reached out and clasped his hand in a warrior's grip. Davy said, "I was just asking what bugged her yesterday."

"Yeah, I saw that one, too."

Of course you did. Bethy rolled her eyes. "You're both imagining things."

"Not fuckin' likely." Davy finished his coffee, pushing back from the table. "I'm out. Got an early meeting. Leavin' her in your capable hands, brother."

"I got this."

Lips brushed the crown of her head. "Y'all travel safe, yeah?"

"We will." Gabe turned over the coffee cup at his setting us Davy walked towards the exit. "Baby, tell me what's bothering you."

The waitress came and left and they sat in silence for a few moments. Bethy knew it was only a matter of time and Gabe would be back questioning her. Dog with a bone. "Jussy," he made a noise of amusement and she grinned, "was raised a world away from where I grew up, but in some ways our lives were a lot alike. It's just weird to realize. We share a father, which means the man I thought of as my daddy all my life…wasn't. Her mother was friends with my mother, while both were with the same man." She tipped her head, watching his expression for any sense of censure. "Did you know Daddy had a series of women when I was little?" He shook his head, lips pursing. "Yeah. I remember this time when there were three in the house at once. They were all best friends, no lie. Like they had to band together to survive the kind of hell the compound was back then."

"Does it bother you about old man Mason not bein' your daddy?"

She shook her head. "I think it makes it better, actually. For me, at least. Davy said he didn't think Irving ever knew. I'd like to believe he did. That would put things into a better perspective, you know? I always wondered how someone who said they loved me could cause so much pain. Like, intentionally set out to hurt me. Makes a body wonder how true their love was. If there was love at all." Appetite gone, she pushed her plate towards him. "You know what? I'm done." The look of confusion, fear, and sorrow that crawled across his features froze her for a moment. "Oh, Gabe. No, honey. I'm talking about Daddy." The breath he released held so much fear. She reached across and grabbed his hand, felt it turn in her grip, Gabe holding on with all his strength. "Baby, I will never leave you. I love you."

"I did things, Beth. Hurt you."

"We're past that, promise." His gaze held hers, steady and patient. "I know what it cost you. You've paid in spades, so much. I know who's in my bed, Gabe. I know that man, and I trust him with my heart. With everything I am, I trust him. I wish you could trust me."

Beth glanced over to watch Gabe driving. His command of the car was confident, easy. He must have felt her gaze because he tipped his head, looking at her for a moment. "Baby?"

She smiled broadly, leaning close as she covered his hand with one of hers, pressing his fingers into her knee, sliding their joined hands higher on her leg. She kissed the corner of his mouth, nibbling gently. Then, keeping her voice quiet and soft out of deference for her sleeping son, she reminded him of something he already knew, but she'd be willing to help reinforce every day for the rest of their lives if necessary. "I love you, Gabriel Ledbetter. I wanna laugh along with you as our children play, and live with you until I'm old and gray. I love you, that's all."

"Oh, is that all?" He met her lip brush with his mouth, kissing her softly while his fingertips stroked the tender flesh inside her thigh, raising goose bumps on her arms. When she pulled back there was such a look of peace and relief on his face she buried her face against his shoulder to hide her tears.

"Yeah, that's everything," she choked out as he chuckled. *God, I love this man.* He was worth everything they'd gone through to be together. "Everything."

Keyword: Redemption

Fury

"What in the fuck do you mean he rolled out?" Fury gritted his teeth and reminded himself for the hundredth time he was on video and couldn't react the way he wanted, by rolling his eyes and staring at the ceiling while waiting on a response that made sense. "Rolled out where, exactly? You—and I know we had this conversation, Opie—were supposed to be keeping him locked down with escorts. What the fuck happened?"

"What happened is Spider's a grown-ass man who decided he didn't want a babysitter. And yeah, he figured that out about a day into it, so I should count myself lucky that he let us stroll along this long without bolting." Opie pressed his palms flat to the table in front of the laptop camera, and Fury figured that was his version of suppressing an emotional reaction. "Not a one of us would have stood it this long, and you know it. Weeks and weeks since we got Juanita and Mela home, and nothing to point to that said he had fuck all to do with what Diamond did."

"Nothing except the Florida boys who said they'd seen him and Diamond with Lalo, and you know how deep Lalo was with Deacon and

Morgan. Deacon was Diamond's old man, brother. Lalo an enemy." Fury gestured to the side, knowing Chismoso was within range of the camera. "Chismoso recognized a picture of the man, which tells us all that he'd been around more than once. We needed to keep Spider locked down, and now he's in the wind." He shook his head. "So that means you need to find him, like yesterday. Jesus." He turned from the camera, giving the people on the other end a view of his patch as he faced the group filling the back of the room. *Mason is a fuck of a lot better at handling this shit.* "Bear, get on the app and call Myron, tell him to join the call." He ran through other members and officers in his head. "Gunny, call Bones and Tater." He whirled and stared at the image on the screen. "Get Hurley in there. We cannot be assured of anyone's safety at this point, but the most at risk are the ones already under this man's eye. Who's with Juanita?"

"Devil." Opie had a quick response, and that told Fury he'd been thinking the same thoughts. "They're in town shopping. I've already recalled them."

A window popped up on the screen and the video resolved into a close-up of Myron. Fury stared because the backdrop wasn't familiar. "You on your phone, brother?"

"Yeah, I'm out. Bear texted this was critical, so here I am." Voices off camera filtered through and Myron grimaced. The phone jiggled a moment, then the sounds went away, and his face turned to the side, mouth moving soundlessly. A shadow crossed the wall behind him, then a man with short blond hair entered the image and exited through an open door, closing it behind him. The phone jiggled again and Myron said, "I'm good here now. Sorry about that."

Before Fury could respond, another window popped up with the iconic club patch on a flag hanging in the background. That was the meeting room behind the bar at the Mother clubhouse in Chicago. Off screen someone made a sound that was a cross between a growl and a laugh. "I got no idea, brother. Myron usually does this shit. I think I got connected, anything on the screen?" A second voice, this one distinctively Bones, said, "I see only blackness, my friend. Clearly you have not worked the device correctly."

Myron grinned and rolled his eyes. Fury watched him, thinking, *Why does he get away with that shit, and I never would be able to?* Myron said loudly, "Turn on the TV, Tater. You can use the little remote with the word TV on the back, or just punch the red button along the bottom right-hand edge."

A red blob came into the window, the color gradually resolving into a view of Tater's beard seen from the side. "I don't see a red button."

"One moment. I have it in hand." Bones stepped around the table and into the foreground with his hand outstretched towards the camera. "Ah. There we are. Tater, you are in the way of the camera. Move back, *por favor*?"

Fury shook his head. "It's like a comedy show in here. Opie, you get Hurley in there yet?"

"Yo, boss." A blond head popped into view over Opie's shoulder. "Present." It seemed Opie's habits were rubbing off on the freshly-patched man.

"Now that we've got a full house, let's get back to it." Fury stared at the camera, hoping he looked as serious as he felt. Being on video like this was weird. "Diamond and Lalo had friends, one of those friends looks to be Spider. Myron found some information we've been sitting on, because it was unclear what it meant. Years ago, Spider was down in Mexico and got involved in a drug trade that went bad. He somehow skated free, but in the years since, he's made regular trips down country. Always alone, and always short, like he didn't want to be gone long enough to be remarked on. Opie's told us how his wife died, and the things he said when he went out of his mind. The fact she died on the border bridge when she had no reason to be there is enough for me, honestly. I think Spider's under someone's thumb and has been working both sides of the river. Is it hurting the club? I got no fuckin' idea. But I do know him not fronting it out when Danger got snuffed down in Mexico is troubling. Him not coming forward and talking about it when Mela was found and fostered at Watcher's is troubling. And finally, him not coming clean about any connections when fucking Lalo had Bella and the Soldiers' entire club was tearing up Mexico looking for her, that's beyond troubling. I got a list of things that are oddities, one me, Opie, and Bones have put together, and I'm happy to go through them, but wanted to have all the players here before I did so."

"Where's Mason?" Myron's face was blank as he asked the question, but it still rankled Fury.

"He's having a goddamned sitdown right now with the boys from Florida who brought news that Spider'd been seen with Lalo and Diamond in Adkens back before all the shit went down. That's where the fuck Mason is right now." It was the second trip the local dominant had made to Fort Wayne, and Mason was feeling them out about an acquisition. They were looking for something, no doubt, but what it was seemed hard to pick from the threads of their stories. Mason had sent Chismoso out with the information and instructions for Fury to start this conversation. "You got a different question sittin' in your mouth, Myron?" *Always have to prove myself.*

Myron shook his head. "No, I'm just failing to see the urgency here. Spider and Diamond were a common sight. You sure they were seen with Lalo?"

A chair scraped behind him, and Fury stepped to the side, letting the camera focus in on Chismoso. "I am certain it's urgent because Mason made it so." Not a ringing endorsement, because he and Chismoso had shared a patch at one point, leaving separately, but for the same basic reasons. "And what you haven't heard is that Spider has left Las Cruces, headed south. He was last seen crossing the bridge. Alone, when he hadn't been granted permission to leave the country. Opie, this is your territory. I think it's time for you to pick up the story."

Opie's head tipped down, and it looked as if he were staring at his hands. Without looking up, he spoke. "Some of this is shit Myron dug up, some if it's from conversations me or one of the brothers had with Watcher over the years. Some of it is shit I've seen. I have something that looks like a laundry list." He reached out and clicked something on the laptop and his screen split, showing a text document to the side. "Easier if I don't have to read it, but I can if it's hard to see."

Fury scanned the text, seeing everything he'd expected, and one extra thing. "Cameras?"

Nodding, Opie said, "We never found out who planted the cameras in Watcher's place. Myron helped out by tracking the feed to a truck." He looked up. "Y'all have heard that story, right? Speak up if you haven't." He paused a moment, then continued, "I added that one while we were waiting on everyone to connect. The timeline matches up. Spider was in Florida, and fuck, I didn't even remember him going. Diamond had headed down for some family thing and broke down. Spider took the truck and trailer, hauled his bike back for him. A week before I found the cameras and those were fresh installs. He had full access, man. Watcher never wanted any of his men to feel anything other than welcome, so it didn't matter who was here or what time we'd show up, the door was always open."

"The roadside drive-by." Bones spoke up. "Spider was not with anyone when Watcher was fired upon?" Opie shook his head. "That is troubling, because as Watcher recounted it for me, the club entire came to his assistance, riding the wrong way on the highway like they were set to rescue the prince from harm."

"Our king, and yeah, we did." Opie made a face. "Except for Spider."

"When Machos started breathing down your neck, wasn't he the man sent down to Mexico to talk to Carlos Estavez?" Chismoso hadn't retaken his seat, was still standing, leaning one hip against the table. "When looking for Mela after Watcher's death, who did you send to Mexico to my village?"

"Spider, among others." Opie sighed, and the cursor on the screen moved, a slow tapping translated to a line of text added to the document.

"I think we're missing something." Myron's voice was low and intense. "We cannot tar and feather the man based on a list of supposed coincidences. He's rolled out, gone south. There's nothing innately dangerous in that." The picture on his video shifted, and it looked like he'd been about to gesture, aborting the movement. "Let's see where he goes, and who he talks to. Let's see what's real and not ghost stories told around a table in a dark room."

"How do you propose we do that?" Fury glared at the screen. "The man isn't in the country as of two hours ago, so exactly how do we accomplish that?"

Myron grinned. "Chismoso, you remember how I always knew where you were? And I showed you the tracker?" A grunt from beside Fury was Myron's only answer. "It's in the top drawer of the desk behind you. Get it out, turn it on." Chismoso disappeared, and Myron squinted for a moment, nearly closing his eyes as his lips moved. "He's number fourteen. Acquire the signal for number fourteen."

Holding a small device shaped like a brick, Chismoso reappeared beside Fury. He fiddled with a knob on the side, then tapped a button. "Okay. Got it. What now?"

"Tell me where he is. The dot on the screen is Spider. His phone died last week, so I took the opportunity to send him one of the club phones. We all know they're tracked, but he might have forgotten."

Chismoso angled the screen so Fury could see, too. The dot was holding steady, not blinking or moving, but the map was zoomed in so close only a road crossroads was visible, the numbers showing not meaning anything to Fury. Chismoso tapped a button on the side once, twice, and the image zoomed out until the shape of the locale was clear. Fury looked up at the screen, staring into Myron's eyes. "Mexico."

"What do you want to do, boss?" Opie's gaze didn't waver, holding as steady as the blip on the screen representing Spider. He was looking to Fury for an answer. Fury glanced around the room to find every man's eyes on him, no question in their mind who was the shot caller for this gig. *Maybe most of the problems I see are in my mind.* Maybe Myron hadn't meant anything earlier. Maybe. *Maybe not.*

"I want you to roll to the bridge and hold. Wait. We see him moving your way, we'll get word to you. Intercept and detain, take him to the clubhouse by whatever means you deem necessary." Opie winced and Fury remembered that only months ago he'd been the second in command, standing alongside Spider at most functions. "Go easy if you can, but once you get him, you keep him."

***

"How long ago?" Fury held the phone to his ear, waiting.

"Ten minutes. He's a fuckin' mess, brother. Not sure how he's breathin'."

"Get him there alive." He disconnected the call, noting absently that his hands were shaking. Swallowing hard, he dialed another number and waited. The call connected and before they could say anything, he started talking. "Spider's back. Glad I put the Las Cruces guys at the bridge, and even more glad they took a cage for some unknown fucking reason. Spider's back, but he's bad off, Mason. He brought home a package, though. A fucking package that we've been looking for a long time."

Taking a breath, he paused, and Mason waited, the pause pregnant with tension.

"Tucker. He fucking brought fucking Tucker back, man."

Drawling the words slowly, Mason asked, "Upright, or planted?"

"Fucking upright, brother. No clue why he'd risk so much."

"Tucker unscathed?" Still slow, with the distinctive Kentucky accent, Mason questioned him. "Spider fucked up, but Tucker breathin'? That don't make sense."

"No, Tucker's down, too. Opie's getting them both to that church they deal with there in El Paso. He's already rolling medics. They'll meet them there. Juanita's on her way, too. She wouldn't hear no for an answer, and the boys there, they won't put hands on the queen, brother. You know how it is."

"Oh, yeah. I do."

Noise in the background resolved to a child's rising laughter, broken off in a scream for "More, Ace, more." Mason's voice sounded like he'd covered the receiver, but Fury could still hear him. "Take 'em to the living room, Chase. Thanks, son." Back in the speaker, he asked, "We got time to get there before things go south?"

"No idea, brother. I'd vote we wait for them to get situated, and see from that."

"Sounds like a plan." Mason paused, then said Fury's name like a question. "Fury?"

"Yeah, brother?'

"Tell 'em to make sure they keep Tucker incapacitated. He's a fuckin' cockroach, always coming back to life when we least expect it. Tell 'em to keep him down, yeah?"

"Will do." Mason was gone, the line nothing but dead air even before he finished saying those words. He tapped out a text to Opie, knowing if he was on his bike he'd get it as soon as they stopped. "Fuck." He spoke to the empty room, then shoved at a chair, rolling it on a collision course with the wall. "*Fuck.*"

***

Mason

Mason strode up the hallway, Fury beside him. Their strides were in sync, boot heels striking in the same cadence, as if this were a maneuver they'd practiced. The church in El Paso was quiet, so each footfall rebounded down the hall, bending back on them in an echo. Their plane had landed an hour ago, and the van Opie had sent to pick them up would be waiting in the parking lot for as long as needed.

Spider was still alive, even if the off-the-clock doc their EMT had brought in didn't understand how. Alive and mending, picking up strength over the handful of days he'd been laid up in the rough infirmary the church ran for the club. Originally the church had partnered with the Southern Soldiers, something Watcher had set up years ago, an arrangement Juanita fostered, volunteering much of her time here. Human trafficking victims passed through here frequently, brought in by the club as they patrolled what they considered their territory, or by others who knew of the mission. Mason had been here before, when Danger hadn't been long gone, helping Watcher keep his club together as best he could.

They were on their way to see Spider, Mason agreeing with Fury that a face-to-face would help clear up much of the muddy confusion spread by the man's behavior. Mason hadn't liked the man for a while. Not since Spider had been a vocal holdout when Watcher had been balancing on the edge of his decision to bring the Soldiers into the Rebels. Mason still believed Spider was loyal to his old patch, even if he'd put a Rebel skull on his back.

Tucker wasn't here. He'd been put back together more quickly and was waiting for Mason's pleasure up in Las Cruces. The bunker under the barn on Watcher's property was perfect for that kind of imprisonment, deep enough to stay cool even in the heat of high summer, and shallow enough to be accessible. Tucker knew who was coming, and Mason didn't expect their conversation to go easy. He'd already talked to Slate and Bear, spoken with Bones and Shades. Bringing Fury with him was a calculated statement to the entire membership, but an even stronger message for his officers.

Their treatment of Fury hadn't escaped his notice, and even if he understood the idea of a change at the national level was unsettling, he'd lose Fury if he didn't get it under control. So this trip had three goals. Settle the members in his Las Cruces chapter in a way that left no questions about loyalty or responsibility. He knew he'd have to deal with Tucker, and while he didn't relish the idea, he was ready. The man belonged to a different kind of crew, always had, the kind of outlaws who used the label as an excuse to do whatever the fuck they wanted. Mason knew differently, as did every man he trusted and called brother. An outlaw had to ponder their words even more carefully after taking on the weight of that one-percent diamond. When every move is scrutinized and cataloged, their words recorded and held against them, and all deeds possible leverage against every brother—those in the outlaw community learned fast how to hold their tongues.

That was the first goal. The second was to provide express approval for Fury's handling of the situation Mason had thrust him into. He could have stepped out of the meet with the Florida boys, easy. He could have made the calls, dealt with the few he would have involved, and been back at the table in less than an hour. No insult was given to Sparks and his crew. But that wouldn't have lent Fury the opportunity to take the reins. Mason had watched the recording and talked to Myron. It had come down to the two of them, and Myron had bowed to Fury's words. He hadn't liked it, but he'd done it, knowing it was what Mason would want. Myron's loyalty wasn't misplaced, and Mason treasured how the man felt about who is in charge. But Myron's attitude was similar to what Spider had done months ago. Fuck of it was, as soon as Mason called him on it, Myron had seen it, face flushing red in embarrassment. So the second goal was to cut off at the knees anyone else who harbored the same doubts.

The third goal was to convince Fury of the same thing. Mason understood him better than Fury knew. They'd both come up through the clubs the hardest way, with blood and bone paving their paths. When a man winds up at the top of the heap using nothing but wits and fists, it's hard for him to believe he deserves to be there. When a man doubts himself, he begins to see doubt all around him, a vicious circle of uncertainty. The leader of a club like the Rebels can't afford to be uncertain. Not when mens' lives depended on them making the right call every time. So Mason's third goal would see Fury doubled down on himself, transforming the long journey he'd made into a grand win at the end.

They neared the only door with light seeping into the hallway, and Mason's ears caught a gravel-filled muttering, the corner of his mouth curling up into a half grin. A woman's voice responded to whatever the man had said, and Juanita's crisp scold was clearly spoken. "No, you do not need to be on your feet. What you need is to stay where you are. So stubborn. It will not kill you to lie here, but it might for you to keep fighting like you are. I'll tie you down if I have to, Spider. Do not test me."

"Jesus," Fury muttered. "She even sounds like Watcher."

"What the fuck are you doin', woman?" The closer they drew to the open door, the more they could hear. "Leave off with that shit. Dammit, stop it."

"Not until you cease your stupidity, Anthony. Daena would be cross with you if she saw you like this." There was silence for a moment, then Juanita said quietly, "I wasn't thinking, Spider. I am sorry."

"She's been gone a long time, 'Nita. Don't worry about it." Spider sounded subdued, his voice shaking slightly.

Rounding the door, Mason didn't slow when the condition of the man in the bed hit him, didn't allow any shock or concern to show on his face. He just walked up and stuck out his hand, reaching down to grip Spider's thumb. It was about the only part of the man that wasn't covered in gauze, tape, or plaster.

Glaring up at him, Spider twitched his thumb, either in greeting or an attempt to throw off Mason's hold. "This is what it takes to get your ass back out here, Prez? One of your own laid up and dying?"

"You're hardly dying, Spider," Juanita scolded, rising from the chair near his bedside. "You were, at one point. But it was more passive, less active. You only coded once, they tell me. I'm certain there are still ribs unbroken." She reached out, rounding the end of the bed, arms going around Mason's waist from the side. "I can fix that for you. Welcome, Mason. Welcome."

He released Spider's thumb and twisted, pulling her around for a proper hug. "Hey, pretty lady. How are you holding up? I didn't know you'd added nursing to your extensive skillset."

She pulled back without answering, and he let her, watching as she made her way to Fury. "Hello, Gabe. I'm so glad you're here." Her hold on him was just as tight, and Mason watched Fury's eyes close when he wrapped his arms around her in response. "Family shouldn't be strangers." Mason turned away, giving them a moment as he studied Spider.

He'd been beaten, that much was clear from looking at him. Fractured arm, broken ribs, and most of those were likely from before someone was humping on his chest to try and get his heart restarted. Burns, a lot of them, over his torso, neck, and face. Bruises, blooming and dying, those fading to yellow gave him a timeline. Whatever had happened to Spider, it had begun nearly as soon as he crossed the bridge.

"Got your fill of looking?" A mouthful of cotton couldn't have muffled Spider's words more than they were. Mason winced, feeling pained just listening to him. "Well? You want the story or you come here to put on a striped skirt and play doctor?"

"You up to tellin' me a story?" He needed to hear it from the source. They knew what Myron had pieced together, but most everyone's networks fell apart when they hit the border, and tech geeks weren't any different. Chismoso fed him most of what they knew, him and a surprising source: Silly. The tattoo artist from Chicago still had family back in Mexico, and the memories of Estavez and his men ran long in the village where she'd grown up. "I could cop a squat and give it a listen, old man."

"You realize if I could get out of this bed, I'd whip your ass, right?" Mason was shocked to see a smirk lift a corner of the man's mouth, knowing it was as close to a grin as he'd ever seen. "It's not a long story, won't take long, Juanita. Stop your frowning. Go get a coffee or something."

She moved from behind Mason to the other side of the bed, reclaiming her seat. "Stubborn." Spider turned from her to look at Mason, and the plea on his face was clear. He couldn't say what he needed to with her there. Mason nodded, but before he could say anything, Juanita sighed. "I know that look, Mason. I'll take a walk, go to the donation room and sort some clothing for our friend here. The ones he came to us in were tatters, and if he's as focused on leaving as he seems to be, it'll save me some time very soon. I'll give you thirty minutes." She stood and rested her hand on Spider's shoulder. "Don't do anything stupid, okay?"

By unspoken agreement, they waited for the door to close behind her before anyone moved. Spider shifted on the bed and winced. "I got word

Tucker was in Juarez. Bold as brass, hanging out in a bar where I go sometimes. I get on with Duck, talk to him a bit. He saved our Bella. Man is worth his weight if you ask me. His woman still struggles with that gal's death."

Mason nodded. "Essa. There're a few of us who do."

"Yeah. It's harder when the young are taken from us." Spider gestured towards the rolling table nearby. "Water." Fury slid it towards him, then must have realized Spider couldn't hold the cup and picked it up, angling the straw so the old man could sip. "Sucked in smoke and gas, hell on the throat." He waved a hand. "So Tucker was there, not ten minutes from US soil, and I went to collect him. He owed us a death, at least one. Time to pay the piper. What I told him when I saw him. Then they were on me. Hadn't seen 'em, waiting in the shadows around the room. Cowards. Fucker laughed, but I got my licks in before they torqued me down." Spider shook his head. "Hauled me to a ranch in the middle of fucking nowhere. You'll never guess who was there." He paused, and Mason shook his head.

"Not playin' guessing games, old man."

"Yeah, I wouldn't either. I found out I nurtured one traitor and harbored another for years. Decades. Pike." He turned his eyes towards Fury. "Shoulda killed him instead of cuttin' him. Learn from your mistakes." His gaze swung back to Mason. "He had friends with him. They sounded a lot like you."

"Men from Kentucky?" Mason took the cup from Fury and held it close, letting Spider's hand rest against his, holding steady as he drank. "Is that what you mean?"

"Yeah. Sounded like you." What they could see of his face paled, expression turning sad. "Miss Watch, man. More than I'd expect, given how we fought that last year. If I could take it back, take all of it back, I would. New York minute, yank it back and eat it down. Eat my words because he was right."

Lifting his chin, he stared at Mason for a minute. "You'll take care of that assmuncher for me, yeah? He did most of this. Never forget the sound of his laugh when he poured the gasoline. Hear it in my head now." His head dropped back on the pillow and he took a deep breath. "Pike. Something's wrong in that man, Mason. He feels like Lalo to me."

"Did you put the cameras on Watcher's house?" Spider jerked in the bed, head shaking back and forth. "Did you shoot at Watcher on the highway?" Another headshake. "How did you know Lalo?"

"You were a kid when you took over the Rebels. Renamed, we all knew the club still lived, didn't matter what you called it. For years, I waited for Deacon to take it back. Years. He didn't, though. Instead, he visited his brand of asshat on every fuckin' club in the south. His touch spanned from Florida to California, and most of his preachin' was against you." Mason knew this already and lifted his hand to cut the man off, Spider beat him to it. "Let me have my say, dammit. You accusing me of bullshit, you need to know what happened. I didn't do a thing you've listed, not one of them. Watcher was my family. Loved the man. Would never have done a thing that could have hurt him." Mason settled on his heels and nodded. "Deacon came through here a few times, Las Cruces, I mean. After the first one, Watcher barred the doors against him. But I'd meet him and lift a bottle. Us old guys have to stick together. Kids don't know what it took to be an outlaw back in the day, and we'd talk about shit like that. Talk about rallies we'd hit, places we'd seen. Was only a few years ago Deacon brought Lalo with him. Suches hated everything Deacon told him to, and that included you. That was the last time I sat a meal with Deacon, because his brand of bullshit was so deep he was drowning in it. Lalo was fuckin' nuts, man. Fuckin' nuts. And that's how Pike feels now. You'll have to deal with him, I suspect."

"How'd you get Tucker out?"

"That's a long story. Too long for today. Just know I had help. You need to talk to the Silent Death. That's an MC that knows more than they've ever let on about what's going on in Mexico, and right now, they're runnin' scared. One of them was at that ranch, opened a couple of doors for me and then looked the other way when I clocked Tucker." Spider shifted again, pain twisting his features. "Got a truck, hauled him in it a slow inch at a time, trussed him to the gills and kept hittin' him every time he woke up. Thank God it wasn't monsoon season. I'd never have gotten him across the bridge if it were."

Mason tipped his head to one side. "Monsoon season?"

"Yeah, when it's wet and the river's up, patrols are not as scattered. Guy I know was on the bridge and he just cussed me out for driving fucked up like I was. Didn't look too close at the truck." Mason shook his head. "Tucker was looking for information on something that happened in Colorado a few years ago. I think it had to do with that singer your sister brought down to Texas. Tucker's owed the Mexican cartel for a long time, said he's been paying off the interest just to stay ahead of it. He was talkin' to Pike. Sounded like there was a warehouse that burned, and it came to roost on him for the whole of it."

"Benny Jones? Tucker knew Benny?" Fury's question startled both men and Mason turned to look at him. "I thought that story about Colorado was a spun thing, made larger by time."

"Burned a whole warehouse full of product ready to ship," Mason confirmed. "We never could figure out who it was set Benny up. Not for lack of looking on Slate's part. He'll be interested to know this, if you think Tucker played a part."

"Don't think, I know." Mason frowned. The man's breathing had changed. Faster, it was nearly a pant. "Fuck, this shit hurts, Mason. Can you get Juanita?"

On his way back with Juanita trailing him, Mason made out murmurs coming from the room. Quiet with a sense of urgency, the sound conveyed that something of importance was happening. As he came through the doorway, he saw Fury leaned over the bed, Spider's bandaged hand gripping the back of the man's head, holding him close. Fury nodded and pulled back, but Spider clamped down, keeping him in place, mouth moving.

"I got you, brother." That was the first either of them had given Spider the word, and Mason recognized it for what it was, acknowledgement that Spider had never betrayed the club. "I got you. We'll deal with that. He'll answer for her death." Fury stood, and Mason looked around him at Spider, locking gazes with the old man as Fury repeated, "He'll answer for everything he's done."

Unfriendly as fuck

Fury

"What'd he have to say there before we left?" Mason's question didn't surprise Fury; he'd been expecting it.

"Reason he's been rolling south for these many years." Fury motioned towards the driver, keeping his hands low, out of sight of the rearview mirror. "I'll tell you when we get to the Otey compound."

Mason nodded and turned, staring out the side window. Fury did the same on his side of the van. Silence filled the rest of their drive.

"We're here now. Tell me what Spider said." Mason's voice was gruff and quiet. His tone said he felt he had waited patiently.

Fury turned to watch as the van drove up the long driveway, a plume of dust rising in an arc along its wake. "Spider said he had every reason to believe Tucker and Diamond both had a hand in his old lady's wreck. Said he'd had questions about Diamond for a while, but first Watcher, and then Opie, had put his concerns down to being his grief talking. His old lady had no reason to be in Mexico that night, none at all. No reason to be on that bridge. Diamond's girlfriend was watching their kids, and Spider said that was not a normal occurrence. We know Spider went to

Florida to bring Diamond's bike back. We assumed that meant some kind of partnership agreement between the two men. According to Spider, that is not the case."

Mason swept the area with his gaze, then turned back and faced Fury. "So, you're sayin' everybody had it wrong? Every one of us had it wrong? Do you put yourself in that group?"

"Fuck, yeah. I was definitely on the wrong side of the fence where Spider's concerned. But you cannot tell me that you looked at that old man lying in that bed, broke up, beaten and burned near to death so he could bring an enemy of the club back to us, and you didn't waver in your previous doubts. You cannot tell me you looked at him and didn't believe." He stared at Mason.

Mason scoffed, gaze angled down. He stood like that for a moment, and Fury wondered what was going through his head. "Spider only gave you part of the truth. I guarantee. If Juanita would've let me dope him up a little, we might have gotten a straight story out of him. But she didn't, which leaves us with only one other person to talk to." Mason lifted his chin and stared Fury in the face. "Are you letting Spider be the shot caller on this play? That, my brother—" Mason shook his head. "—is not his role."

"Mason, you have no idea what you're doing." He was staggered when hot anger flared in Mason's eyes at his words and angled backwards until his shoulders hit the wall. He squared up and persisted. "This is not me passing on responsibility. This is me trying to do what you told me you needed." He took a deep breath. "If you go back there like this, you'll end him before we get what we need. We're in agreement, we can't get it from Spider, which means we got just one source to plumb. Take a breath, brother. Take a deep fucking breath."

Mason shook his head, silently rejecting the idea. "I know exactly what I'm doing. I know exactly how I'm doing it. I know exactly what he don't want me to know." Taking an aggressive step forward, Mason's hands balled into fists at his sides. "Tucker has eluded me for far too long, Fury." He lifted one fist and flipped the long finger out, pointing out the window to Watcher's house. "Me finding out he had anything to do with that man's death? Signed his own warrant."

Fury stayed still and silent. He waited. Waited until it was clear Mason was finished talking. And then, he waited some more. Finally, Mason rocked back on his heels, and fingers unclenching, he shoved his hands in his back pockets. "You have no idea. None. You're a man who's lived his life, exactly how he wanted to. No regrets. Nothing wrong in your rearview. You got no idea what it's like to live in my head, knowing that I let Tucker walk away not once but twice. If it comes out he worked with Diamond on this...? He won't walk away a third time."

Mason couldn't be more wrong. *He don't know me at all.* Fury's regrets were many, so fucking many it seemed he could drown under the weight of them sometimes. *Your sister my greatest regret of all.* "I would expect nothing less, brother." Mason would do whatever was needed, and so would Fury. He looked towards the back of the barn, where the small circle of men stood, waiting for this conversation to be over. "We doing this right now, Mason?"

"Yeah, let's get it over with." Mason turned on his heel and walked towards the group. His stride was easy and long, unburdened by the emotion that had gripped him a moment ago. Fury lengthened his steps and caught up with Mason. As they had at the church, they walked in sync, two men—one purpose.

***

Fury winced and shook his hand, droplets of blood flinging to the shifting sands beneath his boots. He let go of Tucker's neck and allowed the man to fall to the floor, sprawled on his back. Glancing up and around the room, instead of censure, all he saw were expressions of sympathy and support. He didn't know if this was a true turning of tides for the attitudes he'd been dealing with, or if it was due to Mason standing directly behind him. Whatever it was, he would take it all day long. Looking down, he jabbed the toe of one boot roughly into Tucker's ribs, growling when he received no response.

Mason rested a hand on his shoulder and pulled him back two paces, his mutter quiet, but Fury knew every man in the barn heard him say, "Let him come back to himself. Don't waste your efforts when there's nothing to be gained. Give him a few minutes, and he'll be with us."

Fury nodded, accepted a bottle of water from Opie, and wiped the sweat from his forehead as he lifted and drank. He was exhausted. They had been working on Tucker for more than six hours. The sun had finally set, and the brutal heat of the New Mexico summer was beginning to bleed off as the barn cooled. The man had slipped away from them for the third time in as many hours, and Fury took this chance to steady his breath. He finished the water, handing the empty back to Opie. The three of them were standing in a rough circle, towering over Tucker's body. Fury checked and saw the man's chest rising and falling shallowly. *Still breathing.*

"We gettin' anything we can use, Mason? Fury's doin' his job, but I'm less convinced that this guy can be broken. I mean—" Opie gestured towards the prone figure on the floor. "—look at 'em. We know what it took for Slate to get what he needed, and that was years ago. He's a hard motherfucker."

Spreading the fingers on his right hand, Fury clenched them into a fist again, feeling the ache settling in. He studied Tucker for a moment, surveying the damage wrought by his blows. Face nearly untouched, because they needed him able to talk, and needed to be able to understand any words spoken, Fury had been working his body hard. Kidneys were an obvious target, as were fingers, elbows, knees, and ankles. Nothing damaged in a lasting way, not yet, because a man without hope wouldn't have a reason to talk.

Mason's phone rang and he stepped back, pulling it from his pocket. He squinted at the device, then swiped across it, lifting it to his ear. "Yeah?" Whatever was said on the other end had an immediate effect and Fury watched as Mason stilled, freezing in place. "You're sure? You talked to him?" A pause and Fury became aware all conversations had halted. When he glanced around, every eye was on Mason. "Be certain, brother." That made sense, because whoever it was had to be inner circle—Mason wouldn't have taken the call otherwise. "Copy. Thanks, man. Tell him we owe him." Mason's mouth twitched to the side. "Yeah, Myron. I know exactly what those words mean. Tell Sparks we owe him."

Mason was staring down at Tucker as he slipped the phone back into his pocket, expression contemplative. "We don't need you anymore, Tucker." Movement from the floor drew Fury's attention, and he saw Tucker was wide awake, staring up at Mason. "Got what I needed from your ex-crew in Florida. Them boys don't care much for you. All the bullshit you pulled there, drawing down Fed attention to the club, man...that did *not* make you any friends."

"Sparks reached out?" Fury wanted to ask what Myron had told Mason, but knew Mason would share it or not, on his terms. *Always.*

"Yeah. Myron sent him a pic of Tucker here, spit back that he knew him as Scorch, then Brands. We've heard of Brands, man. He's the one who took out one of Retro's guys last year. Dragged him to death at an event in Ocala. No reason other than a spilled beer. Man left behind three kids. Retro's been callin' in all kinds of markers, tryin' to find this piece of shit." Reaching to the back waistband of his jeans, Mason pulled out his gun and leveled it, aiming down. "I'll let Retro know he don't need to waste no more markers."

***

Juanita

Movement in her peripheral vision made Juanita look up from her book. She froze for a moment at the hulking shape in the doorway, then relaxed as she picked out the shape of a black leather vest against the darkness of the hallway. "Hello," she called, marking her place with a finger tucked between the pages. Glancing at Spider, she saw he was sleeping quietly. *Thank goodness*, she thought. He'd had a rough couple of days, and if he was resting, it would at least give his body the energy and healing it needed to live to fight another day. She wasn't fooling herself into thinking his condition had improved enough to mean he was out of the woods. Not yet. There was so much damage to his body, it meant he would likely have several more crises before he could be proclaimed healed.

The man in the doorway hadn't moved, and she looked back up at him, reaching out to turn up the light on the bedside table. It was an older man, grizzled and unkempt as so many of them were. Those long in the tooth, or "OGs" as Watcher had always termed them, cared little for what the world thought of them. "Are you here to see Spider?"

She was preparing to stand when he spoke, and froze in place for a moment as he ordered, "Shut the fuck up, bitch." More cautious now, because while unfriendly didn't necessarily mean not friends of the club, she finished pushing to her feet, turning to lay the book in her chair.

Spider stirred and Juanita had just glanced down at him when his eyes opened. He focused on her with as much of a smile as he could muster, then his eyes cut towards the door and the expression on his face changed in a way that let her know in this case, unfriendly definitely meant not friends. "Fuckin' asshat," he gritted out. "You hurt her, I'll fuckin' kill you."

Juanita jerked her head up at his implication, staring at the man in the doorway. The gun held in his hand was larger than her pistol. Aimed her way, it looked much larger, darker, and scarier. The speaker bolted to the wall behind her crackled, and she heard, "Yes, senor Spider?"

The hole in the end of the barrel looked huge, big enough to swallow her whole. A trickle of smoke curled up out of it, dissipating nearly immediately. So wispy it looked more like the tendrils of fog that would roll off a chunk of dry ice, one of Watcher's favorite tricks for the girls.

"Call Mason, honey." Spider's voice sounded funny, so far away he might have been in Kentucky for all she knew. "Tell him Pike's here."

Darkness was creeping in at the edges of her vision and Juanita stumbled, sitting down hard, the edges of the book biting into the backs of her thighs.

"Tell him..."

Packing for home

Bethany

"No, Ty. He's not making me. Gabe wouldn't give me an ultimatum like that." Bethy was balancing the phone on her shoulder, trying to press down the top flaps on a box while simultaneously wielding a roll of tape to secure the box closed. "Ow." Fingers working carefully, she tugged a few strands of hair out from underneath the tape. "When are you coming over again? I could use the help."

He laughed, a low rolling chuckle that she smiled to hear. He had come back so close to the Ty she'd known for so long, nearly back to center and being the man he needed to be. She'd spoken with Dot earlier and the woman had wept as she told Bethy about all the positive changes she'd seen in Ty.

"You know I can be there whenever you need me. You tell me when, I'm there darlin'." Ty chuckled again. "Want me to bring a friend? You got big stuff to move today?"

Bethy rested one knee on the floor as she glanced around the small apartment. With boxes scattered everywhere, the space didn't even look familiar. This was the last room to pack. Only a few more containers and she'd be done, not just for the day, but ready to move. "I'm gonna go get the truck in about thirty minutes. Are you sure your friend won't mind helping?"

"Sarge said he already offered, little girl. Pretty sure he's not going to mind." Bethy smiled at the warmth in Ty's voice. "We'll meet you there in thirty."

"Sounds good, Ty. I can't wait to see you."

It was hours later when Bethy yawned and stretched, feeling the strain and pull of muscles well used as she lifted her arms over her head. She called out, hearing footsteps in the apartment again, "Are y'all already for a beer yet?" Male voices muttered something indistinguishable from the background noise coming through the open door. "Since you didn't say whatever that was loud enough for me to hear, I'm going to assume it was not flattering." She turned to face the door just as Ty's face popped around, white teeth shining as he grinned broadly at her. "Now do you and Sarge want a beer, or not?"

"Yeah, Bethy. We want a beer." Ty stepped to the side, letting Sarge come into the room as she opened the refrigerator, bringing out three bottles. They clinked together as she cradled them in her arms, bumping the door shut with one hip. "Sarge was just asking about your man. I told him any stories had to come from you, seein' as how it's your business and all."

Inscrutable as ever, Sarge angled his hips to lean against the countertop, reaching out for the offered bottle. His fingers made grimy stripes in the condensation as he gripped and lifted, taking a long drink. Bethy studied him for a moment, long enough he scowled at her and asked, "What?"

"I don't think I've ever seen you relax like this." She shrugged, lifting her own bottle. "That's all." His brows drew together again, expression turning fierce. "Not saying you relaxing is a bad thing, Sarge. You just always seemed to be on a mission somewhere."

"I usually am." He dropped his frown, seeming to give considerable thought to his response. "I can see how that could be off-putting." He took another drink. "Tell me about this man who's luring you to the frigid northlands. I never thought you'd be willing to leave Nashville."

"It's hard to go, promise." She glanced at Ty, seeing his mouth move in a wry smile. "All my friends are here. My work. But I can do the business part from anywhere. I've done it in the back lounge on a tour bus before. The office I'll have is so much better than that. Being on a bus means dropped calls, paperwork a mess, no chance to fix or file." She shuddered in fake dismay. "My brother has a friend who has already set up a studio for his little brother, who just happens to be one of my clients. I've worked out a deal with him, so when I need to produce, I can use his space. It's kinda perfect. His house is about three blocks from where I'm moving to." She gestured with her bottle, smiling. "Ty's settled and happy now." She grinned at him, an expression he returned. "Michael liked it up there, and Davy is excited about me moving closer."

"How about your man? He gonna be best pleased you're heading up his way?"

"Why, Sarge, I didn't know you cared." She teased, watching the tips of his ears redden. "Gabe would have been okay with whatever I decided to do, whether that was commuting, or moving. He's happier with the move, of course, but—" She shrugged. "—so am I."

"Gabe?" She nodded and watched as his eyes narrowed. "This the same Gabe you and me had a talk about a few months back?" She nodded again, slower. His chin rose until he was glaring down his nose at her. "You're fucking shitting me, right?" Twisting to turn his stare on Ty, he barked, "You know this knobgobbler, soldier?"

Ty's spine straightened and he said, "No, sir," his voice quiet.

"Girl, tell me you're shitting me."

Bethany frowned at how he'd said the word, "Girl," as if she didn't have any sense. "I'm not shitting you, Sarge. What's your damage?"

"My damage—" He leaned back, setting his bottle on the counter next to him. "—is that you seem to be inable to keep yourself out of trouble. What is it with you? You look for the biggest prick around and just tell yourself, 'yeah, this one'll do,' huh?"

"Unable." She held his gaze, unflinching.

"What?"

"Unable. Inable isn't a word. What you were looking for was unable or maybe incapable. And no, Sarge, I'm not incapable of taking care of myself." She tightened her fingers on her bottle, holding tightly in an attempt to keep a similar grip on her temper. "I am fully able to determine the best path forwards for myself. I'm a big *girl*." She threw extra emphasis on the word, angry now. "I've been taking care of myself for a long, long time. I do not need a man like you to lecture me on anything."

"Inable, unable. Whatever. What do you mean a man like me? What kind of man do you think I am?"

"A controlling asshole who liked what he found in the military, so you expect everyone to toe whatever kind of imaginary line you have in your head." She threw one arm out to the side, indicating the breadth of the room. "No matter where you are, you're always the one in charge. Always gotta be the top dog."

He took a step forwards and she noted, not for the first time, just how big Sarge was. Big, and right now, very pissed off. *Maybe it wasn't the right move to poke the bear today.* He took another step, pulling up short when Ty rested a hand on his arm. It was the first time she'd ever seen Ty voluntarily touch the man, and the reaction was immediate. Sarge looked like he was deflating, shoulders lowering and his chin tucking towards his chest.

Ty looked at her, staring for a long moment. "Something you haven't told me about Gabe?" She wrinkled her nose. "Yeah, there's something you need to say, ain't there?"

"He's good to me, Ty." She knew Sarge recognized Gabe from the military, but as tight as Ty had been with Watcher, he'd identify him best from the club side. "Gabe Ledbetter, I've known him nearly my whole life. He's in Davy's motorcycle club." She paused a breath, barely a second, but knew Ty saw it because his brow lowered. "Fury. You probably heard of him?"

Ty blinked and his mouth opened, then closed. He licked his lips, frowning. "Fury? Your man is Fury?" She nodded, waiting. "Watcher's cousin?" She nodded again. "What's Mason say about all this? He even know?"

Bethy rolled her eyes. "His first reaction was to have him beaten up."

"I can see that." Ty's head bobbed up and down. "I can see that, for sure." His tone was sarcastic, biting like acid.

"Stop it. You don't know him and don't know how things have been. Davy's fine with it now."

"Sure he is, little girl." Sarge's sneer wasn't veiled. "Keep tellin' yourself that."

"Sarge, man. Not cool. You can't let your attitude about what you let slide color this shit. If Bethy says Mason's cool, then he's cool."

"Probably more like Bethany told him tough titty and he didn't feel like fighting her on every fucking thing."

Bethy scowled at him, then her attention was pulled to the side when Ty burst out laughing. "What?"

"Yeah, keep tellin' yourself Mason's okay with you bein' with Fury, Bethy girl. Keep it up." He lifted his bottle, smiling at her around the neck.

"Mason's been clearing the decks for years without you knowing what was going on. Do not be surprised if he's already mounting a campaign against your man."

"Brother, watch your mouth." Bethy glanced at Sarge, surprised to see his face and ears burning red, something she'd only seen from him once before. She considered Ty's words, and Sarge's attitude, and everything clicked into place.

"Let me tell you something about my man." She made a fist, propping it on one hip as she glared at the two men, one of who had been her best friend for years, and one she now suspected of carrying the tiniest torch for her. "My man is not content letting someone else dictate what he can and cannot have. His only concern is me. If I'd told him no and meant it, he would have backed off. Hell,"—she flapped her other hand towards the door—"I'm the one who had to go chasing him, aren't I?" Pursing her lips, she thought for a moment. "Davy might not like him, and as much as I love my brother, I don't honestly care if he does, but he respects Fury. It's a meeting of equals when they're both in the room. That should stand for something."

She paused and then decided she was done, letting both hands fall back to her sides. Ty leaned over, hooking an arm around her neck and pulling her close.

"Something I know about my Bethy, she decides she wants something, ain't nothing can stand in her way." His lips brushed the side of her head.

"You got that right," she got out around the tears suddenly choking her. "Damn straight."

***

Fury

"No, baby. I'll be back home in two, three days, max. Just unpack your clothes and shove my shit out of your way. Leave the boxes and furniture

285

where the guys put them, okay?" Fury tipped his head down, aware Mason was listening to every word. "I wanna be there for the rest of it. We'll get you moved in, together." Silence for a moment on the phone and then he heard a sniffle. "Oh, baby. No, no. Honey, don't cry." Mason stepped closer and without looking up, Fury held up a hand, palm out. "Don't cry."

"I'm not." She lied badly, and Fury wondered if this would be beneficial for him in the future. Her not being able to lie worth a shit couldn't hurt. "I'm just being silly."

"Well, stop being silly like that. Two, three days, baby. That's all." Noises down the hallway had him lifting his head to look, and both he and Mason were on the move a moment later. Two doctors had just exited a room and were standing in the hallway speaking to a man in a wheelchair. "I gotta go, Beth. I'll call you tonight, tell you a bedtime story."

She giggled, the sound equal parts watery and bright. "Love you."

"Love you, too." He disconnected, shoving the phone deep into his pocket as they came even with where Spider sat in the chair, hands on the grips that maneuvered the wheels. "What's the news, Doc?"

Accustomed to them after three days of having one or several bikers waiting every time they came out of the room, the female doctor didn't hesitate. It hadn't taken much to have them come down on the side of their patient having a large, supportive family like this. "She's much improved. Her condition is still guarded, but we are pleased with her progress."

Mason tipped slightly sideways, his shoulder brushing against Fury's. When he turned to see what had happened, Fury recognized the dark-haired woman pressed tight to Mason's side, her arm wrapped around his waist. Watcher's near-daughter Carmela asked, "Mama Nita's going to be fine, right? She's going to be okay?"

The doctor repeated her words, "She is much improved, Mela. You can go see her if you want."

"Push me in there, gal. My arm hurts like fuck." Spider kept his chin down, face angled towards his lap. If it were to hide tears, Fury wouldn't blame him. Spider's quick thinking to push the tiny remote and activate the speaker system at the church infirmary saved Juanita's life, and ran Pike off. Even with her having rough medical care immediately, it had been touch and go until they got her into surgery and stopped the bleeding. Afterwards, the docs reported they gave her six units of blood during surgery, which was a fuck of a lot. *Touch and fuckin' go.*

The bullet from Pike's single shot had entered just below her arm, punching through a portion of her lung before hitting a rib in her back. The impact had stopped the bullet, and the docs were happy it didn't bounce around inside her any more than it had.

The door closed behind the pair and Fury turned back to face the doc, seeing the other had left. Mason was staring down at her. "He should have come here." Her voice trembled with anger.

"Couldn't, you know how it is." Mason's tone was offhand, but something about his posture made Fury look closer at the woman. Petite, she had pleasant features, but wouldn't be someone he'd recognize without her white coat. "How you doin', honey?"

"Don't. Don't pretend to be the good guy here, Davis." She shook her head. "Don't insult me."

Fury caught voices from behind the door, Spider's half-heard words a shout, "...damn fool. Anyone..."

The doctor grimaced, interrupting whatever she'd been about to say. Striding towards the door, she was only steps away when it opened, Mela storming out, tears smeared across her face. "*Tu stupido!*" She turned and shouted, then pulled the door shut with a slam, freezing when she saw all eyes focused on her. "Uncle Spider is *crazy*." Hurley moved towards her, wrapping his arms around her. "Mama Nita's going to kill him."

"If she's feelin' good enough to kill the man, we're guaranteed to be taking her home soon." Mason reached out, resting one hand on Mela's shoulder. "I'll just go make sure there's no bloodshed in the room."

"She's gonna be okay." Fury restated what they were all still praying for. "She's gonna be just fine."

Unrest in the West

Fury

He stood in the dark, shoulder angled against the wall close to the back door, watching out the glass into the shadow-filled back yard. Propped up like he was, he could hold steady despite the exhaustion that weighed down every limb. Fury and Mason had gotten back to Fort Wayne late the previous night, climbing off the small private jet owned by a friend of the club and walking into an uproar.

Members from every chapter had contacted them, leaving messages on their phones and at the clubhouse. The content of the communications all followed a central theme: Was their family safe?

Pike had hit a raw nerve by going after Juanita like that. Even before his little piece of douchery, it had been Lalo and the Diamante who had shaken the biker world to their core, attacking and killing not only people on the outskirts of the clubs with which they'd gone to war but actively targeting the old ladies and children of officers. Unspoken in their life as outlaws had always the reassuring knowledge that no matter what, the family would be above it all.

Instead of going home, he and Mason had gone straight to the clubhouse, launching into a series of video conferences to sort out the damage. Fallout so far appeared to be only a few members from a couple of far-flung satellite chapters, new charters who didn't have as deep a history.

Movement in the shadows pulled his gaze into focus, and he watched as a cat crept into view. It played with a tall strand of grass for a moment, rearing up on its back legs and batting at it as if it were a toy. He watched as the cat ceased its activities, dropping to flatten itself to the ground, becoming hardly noticeable in the grass. There were no other animals in view, but the cat behaved as if there were another predator close by, or prey. *Even sharks will abandon a feeding ground when a larger shark goes swimming by.*

He sighed. They'd also fielded a dozen calls from other clubs. Wanna-be sharks, circling, darting close to see if there was blood in the water yet, asking pointed or vague questions by turns, trolling for information more than anything. Still, an annoyance that had to be handled. So many details to hold in his head, and every time he wanted to bounce an idea off Mason, the man had been engaged in dealing with another facet of the threatening implosion.

Bethy hadn't been pleased when she found out how long he'd been back in town before he called her. Not pleased, but she got it, equating what he'd been doing to her working a sticky deal for one of her artists. *I'm a lucky motherfucker*, he thought.

His phone buzzed, vibrating silently in his pocket and he pulled it out, glancing first at the time. It was just after two o'clock, which was way too late for casual calls. When he looked at the caller's name, he lifted his lip in a silent snarl. It was the president of a western club: Chief, from Legends, and for him, it was only midnight.

Shit.

Thumbing the button to accept the call, he greeted the man with a more pleasant tone than he thought was deserved, holding himself on this side of rude. "Chief. Whatcha need?"

"Fury. You with Mason?"

Straight to the business, then. Fine. Fury could deal with that. Keeping his voice low so as to not wake Bethy, he answered, "Nope. He's home with his old lady by now, hopefully sleeping peacefully." The implication was the Rebels didn't have a single thing to disturb their sleep. "You got me for now."

No response for a moment, then Chief said in a tone that bled caution, "I have to let you know of a thing recently done in my club."

"Okay." This wasn't protocol. Not at all. Fury wasn't national and hadn't occupied a seat at any tables where the Legends would be bringing grievances or proposing deals. Chief calling him about anything to do with official Legends' business made the hair on the back of his neck stand up. "Spill."

"You were in Kansas City not long ago. Only recently did the purpose of your trip come to my attention." That chill which had raised his hair settled in his gut, anger warring with an unease. "And then tonight, I received a call from mutual friends in Florida." Chief had to be talking about Sparks and his crew, the Jailbreakers MC. "They spoke at length about an event which seems to be pretty common knowledge, but you need to know it was news to me as of an hour ago." So Chief hadn't wasted any time, picking up the phone quickly to sort out whatever this was he had done against the Rebels. "I've gotta tell you, Fury, I was surprised when they told me you were dogging Mason's footsteps. Surprised, but pleased. You always deserved better than Deacon would be willing to throw your way." Fury made a face, but kept himself silent, letting Chief finish his brownnosing. "Are you the one I should talk to about a Legend misstep where it comes to offending the Rebels, or should I be interrupting Mason's rest this night?"

"Probably better off letting me run interference for you, if that's needed." Fury looked out the window, seeing the cat was still flattened in the grass, eyes shining in the moonlight, but immobile and silent. "Talk to me, tell me what you're looking for." He wouldn't offer to help, wouldn't make anything that could be construed as a promise, no matter how long the Legends had been friendly with the Rebels.

"I patched a man about a month ago. There'd been a lot going on out here. You wouldn't believe the fallout from what happened in Florida." With three sentences, Chief gave him everything he needed to know, but he let him keep talking, sensing Chief needed to talk through the story as he saw it in his head. "He's been in the life a while, sold me a story about moving home to be around family out in Wyoming." Legends were based in Utah, but they had other small chapters dotted here and there, some with only a handful of members. More a riding club than anything the Rebels claimed, still the Legends offered the kind of brotherhood so many men needed. "I knew him, knew his family. His nephew runs a chain of bike shops all along the front range of the Rockies." *Jesus.* "He didn't offer a reason for leaving his previous club, and knowing the troubles the club was facing, I didn't reach out."

"You aren't obligated to, Chief." This was strictly truth but wasn't normal practice. Chief not calling meant his club didn't always vet their members like they probably should.

"But knowing where he came from, I should have."

"Shoulda, woulda, coulda. Pike came to you, did he?" Fury sighed. "And now, you've just heard what he did to Watcher's old lady. Am I right?"

"You are. I did. The story coincides with an absence from my territory, too. He's defenseless, as far as I'm concerned." Chief seemed to settle into a comfortable cadence of information distribution, and Fury was reminded that the man had been a federal agent at one time. *Might need to pick his brain about how to help Mason deal with Justine.* "He returned a few days ago, claimed a breakdown out west, but when I had my guy pull records for the club phone he had on him, we saw the lie. He's made several stops, and I think you're gonna wanna know about all of them." Chief cleared his throat. "I'm hesitant to travel with him in tow, because he's aware of my knowledge now, so the man claims himself entirely unwilling to have any kind of face-to-face with yourself." A chuckle, which was so out of tone with their conversation it caught at Fury's interest, wondering what would be coming next. "Surprisingly, he feels differently about Mason and would welcome a visit. At least, that's the story now. Should I tell him we're going to have company soon?"

"Fuck, man. We just got home from New Mexico." Fury sighed, then shrugged, even knowing Chief couldn't see the movement. "You'll get someone who will have the authority to do anything needful, okay? I can't say who, not until I talk to Mason, and we are both knee-deep in managing various things. But yeah, tell him you're going to have a visitor. Tell him you'll let him know who, soon as you know. Then tell him this, because I doubt he knows one way or the other, but he needs to know we're after his ass in a very real way. Tell him 'Juanita lives,' and see what he says to that."

"What if I leave him in suspense and allow whoever arrives to dispense that knowledge? Keeping him on tenterhooks doesn't bother me at all." Chief paused and cleared his throat again, making Fury wonder if that was a tell he was nervous. "You get me, right? I'm personally down with whatever is needed to satisfy the Rebels. If you have questions about Pike's guilt or his whereabouts, we'll share the logs we have. You want info about the other places he stopped along the way, we'll work to get you what you need. I will say, if you want to censure me for allowing him to patch in without picking up the phone, I'm down with that. But, I'd rather you not include my men, because this is all on me."

"Like the best leaders, you take on the full burden, don't you?" The cat was gone, fled at some point in the past few minutes, the place in the yard where it had been empty now. "I'll pass your thoughts along to

Mason, see what he says." Movement along the edge of the shadows evolved back into the cat, walking daintily across the grass, wending its way between clumps with head held high, tail arched even higher. "And Chief, you're talking to the man who delivered Pike's beatout and let him walk away. You can't be second guessing yourself any more than I am. Hold that package, brother. We'll be in touch."

"See you soon."

Yoked tight

Fury reached out and wrapped a hand around the bottle Mason sat on the table between them. "Thanks," he muttered, not yet certain what his defacto brother-in-law wanted. Mason had shown twenty minutes ago, unannounced, and immediately manufactured a reason for Bethany to leave the apartment. *Can't be good, whatever it is.*

"Yeah," Mason grunted, seating himself across from Fury.

They sat in silence for a minute then Mason sighed heavily and leaned back in his chair. "When Hoss brought you to me, you didn't tell me who you were. Coulda." His gaze met Mason's, and he saw an emotion he couldn't name working in the man's eyes. "Didn't." Shifting in his chair, Mason's vest gaped open, the worn leather wrinkling and bending between the patches. "Won my trust, still not comin' clean."

"Wasn't so much a deceit as self-preservation. I earned my name, but how I earned it wouldn't have gained me any fans back home." Fury sat forwards, elbows to the table, fingers twirling the bottle. "Knew you—fuck, everyone knew you. Fifteen years after you left the hollers you were one of the biggest employers, making sure you took care of what you left behind. I didn't have any kind of legacy like that."

Mason's eyes bored into him, anger flaring for the first time. "We do what we can in different ways." Shaking his head, he lifted his bottle and drank. "Won my trust anyway. Every tread along your path was done with others in mind. Loyalty and brotherhood runs deep in you."

"Brothers are hard to find. Takes work to keep." Fury shrugged. "Worth everything to hold that close."

"Truth." Mason shifted again. "I'm calling for a national vote in four months."

That statement got Fury's attention. A national vote for the Rebels generally sat on a five-year cycle. This was not due for at least two years, by his count. "Means folks will be paying attention, and you know why."

"Oh, yeah. Every fuckin' member is gonna be glued to their phones, no doubt." Mason snorted. "Should be. I'm stepping back."

Fury didn't move, didn't breathe for a moment. Mason stepping back was never part of any equation he'd worked in his head about his place in the RWMC organization. Mason stepping back wasn't part of any world that made sense. "What the fuck you mean?" He finally choked out the question, shocked when Mason laughed.

"Should see your fuckin' face, man. Jesus." One corner of Mason's mouth lifted, but no one would ever say the smile held humor. "Take a breath, brother."

"Jesus. Warn a man before you drop a bomb like that." Fury lifted his bottle, draining half of it in one go. "Jesus."

"Tagging you for national president. This is my official verbal vote."

This time it felt as if all the oxygen had been sucked from the room by Mason's pronouncement. Time slowed, the clock on the stove taking a year between each second ticking away. Mason's gaze held steady. There was no disapproval or judgment, just a patient trust.

"No." Shaking his head, Fury pushed his chair back several inches. "There are a thousand reasons for you to pick any of your inner circle over me, and not a single reason—" He reached out, swiping the bottle off the table and, raising it, drained it as he rose to his feet. There was only one reason he could think of for Mason's pronouncement, and he was angry at the idea Bethany would factor in this decision. He leaned a fist against the edge of the sink, staring out the window.

Proving once again that he thought his way around all corners of an argument, Mason said the only thing that would reassure Fury. "In spite of who you're with, not because of it. If you hadn't bucked me at every turn with Bethy, I would have been talking to you six months ago. You fucked my timing, brother." That last held a note of humor and Fury twisted, looking over his shoulder to see a true smile on Mason's face. "Not an easy ask, knowing how she loves you."

He studied Mason for a moment. *Motherfucker's serious.* "Talk to me. If I can't understand the reasons for this fucked up idea, there's no chance of convincing anyone else it's a good idea." Fury turned, leaning a hip against the counter. "Not that I'm saying this is a good idea, because I want to go on record as it being entirely fucked. This is not a good time for a change in leadership, but if you wanted to step back, then Slate or Bear, fuck…even Tater or Opie would be better picks than me. Slate, for sure."

"You don't want the accolades?" Mason barked a laugh. "Good, because there ain't none."

"Smart enough to know that's truth." Fury shrugged. "Talk to me."

"Slate or Opie'd be a safe pick, either of 'em. They'd be good. Stable officers, well-liked brothers, firmly entrenched in the life and the club." Mason shrugged. "No bad bets there. But this is a club that's got a good history of growing. I've made some bold leaps over the years."

"Some folks would say a few of those big jumps weren't your smartest moments."

"Yeah, but those folks couldn't see the end game for the moves. I did." Mason leveled a finger, pointing at Fury's chest. "You do, too. You see the big picture better than anyone I know. Not quite as good as me, but you got time to hone those skills." His hand angled towards the refrigerator. "Gimme another beer, be a good host."

Fury settled back into his chair, sliding one of the bottles he'd retrieved across to Mason. "So you want the club to keep growing? What's next, international?"

"Fuck, yeah. We got seats at those tables already. The connection with the Hawks in Australia is a big step. Germany is a lock. We got a dozen guys in the service stationed there now and they've hooked up with a local club. I'm ready to pass out support patches to their friends, and we both know that's the first step to rolling a chapter. Italy is the same. We're already international, just not singing about it yet." He looked at Fury from under his brows, eyes dancing. "That'll be your first announcement. I've padded your first few months with a wealth of things like that."

"I agree growing is key, but holding territory here isn't guaranteed. Still think it's a bad time for a change, Mason. We've not solved the Diamante threat, yet." Fury leaned back, throwing an arm over the back of his chair. "We don't want to fight internally, too."

"Won't be a fight. Past president stays active for two years. You and me, we'll be yoked tight together."

"Two years? Since when?" Fury shook his head. "Never heard that bylaw."

"First time we've had a change in national leadership since I handpicked my team. My rules. You saying you don't like my rules? What—" Mason grinned and Fury saw an echo of Bethy's smile. "—you can't stomach having to deal with me for a couple of years? Fuck, man. You're my brother in so many ways now, you're fuckin' stuck with me for life."

Bending his head to hide his smile, Fury told Mason, "Talk to me."

For the next several minutes, Mason outlined his hopes and plans for the Rebels, and as he spoke, Fury grasped the edges of the vision, seeing where a change in strategy would strengthen an idea, and where there hadn't been enough consideration given to local political climates for another. Their back and forth was lively, a meeting of equals in a way Fury hadn't experienced with Mason before. It was heady and exciting, and at the end of the conversation, he had a glimpse of the depth and intellectual scope of the man seated across from him.

They were on their next beers when the talk turned somber again. Mason led the way with a quiet statement that sent a chill down Fury's spine. "You put on that patch, it stops being about you."

"I know that."

"I know, you know. But I want to make sure you understand. A member puts on a patch and every decision he makes while wearing that patch reflects on him and his local chapter. Reflects on the club. For each member, it's about the brotherhood and holding the trust passed to him with the awarding of his center. Brotherhood is all. The bones behind the phrase that rolls so easily off every member's lips, Rebels forever,"—Fury finished with him, their voices overlapping on the final two words— "forever Rebels."

"Accountability is a good thing, and every member knows they're held to the wall by their choices." Fury nodded.

"You put on that national president's patch, it stops being about your choices. It stops being about you. From that point onwards, you are the office. The office doesn't take a vacation, it doesn't sleep, doesn't rest, and never goes away. It stops being about the individual, and becomes about the collective membership. Every word that falls from your mouth is measured and weighed, prodded for hidden agendas and favoritism. Every decision is life and death, because you're a general behind the lines calling for an advance or retreat." Mason pinned him with a stare. "It is a burden that doesn't shift from your shoulders, ever."

"Not painting a picture that makes me want to say yes."

"But, you will."

Fury heard the rattle of Bethy's keys in the front door and climbed to his feet. Without a word he walked out, met her in the middle of the living room and wrapped his arms around her, forcing her to lift her bag-laden hands to the sides. "Well, hello to you, too," she chirped, and he smiled against her neck to hear that sassy tone.

"Missed you, baby." He pulled back and stared down into her face, smiling.

"Aww." She pursed her lips and made a clucking noise. "Kiss me already, then take these bags. There are more in the car."

He leaned in, kissing her deeply as he ran his hands down her arms, unburdening her at the same time. "Go sit with your brother. I'll get the rest." He walked her in and pushed her towards his empty seat, knowing from the tilt of her head she was mentally counting the number of empties and that he'd be answering questions later. "Be right back, boss." Fury walked out, hearing her laugh and already arguing with Mason over who the "boss" was in that scenario.

End of an era

Fury

Fury stood, staring down at the man lying on the ground. With the toe of one boot, he stirred the gravel alongside the body, shocked when his nudge gained a response. A groan, then a cough followed by another groan. "Motherfucker," Fury muttered. "Nine evil lives."

Pike coughed again and his arm lifted to curve across his belly, fingers grasping and holding onto his ribs. Fury waited, expecting that grip to loosen and fall away, but it didn't, and a few moments later, Pike's eyes squeezed tightly shut, then opened in a slit. Not sure if the man saw him, Fury stepped back a half pace, seeing Pike's eyes slide his way, the whites stained with red, burst blood vessels making themselves known.

Bending at the waist, Fury leaned down, putting his face close to Pike's. "You in there, old man?" Age wouldn't save him, not this time.

"What you want, boy?" Filled with gravel and pain, Pike's voice rose, coming through clenched teeth. He coughed again, covering his full-body flinch at the end with a growled, "Fuck."

"Want you dead." Fury told him, seeing the glint in the man's eyes as he stared up. "You're looking at death, right now, old man. Ain't got no reason to leave you livin'. No one here to plead your case. Gonna take care of business what shoulda been dealt with ages ago. Put you out of your miserable existence, filled with hate. Hate that you seem to spread everywhere you go."

"Lotta talkin' for a man who's pridin' himself on doin'." Pike rasped out, and Fury saw his fingers clutching tightly at his shirt, holding on, that action giving away fear that must be boiling inside Pike far more than pain.

"Welp, I ain't talkin' for *you*." Fury gestured to the crowd gathering on all sides. Rebels and a dozen other clubs, coming together for this. "Got things folks need to know. Got a fuckin' list, old man. Listen up."

Straightening, Fury let his gaze skip across every face turned his direction. Patient, horrified, resigned, eager—those last bothered him, but he marked the faces for now, resolving to return to them when he could—determined, and pained. He focused on those, members of Pike's own club, turned to doing his bidding without realizing the cost. "Not without blame," he laid it out there, justified as Chief flinched. "Not without cause, either." Without giving anyone a chance to rebuke him, he pushed forwards. "Man you trust comes to you with an ask, you're a brother, you do what you can to assist. What you did, every bit of it, no more or less than any one of us would do."

Fury turned, looking around the group again. "Pike's not the sole source of our pain. Not by a longshot, but he's the crux that kept things going bad. If he'd left things alone, we'd a been working together rather than against each other. He'd've left things alone, brothers would be home with their old ladies, instead of rotting in the ground. He didn't leave it, and we've all paid a price. Time we stop payin' this piper, brothers. Past time."

Looking down, he saw Pike had pushed to one elbow, neck twisted to keep Fury in view. "Ain't a lie to say he deserves to die. Ain't a lie to say I'm proud to be the shot caller for this one. The list of pain in your past is so fuckin' long, old man, it stretched back decades. Even those alive, you've marked in your quest for vengeance in an imagined feud."

Pike spat, then said, "Ain't imagined."

"Fuck yeah, it is," Fury clipped, staring into Pike's eyes. "You didn't pull your bullshit, officers coulda talked to you, figured out how to keep things from going as far sideways as they did, all those years ago. You picked a side." Fury swung his hands out to the side, palms up. "You lost. You have been losing for years. You lost, old man. Give it the fuck up."

Reaching for the holster at his back, Fury pulled the gun and leveled it at the man. "Got anything to say? Any pithy words of wisdom?"

Pike's teeth bared in a feral snarl as he growled, "*Fuck y—*"

The shot rang out and everyone watched as the body jolted ten inches, jarring down to the dirt, lifting a puff of dust. The round hole in Pike's temple oozed a tiny rivulet of red. And that was it, the end of an era of pain and fear, silenced by a single bullet.

Settling down

Fury

He leaned back in the rickety lawn chair Gunny had set out for him, watching the big man laugh as he lifted both hands out to the side, three kids of varying ages and sizes hanging off each arm. The swing set in the corner of the yard had become overrun with the older children, and now Gunny was acting as a makeshift monkey bars. The grin and big, booming laugh falsified his claim to being annoyed at the activity, and Fury smiled to hear the kids' voices clamoring for more.

Tipping his head up, he stared through the sunlit fabric of the awning Gunny had setup over the table. Brilliant, dazzling even through the layer of material, the sun shone down on what he knew was a regular occurrence. One of the greatest things about the Rebels was how the club effortlessly folded families into the mix of celebrations. Not to say they didn't have brothers-only parties, but since most of the men were building families, it made sense to include them as often as possible. *Happy wife, happy life.* He grinned, because the adage was still true.

In the weeks since he'd made the trip out to Utah, things had settled down. Even knowing how hard Pike had been working to make life hell for the Rebels, it was still surprising to find how much actual effort he'd been putting into the disruptions that had seemed to come from all sides. *Had seemed to, because they fuckin' were.* Myron had spent days putting together a timeline and map of the old man's work, and then trapped Mason and Fury in a room for hours explaining. It was good to know, because the information allowed them to drop the issues that would be dying on their own now that the shit-stirrer was dead, focusing instead on the real threats.

There were threats, of course. Given the paths they'd chosen to follow, the lives they led, there would always be threats. *Always*. He sighed, rubbing the back of his neck with stiffened fingers. Last night had been an example of that always, because there'd been a series of attacks on several clubhouses on the easternmost edges of Rebel territory. Pressure from an east coast club who were responding to the encroaching tide of Rebels. The men on the edges of things knew where they stood, they expected more action than the members in long-established cities like Chicago and Fort Wayne, but it didn't make hearing the litany of injuries easier on anyone back here.

He'd told Mason they would need to push harder, expand a bit more before making a controlled contraction to consolidate clubhouses. Unblinking, his stare still unnerving even after so many months of being joined at the hip, Mason had listened and agreed. They couldn't be seen to backdown from a few hits like last night, but they still needed to protect their men. For now, they'd try patching mostly single members on the fringe cities, redirecting others with interest back to a more centralized city like Columbus, Toledo, Lexington, or Knoxville.

A gliding touch on his shoulder was all the warning he needed and Fury lifted his arms, holding his beer out of the way as Bethy tumbled over the arm of the chair and into his lap, laughing and clutching at his neck as the chair threatened to collapse. "Hey there," she said softly, palm coming to rest on the hinge of his jaw, fingers scratching and threading through his beard. "Food's nearly ready. Want me to make you a plate?"

Luckiest man alive. He stared down into her grey eyes, corners of her lids crinkling up as she smiled. *I'd do anything for you*. He would, too. He'd tackle any task, level any mountain, and clear all obstacles out of the way of her happiness. Anything. "Sounds good."

"Mmhmm." She lifted her chin, brushing her lips across his. "I'm kinda stuck here right now." He tightened his arms around her, chuckling as she gave him a pretty pout. "Help me out, Gabe."

"Pay the toll, woman." She rolled her eyes, lifting her chin again. He slipped a hand between her shoulder blades, lifting her up as his mouth descended, pressing a kiss on the tip of her nose. She made a frustrated noise and he smiled, laying the next kiss on one cheek, trailing soft caresses along towards her ear. "What do you want, Bethy? Tell me."

Her hands twined around his neck, pulling him down as she arched up. "Kiss me."

"You got it," he murmured, mouth hovering over hers. "Whatever you want, baby."

Gunny lifted his arms again, a new batch of kids dangling, bare toes in the breeze, giggling laughter filling the air around the big man.

For today, life was good.

Sammy's ready

Hoss, three years later

"Jesus, brother. Take a fuckin' breath."

Jase's voice startled him, as did the sudden appearance of a heavy hand on his shoulder. Fingers squeezing, holding on to balance himself, Jase stepped over the bleachers from behind where Hoss sat, claiming a place next to him.

"He's good. Kid's not gonna get hurt, man."

Hoss turned his attention back to the arena, tensing up again as he watched the bodies flying across the ice. His focus was on a specific young body, because his son Sammy was one of the skaters.

"Dude, I wouldn't have recommended this workshop for him if he wasn't ready."

Hoss knew that. Knew it to his bones. Jase was one of the most compassionate and caring men he'd ever seen when it came to kids. And he'd helped kids through tough times before, seen them come out the other end and move on to be healthy, young adults. Sammy needed this challenge. Needed so much. Still, seeing his fourteen-year-old son taking on hulking high schooler kids like this, kids who were listed on the hockey prospects websites, was terrifying.

"I'm scared as fuck. All the time." He didn't look at Jase, could have been talking to himself, but he knew Jase was listening. "My boy's lost so much. I can't imagine if he got hurt and lost hockey, too. Jesus, brother, some days I think it's one of the only things that keeps him going." Sammy's skills were undeniable, but so too was a fragility that hadn't been in the boy's eyes before. He'd learned far too young how vulnerable they all were. *Loss does that to people*, he thought. *Breaks us in ways others can't see, but we feel.* Scarred and scared, Sammy's only solace were his dreams, both nighttime and this one, the pursuit of a life on ice. It was working, all his hard work paying off, because Sammy was one of the youngest prospects listed on those websites, arrayed alongside men he revered.

"He's healing." Jase's tone was firm, a statement that he would brook no argument on the topic. It was decided, at least in *his* head.

"He is." It had been four years since Hope died. Together he and Sammy had dealt with the beginnings of adolescent angst, a mini-rebellion when classwork had to take precedence over hockey, and the boy sprouting his first pubes. They'd also handled teething, potty-training, and the sad death of a first pet for Sammy's sister, Faith. Hoss had replaced Goldie the goldfish with a rat terrier puppy, and Sammy was pretty certain he'd gotten the better of that deal. Hoss hadn't known until they pulled away from PBJ's house with the puppy wrapped in a blanket that a dog was Sammy's dream pet.

He'd wrestled with that guilt for a long time, Sammy's tearful recitation of Hope's arguments against a dog spelled out in their son's quaking voice scoring deep. Another thing he hadn't picked up on, and the example Hoss held up to himself on nights when he couldn't sleep, wondering what else he'd missed.

"Are you?" Hoss jumped, so lost in watching his son and his memories he'd forgotten Jase was sitting at his side.

"Am I what?" Before Jase could respond, Hoss jumped to his feet, shouting "Yes! *Goooaall!*" as Sammy deked around one of the high school kids and slipped the puck between the knees of the also-a-high schooler goalie. "Way to go, Samboni!" He stood, clapping until Sammy glided off the ice, one mitt lifted Hoss' direction in acknowledgment of the applause. "Did you see that?"

"I did." Jase chuckled. "Told you he was ready." They sat for a moment, then Jase asked again. "Are you?" Hoss twisted his neck, one eyebrow raised, looking his question at Jase. "Are you healing?"

Hoss didn't have to wait. The grief of losing his wife swept over him, the edges of his vision blurring while he turned to stare straight ahead, ignoring the emotion as best he could, hoping Jase would do the same.

"Brother." Anguished, filled with a breathy pain, Jase tried to set what he must see as his misstep back straight. "I didn't mean to make it harder. But," Jase's voice grew stronger, that same conviction returning from before, "you can't keep on like this. You need something."

"I went in my studio last night," he blurted, mouth running away with him. "Haven't been in there in months, maybe years. I've done only a few things since Hope—" He stopped, breathing as if he'd run a mile. "It just, made things fresh, brother. You didn't do or say anything wrong. It just made it fresh."

"You think you need to be going in there and stirring things up? Is that a good thing?" Jase sounded doubtful.

Hoss wasn't. He knew the cost of not going back to work. His art had always been a part of him. Much as anything could, he believed if he let it, art could help him come to terms with the loss of the light that had filled his days for such a short time. "Yeah. I think it's what I need, now." He inclined his head, indicating Sammy seated on the bench, awaiting his next shift. Following the dream that made him stronger, more resilient. Made him whole. "I think...maybe we're both ready for this next step."

"Then take the fucking leap, brother." Jase held that same confidence and conviction out like a lifeline. Hoss smiled.

"Maybe I will."

Foreseeable future

Mason, three years later

"Babe?" Looking for Willa, Mason held Garrett's hand as they walked through the house. Smiling wryly, Mason knew his youngest son's steps were steady, no longer needing his daddy to hold to. Gar ran at full tilt most days, racing from thrilling experience to exciting event without looking back. At seven, he didn't yet have the heft to back up his attitude of "don't fuck with me," but Mason knew he'd get it sooner rather than later, grinning each time Gar ran up against something that set him back on his heels. Those were the teaching moments, and Gar grabbed hold of them with both hands, wrestling knowledge to work on his side.

"In here," Willa called, and Mason turned up the kids' hallway, Gar's hand slipping from his grip as the boy pulled away, angling towards his room.

"Don't make a mess, Gar-boy." His son lifted one hand in acknowledgment, not turning around. "We got company comin'." Walking into the next room along the hallway, he found Willa seated on the bed with brush in hand, Dolly standing in front of her. Decorated in soft pinks and purples, there was no doubt whose room this happened to be.

"Daddy!" Dolly wriggled free of Willa's grasp and darted towards him. Mason lifted her, tossing her in the air once, then bringing her down for a hug before setting her feet on the floor. "Momma's makin' me pretty."

"You're already pretty, baby girl." He rested a hand on top of her head. "She's just polishing the raw beauty to a shine."

Grinning at her mother, Dolly ordered with her own slice of "don't fuck with me" attitude, "Shine me, Momma!"

Rolling her eyes, Willa didn't have to say a word. He read her "see what you started" look and laughed. "Hey, babe. You gals nearly done in here? I'm gonna go out back and get the grill started." There were a half a dozen Rebels coming tonight, all past and present officers in the Fort Wayne chapter, celebrating a couple of birthdays. Faith Inez was seven, only a few weeks younger than his and Willa's Garrett, and having a joint celebration had become something of a tradition. In the beginning, it was more that the women worried Faynez, as her brother Sammy called her, wouldn't have enough of a female influence if they didn't stake their claim. Now, the party was just what they did.

"Yeah." The tip of Willa's tongue had escaped the corner of her mouth, an aid in her concentration to try and corral Dolly's mass of curly hair. They weren't certain where the girl had gotten her hair from, but it was uniquely Dolly, as unruly as the child could be. "In a minute." The band snapped, flipping out of her fingers and she shook her head. "Dang it. A minute more than the last minute I talked about, then."

She was still muttering as he made his way back down the hallway and back to the living room. The roar of pipes led him to the windows, and he looked out to see about three dozen bikes parking on both sides of the road. They were a mix of traditional and sport bike models, and he shook his head, yelling an answer to Willa before she even finished asking who it was. "Chase made it home. Looks like he brought a few friends over." She'd see the numbers as soon as she came out, and that would be soon enough to worry about ordering pizza for the boys. *Men*, he corrected

312

himself. Chase was nearly twenty-five and had carried that title for a long time now.

Need that boy to settle down. His oldest son hadn't yet found his niche, trying his hand at a dozen things and doing well at all of them, but not sticking with anything. *Except the music*, he mused. Chase still played with Slate's brother, Benny.

It wasn't long before the backyard filled up, men sitting or standing as was their wont, women traveling back and forth between the house and tables outside. The kids were running rampant, a roiling mess of shrieks and scraped knees, dirty hands and wide grins. Mason was holding his second beer, having surrendered the grill to Chase who had promised him dibs on the first burger. He was talking to Fury, ironing out a shift in protocol the man wanted to put into place when Jase and Hoss walked up.

Grinning broadly, Jase elbowed him hard, catching him on the ribs. "*Ow*, motherfucker. What the hell?"

"Check it out, man." He lifted his chin, pointing towards the house. "Hoss, did you see?"

"What?" Hoss and Mason asked at the same time, turning to look through the sliding glass doors and into the living room.

Mason froze, staring at the scene in disbelief. Faynez had a napkin or something pinned to the top of her head. Standing nearby and holding up what looked like a sheet knotted around her waist were Dolly and either Hayley or Kayley—Slate's youngest set of twins were hard to tell apart on a good day, much less from twenty feet away. Faynez was solemnly marching towards where Gar stood next to Graham Williamson, Deke's boy.

"Are they...?" Hoss' voice trailed off.

"It looks like they are." Fury's laughter was scarcely contained. "Hey, Mason. Didn't you call this wedding back when the kids were still in diapers? I've heard stories.'

In that moment, Mason was struck by how beautiful Faynez was, and would be, and how handsome his son would become. He looked at all the kids with fresh eyes, seeing in the hurtling bodies around them the wealth of experiences to come. *This right here is where the future begins. We've been holding it in the palm of our hands for a long time.*

"My boy looks good next to your girl," he said to Hoss, keeping his tone offhand. "Kids might be onto something, man."

The kids had lined up in front of Slate's boy Allen, who was only a year older than Garrett, but already half a foot taller. Without taking his eyes off the evolving scene, Hoss responded, his words careful, tone reverent. "That's beautiful."

"Yeah, it really is." Mason reached up, gripping Hoss' shoulder with one hand. "Pretty as a picture."

The end (of this story)

THANK YOU FOR READING *Fury*!

This is book #11 in a series. Throughout this series we've been introduced to so many wonderful characters. People who live in my head in a way that makes them seem real in many aspects. I hope you fell in love with Fury and his pursuit of Bethany, and will continue in this saga along with me. Next up will be Cassie's story, which is mostly Hoss' story, if I were being honest. Available now.

MUSIC PLAYLISTS

I put together playlists of music both mentioned in the book, and used during writing and editing. Want a peek into the mind of me? Be sure of your decision, it's not always normal here!

Playlist: bit.ly/fury-playlist

ABOUT THE AUTHOR

Raised in the south, MariaLisa learned about the magic of books at an early age. Every summer, she would spend hours in the local library, devouring books of every genre. Self-described as a book-a-holic, she says "I've always loved to read, but then I discovered writing, and found I adored that, too. For reading...if nothing else is available, I've been known to read the back of the cereal box."

Also by MariaLisa deMora

Alace Sweets

A dark thriller, this book is not a light read. Filled with edge-of-your-seat suspense, this intense story commands the reader's attention as it drives towards the explosive ending. Alace Sweets is a vigilante serial killer, with everything that implies and is sure to trip all your triggers. Be ready.

At seventeen, Alace Sweets turned a corner in her life, taking the wrong shortcut home from school.

Resisting the harsh knowledge her attackers will never be made to pay for their actions, Alace takes a stand. Justice must be served, and if fate's scales are out of balance, she's determined to set things right as best she can.

When the laws of men fail, the rules of Alace prevail.

5-Star Reviews for Alace Sweets

"deMora has a superb story-line and exceptional character development. All of her characters have such depth that will intrigue the reader..."
~Turning Another Page

"Hot, sweet, dark thriller."
~Beth D

"It will keep you on the edge of your seat and give you chills."
~Escape Reality Book Blog

"Disturbing, haunting, sickly; yet hot, sexy and heart racing!"
~Amanda L

"From the first page [deMora] pulls you into the world she has created and you do not even try to escape…"
~Little Shop of Readers Blog

"A must read for all those dark, gritty romance fans out there."
~Sweet & Spicy Reads

"You will find yourself so drawn into the story that the outside world is blocked out and your locking the doors and turning on all the lights."
~Danena F

"Don't judge me for bonding with a vigilante serial killer, she's more than what she does."
~iScream Books

"Thrilling…chilling…full of suspense, nail biting edge of your seat excitement."
~Tracey H

"Every time MariaLisa deMora picks up her pen (or opens her computer), she creates characters you want to believe in."
~Gail S

"Intriguing dark storyline, beautiful love story and nail-biting conclusion, what more could a reader ask for?"
~Manda M

"This book takes you a dark and twisted ride that is gripping…"
~Renee Entress' Blog

"This book is dark and gritty and I literally had to take a day off from reading it because it's that intense."
~My Girlfriend's Couch

"This is my favourite book so far from this author … I recommend this book if you enjoy dark romantic thrillers."
~Cheekypee Reads and Reviews

"There's not enough stars to give this book and 5 just doesn't really do it justice!"

~DeLane C

"I couldn't put this book down from page one! Tried to stop & go to bed but couldn't sleep thinking about Alace and got up & finished the book."
~Debbie M

"MariaLisa DeMora, wordsmith that she is, made this a story of the enlightenment of a woman and finding love in a life where she has had none."
~Kat W

"Whatever deep dark trench [deMora] pulled a character like Alace from should be revisited again and often."
~Confessions of a Serial Reader

ADDITIONAL SERIES AND BOOKS

Please note that books in a series frequently feature characters from additional books within that series. If series books are read out of order, readers will twig to spoilers for the other books, so going back to read the skipped titles won't have the same angsty reveals.

Rebel Wayfarers MC series:

Mica, #1
A Sweet & Merry Christmas, short story #1.5
Slate, #2
Bear, #3
Jase, #4
Gunny, #5
Mason, #6
Hoss, #7
Harddrive Holidays, short story #7.5
Duck, #8
Biker Chick Campout, short story #8.5
Watcher, #9
A Kiss to Keep You, novella #9.25
Gun Totin' Annie, short story #9.5
Secret Santa, short story #9.75

Bones, #10
Gunny's Pups, novella #10.25
Never Settle, short story #10.5
Not Even A Mouse, short story #10.75
Fury, #11
Christmas Doings, #11.25
Gypsy's Lady, #11.5
Cassie, #12
Road Runner's Ride, novella #12.5

Occupy Yourself band series:

Born Into Trouble, #1
Grace In Motion, #2 (TBD)
What They Say, #3 (TBD)

Neither This, Nor That series:

This Is the Route Of Twisted Pain, #1
Treading the Traitor's Path: Out Bad, #2
Trapped by Fate on Reckless Roads, #3 (TBD)

Other Books:

With My Whole Heart
Alace Sweets
Hard Focus

More information available at mldemora.com.

www.ingramcontent.com/pod-product-compliance
Lightning Source LLC
Chambersburg PA
CBHW070044030726
47506CB00002B/329